"Welcome, my Lord Ranulf," she said. " 'Tis a fine day for a duel."

He stared unblinkingly at her for some moments, then let a frown settle between his eyes. "I did not expect you to attend this bloodletting," he said. "I must remember you are not a lady."

Her jaw hardened. "I assure you I would not miss this for anything."

Ranulf looked at the weapons she carried. "And where is this man who would champion your ill-fated cause?" he asked.

"Man?" She shook her head. "There is no man."

Ranulf considered this with an arched brow. "You were unable to find a single man willing to die for you, my lady? Not one?"

"Nay," she said, her eyes unwavering, "but your opponent is here before you now."

Ranulf took some moments to digest this and then burst out laughing.

"I find no humor in the situation. Perhaps you would care to enlighten me, Lord Ranulf?"

"Doubtless you would not appreciate my explanation, my lady."

Her chin went up. "Do you think I will not make a worthy opponent?"

"With your nasty tongue perhaps, but . . ."

"Then let us not prolong the suspense any longer," she said as she removed her sword from her scabbard.

Warrior Bride

Tamara Leigh

BANTAM BOOKS
New York Toronto
London Sydney Auckland

WARRIOR BRIDE
A Bantam Fanfare Book/April 1994

FANFARE and the portrayal of a boxed "ff" are trademarks of Bantam Books,
a division of Bantam Doubleday Dell Publishing Group, Inc.

ISBN 0-553-56533-8

Published simultaneously in the United States and Canada

Bantam Books are published by Bantam Books, a division of Bantam Doubleday
Dell Publishing Group, Inc. Its trademark, consisting of the words "Bantam Books"
and the portrayal of a rooster, is Registered in U.S. Patent and Trademark Office
and in other countries. Marca Registrada. Bantam Books, 1540 Broadway, New
York, New York 10036.

PRINTED IN THE UNITED STATES OF AMERICA
RAD   0 9 8 7 6 5 4 3 2 1

"To everyone who made this dream a reality, and most especially David, who taught me there is no limit to love."

Prologue

*G*ilbert!" *Lizanne screamed.* Paying no heed to the marauders ransacking her dowry wagons, nor giving any thought to her own safety, she pulled free of her maid and rushed past the torn and blood-strewn bodies scattered about the ground. The old woman called to her, but Lizanne disregarded the desperate pleas.

Sinking to her knees beside her brother, she reached to him, her gaze searching his shuttered face. "Nay," she cried, refusing to believe he was gone from her. Taking hold of his shoulders, she shook him. "Pray, open your eyes!"

His head lolled on his neck, but naught else.

Whimpering, she forced her gaze down the length of his body. His hauberk lay open, its fine mesh brilliant with the blood seeping through. And his leg . . .

God help his leg. Swaying, she lifted her hands and stared dazedly at the crimson covering her palms.

Suddenly, she was wrenched upright, rough hands hauling her back against a coarsely clothed chest. Coming out of her stupor, she flailed against her captor.

"Nay!" she cried as she was lifted off her feet, her hands reaching again for Gilbert but grasping only air.

Her frayed senses barely registered her release moments later as she was shoved into the waiting arms of her old maid. Kneeling in the dirt, she clung to Hattie and wept as the villains began a boisterous, albeit short-lived, argument over who would be the first to have her.

Of a sudden, the clamoring of voices subsided to a curious hush that Lizanne did not immediately register. It was her maid's response, a trembling that shook her entire body, that forced it to her consciousness. Lifting her face from Hattie's bosom, she peered over her shoulder and saw muddy boots.

"Nay, milady," Hattie murmured, trying to press her mistress's face back to her. "Be silent."

Lizanne resisted the woman's urging, pushing aside the hands that had delivered her from her mother's womb four and ten years ago.

With a daring she had not known she possessed, she lifted her gaze up the length of the lean, muscled body standing over her. The man was uncommonly tall—near as tall as Gilbert, and every bit as broad.

Hatred, more intense than she had ever known, suffused her being and set her limbs to trembling. It was he who had laid the final blow to her brother.

Uncaring that her eyes mirrored her loathing, she slid her gaze from a wide, generous mouth, up over a long, straight nose, to cruel, glittering orbs as dark as his hair was light.

Aye, that hair. Not quite flaxen, not quite white, it fell about an angular face deeply tanned from hours in the sun. Staring at him, Lizanne could not help but question God's infinite wisdom, for He had wielded no foresight in bestowing such a handsome face upon this spawn of the Devil. Doubtless, many women were rendered agape by the mere sight of him.

Not Lizanne, though. She found nothing captivating

about him. Nay, that was not entirely true, she corrected herself. That telling streak of blood matting a length of his hair was fascinating. Gilbert's blade had done that. . . .

"God's teeth, men, what delights have we here?" the man said in the halting, imprecise English of a commoner. As his men guffawed, a slow grin spread his lips to reveal straight but discolored teeth.

Reaching out a hand, he lifted a lock of Lizanne's black hair. "Aye," he purred, pulling his fingers through the heavy hair. "Yer a rare beauty, lass—a fine prize."

His eyes met hers, and their fathomless depths charged her anew with fear.

Feeling the tremors that racked her young charge's body, Hattie clutched her nearer. "Take that which ye came fer and leave the child be," she said daringly.

The man threw his head back, harsh laughter rumbling from him. He was joined by the others.

Her heart quickening, Lizanne stared at her captors.

The man sobered. "Aye, old woman," he sneered. "I'll take that which I came fer." He raised an arm, then swung it down, striking Hattie alongside the head. With barely a sound, she toppled backward to lie motionless.

"Nay!" Lizanne cried, her breath lodging in her throat as she reached out to the still form. Even as she touched Hattie's rough woolen tunic, she was hauled upright, a heavy hand biting into her arm. She struggled against it, but there was no freedom to be had, and a moment later she was staring into that evil visage again.

She loathed the grin that widened his mouth as his gaze dipped to the high neckline of her gown. Still, she was unprepared when he reached up and ran a seeking hand over her breasts.

"Do not!" she shrieked, striking out at him even as she recoiled from his vile touch.

His grip tightening, he hauled her against his length and imprisoned her there. "Aye, my beauty, ye will bend to me," he muttered, then lowered his head to take possession of her untried lips.

Laughter roaring in her ears, Lizanne fought to free herself as his hands roamed over her most private parts—her breasts, buttocks, the soft juncture between her thighs. She thought she would die—at that moment would have even preferred it.

As hot tears spilled upon her cheeks, other hands materialized to obscenely touch, claw, and pinch her delicate flesh.

But it seemed the man was averse to sharing.

Growling at those who sought to sample his booty before him, he swept her from the ground and, settling her against his broad chest, began to shoulder a path through the throng of men.

Panic-stricken, Lizanne could only hold tight, pressing her face to his tunic as she was carried past those terrible, leering faces.

They had only just cleared the gathering when the man suddenly lurched sideways, jarring her as he dropped down upon one knee. Still, he managed to retain his hold on her, gripping her tighter as he shook his head, as if to clear it.

So near him, Lizanne saw that blood still coursed from his head wound, and that it was no mild injury as she had first imagined. Mayhap God had not abandoned her after all, and the man would simply drop dead.

But neither God, nor her captor, was of a mind to oblige her.

Recovering amid mocking laughter and jeers, the man surged to his feet and spun around to face the others. "Do ye laugh again, I'll see the lot of ye gutted," he snarled.

His threat hanging on the air, he strode from the camp toward the moonlit woods.

"When ye finish with 'er, Darth," one called after

him, "I'd like a taste meself." Loud, raucous laughter followed.

Darth. Lizanne clung to that, finding a niche for this one bit of information in the turbulence of her mind.

Looking up at a canopy of trees as she was carried deeper into the woods, she at last acknowledged her desperate circumstances. The animal meant to steal her virtue—to defile her!

With newfound strength, she resumed her struggles, bucking her body and letting her hands fly. When her nails raked his rough, unshaven face, drawing blood, she was immediately dropped to her feet and repaid with a slap so weighty, it rocked her head back.

Dazed, she stumbled backward, her hand covering her stinging cheek. Regaining her balance, she forced herself to look up at the devil where he stood with the moonlight full upon his face. He was unmoving, his body rigid with anger.

Feeling very much the prey, Lizanne stepped farther away, her eyes shifting frantically from side to side. Mayhap she could run. The castle of her betrothed lay less than five leagues to the west. She could hide herself in the dense woods until the sun rose to guide her there.

Embracing that course, she turned to flee, but in the next instant, the needled ground was at her back, and looming over her was the man called Darth. Before she could react, his lips fell to her throat and his hands roamed over her, familiarizing themselves with her every curve.

Realizing she was powerless against such a giant, she squeezed her eyes tightly closed, shutting out his face and attempting to withdraw inside herself. *'Tis but my body,* she assured herself over and over, willing her soul to rise above the invasion he intended.

Then his weight lifted from her.

Eyes flying open, she watched, horrified, as he dispensed with his garments. Never before had she seen a man unclothed, and even in the moonlight, his powerful build was graphically exposed.

She started to look away, but of its own accord, her gaze was drawn to a long, jagged scar that slashed across his lower abdomen.

Unsightly . . .

He moved to stand over her. "Fight it and 'twill only go worse fer ye," he growled.

She saw him shake his head once more and lift a hand to it, obviously suffering from his injury, but a moment later he again lowered himself onto her. Throwing up the hem of her chemise, he forced a leg between hers.

As she tried, in vain, to bring her thighs together, her gaze fell upon that part of him that differentiated man from woman. Knowing only the bare essentials of copulation—those things Hattie had deemed requisite for a lady about to become a bride—she had not fully understood it until now.

Gasping, she threw herself sideways, her hands frantically pushing her chemise downward. She could not allow this. Could not! 'Twas to be her husband's privilege—Philip's.

"Listen well!" the man said, his hand on her throat roughly bringing her face to his. "I mean to have ye, and I would not want to spoil yer beauty unless 'tis necessary. Do ye understand, wench?"

She understood, but it did not stop her from prying at the fingers about her neck. What did still her hands was the visible pain that lanced across his face.

Of course! Before she could consider the prudence of such an act, she swung a clumsily bunched fist upward.

"For Gilbert!" she cried.

Her fist connected solidly with his head, just where the wound was, then a searing pain shot through her hand. The man slumped down on top of her, but she hardly noticed as she cradled her injured hand beneath her chin, shards of brilliant blue light dancing behind her closed eyelids.

Why did it hurt so much? What was this pain that made it feel as if she had laid her hand upon a fire?

As the colors receded, she tried to open her eyes, but it was some minutes before she was finally able to.

She slowly lowered her chin and settled her gaze upon the pale head pressed to her shoulder. Except for the shifting of the man's hair by the gentle breeze meandering through the trees, he lay unmoving.

Reality pressing in upon her, she gasped, the sound strangled by the man's weight. She drew another labored breath. Had she truly succeeded? Was it possible she, who had never before struck another being, had knocked the man unconscious? How—

Run! her mind screamed, thrusting aside its fruitless ponderings.

Ignoring the terrible pain in her hand, Lizanne twisted beneath the body that pinned her to the ground and used her forearm to push the man off her. He groaned as he rolled away, making her heart race furiously. But he did not regain consciousness.

Nursing her hand to her chest, she stumbled to her feet, sparing the man one last glance. Had she but a weapon—and the courage—she would have put a quick end to him. But she had neither.

Lifting her skirts high, she plunged into the woods. Deeper she went, oblivious to the sharp rocks and pine needles that tore at her feet, the branches that tangled her hair and scratched her face.

She did not know how far or how long she ran. Only when she finally tumbled headlong into a narrow ditch, her lungs raw from exertion, did she notice the first rays of dawn penetrating the sky above the woods.

Drawing deep, ragged breaths, she peered between the branches at the streaks of lavender and orange that

shot through the inky sky and listened for the sounds of
those she was certain pursued her. All she picked out
were the innocent noises of an awakening wood—the
buzzing of insects, the twittering of birds, and somewhere, the gurgle of water.

Would they come? she wondered frantically, her fingers raking through the wild hair falling about her face
and shoulders. Mayhap she had outdistanced them. . . .

Knowing she should continue on, Lizanne fought
the fatigue enveloping her and tried to raise herself. Failing, she tried again, but to no avail. She simply could go
no farther. Admitting defeat, she eased herself more
deeply into the concealing undergrowth, grateful her
clothing blended so well with the greenery.

Before giving in to sleep, though, she first had to
answer the insistent call of survival. She unearthed a
smooth, rounded rock with her uninjured hand; it was a
weapon of sorts. Clasping it to her bosom, she let her
lids drop over sore, reddened eyes.

Sleep came easily, though it brought with it disturbing images of the night past. Sinking deeper into its
frightening embrace, Lizanne saw again her beloved
brother's ravaged body. "Ah, Gilbert," she sobbed, " 'twill
not go unavenged."

Chapter 1

By degrees, Ranulf Wardieu became painfully cognizant of his surroundings. A fetid, musty odor assaulted his senses first, the taste of it on his indrawn breath causing his throat to constrict tightly.

Lord, but he was thirsty.

Swallowing hard against the parched tissues lining his mouth and throat, he lifted his chin and leaned his head back against the cold, weeping stones. There was a dull, aching throb where his head rested, but before he could question the reason, he was alerted to stirrings around him and lowered voices.

Cautiously, he opened his eyes and peered out at the dimly lit room. Though it was too dark to be certain, his wakening senses told him it was a cell. As his eyes grew accustomed to the darkness, he watched as indistinct shadows moved in and out of the light cast by a single torch.

'Twas a dream—nay, a nightmare, he told himself, straining forward to catch a piece of the conversation. The unmistakable rattle of chains on either side of him brought full alertness. At once, his mind protested the excruciating pain in his outstretched arms and the numbing chill throughout his body. Although his senses screamed with a mixture of shock and outrage, the warrior in him forced his body to predatory stillness.

His shadowy companions grew quiet as well at the sound of their wakening captive, and the flickering torch was the only movement for interminable minutes.

Although he remained motionless, his own face in shadow, Ranulf continued to watch the silhouettes through narrowed eyes.

Why did they not show themselves? he wondered. Who were they?

Then, suddenly, they were moving again, their voices louder, but not so that he could make out their words.

Would they come closer?

A frown knit his eyebrows as a door was thrown open on the far side of the cell, and the shadows transformed themselves into three men-at-arms. In none too orderly fashion they filed out, then firmly closed the door behind them, returning the cell to its former state of near-darkness.

God's mercy, he truly was in a cell!

Was he alone? His eyes and ears told him so, yet his instincts denied it—instincts that many a time had saved his life.

Nay, he was not alone. He could feel another's presence. He silently cursed the torch that cast its shadowy light across the floor and illuminated little else in the cell save himself.

He would wait. . . .

To occupy his mind and curtail the agony of his bondage, he set about assessing his situation.

He was imprisoned—stripped of all clothing, save his braies, and chained upright to a wall. His arms were stretched up and out to the sides, the steel manacles biting into his wrists. Beneath him, his knees were buckled, his arms having carried the full weight of his slumped body for ... how long?

Although he felt the grip of manacles around his ankles, there was not the same tension there. Lowering his head, he peered down the length of his body, straining his eyes to pick out the dark shape of a chain running from one manacled ankle to the other. The excess lay pooled between his feet.

Ignoring the pain in his limbs, he searched for an answer to his predicament. His memory rebelled, but then, slowly, unfolded.

He'd been at Langdon's Castle. At the beckoning of a comely maid, he, full of wine, ale, and a burgeoning sexual appetite, had followed the wench down a narrow corridor. She had teased and cajoled him, allowing tantalizing glimpses of a sizable bosom and long, slender calves as she danced ahead of him—always just out of reach. It had only served to whet his appetite ... and dull his senses.

As he'd rounded a corner, he had been set upon. He'd had little time to react, and after he had delivered only one retaliatory blow, his assailant had struck him on the back of his skull. Dropping to the stone floor, he'd barely had time to focus on a darkly hooded figure bending over him before a sea of black had sucked his consciousness away.

Now, he was more acutely aware of the pain in his head than any other. He tried to move his head, and a sharp sensation assailed his senses and sent his anger spiraling. At once, his entire body protested its abuse, his joints burning like a thousand fires.

Determinedly, he clenched his jaws to arrest the groan that rose to his lips. Though he wanted nothing better than to get his legs beneath him and take the weight off his aching arms, his battle-proven instincts forbade him the comfort until he could better determine his plight.

Trembling from the effort to contain his rage, he turned his head and began a search of the darkened cell. He forced his eyes to adjust to the darkness—to see into those cloaked corners. Though they revealed to him nothing he had not seen before, he still felt that other presence straight through.

After a thorough battle with his inner voice, he finally lowered the heels of his bare feet to the cold, earthen floor. One foot nudged something soft and warm, which shrieked and scuttled noisily across the floor. He hardly noticed.

Straightening, he narrowed his focus on the manacles above him. Thick bands encircled wrists raw and darkened with blood. As he was large-boned, they cut deeply into his flesh, very nearly cutting off the laborious upward flow of blood to his fingers.

Clenching and unclenching his hands, he was gradually rewarded with a prickly warmth that spread from his aching shoulders to the tips of his fingers. With it came a measure of strength, and eager to test it, he propelled both arms forward. Not surprisingly, the restraints held fast, drawing fresh blood as they clattered loudly in the silence.

As the noise died, he heard something—a movement to his left. He stilled, his body bunching in readiness, his eyes narrowing as they swept the cell again.

"Show yourself!" he demanded, his voice harsh as it echoed against the stone walls. He waited, but nothing. So, 'twas a game they played. . . .

Straining to the right, Ranulf put every ounce of strength into his left arm and wrenched it forward. The manacle bit more deeply into his already broken flesh, easily resisting his efforts.

A growl rose from his throat as he felt the sticky trickle of blood course downward from his wrist.

Where in God's name was he, and who dared chain

him like an animal? With his own hands he would crush the heinous offender.

Anger surfaced, fueled by the images of his revenge, and of such intensity, it surprised even him. Unleashing it, he roared and thrust his body forward, uncaring of the searing pain in his shoulders or the punishing bite of the manacles.

Time and again he fought the chains until finally his energies drained. He collapsed back against the wall, curses issuing from his hoarse throat.

"What ails you, my lord Ranulf?" a sweetly sarcastic voice queried, cutting through his stream of expletives.

He snapped his head to the left and there, less than an arm's reach away, emerged a darkly clad figure. It was nigh impossible to make out the features of the upturned face hidden in the shadows of a hood, but the woman's eyes caught the barest light and glittered coldly at him.

Familiarity tugged at him, his mind thrusting itself back to the moment before he'd lost consciousness at Langdon's castle. It had to have been her—

"A lord, indeed," she continued, then added, "I never suspected such."

Though size and gender could be deceiving, Ranulf's sixth sense told him this woman was his captor. "Who are you?" he demanded.

Although she was nearly a head shorter than he— still tall for a woman—she confidently stood her ground. "An old acquaintance, 'tis all," she said, her voice vibrating through the chill air. Stepping nearer, she raised herself on tiptoes and boldly tested his chains.

'Twas maddening! Close enough for him to smell the sweet scents of her womanly body, yet he could not so much as touch her. His hands tightened into fists with the fervent desire to close around her neck.

"It holds well," she said, her gloved hand grazing his before she stepped back. "Best you not waste your strength so foolishly . . . my lord." Her words were so heavily laced with sarcasm, the title fairly oozed from her lips.

Defiantly, Ranulf jerked at the chains again. "I demand to know the grounds for my imprisonment!"

Wordlessly, the woman slid her eyes from his and down his bared chest before turning and walking away.

Forcing himself to a calm he did not feel, Ranulf followed her progress. When she stopped before the wall sconce with its single torch, it became evident she was not clothed as the lady her voice proclaimed her to be. Indeed, she wore the leggings and oversized tunic of a man, which hid all imaginable feminine curves, save the narrow, belted waist.

He continued to watch as she removed the torch and used it to light three others about the cell. Soon, every corner stood out in sharp contrast to its former self.

Aye, 'twas empty except for himself and the woman.

Promptly, he imprinted every detail of the dungeon upon his mind. He was chained to the wall of the main room, where guards could be stationed. To his left, beyond an iron-banded door with its grate set at eye level, was a row of individual cells. On his right was a draughty corridor pit that stretched into nothingness, and from which he was certain he detected the sound of running water.

When he turned his attention back to the woman, he found she now faced him. She had assumed a bold, manly stance, legs spread wide and hands clasped behind her back. Still, he could not make out her features, and wondered if she kept them hidden for a reason. After all, what kind of woman dressed as a man and tended a cell with such apparent ease?

For the first time since regaining consciousness, he felt the corners of his mouth tug upward. Never in his life had he been intimidated by a woman—not even his strong-willed mother—and this woman's display served only to spark humor in him in an obviously humorless situation.

Shaking off the queer, misplaced emotion, he asked, "Am I to be told of the charges against me?"

Unhurriedly, the woman traversed the earthen floor and came to stand before him once more. The hood continued to shadow her features, though he could now make out the line of her straight nose and the curve of her full lips.

Lower, something caught his eye. There, suspended about her neck, was a pair of keys on a thin leather thong. Worn to taunt him, they would fit the manacles binding him. His anger quickened.

"You are here, Lord Ranulf," she began, lifting her hand to push the hood back, "to do penance for the sins you have visited upon others."

His eyes narrowed on her lovely pale face. It struck a deep chord of familiarity in him—a recent one. He shifted his gaze from her intensely green eyes, which were regarding him with immortal loathing, and raised it to the blackest hair he had ever seen—like the starry night of a new moon, he thought.

Of a sudden, recognition flew at him. Aye, well he remembered the Lady Lizanne. He had made inquiries about her the one and only time he had caught a glimpse of her at Lord Bernard Langdon's castle. His mind drifted back to that brief encounter.

Shortly after his arrival at the castle, he and his vassal, Sir Walter Fortesne, had been seated with Lord Bernard and his steward in the hall, when a commotion at the opposite end had interrupted their discussion. Exhausted after two sleepless days of riding in the constant drizzle of the season, Ranulf had been more than annoyed at the rude intrusion. Scowling, he had turned in his chair to observe the perpetrator.

There she had stood, all that glorious, unconstrained black hair flying out behind her as she loudly berated a servant who, it seemed, had dared lay a hand on her maid. Even in the drab bliaut the lady had worn ungirded, he had been intrigued.

"Lady Lizanne!" Lord Bernard had bellowed, rising so abruptly, his chair was sent crashing backward.

Midsentence, the lady's harsh words had ceased. She had turned and looked across the hall, her eyes widening in disbelief.

"Apologies, my lord, I knew not . . ." Her voice had trailed off as her gaze lit upon Ranulf. He had swiftly risen from his chair to tower over Lord Bernard's plump figure.

Ranulf had smiled at her, making no attempt to conceal his interest. Her eyes had widened farther, her mouth gaping as the high color drained from her face.

Puzzled by her reaction, and wondering if he dared take it as a compliment, he'd watched her take a halting step toward him. Then, with a strangled gasp, she had spun around and fled the hall as if the Devil himself were at her heels.

Grunting with disgust, Lord Bernard had dismissed the lady's unseemly behavior with a fluttery wave of his hand. "My apologies for Lady Lizanne," he had muttered, reseating himself in the chair his steward had rushed to upright. "Would that you know what a trial she is to me."

"Your daughter?" Ranulf had inquired, thoughtfully lowering himself back to his chair as he gazed in the direction the lady had disappeared.

Lord Bernard had burst out laughing. "God's mercy, nay! A daughter such as that? No worse curse could be visited upon me. Nay, 'tis my wife's cousin. 'Twill be nothing short of a blessing when she returns to her brother on the morrow."

Interested, Ranulf had pried further. "The lady is not wed, then?"

Clearly taken aback, Lord Bernard had stared at

him, his smile disappearing. "Take my advice, young Ranulf, and ease yourself with any one of the willing wenches of my castle. But stay you away from that one. She is mean-spirited."

His advice had done little to cool Ranulf's ardor. Indeed, his curiosity had only increased tenfold. However, the lady had not appeared in the hall that evening for the meal, and Ranulf had not seen her again. Instead, he had followed the skirts of an enticing little maid straight into an ambush.

But why? Penance for what sins? Desire?

Abruptly, he pulled himself back to the present. "The Lady Lizanne," he said, still groping for an explanation of his predicament.

Her dark brows lifted inquiringly. "My lord knows me?" she asked in mock disbelief. Tauntingly, she stepped closer, raising herself on tiptoes so that her face came within bare inches of his and her warm breath fanned him.

Forcing an indifferent expression, Ranulf searched for an advantage to her nearness. In the end, there seemed none. Even if he lunged forward, he knew he could do no more than brush against her. For the moment, he was pitifully without recourse.

"I do not know you," he answered, stamping down the rage threatening to resurface, "but I know of thee."

One corner of her mouth lifted as she set herself back on her heels and began to peel the gloves from her hands.

"Ah," she sighed, "my good cousin Bernard has been wagging his tongue." She clucked her own. "One day someone will no doubt cut it out for him. Would that it could be me."

Expressionless, she lowered her eyes down the length of his body again. "I wonder . . ." she began, then swallowed hard before continuing. "Do you not remember our first meeting?"

Did her voice break, or was it his imagination? Ranulf stared hard at the top of her head, his brows drawn together.

Slowly, she lifted her head and thrust her chin forward, her eyes pinning him with their impossibly green depths.

He glared back at her. "Aye, and most memorable 'twas," he answered, his sarcasm evident as he again reflected on her less than proper display in Lord Bernard's hall.

At his admission, her eyes opened wide, her head snapping back as if she'd just been delivered a mighty blow.

In spite of himself, Ranulf was beginning to enjoy the game. Smiling broadly, he leered at her. "Tell me, are you in the habit of imprisoning men you desire to bed?"

She merely blinked, then plodded on as if he had not spoken. "Do you not deny it, then—that first meeting?" Her voice was hoarse with disbelief.

Ranulf frowned, both baffled and angered by her refusal to rise to the bait he dangled before her.

"Deny it?" he asked in a dangerously soft voice. Shaking his head, he snarled, "Why should I? 'Twas you, not I, who made a spectacle of yourself before Lord Bernard."

Again, she recoiled, her face suffusing with angry color. " 'Tis not the meeting I speak of!"

Ranulf lowered his own face to within an inch of hers, a stray lock of his long hair springing forward to fall between them. "I recall no meeting other than our brief one in Langdon's hall—could that be called a meeting."

A bitter laugh unexpectedly issued from the lady's lips, then died. She reached out and touched the fingers of the gloves she held to the base of his throat. Her eyes following the movement, she trailed them down his chest.

Ranulf stiffened. He was not accustomed to being touched so brazenly by a lady who was not already sharing his bed.

"I shall never forget our first meeting," she said in a small, level voice. " 'Twould appear, though, that you have."

Catching her lower lip between even white teeth, she dropped her eyes farther and stared at the chain binding his feet.

He watched as a frown knit itself between her brows. Aye, she was lovely, more lovely than he had first thought. Like a wild, angry rose with sharp, nasty thorns. Though the petals would surely be fragrant and soft, the thorns would likely be a man's undoing. In that instant, he very much wanted to be the man to strip away her prickly defenses. He—

The sudden realization that his initial attraction to this woman had not abated with the turn of events both shocked and disgusted him. He had placed bedding the wench above exacting revenge for the injustice done him.

Sickened by the dominance of his baser needs, he thrust himself forward. "I demand to speak to the lord of this castle."

So intent was she upon the ground at his feet, the lady hardly noticed his rebellion. "Hmm, well," she began absently. "If you are referring to Lord Bernard, then I must disappoint you. You are no longer under his roof, Lord Ranulf. You now reside under mine."

Truly, Ranulf was not surprised. "Then I would speak with the lord of *this* castle!"

She sighed. "Regrettably, 'tis not possible. 'Twill be a sennight hence he returns. And then . . ." Her words trailed off.

At the same moment, her gaze flew back to his, and before she could step away, realization dawned upon Ranulf. He gave his arms his full weight again and thrust his legs out before him.

His powerful thighs trapped her around her slender waist, the looped chain between his feet striking her shins and buckling her knees. With a cry, she fell heavily against him, her face slamming into his chest, her long black tresses cascading from the collar of her man's tunic.

"Now," he muttered at the crown of her head, "take those keys from round your lovely neck and release me."

Defiantly, she pushed her hands against his chest and tossed her head back. A trickle of blood trailed from her nose. " 'Twill do you no good," she warned. She wiped the blood away with the back of her hand, then dragged it across the front of her tunic. "You would not be allowed to leave alive." Her eyes blazed with challenge, her mouth held in a tight, unyielding line.

"Do it," he rasped, "or by all that's holy, I swear I will crush the life from your accursed body." Making good the threat, he tightened his legs around her.

Swift as a cat, she countered. Bringing both arms up, she raked his face with her nails.

Chained, Ranulf's only defense was to crush his legs tighter about her.

With a strangled groan of pain, she arched backward, her hands dropping to try to pry his thighs apart. In her struggle, her hand fell to the hilt of the small dagger belted at her waist. Hesitating only briefly before withdrawing the weapon from its sheath, she raised it high, then buried its tip in Ranulf's thigh.

His roar of pain was followed by her release.

Crying out as she was propelled backward, Lizanne threw her hands behind her to cushion her fall onto the hard earthen floor. The dirt tore into her bare palms as she skidded on her buttocks and landed flat on her back, her breath momentarily torn from her chest. She allowed herself only a moment to fill her lungs before pushing herself to her feet. Clutching at her aching ribs, she faced her attacker.

"You!" she gasped, staggering forward on uncertain legs. "I will see you in hell for this."

Ranulf looked up from the dagger protruding from his thigh, his thoughts murderous. "Am I not already in hell?—witch!"

Her gaze fell to the dagger, and to Ranulf's amazement, she visibly started at the sight of her bloody handiwork. Hand flying to her mouth, she spun on her heel and flew to the cell door. Throwing it wide, she disappeared through it without a backward glance.

Breathing deeply through clenched teeth, Ranulf fought the void of blackness threatening to engulf him once more. Dropping his head to his chest, he imprinted the image of the dagger protruding from his flesh upon his mind, allowing it to feed on the hatred engendered by it. Never in his one score and nine years had he so desired to bed and to physically harm a woman at the same time. Nay, women were meant for pleasure. They were to be protected, not set upon as he was plotting.

This woman was different though—mean-spirited as Lord Langdon had warned . . . but more. He nearly laughed aloud at the traitorous desire.

A long, thick shadow falling across the floor heralded the arrival of a large man. He stepped through the doorway and hesitated briefly before crossing to Ranulf's side.

"Me name's Samuel," he said, his large hands splayed self-importantly on his hips, "an' I be yer jailer." His expressive face pinched as he leaned closer to inspect the scratches Lizanne's nails had inflicted. "Hmm," he muttered, his eyes twinkling mischievously.

At Ranulf's deadly silence, Samuel sighed regretfully and bent over to inspect his thigh, his great bald head gleaming in the light. "Aye, she got ye good, that she did. Ye must have made her right angry."

"I'll need a physician," Ranulf bit off, ignoring the man's ramblings.

Samuel straightened, bringing him eye-to-eye with Ranulf. "Well now, Lady Lizanne ain't ordered no physician for ye. But I've had some experience if ye'd like me to give it a try...."

"I have no desire to lose my leg!" Ranulf exploded.

"Mayhap that be what she wants. She do seem to hold a mighty grudge again' ye."

Ranulf calmed himself enough to ask the burning question. "Why?"

Samuel shrugged. "Milady's reasons I ain't privy to."

"Then do not speak to me of them!"

Samuel's face split with a grin, showing a surprisingly full set of teeth. Chuckling, he leaned over again. "It ain't such a deep wound." He tapped the hilt of the dagger, then strode across the earthen floor and back out the door.

Some minutes later he returned with a fistful of rags. With one swift movement, he pulled the dagger from Ranulf's flesh and tossed it aside. Immediately, he pressed a rag to the wound to stanch the flow of blood.

Awash in pain, Ranulf groaned loudly. 'Twas worse than the actual inflicting of the wound. Squeezing his eyes shut, he gnashed his teeth as Samuel continued his clumsy ministrations.

"Now hold still!" the man commanded, making quick work of applying a crude tourniquet.

Taking deep, steadying breaths, Ranulf looked down at his bandaged leg and scowled. " 'Twill take more than that to save my leg."

"Ungrateful, are ye?" Samuel admonished. His lips twitched humorously, somewhat at odds with his tone of voice. "Well now." He stood back and cocked his head, his bald pate reflecting the light. "Methinks it'll do just fine."

At Ranulf's thunderous expression, he grinned broadly. "Now don't ye worry. After the nooning meal,

I'll have me missus come and clean it right fer ye. She knows plenty 'bout tendin' wounds." Another grin and the man was gone, returning only moments later to secure the forgotten door behind him.

Imposing though he might be, Ranulf knew this Samuel was no jailer. Perchance an ally . . .

Alone, Ranulf visually searched the dirt floor until he spotted the jeweled hilt of the dagger where the man had carelessly tossed it a good distance away. It could be useful later.

Balancing himself on the injured leg, he twisted his other foot into the hard, packed dirt of the floor and kicked a spray of granules in the direction of the weapon. It took much concentrated effort, but when he finished, the dagger was no longer visible. In its place stood a nondescript, loosely mounded pile of dirt.

Smiling derisively, he leaned his head back and through a haze of pain began plotting—from his escape to the revenge he would take upon the Lady Lizanne. He would not leave this place without her.

Chapter 2

Scarcely *noticing the* shocked faces of the castlefolk as she rushed past, Lizanne barely reached the sanctuary of her chamber before giving up the simple meal she had partaken of that morning.

Kneeling, she held her head in trembling hands and rocked her body for long minutes. "Why?" she groaned aloud. Why should she suffer such remorse at having defended herself against that beast? Why had it bothered her to look upon the wound she had inflicted on him? It was certainly no less than he deserved—a ruthless man who had taken from her everything she held dear. Still, it sickened her.

Drawing a deep, shuddering breath, she finally drew herself upright and, on shaky legs, crossed the chamber to the door. With hands that did not feel like her own, she barred the door, then turned and walked over to a large window. Earlier that morning she had removed the oilcloth that covered it to let in the light of a cloudless day. Considering the past six days had seen overcast skies and constant, miserable drizzle, it was a godsend.

Though its descent into the west had begun, the sun was still high, casting a warm column of light over her. With a murmur of submission, she closed her eyes and felt the heat through every pore of her icy skin. Although she began to warm outwardly, she was unable to shake the chill at the very core of her being. It was a different kind of cold she had carried with her for nigh on four years. . . .

Drawing a weary hand across her forehead, she slid into the window embrasure and looked uninterestedly down into the inner bailey. She noted, put paid no heed to, the young squire engaged in swordplay with one of the men-at-arms.

Clasping her hands to her mouth, she began chewing the edge of a thumbnail. For the first time, the implications of her abduction of Ranulf Wardieu began to burden her. Previously, she'd given no thought as to what the consequences of exacting her revenge might be. She'd known only the burning need to free herself from years of painful memories. To avenge Gilbert.

It had taken her by surprise to discover that Ranulf Wardieu was of the nobility, but how easily she'd put that aside in her consuming hunger for retaliation. It had not mattered that he had been personally sent by King Henry to preside over a dispute between Lord Bernard and one of his vassals.

It would have been so simple had he been but the common villein he had portrayed himself to be years ago. But now . . . Dare she believe her taking of him would leave her and her brother, Gilbert, unscathed? Little she knew of Ranulf Wardieu, but she was certain he would be missed. And soon.

Unbidden, his larger-than-life image forced itself upon her. At least physically, he appeared to have changed little in four years—perhaps a bit huskier.

His rank of nobility with its accompanying speech, mannerisms, and clothes might have thrown another, but Lizanne would have known him anywhere. That long, shockingly pale hair. The large, powerfully muscled frame. And those eyes that had stared at her with such anger—as black as she remembered them, yet somehow different. It was almost as if . . .

"Damn him to perdition!" she cursed, her voice tight with raw emotion. It was he. It could be no other! Squashing the childish desire to kick her feet and pound her fists against something—anything—she drew her knees tightly against her chest and wrapped her arms around them.

The revenge she had envisioned these past four years, while she had obsessively honed her body and weaponry skills to a level that vied with the best of her brother's men, was so close. She had but to raise a hand to fulfill her destiny. But could she? Dared she?

If only Gilbert had not been waylaid in his return from court. Surely, he would have challenged the man properly and seen justice done. Had he not more reason to hate him than she? Was it not he who bore the marks of that fateful night forever upon his lame body? Well she knew the depths of his anger.

Her weakening resolve found strength in the memories that had driven her these past years. Eyes narrowed, she forced to mind the image of her brother and his pronounced limp. His agony. The lost laughter that had once lit eyes now rendered empty of all but suffering. Wardieu had done that to him.

And what of her? Had she not suffered as well? Had not her betrothed, a man she had thought herself in love with, broken the marriage contract, believing her no longer chaste? A bitter laugh parted her lips. Aye, she had suffered, but not as Gilbert had. Naught compared to his loss.

Biting into the tender flesh of her lower lip, Lizanne searched frantically for a solution to her dilemma. Exactly how was she to exact her revenge? For exact it she must.

Tears of frustration welled in her eyes. Sniffling, she wiped them away with the backs of her hands, then tossed her head. Out of the corner of her eye, she caught another glimpse of the duel in the inner bailey below. The young squire had backed his opponent into a corner and was taunting him as he prepared to deliver the final mock thrust that would name him the victor.

With sudden interest, she stared transfixed as the squire thrust gracefully forward, withdrew, then laughed joyously and waved his sword heavenward. Foolish, she told herself as the idea came together. Terribly foolish.

Then she shook her head, a small smile tracing her lips. "Nay, 'tis perfect," she breathed. She would have her revenge. She would—

A persistent knocking broke into Lizanne's thoughts. "Milady!" Her maid Mellie's voice floated into the chamber. "Ye are needed."

As distinct as her words were, Lizanne knew the girl was on her hands and knees in the corridor outside, her mouth positioned near the large gap created between the floor and the bottom of the door.

"Can it not wait?" Lizanne called, reluctant to abandon the plans she had yet to formulate.

" 'Tis a child, milady. She's been hurt."

A healer, Lizanne was immediately on her feet, rushing to the chest that contained her medicinals—a chest that had once been her father's.

"A moment," she called to Mellie. As happened each time she opened the chest, memories flooded over her as the lid fell back against the wall.

Though more often a woman's domain, her father had always been fascinated with the healing properties of herbs. He had encouraged his daughter's interest in healing, taking her "herbing" with him from a very young age.

In the end, though, nothing could save the old baron from the terrible sickness that had eaten at his body. The attack on Lizanne and Gilbert's camp had wrested his last hold on life from him. Another reason why Wardieu must pay for his crimes . . .

Sweeping away the tears that had again fallen to her cheeks, Lizanne gathered the various pots she might need, her fine sewing needle, and strips of clean linen. Bundling them together, she closed the chest and ran across the chamber to throw the door wide.

"Where is the child?" she asked as Mellie straightened from the floor.

"In the hall, milady. 'Twas a dog that bit her."

Though Mellie kept pace with her all the way to the hall, relating the details of the attack, Lizanne did not pause to ask any questions.

The child's weeping mother sat upon a bench at the far end of the hall, her precious one clutched to her bosom as the servants clustered around her.

At Lizanne's approach, all stepped aside to allow her access to the sobbing child, who clung to her mother. "Send for Lucy," she instructed Mellie as she sank down upon her knees.

"She has been sent fer, milady," the maid informed her.

"And what is keeping her?" Gently, Lizanne pried loose the mother's arms and turned the child about. She was a pretty little thing, mayhap all of four years old. Pushing back the bloodstained cloth from the child's arm, Lizanne moved closer to examine the injury.

Bending near so that no others might hear, Mellie whispered, "Lucy is tendin' that other's wound, milady."

Other? Frowning, Lizanne stretched out the child's arm and carefully wiped the blood away. The wound was not as bad as she had feared, but it would require many stitches. And there would be a scar. Suddenly, her head came up as realization dawned upon her. Looking over her shoulder, she stared hard at Mellie. "Other?"

Shrugging apologetically, the maid nodded, confirming it was Wardieu whom Lucy was tending.

Lizanne's anger was short-lived as the healer in her pushed it aside. The man, evil though he was, had been wounded. It would be unseemly to leave him uncared for, even if she could not bring herself to see to his needs. Not even an animal deserved to be left bleeding and in pain.

Nay, her revenge would be carried out properly. Wardieu would be given the opportunity to defend his person.

Lizanne turned her attention back to the child. "And what is your name?" she asked, pushing damp golden hair back from tear-swollen eyes.

The little girl stared at her, her bottom lip trembling as she bravely fought back the tears. "A-Anna," she whispered.

"Anna," Lizanne repeated, forcing all thoughts of Wardieu out of her mind so that she could smile genuinely at the child. "You are such a brave little girl," she added as she reached for her medicinals.

A wavering smile lifted Anna's mouth. "I—I am?"

"Aye, you fought that mean old dog and won, did you not?"

Sniffling, Anna turned questioning eyes upon her mother. "Did I win, Mama?"

The woman met Lizanne's gaze first, her gratitude shining in her eyes, then smiled at her daughter and nodded.

"Now," Lizanne said as she deftly unstoppered a bottle with one hand, "I want you to tell me the whole story."

Anna looked uncertainly from Lizanne to the bottle that wafted a pungent odor upon the air, then back to Lizanne. "Will it hurt?" she asked.

Reassuringly, Lizanne touched her fingers to Anna's cheek. "Mayhap a little," she said honestly, "but you are brave, hmm?"

After a brief hesitation, Anna nodded.

Chapter 3

It was not simply the cold that awoke Lizanne with a violent start, but the nightmare. Although it had faded considerably over the years, it had taken this most recent opportunity to return with a vengeance—frighteningly vivid in its every painful detail.

She was huddled again in the window embrasure, having returned there after stitching little Anna's arm. The afternoon and evening had slipped away while she contemplated her plans for revenge, and she had fallen asleep. Drawing a hand across her face, she was surprised to find it damp with tears. She dried her cheeks, then looked out at the dark night. A cold breeze buffeted her face, lifting strands of her long, unruly hair.

Though unwilling to admit her fear, she searched for and finally spotted the dark, shadowed figure of a man as he slowly traversed the parapet of the inner bailey's wall. Disconcerted, she looked for more men-at-arms, but saw none. In all likelihood, there were no others.

It was a relatively peaceful time under the reign of King Henry II, and Gilbert, having seen to his sister's safety by placing her under the protection of Lord Bernard, had virtually divested the castle of its defenses, taking the bulk of his men with him to court. He had left only a minimum capable of offering a token resistance in the unlikely event the castle was set upon. Unfortunately, he had not anticipated the delays that had resulted in her return ahead of him, and most especially, her recent venture.

Lizanne knew that, should Ranulf's presence at Penforke be discovered and a campaign be undertaken to free him, the defense of the castle was less than questionable. It was practically nonexistent.

Shifting her cramped muscles, she grimaced at the chilling numbness that had settled in her limbs, and most especially her right thumb. It had never set properly and was wont to bother her from time to time.

Easing her feet to the cold floor, she thrust a hand out before her and felt her way across the darkened room. Familiarity guided her, and she found her bed without mishap. She began to disrobe, and not until she stood in her thin shift and soft braies did her woolly mind register that her precious dagger, given to her by Gilbert, was absent. Hands stilled in midair, she shook the last of the cobwebs from her mind and tried to remember what she'd done with it.

Her brow furrowed as she recalled she had used it against Wardieu. What had become of it after she had fled? Surely, Samuel would have put it aside for safekeeping, she assured herself, but she remained doubtful. Not only was the dagger sentimentally valuable, it posed a threat should it fall into the man's hands.

Throwing on a robe, she crossed to the door and pulled it open, then stepped out into the drafty, dimly lit corridor. She snatched a flickering torch from the wall and hastened down the corridor, miraculously descending the stone steps to the Great Hall without mishap.

As quietly as possible, so as not to awaken those sleeping on the rushes and benches there, she crossed the room. Hurrying down a narrow passage and a long flight of stairs, she came to the door of the main cell.

Although she had ordered that a guard be posted,

there was no sign of one. Stamping down an anger that threatened to erupt, she peered through the grate into the darkened cell. The torches had long since expired; the cell was pitch-black.

Unbolting the door, she pulled it open just enough to squeeze through, holding the torch before her as she stepped inside.

Her heart leaped in her throat as she focused on the still figure across the room. Cautiously, she stepped forward and saw that not only was her captive fully clothed, he now sat on the earthen floor, his head resting on his chest as he slept. Though he was still manacled, his arms were comfortably suspended by chains mounted lower in the wall on either side of him.

"Damn you, Samuel!" she hissed just beneath her breath.

Quietly, she withdrew to the far side of the room where a few tables and benches were set. Samuel might have left the dagger there. The light from the torch clearly illuminated the bare surfaces, and after a few minutes of searching, she resolved that Samuel had taken the dagger with him.

Although sense told her that she should leave, she was inexorably drawn to stand before her enemy. Her gaze drifted downward from the pale crown of his head, to his bandaged wrists, and finally to his left leg. There, the material of his coarse russet leggings was torn open, revealing the bandaged wound.

She could not help but wonder if he would be forever constrained by an ungainly limp such as that which Gilbert suffered. It would be fitting. . . .

Taking stock of her defenses and concluding that the man was less of a danger to her sitting than he had been standing, she knelt beside him and lowered the torch to better see his leg. The bandages were not bloody, nor were they damp to the touch, as they might have been had the wound been festering.

It was definitely the handiwork of Lucy, Samuel's wife. Lizanne wondered how they had managed Wardieu, though. Even injured, he would be a worthy adversary. But then, Samuel was a strong man, and undoubtedly he'd brought armed men with him for the task.

Nay, the wound had not been deep, and now that it had been properly cared for, it would likely heal fine.

Sighing with what she quickly denied was relief, Lizanne lifted her head and looked straight into black black eyes.

Gasping, she arched backward. The torch flew from her hand and rolled across the floor, flickering uncertainly as it came to rest against the leg of a table.

Disconcerted by her unusual clumsiness, she scrambled to her feet, scowling as deep, satisfied laughter echoed around her. Heart pounding, she retrieved the torch and was relieved when its flame sprang upward again.

There he sat, his head thrown back, a sinister smile stretching his lips wide as his laughter faded to a deep-chested rumble before subsiding altogether.

The silence that followed stretched interminably. Even when Wardieu began an insulting perusal of her less than appropriately clad figure, she could think of no words to put him in his place. A tremor of fear rocked her body when his eyes met hers again.

Mayhap she was a witch, as he had called her, but verily he was the Devil himself! Heart in her throat, she turned, eager to be away.

"Nay!" he bellowed, halting her flight.

Stiffly, she turned to face him.

"Come here!" he commanded, his harsh voice echoing through the cell.

She hesitated, clutching the torch in one hand and the lapels of her robe with the other. Why should she feel vulnerable—childish—standing before him? Was he not *her* prisoner?

"Surely, I can do you no harm," he continued in a

tight, sarcastic voice. He punctuated his words with a rattle of his chains.

Suspicious, Lizanne regarded him for a long moment. Then, summoning her courage, she lifted her chin and walked back to stand at his feet. "Aye, my lord?" she asked in a voice she hoped sounded confident.

Ranulf considered the dagger pressing against the backside of his thigh where he sat upon it. It was undoubtedly the reason for her visit to the cell.

Following the dinner Samuel had brought him, and which he had hungrily devoured, he had been overcome by darkness—drugged, no doubt. Upon awakening, he had found himself clothed and repositioned on the floor of the cell, his leg skillfully bandaged and curiously painless.

It had taken him only minutes to retrieve the dagger with his right foot, but far longer to work it up beneath his left leg. As the weapon was of little use to him until he could actually lay his hands on it, he reluctantly forced the thought to the back of his mind.

"Do sit," he invited.

Lizanne shook her head, her eyes narrowing to watchful slits. "Nay, I prefer to stand."

Conveying a measure of indifference, he shrugged. "I've a boon to ask of you."

"A boon?" she repeated, incredulous.

"Aye." A crooked smile slanted his lips. "I would know the grounds for my imprisonment—and where I am being held."

She crouched down at a safe distance and regarded him with something akin to puzzlement. "Would it give you comfort, my lord?"

Her deliberate "my lord" taunts made his palms itch for the feel of her throat between them. Fighting to keep a rein on emotions that were normally in control, he answered in a tight, raspy voice, " 'Tis mere curiosity, *my lady*."

He watched with undisguised interest as her lips

tightened and her eyes flashed with outrage. "Do not call me that!"

"My lady?" he repeated with mock innocence. " 'Tis simply a polite form of address—respect for your station."

"I am not your lady!"

"Nay," he was quick to agree. "You are not a lady at all."

His words cut more deeply than Lizanne would ever have imagined possible. Doubtless, there were others who would heartily agree with him—such as all of Gilbert's knights, who thought it unseemly for a woman to bear arms and clothe herself in men's garments. Still, none had ever spoken such words to her, though their feelings were conveyed readily enough. It did not seem to matter that, more often than not, she clothed herself as a lady and carried out her role as lady of the castle, a role she had been trained for from an early age. They saw her only through the eyes of men threatened by her ability to protect herself. But she was a lady too.

"And I . . ." Ranulf continued, baring a set of even, white teeth, "am not your lord—yet." His last word fell softly from his lips like warm honey.

A cold hand closed over Lizanne's heart. How was it he was able to arouse in her such misgivings? Had she not resigned herself to the task at hand? Was it not she who was in control?

Unsteadily, she rose to her feet, her hand falling from the lapels of her robe. "I have a proposal for you."

He met her eyes, but remained silent.

"I shall set you free if you can best the opponent of my choice in a duel of swords," she said in a rush, then waited anxiously for a response.

She got none. He simply stared at her, some ominous emotion building in the depths of his eyes and thinning of his lips.

Uncomfortable, she glanced away, then back. When

she spoke again, her voice was tight, constricting her throat as it pushed its way out. " 'Twill be a fight to the death."

Ranulf's eyes narrowed. "And who is this witless man who would die for you?"

She raised her chin. "Do not worry," she said with feigned nonchalance. " 'Tis a worthy opponent I have chosen."

His anger surfaced with the unexpectedness of a bolt of lightning. "Bitch!" he roared as he strained against his chains. "Do you think there will be no retribution for what you have done when I have killed this man who will die needlessly?"

Lizanne held her ground. "I have faith in my choice. Besides," she added, " 'twould not be difficult to best one in your condition. After all, what good is skill without speed? Need I remind you of your recently acquired lameness?—a decided disadvantage, my lord." Pointedly, she looked at his bandaged leg.

He erupted again, bright red suffusing his face. "He will die a bloody death," he barked loudly. "Then you and your family will suffer for the injustice done me!"

Of course, there was always the chance he would be the victor, but she had already considered that very real possibility. " 'Tis part of the bargain," she said. "To the death, and should you be successful, there will be no retaliation against my family."

Obviously enraged, Ranulf slammed his body hard against the wall, once again testing the strength of the chains.

Lizanne stood firm, coolly observing his struggles, yet drawing no pleasure from them. Though she was loath to admit such a weakness even to herself, she was more than a little frightened.

It was several minutes before he stilled again. Thrusting his lower jaw forward, he threw back his head and pinned her with those murderous, loathsome eyes.

Though greatly unnerved, Lizanne stepped closer. She stared at him for a long moment, a terrible silence hanging between them.

"So much anger," she murmured.

Her tone lacked the familiar sarcasm, and Ranulf was baffled as she seemed to withdraw within herself. It was almost as if she were someplace else, even though her eyes, suddenly flat and lifeless, still met his.

Mayhap the lady was mad, he considered. It would certainly explain a few things. . . .

She spoke again, her voice so soft he had to strain to catch it. "I, too, know such anger, my lord. 'Tis verily the reason for my bringing you here." She stared hard at him, then closed her eyes.

Ranulf remained silent.

"I will have my revenge," she said, her voice calm and level when she looked at him again.

She stepped closer, casting only a brief, wary look at his legs thrust out before him. Reaching down, she touched his unshaven jaw. He did not flinch, though his muscles tightened.

"Believe me, Ranulf Wardieu, my family and I have already suffered greatly for your crimes," she whispered. " 'Tis our due."

The two adversaries locked eyes, and something deep and unspoken passed between them. It was more than revenge, more than past aggressions. Ranulf gave it the name of desire, but Lizanne denied it, violently snatching her hand away.

The spell was broken.

"You think I do this only to amuse myself?" Her voice rose shrilly in the cell, her mouth compressing into a tight, unyielding line as the fire returned to her luminous eyes.

"I will have your word," she demanded. "Now!"

Ranulf resolved that he would not beg again for an explanation of his crimes. Instead, he stared up at her and shook his head. "Nay," he said in a deep, harsh voice born of stubborn conviction. "Like you, I will not be cheated of revenge. 'Tis also my due."

She stepped closer, and the light of the torch was full upon her face as she spit, "Your word. Else you will die the death of a coward on the morrow. I swear it!"

He missed nothing—from the sudden wash of color suffusing her face to the shallow breaths she drew. For a moment, he stared at her, doubtful of her threat.

Still, he found himself reconsidering her challenge. Mayhap what she proposed was merely a way out of the mistake she'd made in imprisoning him. Aye, he had put the fright into her. He had not missed the red puffy eyes she had unsuspectingly allowed him a glimpse of. The woman who stood before him now was not the same who had been so arrogantly confident before him earlier.

His brows drew together. Her proposal was not entirely without merit, as he had no desire to remain chained in this godforsaken cell a moment longer than necessary. Perhaps what she offered would be enough . . . for now.

Thus consoled, he laughed shortly as his gaze slid over her soft white neck and down her robe, which revealed a glimpse of the feminine undergarment beneath.

"Aye, you've my word, witch," he said. "Though it remains to be seen whether I keep it." His smile was wicked, feral. "Mayhap I will leave your family be, but it remains to be seen whether you yourself will be so fortunate."

Feeling burned by his dark gaze, Lizanne reached up to grasp the lapels of her robe together. " 'Tis enough," she said, knowing it was the best she could coax from him.

"On the morrow, then," she threw over her shoulder as she beat a fast retreat to the door.

Chapter 4

$\mathcal{R}$*anulf was awakened* the next morning by Samuel's ungainly clamor and the smell of food. He watched as the big man, two men-at-arms close on his heels, traversed the cell.

"You," Samuel addressed the men. "Go yon and light the torches." There was a murmur of assent, then the men moved away.

"Yer awake bright and early," Samuel cheerfully greeted Ranulf as he lowered a tray to the floor. Straightening, he planted his hands on his hips and looked down into Ranulf's face. "Appears ye didna sleep well last night—an' after all me trouble to make ye comfortable." He shook his head.

Ranulf lifted an eyebrow. " 'Twas unkind of you to drug me."

Shrugging, Samuel lifted a palm heavenward. " 'Twas only a mild sleeping draught. Seeing as I had only me wife's help, 'twas the easiest way to tend to yer wound and clothe ye."

"Surely, you are not frightened of me?"

The great man scowled, clearly affronted by Ranulf's taunt. "Ain't no man that frightens big Samuel. 'Twas me wife, Lucy, who insisted on it. Saw that bloody nose ye gave to our lady and wouldna come down till ye were out fer certain."

Ranulf was unable to suppress his smile. A bloody nose. It was the least he intended to do to Lady Lizanne.

"Forsooth, I am grateful to you, Samuel—and your Lucy. My leg does not pain me as it did, and 'tis by far more comfortable sitting than standing."

Samuel warmed visibly, his chest puffing with pride. "Lucy's good with medicines and herbs. Taught by the lady herself."

"The Lady Lizanne?" Ranulf asked, his tone infused with disbelief.

"Aye. Fer all her wildness, that one has a mighty gift fer healin'. Takes care of everyone, she does.

Ranulf attempted to fit this odd bit of information among his other impressions of the woman. After a few moments' deliberation, he gave up and lumped it with a growing number of unclassifiable oddities.

"Here now!" Samuel raised his voice as he crossed the cell in a half-dozen strides. "Do I have to do it meself?" Taking the torch from the men, he quickly lit the others.

"Simpletons," he grumbled, returning to stand before Ranulf. " 'Twill be a relief once Lord Gilbert returns. Gone off to court and took his best men with him, he did. And now him delayed." He heaved a great, disgusted sigh.

Ranulf pretended an interest in the food as he pondered Samuel's words. The man was proving to be an excellent source of information. Mayhap he could learn more. . . .

Samuel did not disappoint him. "Highly improper, I would say, to let the Lady Lizanne come home to Penforke with all this disorder. And she only makes matters worse with all her lordin'."

Penforke . . . Ranulf searched his knowledge of the southern lands in an attempt to determine his location. 'Twas not so far from Langdon's castle, he realized.

Samuel leaned down and deftly removed the manacle from Ranulf's left wrist. "Knows she can get away with it, of course. Ain't a one ceptin' her brother that'll tell her nay, and even he usually gives in to her. Ain't ne'er understood it. Been that way since me Lucy and I came here."

Intrigued, Ranulf accepted the hunk of warm, freshly baked bread Samuel shoved into his freed hand.

"He knows better 'n to leave her to her own devices. That one needs supervision, I tell ye. And look what she's done bringin' ye here. Can't say as I like it much. Nay, canna say as I do."

Ranulf was tempted to insert his own comments on that subject, but, fearful of alerting Samuel to his loose tongue, squashed the idea. Absently, he took a bite of the bread, listening as his eyes sought out and found the two other men. They were bent over a table engaged in a game of dice.

Samuel shook his head and heaved another sigh. "Have a taste o' that brew. 'Tis the best fer miles around."

Ranulf lifted the pot of ale to his lips and took a deep swallow, waiting patiently for Samuel to speak again.

He did not. Hearing the exultant cry of triumph across the cell, the bald man looked over his shoulder and eyed the taller of the two men, who was tossing his newly won wealth from one hand to the other. Grunting, Samuel turned back to Ranulf, smiled apologetically, then trotted off to join in the game.

Ranulf was more than satisfied with what he had gleaned from the man's grumblings, and now that he found himself forgotten, the need to secure the dagger was uppermost in his mind.

Never taking his eyes from the three men, he retrieved the sharp, bejeweled object from beneath his leg and, lifting the hem of his tunic, slid it into the top of his leggings. Then he calmly reached for another piece of meat, looking every bit as if nothing untoward had occurred.

* * *

Attired in men's garb, Lizanne sat atop her gray palfrey and peered through the trees bordering the meadow. On a baldric passing from her right shoulder to her hip hung a two-edged sword. In a scabbard attached to the saddle was a second. Beneath her, the mare shifted restlessly, throwing her head to the right to pull the reins held loosely in gloved hands.

"Shh, Lady," Lizanne soothed, pressing herself low over the mare's neck to stroke the favored spot between the pert ears. " 'Twill not be long now."

The mare was only recently saddle-broke, but she had a spirit and grace that had immediately caught Lizanne's eye. In spite of his misgivings over the animal's flighty temperament, Gilbert had gifted the beautiful horse to Lizanne for her seventeenth year.

Straightening, Lizanne glanced up at the sun's position, wondering not for the first time if Samuel had misunderstood her instructions, mayhap intentionally. The thought did nothing to improve her disposition.

Then she heard the thundering of hooves. Swinging around in her saddle, she saw three horsemen enter the meadow from its southernmost corner. At the fore rode Samuel, and pulling up the rear was the armed escort. Ranulf Wardieu rode between the two, a long mantle about his shoulders, short boots on his feet.

Lady whinnied in welcome, taking a step forward before Lizanne firmly yanked the reins. Thankfully, the noise went unnoticed, eclipsed by the beating of hooves. At its mistress's command, the mare pranced backward and assumed a detached stance to await the next instruction.

Leaning over Lady's neck, Lizanne watched as the horses were reined in at the center of the meadow. Crouching lower, she held her breath when Samuel scanned the border of woods.

Samuel clearly had not liked the orders she had delivered to him that noon and had suggested they await her brother's return before doing anything further. Lizanne had been adamant, though, instructing him to escort the prisoner to the meadow east of the castle and releasing him. Though Samuel had been suspicious, he'd had no choice but to agree.

At long last, Ranulf was dismounting with an ease that belied the injury he had suffered the day before. Tossing the reins to Samuel, he said something that made the other laugh uproariously. A few more words were exchanged, then a sack was handed down— provisions, no doubt.

Lizanne drew in a sharp, angry breath. Samuel had disregarded her orders again! It was small wonder he was not providing the cur with a horse as well.

Lady felt her mistress's mounting tension and nervously tossed her head, her great, soulful eyes rolling back to show white. With whispered words of reassurance, Lizanne soothed her, though her gaze never left the men in the meadow.

Moments later, the horses were galloping away, leaving the lone man standing amid the long grass. Hands on his hips, he turned to watch the departure, his pale hair lifting in the warm breeze of early summer.

Even when the riders had disappeared and the pounding of hooves had faded to a distant rumble, Lizanne did not move, suddenly less than eager to finish what she had started. Gripping the mare's silky mane, she fought down the panic that threatened to overwhelm her and send her fleeing back to the safety of the castle's walls.

It was Lady who finally decided the matter for her, jumping from the cover of the trees and into the meadow.

Providence, Lizanne concluded with new-found courage as she spurred the mare into a gallop. The hood of her short mantle slid off her head, and her braid flew out behind her.

Ranulf turned and stared at the horse and rider, feeling the ticklish vibrations of their approach through the thin soles of his borrowed boots. He tried to assess his opponent; however, the man was not only distanced, but the glaring sun was at his back.

As the horse drew steadily near, the glint of steel caught Ranulf's eye, making him grimace at the grisly task that lay before him. A vision of the lady sitting safe within her castle's walls while she nonchalantly sent another to likely death only served to deepen his anger and resolve.

He did not want this man's life. Nay, he would be satisfied only with avenging himself upon the Lady Lizanne. And though he would keep his vow to render her family blameless, he had determined she would be his. If, ultimately, that meant doing battle with the brother, then so be it.

So it was with great astonishment that Ranulf found himself staring up into the flushed countenance of that lady when she brought her horse to an abrupt halt before him. It was the first time he had seen her face without the cover of her unkempt hair, and he could not help but be pleased by the flawless oval above a slender throat.

"Welcome, my Lord Ranulf," she said. " 'Tis a fine day for a duel."

He stared unblinkingly at her, then let a frown settle between his eyes. "Forsooth, I did not expect you to attend this bloodletting," he said. "I must needs remember you are not a lady."

Her jaw hardened. "I assure you I would not miss this for anything."

He looked at the weapons she carried. "And where is this man who would champion your ill-fated cause?" he asked, looking past her.

"Man?" She shook her head. "There is no man."

Ranulf considered this, one eyebrow arched. "You

were unable to find a single man willing to die for you, my lady? Not one?"

Refusing to rise to the bait, Lizanne leaned forward, smiling faintly. "Alas, I fear I am so uncomely that none would offer."

"And what of our bargain?" Ranulf asked, suspicion cast upon his voice.

"It stands."

"You think to hold me till your brother returns?" He shifted more of his weight onto his uninjured leg. "Do you forget that I am an unwilling captive, my lady? 'Tis not likely you will return me to that foul-smelling cell." He took a step toward her.

At his sudden movement, the mare shied away, snorting loudly as it pranced sideways. Lizanne brought the animal under control with an imperceptible tightening of her legs.

"Nay," she said, her eyes unwavering. "Your opponent is here before you now."

Ranulf took some moments to digest this, then burst out laughing. As preposterous as it was, a mere woman challenging an accomplished knight to a duel of swords, her proposal truly did not surprise him, though it certainly amused him.

And she was not jesting! he acknowledged. Amazingly, it fit the conclusions he had wrestled with, and finally accepted, regarding her character.

Had she a death wish, then? Even if that spineless brother of hers had shown her how to swing a sword, it was inconceivable she could have any proficiency with such a heavy, awkward weapon. A sling, perhaps, and he mustn't forget a dagger, but a sword?

Slowly, he sobered, blinking back tears of mirth and drawing deep, ragged breaths of air.

She edged her horse nearer, her indignation evident in her stiffly erect bearing. "I find no humor in the situation. Mayhap you would care to enlighten me, Lord Ranulf?"

"Doubtless, you would not appreciate my explanation, my lady."

Her chin went up. "Think you I will not make a worthy opponent?"

"With your nasty tongue, perhaps, but—"

"Then let us not prolong the suspense any longer," she snapped. Swiftly, she removed the sword from its scabbard and tossed it, hilt first, to him.

Reflexively, Ranulf pulled it from the air, his hand closing around the cool metal hilt. He was taken aback as he held it aloft, for inasmuch as the weapon appeared perfectly honed on both its edges, it was not the weighty sword he was accustomed to. Indeed, it felt awkward in his grasp.

"And what is this, a child's toy?" he quipped, twisting the sword in his hand.

In one fluid motion, Lizanne dismounted and turned to face him. " 'Tis the instrument of your death, my lord." Advancing, she drew her own sword, identical to the one he held.

He lowered his sword's point and narrowed his eyes. "Think you I would fight a woman?"

" 'Tis as we agreed."

"I agreed to fight a man—"

"Nay, you agreed to fight the opponent of my choice. I stand before you now ready to fulfill our bargain."

"We have no such bargain," he insisted.

"Would you break your vow? Are you so dishonorable?"

Never before had Ranulf's honor been questioned. For King Henry and, when necessary, himself, he had fought hard and well, and he carried numerous battle scars to attest to his valor. Still, her insult rankled him.

" 'Tis honor that compels me to decline," he said, a decidedly dangerous smile playing about his lips.

"Honor?" She laughed, coming to an abrupt halt a few feet from him. "Methinks 'tis your injury, coward. Surely, you can still wield a sword?"

Coward? A muscle in his jaw jerked. This one was expert at stirring the remote depths of his anger. "Were you a man, you would be dead now."

"Then imagine me a man," she retorted, lifting her sword in challenge.

The very notion was laughable. Even garbed as she was, the Lady Lizanne was wholly a woman.

"Nay, I fear I must decline." Resolutely, he leaned on the sword. " 'Twill make a fine walking stick, though," he added, flexing the steel blade beneath his weight.

Ignoring his quip, Lizanne took a step nearer. "You cannot decline!"

"Aye, and I do."

"Then I will gut you like a pig!" she shouted and leaped forward.

Instinctively, Ranulf lifted his sword and swung it upward to hers. The strength behind her controlled thrust surprised him. Had he not been prepared, her blow might well have landed across his neck, he realized with amazement. It shook him momentarily to be faced with such an unlikely opponent.

Still, he was confident she presented no real threat. It would be easy enough to disarm her, but perhaps he would humor her for a few minutes until she tired of the sport.

He smiled and, with a great shove forward, pushed her sword off his.

She fell back a step and immediately countered with a wide, arcing swing upward. A moment later, the point of her sword found its mark just shy of his right eye, leaving a long, thin tear up into his hairline.

Shocked, Ranulf clapped a hand to the wound and stared at the blood his hand came away with.

"Do not underestimate me, my lord," she warned before resuming her attack.

Although he was more angry with himself than with her, Ranulf's tolerant disposition altered significantly. He had indeed underestimated her ability—and her conviction. It had been ages since an opponent had landed him a blow, and to have a woman do so deeply injured his warrior's pride.

Even as he castigated himself for his former nonchalant attitude, he assumed a proper dueling stance and thrust his sword forward, easily knocking her next offensive blow aside.

She recovered instantly and, snarling in a most unladylike manner, came after him again.

She was swift and accurate, taking full advantage of his disability, as promised. Though she was well practiced and proficient with a sword, her chief advantage lay in the ease and grace with which she maneuvered. One moment she was fully to his right, and in the blink of an eye, she was attacking from the left. Even so, with Ranulf's powerful body mass and years of experience behind him, he easily deflected each of her blows, wearing her down with the forceful impacts he countered with.

At one point, she stumbled. Though she quickly recovered, he pressed the moment of advantage and slashed his sword diagonally across her chest. It could have meant her death, but he was too precise for such an error. Instead, it cleanly opened her tunic and scored a thin, neat line from her collarbone to the swell of the full breast opposite.

She spared only a brief glance downward before recklessly raising her sword and swinging near his midline.

Ignoring the protesting throb in his leg, Ranulf sidestepped, then advanced on her, determined to yield no ground. With deliberate acceleration, he drove her back, but still she fought, her tenacity sustaining her in the face of failing strength. Even when she labored for breath, now using both hands to guide each swing of her sword, she pressed on.

With growing satisfaction, Ranulf watched as her sword grew heavier with every stroke. He noted the perspiration upon her skin and the frenzied look that entered her eyes as he forced her out of her offensive posture and into one of pure defense.

She was his. . . .

Thinking to bring an end to the senseless exhibition, he hoisted his sword a final time and, putting his whole body behind it, brought it forcefully down upon her steel.

The unthinkable happened.

At the juncture where blade fused with hilt, his sword snapped, leaving him staring at his suddenly useless weapon.

Shaking off his surprise, he looked up to find Lizanne, her sword frozen in midair, gaping at him. In complete disarray, she stood motionless except for the widening of her eyes.

Her cheeks were flushed scarlet, her lips softly parted, and much of her hair had loosed itself from the braid. Rivulets of moisture meandered down the flawless skin of her face and neck, and lower, to the gleaming curve of flesh he had exposed with the point of his sword. The light material of her ripped tunic clung damply to her, clearly outlining the proud, thrusting breasts that rose and fell with each hard-won breath.

She was splendid.

With a deep sigh of regret, he tore his gaze from the sight. "Inferior steel," he said dryly, shattering the silence. Carelessly, he tossed the hilt aside.

Feeling the press of her dagger where it rested against his abdomen, and knowing he might have to use

it to subdue her, he boldly stepped forward. "I am resigned to my fate, witch. Do have mercy and be quick
about it."

She blinked once, twice, three times, then took a
halting step backward, her sword thrust before her.

One corner of his mouth quirking, Ranulf advanced
on her. For each step he took, she retreated two, her indecision written clearly in her eyes. He could not help
but be pleased.

Her moment at hand, Lizanne's thoughts of revenge
deserted her completely. She had never killed a man. For
that matter, she had only ever taken small game—and
with her bow. That instant, she knew what Ranulf had
already recognized. She could not take his life.

"To the death," he taunted, lengthening his strides.
"Was that not our bargain?"

She shook her head and in the next instant bolted,
making straight for where her horse had wandered to
watch the skirmish from a comfortable distance.

Ranulf stared after her a moment before giving
chase. Though he tried to ignore his injured leg, it
slowed him, gaining for Lizanne the time she needed.

Winded, she resheathed her sword and hoisted herself onto the mare's back. Gathering the reins, she pulled
hard, causing Lady to rear and cleave the air with her
hooves. That halted Ranulf's pursuit.

"I give you back your life, Ranulf Wardieu," she
shouted above the horse's agitated cry. " 'Tis over ...
over." Veering away, she pressed her heels sharply to the
mare's sides and galloped across the meadow without a
backward glance.

Ranulf's eyes followed her until she passed from
sight. "Nay," he breathed, "it has only begun, Lizanne of
Penforke."

Chapter 5

"Ah, Mellie! 'Tis my brother that comes, not a suitor," Lizanne protested as the young maid pressed her down upon a stool and began combing her mass of errant hair.

"Aye, and ye've not seen him for nigh on two months now," Mellie reminded her as she tugged at a particularly troublesome snarl. "Ye know he prefers it when ye look the lady. Now would ye rather be pleasing to the eye, or woeful?"

Mellie was right, of course. Though Gilbert did not voice his objections, it was no secret he disliked the austere hairstyle and man's garb she favored.

Aye, for him she would do it—but none other! She only hoped it was not all in vain and that he would, indeed, return on this, the sixth day since she had released Ranulf Wardieu. Her insides churned at the mere thought of that man.

As each uneventful day had passed, she had grown increasingly confident her brother would return in time to quell any retaliation Wardieu might think to undertake against Penforke. Still, in the event she was wrong, she had seen the castle's defenses strengthened as best she could. But Wardieu had not come, and now it seemed unlikely he would.

At last the torturous tugging ended. Heaving a sigh of relief, Lizanne began to stand but found herself urged back down. Glowering, she resumed her seat and squirmed as Mellie carefully applied hot irons to her hair, creating orderly curls that flowed softly down her back. Last, a short, light veil was placed over her head and secured with an unadorned silver circlet.

Lizanne would have left her chamber then, but Mellie pressed a small mirror into her hand. As she viewed her reflection from different angles, Lizanne was ashamed at the twinge of pleasure coursing through her. Arrayed in her best bliaut, an embroidered garment of green samite slit up each side to reveal the saffron-colored chemise beneath, she looked every bit the lady ... every bit the picture of femininity that she, as a gawky girl, had dreamed of becoming. Thoughtfully, she fingered the ornamental girdle settled loosely upon the curve of her hips.

You are vain, she reproached herself, but could not refrain from staring. Truly, Gilbert would be pleased.

"You are lovely, milady," Mellie breathed, more than a little pleased with her contributions.

Lizanne felt the heat rise in her face. Scowling, she swung away, swatting at an unruly lock of hair that had sprung forward across her cheek. "Come," she said. "I must be certain all is in order for my brother's return."

As she descended to the hall, a lad of no more than a dozen years rushed forward and placed himself squarely in her path. Looking up, he was momentarily dumbstruck by her appearance, his head jerking back as if he'd been firmly smacked.

His reaction was almost enough to send Lizanne flying back up the stairs to rid herself of the garments, but his words immediately set aside any thoughts of flight.

"Riders approaching from the east, milady," he panted, excitement and exertion staining his cheeks scarlet.

Lizanne broke into a run, unmindful of her unladylike behavior as she crossed the inner bailey, sprinted over its drawbridge, and sped across the outermost bailey. At the gatehouse, she threw the bulk of her skirts over one arm and ascended the stone steps two at a time. Shouldering her way between the gathering of men on the roof, she looked out between the crenellations to the large group of riders approaching from the east.

Though they were still too distant for her to make out the pennants they flew, she knew it would be Gilbert.

The riders disappeared momentarily as they plunged down a distant hillside, only to reappear moments later when they crested another hill.

Shading her eyes against the glare of the sun, Lizanne leaned out over the stone wall. She was charged with a peculiar mixture of excitement and uncertainty over her brother's return.

These long weeks had not been easy for her. In spite of her disdain for court life, she would gladly have accompanied Gilbert if not for her overwhelming fear that the king would once again undertake to match her with one of his knights. He had done just that the previous year, and it had not been a pleasant scene she'd caused. In fact, so great was his humiliation, Gilbert had not spoken to her for days thereafter.

Her uncertainty was firmly rooted in what Gilbert's reaction would be to her abduction of Ranulf Wardieu and his subsequent release. She'd had too many days to reflect on her deed and had finally accepted the truth of the matter. In her impatience to exact revenge, she had acted rashly. It was a difficult thing to admit, but nonetheless true.

Again, the riders disappeared.

In the lull, Lizanne turned to find Robert Coulter, the captain of the guard, behind her. A heavy frown marred his aged countenance as he looked past her, his squinting more from failing eyesight than from the sun's glare.

"Lower the drawbridge," she ordered.

"But, my lady—"

"Nay, do not argue," she interrupted. "Prepare a proper welcome for my brother."

His mouth tightened perceptibly. Grumbling, he spun on his heel and went to do her bidding.

Lizanne turned her attention back to the hills. Over the next rise, the lofty pennants were visible before the riders, their vivid blue, red, and gold colors backlit by the sun that glinted off the armor of the men that followed.

Lizanne beamed, but only for a moment. Realization swept the smile from her face as her gaze flew back to the fluttering pennants. Her breath caught in her throat, her eyes widening as the color drained from her face. An anguished denial tore from her lips at the same moment the drawbridge began its descent with a reverberating rattle of its enormous chains.

The sound brought her instantly to life. Rounding on the man nearest her, she grasped his arm. "Send word to raise the bridge—run!"

The startled man blinked. Then, assisted by a thrust from his mistress, he sprinted to the stairs.

The drawbridge was fully three-quarters lowered before it came to a wrenching halt. Moments later it began a laborious ascent. Amid a flurry of confusion, Lizanne watched its return with bated breath, her eyes sweeping back and forth between it and the swiftly approaching riders.

On level ground now, the army, more than a hundred strong, spurred their horses forward. The thundering of hooves rose menacingly above the land, striking fear in the inhabitants of Penforke. Having discerned that something serious was afoot, they were quickly making themselves scarce.

Though she knew not the colors of Ranulf Wardieu, Lizanne did not delude herself into thinking that these could be any others.

He had returned.

Frantically, she searched among the riders for their leader, shrewdly eliminating those whose horses were void of the trappings emblazoned with the same colors as the pennants. After a moment, her gaze settled upon one who rode in the center before the others, a man who was large even from this distance. Though his telling hair was covered by a mail hood and helmet, she knew it to be he.

The skin of her forearms pricked with a sudden chill that raised every hair on her body and threatened to buckle her knees beneath her. Grasping the ledge of the stone wall, she drew in deep, calming breaths and squeezed her eyes closed, hoping that when she opened them again, a far different sight would greet her.

It did not.

Although it was tenuous, she summoned enough composure to begin weighing the alternatives she would soon be forced to choose among. Repeatedly, she returned to one—Gilbert. If she could only keep Wardieu at bay, her brother's return would surely send him running. Not for one moment did she doubt he would return this day. She had to believe it.

Even as the infidels flanked the castle's curtain wall, reining in at a distance beyond the range of arrows, the drawbridge completed its return journey. An unbroken silence, save for the labored breathing of the great warhorses, ensued.

Mounted astride an enormous destrier as dark as he was light, Ranulf raised his gaze to the top of the wall and searched out the few men-at-arms visible there.

Having expected Gilbert Balmaine to precede his own arrival, he was taken aback by the castle's seemingly inadequate defenses. Still, appearances could be deceiving. Considering this, he shifted his attention to the drawbridge that had so recently been raised against them.

"What make you of this?" Sir Walter Fortesne asked,

breaking into his lord's thoughts as he urged his mount nearer to Ranulf's.

Ranulf brushed aside the question and continued his inspection of the castle's fortifications. Although it appeared solid and in good repair, it would be nigh impossible to defend were it lacking an adequate supply of well-trained men. Methodically, he considered the avenues of attack available to him should one be necessary. There were several.

"'Twould appear the lord of the castle and his men have not yet returned," Walter commented. "It looks to be an easy conquest."

Ranulf smiled, and at once he was reminded of the healing cut near his right eye where the chain-mail hood grazed it. "If 'tis so, I vow to have that which I came for ere the noon hour."

He lifted his gaze farther up the gatehouse and counted half a dozen men-at-arms stationed between the crenellations of the tower. Which one was she? he wondered, searching for a glimpse of unruly black hair. As he considered each person, a lone figure to the left caught his attention.

He had only to shift his eyes to see the richly garbed woman who stood on the roof of the tower, motionless except for her white veil, which shifted gently in the breeze. Fleetingly, he wondered who she was. He had it from a particularly reliable source that there were no other ladies at Penforke besides Lizanne.

Considering the woman unworthy of his immediate attention, Ranulf averted his gaze, but not before the air stirred briskly and lifted the lower edge of the veil. And then he knew.

Drawing in his breath sharply, he fixed his eyes upon the Lady Lizanne. Though he couldn't be absolutely certain from this distance, he was sure her attention was turned upon him as well. At that moment, he would have given much to be able to see her face up close, to witness her reaction to his coming. She would know it was he, although from her manner of dress, in all likelihood she had been expecting her brother. Aye, Gilbert had not yet returned. It would take little effort to capture Penforke.

The silence continued for interminable minutes as each opponent took measure of the other. Outside the castle's walls, Ranulf's men patiently awaited their orders, while inside, Lizanne's grew increasingly restless.

Following Ranulf's steady gaze, Walter spied the lady. "My lord, be that her?"

Ranulf blinked and turned to meet Walter's questioning eyes. "Aye, that is the Lady Lizanne."

A true friend and fiercely loyal to his lord, Walter was the only one Ranulf had entrusted with a brief accounting of his disappearance. Only he could possibly guess at the strictly checked emotions that ran beneath Ranulf's grave composure.

The day following his release, Ranulf had met up with the search party Walter had organized to find him. Forcing logic to dictate his actions, he had temporarily set aside his plans for revenge and returned to Langdon's castle to conclude his business there.

He had offered no explanation of his disappearance to the overwrought Lord Langdon but had worked day and night to resolve the differences between the lord and his vassal. And over supper he had made a point of spending as much time as possible with the man's wife, Rachael—Lizanne's cousin. Though the woman had been fairly close-mouthed on the subject of Lizanne, obviously from dislike of her, when pressed, she had finally enlightened him.

Of particular interest was the unusually close relationship between Lizanne and her brother. Ranulf had learned that the two were practically inseparable, and that it wasn't uncommon for Lizanne to accompany Gilbert on his campaigns. That small bit of information explained her facility with weapons, but it did not explain why the man would allow his sister to conduct herself in such an unladylike manner. By all rights, he should have wed her off long ago and been done with her.

Ranulf could not help but wonder if Gilbert Balmaine would appreciate the favor he was about to do him.

When he turned back to the gatehouse, he was unsettled by Lizanne's disappearance. Where had she gone? He urged his mount forward, motioning for Walter to accompany him.

A select portion of his retainers drew their weapons and followed until they were within arrow range. Taking the shields their squires passed to them, Ranulf and Walter proceeded to within several feet of the arid moat.

"I am Baron Ranulf Wardieu," he announced in a booming voice that carried to all within the outer bailey. "I command you to surrender and lower the drawbridge without delay."

Silence.

"Who speaks for this castle?" he demanded when the silence threatened to stretch endlessly.

"I do!"

In unison, Ranulf and Walter turned their heads and caught a flash of green fabric between the crenellations of the gatehouse.

Truly, Ranulf was not surprised. "Do you yield?"

Her answer was an arrow that sliced shrilly through the cool morning air and cleaved the ground directly before his destrier. With a startled cry, the horse reared and would have bolted if not for its master's skillful handling.

At once, Ranulf's men loosed a barrage of arrows at Lizanne, but she had dropped from sight. Angrily, Ranulf signaled his men to suspend their counterattack.

Silence fell again, but was soon broken as her voice carried over the wall.

"That was but a warning, Ranulf Wardieu. The next will find your heart."

"I would not test her, were I you," Walter cautioned, peering at Ranulf's grim countenance from the cover of his shield.

Tight-lipped, Ranulf cast him a look that effectively silenced any further advice.

"Show yourself, Lady Lizanne," Ranulf ordered.

"I regret that I must decline."

"Show yourself," he repeated. "No harm will come to you."

"Ha!"

Ranulf fought down his rising anger. "Blood need not be spilled over this matter," he warned.

"'Tis your blood that will spill," she challenged him. "Even now my brother rides to defend his home."

As he'd guessed.

"I think not," Ranulf returned. He had not previously considered this deception, but it rose so easily to his lips, he could not refrain.

His words achieved the desired effect. Cautiously, Lizanne moved into the open, the drawn bow with its nocked arrow held before her and trained on him. She stood alone among the crenellations, her men-at-arms having long since disappeared from view.

At the sight of her, an involuntary smile tugged at Ranulf's lips. He suppressed it.

Though she was suitably attired as the lady of the donjon, the picture she presented of soft femininity was at odds with her defiant bearing, made even more prominent by her state of dishabille.

He narrowed his eyes as he studied the face behind the bow. A long dark smudge stood out against her skin, slashing diagonally across her face to disappear beneath the hand grasping the bow's string. Her curled hair sprang from beneath the veil that, having slipped from the restraining circlet, hung unevenly. One eye was closed, but the other was leveled unblinkingly down the arrow's shaft.

"Good God, Ranulf, shield yourself!" Walter exclaimed. "She means to run you through."

Ranulf made no move to raise his shield, refusing to break eye contact with her. It was a test of wills, and one that he was determined to be the victor of.

"What have you done with my brother?" she finally asked.

"He is alive," Ranulf answered noncommittally, ignoring Walter's visible start of surprise.

Lizanne's aim wavered noticeably. "Where is he?"

"I assure you he is quite safe—for now."

Her gasp was audible. "Where is he?" she demanded a second time.

He urged his mount closer to the edge of the moat. "Mayhap I will take you to him," he offered.

"I have no intention of going anywhere with you!"

"And I have no intention of leaving without you, even if it means the lives of your people." He allowed this to sink in before continuing. "Their fate, and that of your brother, lies with you, Lizanne of Penforke. Yield and I give you my word there will be no blood shed this day."

Although Lizanne maintained her offensive stance, she did not immediately answer his demand.

For the first time, Ranulf began to worry about the arrow aimed at him. Not that he thought she meant to shoot him, but the sustained effort of keeping the string taut was surely wearing on her. She just might accidentally loose it upon him. In readiness, he tensed the arm that carried his shield.

When she did speak again, he had to strain to catch her words.

"I would bargain with you."

Sensing victory, he thinned his lips into a hard smile. "You are in no position to bargain, Lady Lizanne."

"Would you have me dead or alive, Ranulf Wardieu?" she angrily threw back, her veil slipping farther.

"Naturally, I would prefer you alive."

"Then you will honor my demands."

He did not like being forced to make concessions, particularly to this woman, and certainly not before his men. Incensed, he tightly clenched and unclenched his hands.

"And what would they be?" he asked.

A brief pause, and then: "Willingly, I will come with you. In exchange you are not to enter these walls."

He considered this, found it agreeable, and nodded. "And?" There had to be more.

"You will release my brother and hold him blameless for my actions."

"And?"

" 'Tis all."

Ranulf grimaced. She had made no demands for her own safety—a miscalculation on his part. It would have pleased him to refuse at least one of her demands, but she had made it impossible for him to do so. He looked to Walter, who had been following the discussion with undisguised interest. The man was clearly amused. Ranulf was not.

He looked back at Lizanne.

"My quarrel is with you, Lizanne Balmaine. Hence, I will honor your terms. Now present yourself. No harm will come to Penforke."

"And my brother?"

"Aye, Gilbert as well."

"I would have your word now," she insisted.

He grasped the hilt of his sword. "I give you my word."

She began to lower the bow, then caught them all off-guard as she swiftly raised it and released her arrow in an act of sheer defiance. It found its target, rending the fabric of a raised pennant.

"I will not make this easy for you, Ranulf Wardieu," she vowed before disappearing from sight.

"I did not expect you would," he muttered. Nevertheless, he had won.

Alone atop the gatehouse, Lizanne dropped her bow and knelt behind the battlements. Steepling her hands before her, she sent a silent prayer to the heavens, hoping that God had not set her aside as she'd done Him four years ago. "If You are there," she breathed, "I need You now."

The very thought of what Wardieu intended to do to her made her knees quake and her heart skip. When she gave herself over to him, he would surely take that which she had wrested from him four years past—and more. And when he was finished with her, he would kill her. Wouldn't he? Or give her over to his men ... Tears squeezed out from beneath her lids. More than anything, it pained her that her thirst for revenge had brought her to this.

Her feet dragging, she descended to the outer bailey. Before the gatehouse, the castlefolk had gathered, awaiting her. Silently, she gazed at them.

They were frightened, the women wringing their hands and clutching their children to them, the men ashamedly bowing their heads and looking anywhere but at her. Even Robert Coulter could not meet her eyes.

"All will be well," she said in as reassuring a voice as she could manage. "Lord Gilbert will be returned shortly. He will know what to do."

A murmur of opposition rose from the gathering, but died quickly as Samuel and Lucy pushed their way through.

"My lady." Samuel lifted her hand and enveloped it in his much larger one. "Surely ye canna be thinkin' of givin' yerself over?"

"There is no other course, Samuel. I must consider the welfare of these people—and Gilbert."

"Methinks he bluffs. Lord Gilbert wouldna allow himself to fall prey so easily."

"I cannot be so sure." Gently, she pulled her hand free. "'Tis too great a risk." She turned to the captain of the guard. "Robert, lower the drawbridge."

He nodded and reluctantly moved away.

"And raise the portcullis no more than what is necessary for me to slip beneath. Once I am through, secure it. Do you understand?"

"Aye, 'twill be done."

"Nay, milady," Mellie cried, rushing forward and throwing her arms around Lizanne's waist. "Ye cannot!"

Lizanne returned the girl's hug, then disengaged herself. "Aye, I must."

"Then I will go with ye."

"Nay, I go alone."

Mellie stepped back, her bottom lip caught between her crooked teeth. Emotions flitted across her face as if she were considering a matter of grave importance. Then, having reached a decision, she dipped her head.

"Ye will have need of protection," she declared, brazenly lifting her skirts and rummaging beneath them. Moments later, she proudly produced a meat dagger that she pressed into Lizanne's palm.

After a brief hesitation, Lizanne accepted it. She lifted her own skirts and concealed the nasty little weapon in the top of her hose as, for the second time that morning, the drawbridge lowered.

Smoothing her skirts, she tried to smile. "Thank you," she said, unable to meet Mellie's level gaze.

The girl reached up suddenly, startling Lizanne, and straightened her veil.

"Do ye look the lady," she explained, "he will have no choice but to treat ye as one."

Lizanne did not think so but hadn't the heart to disillusion the girl. She allowed Mellie to adjust the circlet and smooth her hair. However, when Mellie began to rub at the dark smudge, Lizanne objected. Stepping away, she absently drew the back of her hand across the mark.

"Ye did not get it all," Mellie said, moving forward to assist her once more.

"Nay." Lizanne waved her off. " 'Twill do."

The drawbridge was nearing its end. Squaring her shoulders, she turned and walked to the arched portal and positioned herself before the portcullis. For the first time in years, she mentally recited a paternoster, stumbling over the barely remembered words as she delved into the reaches of her memory. It had been so long. . . .

As the drawbridge revealed, bit by bit, the two knights positioned before the moat, her heartbeat quickened, the blood pounding loudly in her ears. With a rumble, the large, planked device joined with the stationary bridge that spanned half the moat.

Drawing from deep within herself, Lizanne found the courage not to flee. Jealously seizing it, she lifted her chin and stared unseeingly straight ahead.

With a groan, the portcullis raised, coming to a shuddering halt level with her waist. Bending, she ducked beneath it and stepped out onto firm wooden planks. As she'd directed, the iron gate immediately fell back into place.

Stiffly erect, Lizanne met Ranulf's penetrating gaze across the breadth that separated them. Neither moved.

At an impasse, it was Lizanne who took the first step—the most difficult. Determined to maintain a measure of dignity, she thrust her chin higher and crossed the bridge without further delay. However, drawing even with the bridge's threshold, she went no farther, determined he would have to meet her at least part of the way.

Obligingly, Ranulf dropped the reins and dismounted. The metallic ring of his great hauberk echoing before him, he strode toward her.

Lizanne noted the absence of a limp, though he was, perhaps, a bit stiff in the leg. Apparently, he had suffered no lasting ill effects from his wound. But then, it had not been deep, she reminded herself.

He stopped before her, somehow managing to tower over her even though she, too, was tall. Truly, he had not seemed so large chained to a wall. It was the armor, she was certain.

Crossing her arms over her chest, she tilted her head and defiantly studied the face partially concealed behind chain mail and the wide nasal guard of his helmet. Though she refused to allow her fear to show, secretly she was in the midst of an inner battle that threatened her very consciousness.

Ranulf was struck by the incredible bit of femininity before him. Aye, she was tousled and rebellious, but wholly woman. He liked the sparkle of her very green, very candid eyes, and the thick fringe of sooty lashes that threw shadows beneath her delicately arched brows. And those lips, perfectly bowed and rose-hued—though without benefit of rouge.

His body stirred, and he clenched his fists as he fought down the desire to touch the lustrous length of sable falling past her shoulders. It did not even begin to resemble the wild mane she had sported all those days past.

God's teeth, was this truly the same woman? Or had she a sister? His eyes strayed lower and settled on the swell of her breasts beneath the well-fitting bodice. Frowning, he watched them rise and fall with the force of her short, rasping breaths. Lower still, the ends of her curling hair caressed the gentle flare of her hips. Again, his self-control was put to the test as he fought the overwhelming urge to sample her then and there.

Just barely, he won.

Giving no warning, he reached up and yanked the veil from her hair, sending it and the circlet plummeting to the dry bed of the moat.

Caught off balance by his unexpected action, Lizanne was unable to control the start that propelled her backward, but Ranulf did. His large hands descended to her shoulders and wrenched her forward, bringing her face within inches of his.

Unblinking, Lizanne raised her lids. Here were the

cold, angry eyes that had haunted her sleepless nights, so dark 'twas nigh impossible to determine where color ended and pupil began.

"Surely, you are not frightened of me?" he taunted, his warm breath stirring the wisps of hair at her temples.

Aye, she was, but never would she admit it. "Frightened of you?" she threw back, her voice rising. "Does your flesh not bear my mark, Ranulf Wardieu?"

His fingers tightened their hold on her, a fine white line of tension appearing around his lips.

She flinched beneath the pressure but refused to back down. "Nay, I will never fear you," she lied, "and lest you forget, I offer fair warning. Do not show me your back." Or what? she asked herself. You'll put a knife in it? Coward. Even when you held him at the point of your sword, you could not finish what you'd begun.

Aye, it was the same woman, Ranulf thought, though cleverly disguised as a lady. He had not expected her to grovel, but he'd believed she would be sensible enough to suspend her hostilities. Any other woman would have attempted to use her beauty and charm to soothe his anger, but not Lizanne Balmaine. She was unlike any he had ever before encountered. He still had much to learn about her.

"You are indeed fortunate we are not alone," he warned, easing his hold on her.

Her brows lifted. "You would not beat me in front of your men?" She smiled thinly. "You are truly gracious, my lord."

"You learn fast," he said, smiling at her unintentional form of address.

As her puzzled stare turned to one of outrage, he reached up and caught her chin in his leather-gauntleted hand. "You would do well to remember that I am indeed your lord now, Lizanne. You belong to me."

It was on her lips to refute his claim, but his next words made her swallow hers.

"Are you armed?"

She hesitated, perhaps too long. "You need not worry. I left my bow behind," she hedged. It was the truth, after all.

He saw the lie. Abruptly, his hands dropped to her waist, probing beneath the material of her garments as he worked his way down the curves of her body.

"Oh!" With wide-eyed indignation, Lizanne twisted out of his grasp, deftly evading the hands that reached to recapture her.

Straightening, Ranulf removed his gloves. "I would see what you've hidden beneath your skirts," he said. "Lift them."

Hands on her hips, she stood defiantly before him, her eyes glittering. "Nay!" she spit.

He took a step toward her. She took a step back.

"Obey me, Lizanne," he commanded, "else I will tear the clothes from your body."

"You would not!"

"Aye, I would," he vowed in a dangerously soft voice, bridging the distance between them in one long stride.

She would have refused anew, but a look at his face told her she did not dare. He would have no remorse in carrying out his threat. Setting her teeth, she hiked her skirts up to her knees.

Bending, Ranulf ran his hands up from her ankles.

Flushed with humiliation, Lizanne stared straight ahead, training her eyes on Ranulf's companion where he languished astride his mount.

Damn the knave, she thought. He was thoroughly enjoying her disgrace. She scowled at him, then turned her attention to the mounted soldiers flanking the moat. It appeared they, too, were amused by her plight.

She was shocked and dismayed by the palpable thrill that coursed through her when Ranulf's warm fingers settled upon, and began to stroke, the inside of her thigh. Wide-eyed and breathless, she stared down at him.

He smiled! The cur simply smiled—a wicked, crooked smile that flashed white at her. Then, without surrendering her eyes, he removed the dagger from her hose, drawing the flat of its warm blade across her skin.

When he straightened, she let go a shuddering breath and hastily averted her eyes. Though she was not sure what he might read in them, for she did not know herself, she knew it to be a vulnerability.

Ranulf turned the puny weapon in his hand, examining it, before raising questioning brows.

Smoothing her skirts, Lizanne stole a glance at him and shrugged. "I had to try."

"You disappoint me," he said. "I would have thought you could have done far better than this."

Her eyes flashed. "The particular weapon is of less consequence than the person behind it."

"Hmm." He considered her veiled threat, then he smiled. "As you say, 'tis the person behind it."

He tossed the dagger aside and pinned her with his penetrating eyes. "Three times, Lizanne of Penforke, you have had the chance to slay me. Once with a dagger, once with a sword, and finally an arrow. And three times you failed."

"A mistake I intend to remedy!"

"Aye, I am sure you will try." He was done speaking. Grasping her arm, he pulled her toward his horse.

Lizanne dug her heels in, but for all her effort suffered the indignity of being half-carried, half-dragged across the short distance.

"What of my brother?" she demanded.

Ignoring her question, Ranulf turned to Walter. "She will ride with you," he said, sympathizing with the man's obvious aversion to the task.

However, he did not trust himself with her. Though it was not in his nature to strike a woman, he had felt very near to it more than once in the last few minutes. Doubtless, she would be inclined to continue her verbal assault were she to ride with him. All too aware of his simmering anger, he accepted his need for a respite from her waspish tongue.

Drawing Lizanne forward, he easily lifted her onto the back of Walter's mount to ride pillion. Immediately, she scooted backward and very nearly unseated herself.

The great destrier pranced sideways. Ranulf had no choice but to transfer Lizanne, none too gently, before Walter.

Distastefully, Walter encircled her waist with one arm and drew her back against his armored chest.

In spite of the iron band around her, Lizanne began to squirm, unladylike invectives spilling from her lips.

Ranulf gripped her thigh. "You would do well to remember these are your terms, Lizanne," he said tightly. "You keep your side of the bargain, and I will keep mine. Now, show some dignity and gracefully accept your fate."

She stilled. Nevertheless, that damned chin of hers went up. "Will you take me to my brother?" she persisted. "I would see that no harm has befallen him."

Ranulf released his hold on her. "Nay," he answered, and turned away. It was neither the time nor the place to disabuse her of her brother's capture. He didn't doubt that she would prove to be far more difficult when she learned the truth.

Disregarding the onslaught of questions and demands she tossed at his back, he effortlessly swung himself up into the saddle and spurred his horse away from Penforke.

Unmindful of his burdensome baggage, Walter followed at a brutal pace, matching Ranulf's.

Lizanne looked over her shoulder to her home, sudden tears blurring her eyes. The drawbridge was being raised again, the finality of its groan and creak silenced by the thundering of hooves. Stifling a sob, she leaned back against the knight and squeezed her eyes closed.

Chapter 6

$\mathcal{L}$izanne *had not* intended to fall asleep. In fact, she was astonished that she'd been able to, considering the rigorous, breakneck pace Ranulf had set for his men.

Still muddled from sleep, she yielded to the hands that lifted her from the horse's back, allowing them to support her when her knees buckled beneath her and toppled her forward against a firm, armored chest. Her cheek smarting from its brush with the rough links of armor, she lifted her head and gazed into Ranulf's glowering face.

Neither spoke for a long moment, each studying the other.

As he held her, Ranulf's hostility began to ease, his body instinctively responding to the soft, feminine curves pressed against him. He had known it the moment he'd first laid eyes on the wild-haired hellion—he liked the feel of her. There was something so incredibly feminine beneath the hardened exterior she hid behind.

It unsettled him to admit the desire he'd felt for her upon their first meeting had not diminished, although he'd tried to convince himself of it during the past days. Indeed, it had only increased. Having spent every spare moment since his release planning his revenge, he was surprised at the intensity of his feelings. Though he tried to push them to the back of his mind, he was unsuccessful.

Still sleep-befuddled, Lizanne kept staring at Ranulf. He'd removed his helmet and unbuckled his chain-mail hood. The hood hung loosely over the collar of his hauberk, revealing his incredible hair, the length of which was still tucked beneath the neck of his armor.

For a few moments, she was captivated by the effects of the setting sun behind him. Like a halo, it surrounded him, setting fire and bringing color to his colorless hair. Had his eyes softened perhaps? Was that a hint of a smile curling the corners of his mouth? For the first time, she looked at him without bias and sleepily wondered if a heart as black as his could ever purge the evil there.

Impulsively, she reached up and traced the cut above his eye, her finger following its path into soft, flowing hair.

Though his eyes revealed astonishment at her daring, Ranulf remained motionless.

" 'Twill not even scar," she murmured, her fingers twining themselves in the hair at his widow's peak. Then, with a jolt, she snatched her hand away as if burned.

Aye, he was evil personified. His past could not be put aside. Fully awake now, she was very much aware of her proximity to the enemy and horrified that she had willingly touched him!

Thrusting her hands against his chest, she began to struggle and was surprised when he released her. His face was hard again when she tossed her head back and defiantly met his eyes.

Ignoring her challenge, he turned on his heel and retrieved his horse's reins. "Come!" he said to her, already leading the destrier to where the others were tethering their horses.

Charged with rebellion, Lizanne folded her arms across her chest and stared after his retreating back.

"I will drag you if needs be," he added without faltering in his stride, not once looking behind.

That humiliation forced Lizanne's capitulation. Drawing a deep, calming breath, she started after him but maintained a safe distance as they crossed the meadow where camp was being erected for the night. She noted half a dozen wagons grouped near the horses that had not been present earlier. They had obviously joined up with the party while she'd slept.

Staring straight ahead, her eyes level at the spot between Ranulf's shoulder blades, she sidestepped the soldiers in her path. For each interested look she received, her chin lifted a degree, until it was held so high, she stumbled and nearly fell over an exposed root. Her muttered string of curses was immediately suppressed when she became aware of her audience.

Gritting her teeth, she glared at the snickering group of men who had paused in the middle of raising a tent to witness her clumsiness. They only grinned wider. Lizanne's face warmed uncomfortably.

"My lord," Ranulf's squire called, hurrying forward, "I've the rope you asked for."

Ranulf halted and accepted the rope, his head lowering as the animated young man spoke to him. His words were hushed, and Lizanne could not discern them across the distance that separated her from Ranulf. Curious, she took a step closer, then another, but pulled herself up short when Ranulf straightened.

"See he is given plenty of oats and water, Geoff," Ranulf instructed, stroking his horse's neck.

"Aye, my lord." Stealing a glance at Lizanne, the squire led the horse away.

Ranulf watched their departure before turning back to Lizanne. He had been aware of her approach and the curiosity that had compelled her to draw nearer. The indifference she feigned now amused him.

Legs spread wide, his attention never straying from her, he looped the skein of rope beneath his belt, then settled his fists on his hips.

At once, Lizanne took offense. Crossing her arms beneath her breasts, she turned her back to him and pretended an interest in the flurry of activity around her.

In less than three strides, Ranulf covered the distance between them and closed a hand over her upper arm. Without a word, he pulled her toward a copse of trees.

Lizanne stumbled behind him, wildly searching for scathing words to throw at his back. Then she looked to where she was being led. What he had done four years past, taking her into the woods with the intent of defiling her, came thundering back to her. Fearful, she began to resist.

"Nay!" she loudly protested, digging her heels in as she attempted to pull free of his hold. This could not be happening to her. Dear God, not again!

He simply gripped her arm tighter and increased the length of his stride, forcing her to match his pace in order to keep her feet beneath her.

Surprisingly, at the edge of the meadow he released his hold on her and pushed her forward. "Relieve yourself," he commanded. "But be quick about it, or I may feel it necessary to interrupt your privacy."

She could only stare uncomprehendingly at him. Then he did not mean to . . . ?

Her relief immense, she ducked beneath a low-hanging branch and hurried into the woods, eagerly putting distance between herself and the hateful man. It occurred to her that, were she of a mind to escape, she might just outrun him, given the hindrance of his massive proportions and the extra minutes' lead she would have on him. But, she admitted grimly, until Gilbert was released, escape was not an option.

Not wanting to give Ranulf an excuse to humiliate her further, she finished quickly and hastened back to where he awaited her.

"You do try my patience," he admonished. "Another minute and I would have come after you, regardless of your state."

" 'Tis not so easy for a lady!" she exclaimed.

"Were you one," he reminded her, "I would make allowances for it."

Again, that sharp pain. Though she wanted very much to argue the matter, she knew it would be pure folly to attempt to persuade him she was a lady. "Nevertheless," she said, throwing her chin into the air, "there are differences."

"I assure you I am well aware of them."

"I do not believe you are," she recklessly challenged.

Without warning, his hand shot out and caught hold of her. Dragging her back into the shelter of the trees, he pulled her firmly against his body.

"If you would like a demonstration of my knowledge," he said from between tightly clenched teeth, "I am more than willing to oblige."

As Ranulf lowered his head, intent on her parted lips, he missed the terror that leaped into her eyes. Roughly, he captured her mouth and began an assault of the sweet, tender flesh she surrendered to him.

He meant only to punish her for her willful defiance, but at the taste of her, his anger receded, supplanted by desire. His touch gentled, his tongue lightly circling the inner recesses of her lips as he attempted to persuade her to open her mouth to him.

Pressing her closer, he lifted a hand to cup her neck and ran the other lightly down her back, then lower to her firm buttocks. She neither resisted nor responded to him, her previously rigid body pliant and unmoving beneath his touch.

Frowning, he lifted his head and looked down at her. Immediately, his ardor subsided. Wide-eyed, but otherwise expressionless, she stared at him.

Nay, Ranulf amended, she was staring straight through him! The infuriating woman had managed to remove herself completely from the situation. Doubtless she had not felt one of his caresses. In fact, were he to release her, she would certainly crumple to the ground.

It had never occurred to him that she might be frigid, and even now, with the evidence before him, he was unable to accept such a possibility. There was far too much fire and spirit in her.

Aye, it was a defensive ploy. Verily, it was an effective means of cooling a man's ardor, but he was a patient man.

"Lizanne!" He gripped her arms and gave her a shake, then another when she remained unresponsive.

Pulled back from the scenes that had been unfolding in her mind, Lizanne blinked. The past and present melded as she focused on the face above her own. It was the same as that which plagued her dreams . . . yet somehow different. The realization unsettled her. Instinctively, she knew it to be more than the intervening years that were responsible for the discrepancy. It went far deeper than that, and that confused and frightened her.

Ranulf was smiling now, though it did not quite reach his eyes. "I think 'tis you who do not understand the difference between the sexes," he said as his gaze flitted to her lips.

Her hand flew up and pressed against her swollen mouth.

"You have much to learn," he went on, "but I shall enjoy instructing you."

It was all she needed to jolt her out of her stupor.

Immediately, she flew into a rage, attacking him with hands, feet, teeth, and profanity.

Prepared for her reaction, Ranulf simply pulled her against him and held her while she vainly thrashed about. It took longer than he expected for her to quiet down, but she finally exhausted herself and stilled.

Sighing, he grasped her chin and tilted her face up, lightly touching the corner of her mouth with his thumb. "Lesson one," he began, pausing until she lifted her lids and met his stare, "you will open your mouth when I kiss you."

"Oh! You are—you are insufferable," she sputtered.

He laughed, a deep, rumbling sound that echoed throughout the woods. Then he released her and swung away, leaving her no choice but to follow.

Fuming, she lifted her skirts and tramped after him, emerging from the thicket to find him uncoiling the length of rope.

He motioned her forward.

Suspicious, she watched him untangle the rope but made no move to come closer.

"Must you defy me at every turn?" he asked impatiently. "I grow weary of your games, Lizanne. Now come here!"

Fully aware of his intention, she shook her head and remained firmly rooted to the spot.

He stilled. "I warn you, 'twill not bode well for you if I have to collect you myself."

She did not move, pushing him just a bit farther, then acquiesced—albeit resentfully.

"Your hands," he ordered.

She held them out, swallowing hard as he quickly bound them together. "'Tis not necessary to fetter me," she said.

He ignored her.

"You bind them too tight," she complained, attempting to pull her hands free.

"I repay in kind." Pointedly, he glanced down at his own wrists. They still bore the marks of healing flesh.

Having a particular dislike for his reminder, she averted her eyes. "So long as you hold Gilbert, I would not escape," she said in a small voice.

Deftly, Ranulf knotted the rope, then pushed her down to a sitting position, her back against a tree. "'Tis precisely the reason I must do this," he muttered as he lashed her to the trunk.

Suspicion nagging at her, Lizanne puzzled over his words.

"Moreover," he continued, sitting back on his heels to regard her, "I would not want you causing mischief among my men. There is much to be done before nightfall, and you would only serve to distract them from their duties."

She looked at the ropes that bound her. "Think you I cannot work my way out of this?" she defiantly tossed at him.

His eyes narrowed, then closed for a moment.

"You may try, if you like," he said at last, "but 'twill only waste your strength."

"What of Gilbert?" she demanded when he started to rise. "You agreed to release him. Have you done so?"

With clear reluctance, he lowered himself again and rubbed a hand over his mouth and chin. Then, slowly, he shook his head. "Nay."

It was not the answer she had expected. A new surge of anger knotted her stomach as she groped for words to express her outrage.

"You are turning a most unbecoming shade of red," he noted.

The color deepened. "You gave me your word!" she finally managed.

"Aye, I promised no harm would come to Penforke—or your brother. None has."

Vehemently, she shook her head. "You also agreed

to release Gilbert. This you vowed before your own men!"

Ranulf looked down at his hands, thoughtfully considering each knuckle before answering. Truth be known, he would have liked to avoid the subject of her brother a while longer. The leverage the deception had given him was appealing in its simplicity. It had, after all, delivered her to him without a single drop of blood being shed. However, he was nothing if not an honest man, and she would have to be told eventually. It was not in her nature to be satisfied with evasive answers.

When he finally spoke, his voice was matter-of-fact, his eyes level with hers. "I cannot release a man I do not hold."

It took some moments for his words to sink into Lizanne's consciousness, but when they did, her face contorted with such fury, she looked comical.

"You deceived me!" she spit.

He shrugged.

Though she was bound securely to the tree, she lashed out with her legs, stirring up a cloud of dust and scattering stones in his direction. "You dishonorable swine!" she shrieked.

He held up a hand to stem the flow of curses he was certain was forthcoming. "Lest you forget, 'twas you who assumed I had captured your brother. I neither confirmed nor denied this."

His explanation only heightened her anger. "Nay, you deliberately misled me."

"Aye, that I did." He straightened. " 'Twas necessary to use your assumption to protect your people from foolishly giving their lives for such an unworthy cause."

She stilled. "Unworthy?" Her voice was harsh, strained.

Ranulf saw she was fairly shaking with rage—her eyes huge, her lips pale, her jaw thrust forward. He was intrigued by the transformation. True, she looked fierce, but she was also exceedingly beautiful.

"Aye," he answered. "Though I would have done whatever was necessary to capture you, 'twould have been a senseless slaughter had you not surrendered. You are not worth dying for, Lizanne of Penforke."

He was surprised at her reaction to his words, glimpsing a raw vulnerability before she masked it with a sweep of her long lashes. Lips tightly compressed, she dropped her head back against the tree and pinned him with her most hateful expression.

He was unmoved by it, though he did imagine that were it possible to lay a man down with such a look, he would certainly be dead. There was far too much hate in her.

"When you come to my tent tonight," he went on dispassionately, "I expect you to have all this anger worked out."

"Then you had best not send for me!"

"Get over it, Lizanne," he said before abruptly turning and starting back across the meadow.

Immediately, Lizanne resumed her tirade of profanity, throwing every foul curse she could dredge up at his departing back. A particularly vile word halted him and brought him back around.

"If needs be, I will gag you as well," he warned before resuming his course.

She stifled the words that rose to her lips and, clamping her mouth firmly shut, followed his progress until he disappeared. Then, and only then, did she give way to the well of pent-up emotions that hammered with such intensity at her temples, she was certain her head would split in two.

"Ah, Gilbert," she lamented as tears coursed down her face, "what have I done?"

There was none to answer her. None to offer hope for the wrong she had sought to right. A great sorrow, rooted in years of anger at the injustice done her and her brother, settled itself upon her burdened shoulders as the first of her sobs broke from her throat.

It was dark and growing cold before anyone came for her. Her tears having long since dried, Lizanne squinted up at the two sent to fetch her to Ranulf.

Their torches revealed youthful, somber faces. One, however, a young man she recognized as Ranulf's squire, was clearly trying to mask a grin.

Her mind working furiously, Lizanne favored each with a smile, flirtatiously sweeping her lashes down over her eyes. The deception she was about to work on them nearly made her retch.

In unison, both youths broke into smiles.

The taller one stepped forward. "I am Geoff, Lord Ranulf's squire. And this is Roland, Sir Walter's squire."

Lizanne nodded. "Geoff and Roland," she murmured, forcing her smile wider. "You may call me Lizanne."

Blushing, Roland moved closer. "L-lord Ranulf has instructed us to escort you to him."

She cocked her head in feigned bewilderment. "My ... Two of you? I am deeply honored."

Geoff nudged Roland and winked, then dropped down beside her. There ensued a struggle to untie the rope that bound her to the tree, but at last it fell away. A hand beneath her elbow, Geoff assisted her to her feet.

"Thank you," she said, leaning against him as she entreatingly thrust her joined hands forward.

Shaking his head, the squire stepped back. "Nay, Lord Ranulf did not say we could."

Her eyes widened. "Then how will I relieve myself? Surely, he did not set you that task as well?"

Both Geoff and Roland shifted uncomfortably from one foot to the other.

"Nay, but—" Roland began.

"Lord Ranulf said we were to bring you straight to him," Geoff interrupted.

Lizanne bowed her head. "I fear I shall not make it that far." She allowed them a long moment of discomfort before offering a solution. "Mayhap one of you can accompany me—though you must vow not to look."

Though they were obviously uncomfortable with this arrangement, they agreed.

Unsheathing his dagger, Roland moved forward.

Fearful of losing a finger as a result of the young man's clumsiness, Lizanne grimaced as he cut the rope from her hands. She sighed with relief when she was freed without mishap.

To her chagrin, it was the larger one, Geoff, who volunteered to accompany her to the woods. Rubbing her wrists, she demurely followed.

"There," he said, pointing to a row of low-lying bushes several feet away.

She shook her head. "Nay, they are poisonous. Did you not know?" Without a glance his way, she walked past him and headed deeper into the woods.

"This will do," she announced once they were out of sight of Roland's torch. Peering around a large oak tree, she motioned for him to turn around. Immediately, he obliged.

Lizanne could not believe her good fortune when he began to whistle, masking her noisy movements.

She wasted no time shedding the cumbersome chemise and bliaut, leaving them strewn about the leafy bed at her feet. Clad in only her shift and braies, she groped along the ground for her weapon. Hefting a decent-sized branch, she weighed it for ease of swing. Though she did not like the leaves that still clung to it, for they were bound to rustle noisily, she decided it would suffice.

Verifying that Geoff still had his back to her, she crept from behind her cover, wincing each time the leaves beneath her feet crackled.

The young man did not hear her approach, though, did not even realize he had been struck when he toppled to the ground at her feet.

Retrieving his fallen torch, Lizanne thrust its tip into the ground, then knelt beside the fallen youth. His pulse was strong, she discovered a moment later, and was relieved she had not struck him too hard. Quickly, her probing fingers found the lump forming upon his skull. She grimaced. It would be of a good size when he came to.

"Forgive me," she said; then, without further delay, she began to disrobe him. The new energy surging through her facilitated her task, and within minutes she was outfitted in his garments. Finally, she belted on his dagger.

Backing away, she turned and fled deeper into the woods. Though there was not much of a moon to guide her, she made do with what there was.

With barely contained rage, Ranulf stared down at his unconscious squire. It took every last ounce of patience he had not to wring Geoff's miserable, foolish neck. His hands clenched and unclenched as he envisioned doing just that.

In spite of the long years of training, first as his page and most recently his squire, the lad had failed him. He had ignored a direct order, and as a result, had allowed Lizanne's escape. Mayhap, he had overestimated Geoff's ability. . . .

Nay, he harshly corrected himself, he had underestimated Lizanne's—and not for the first time. Growling deep in his throat, he clapped a hand to his forehead and drew it roughly back through his hair.

Truth be known, he was more angry with himself than with the gullible squires he had sent in his stead. He had foolishly believed that two nearly grown men would have no difficulty in bringing one woman to him. That had been his greatest mistake. Aye, the lads would be disciplined for disregarding his orders, but he alone would take responsibility for this particular incident.

Impatiently, he wondered at the time it was taking Roland to alert the camp and assemble a search party. He had sent the cowering squire for them many minutes ago. If they did not arrive shortly, he would go for them himself.

When Geoff groaned and raised his head, Ranulf stepped closer and flung the bunched-up chemise and bliaut into his face. Still dazed, the squire emerged from the garments and, rubbing the sore spot at the back of his head, looked up.

"My lord!" he exclaimed, shaking his head to clear it. As realization dawned, his bewilderment turned to horror. Sputtering, he scrambled to his feet, then pitched forward and fell to his knees. Only then did he realize his state of undress.

Wearing only his braies, every other garment having been stripped from him, he gaped in disbelief. Then he reddened, the color sweeping from his chest up over his neck, to the roots of his hair. Groaning, he forced himself upright and bowed his head.

Ranulf knew well his squire's discomfort. Had Lizanne not done the same to him? Still, 'twas necessary to impress upon him the seriousness of his error.

"What say you?" he demanded.

"My lord, the lady claimed she had need of privacy—"

"And you believed her?"

"She tricked me," Geoff said weakly.

"Nay, you allowed yourself to be deceived. What did she do? Smile at you?"

The squire shuffled his feet in the crisp, fallen leaves.

At that moment, two dozen of Ranulf's men noisily entered the woods. Leading Ranulf's horse, Walter arrived ahead of the group. Shamefaced, Roland rode behind him, his eyes downcast, his shoulders hunched.

Bearing torches, the men assembled before Ranulf and awaited his instructions. Though their eyes reflected amusement at the sight of Geoff, they wisely held their tongues.

Taking the reins Walter passed to him, Ranulf fluidly mounted his horse. "Geoff, you will ride with Roland," he said, then frowned. "He has brought clothes for you. Be thankful I don't make you wear Lizanne's."

As the squire abashedly turned away, Ranulf gave his commands to his men, dividing them into two groups. With himself leading one group and Walter the other, they broke and rode in opposite directions.

Ranulf guided his men through the densely wooded region, their progress frustratingly slow. Nevertheless, they covered ground more rapidly than Lizanne would be able to on foot.

Ranulf cursed the night and the weak sliver of moon. Under cover of dark it would be easy to overlook her were she hidden among the trees. He forged ahead grimly, growing increasingly tense with each passing minute.

Lord, had she truly escaped him? Immediately, he chastised himself for having told her of Gilbert. Why hadn't he waited? She would not have dared attempt an escape so long as she continued to believe he held her precious brother. By God, if she managed to elude him all the way back to Penforke, he would bring her out again—even if he had to topple the walls down around her.

"My lord!" a voice called. He heard the sounds of a horse speeding toward them through the trees. A moment later, one of the men from the party led by Walter emerged from out of the darkness.

"We've found her!" he exclaimed.

Though Ranulf kept his expression hard, relief swept him. "Where is she?"

The man hesitated. "I fear she has gone over the side of a ravine."

Ranulf's chest tightened. "She is unharmed?"

"For the moment, my lord, 'twould appear so. Sir Walter has sent someone down to bring her up."

The ride was a short one, though for Ranulf it seemed unending. When he spotted the faint glow of torches atop a rise, he overtook the messenger and covered the remaining distance alone.

Walter hurried forward as Ranulf dismounted. "Kendall is with her, my lord."

Ranulf nodded. The men who peered over the edge of the sheer drop moved aside at his swift approach. Leaning out over the edge, he looked down. He heard the rush of water before he caught the play of light over its surface. It was a very long way to the bottom. Worse than he'd expected.

It took his eyes a few moments to adjust to the shadowy scene below. When they did, he first saw the knight who had been lowered a good thirty feet down the side. Then, following his progress to the right, he located Lizanne. Though she appeared to have a firm hold on an outcropping of leafy vegetation, she was practically vertical against the cliff, suspended God knew how many feet above the loud, breaking water below. His heart constricted.

When she lifted her head in response to the commotion above, the light from the torches danced over her features.

Ranulf saw the wild mass of hair strewn across her filthy face, but what held his attention was her expression. Most amazingly, she looked to be positively furious. His brows drew sharply together. She should be screaming, weeping, pleading . . . anything but defiant.

She should be frightened, dammit!

She must have noticed him, for a moment later her voice rose clearly through the chill night air. "Well, you certainly took your time getting here!"

Had he heard right? Was she actually chastising him? He dragged a hand across his eyes and sighed loudly. At least he could be fairly certain she was unharmed.

Having worked his way along the wall, Kendall was now beside her. "My lady," he said, "give me your hand."

"Nay," she answered sharply, her voice carrying up the ravine.

"I would only help you," the man patiently explained, reaching out to grasp her arm.

Ranulf watched with amazement as Lizanne shrugged his hand off. "I do not ask for help," she said.

"Lizanne!" Ranulf bellowed, having completely lost control of the last vestiges of his patience. "This is not the time to argue. Give Sir Kendall your hand—now!"

Shaking her head, she looked up at him. "Leave me be. I will find my own way back up."

The knight reached for her again but immediately withdrew when her struggles sent a shower of rocks flying from beneath her feet. A moment later, all watched in horror as the undergrowth she clung to snapped in her hands.

A collective gasp went up as she slid farther down the wall, scrambling wildly for another hold. Miraculously, her descent was arrested only a few feet below her original position when she caught hold of a thick root that forced its way between a layer of rock.

"Bring him up!" Ranulf shouted.

When Kendall was pulled back over the side, Ranulf cut the rope sling from him and quickly fashioned another about himself. Without delay, he dropped over the edge and was quickly lowered.

As he drew near, Lizanne turned her head and concealed her face in the vegetation. She said nothing as he was lowered the last few feet to her side.

Taking her silence as a further act of defiance, Ranulf felt his ire rise. However, having no intention of wasting any more time arguing with her, he reached out, clamped an arm around her waist, and began to pull her toward him. Though her lower body followed, her upper did not.

"For the love of God, Lizanne, let go!"

When she did not comply, he clamped her legs between his thighs and began to pry her hands free. He was amazed at the tenacity of her hold and cursed the disadvantage of having only one free hand. The other was occupied with steadying the rope.

"Lizanne!" he roared when no amount of prying loosed her grip. "Obey me, or I swear I will beat you when this is over. Release your hold."

She lifted her face to him, and to his amazement he saw tears spill from her eyes and course a dark path down her mud-streaked face. "I—I cannot," she croaked.

She was terrified.

Ranulf was taken aback, his anger cooling instantly. Reaching to his belt, he removed his dagger and began slashing at the root she held. Still grasping her lifeline, she fell against him a moment later. A murmur of relief from the men above carried down the ravine.

Wrapping an arm securely around her, Ranulf pulled her close. "Put your arms around my neck," he said, not truly expecting her to obey.

Her head pressed beneath his chin, she slid her arms up his chest and encircled his neck.

Bewildered, Ranulf stared at the crown of her head and wondered if he would ever understand this beautiful, wild creature.

They began a slow ascent, during which time neither spoke. At the top, Ranulf's men rushed forward to assist him over the edge and to his feet. Standing, he set

Lizanne down, but she immediately collapsed back against him. Supporting her lax frame, he allowed his men to extract him from the sling.

He was utterly baffled by her reaction. From what he knew of her, he would have expected her to have recovered somewhat from the ordeal by now, but she continued to cling to him——her despised enemy. Mayhap she was only acting to avoid his wrath. The thought deepened his frown.

Swinging her up against his chest, he carried her to his horse. There, he ducked beneath her arms and quickly lifted her into the saddle. Geoff rushed forward to assist him, steadying Lizanne astride the mount as his lord climbed up behind her.

Ranulf started to pull her back against him, but she turned suddenly. Drawing her knees up, she slid her arms around his waist and buried her face in the soft wool of his tunic. Nay, he did not think she was acting at all.

For Ranulf, the ride back to camp was torturous. His awkward baggage clung to him, pressing her body so tightly against him, he had to exercise strictest control to prevent himself from responding.

Though she still held fast to him, she was sound asleep when they finally reached the camp. He carried her into his tent, and gently lowered her to the cot. In repose, she appeared so incredibly childlike, he felt an involuntary surge of protectiveness envelop him.

From the corner of his eye, he saw the root she still grasped in her white-knuckled hand. Though he half-heartedly attempted to remove it, he gave up for fear of wakening her. He did, however, remove the belt about her waist that held Geoff's dagger.

Wearily, he crossed to the small, squat table that held an assortment of meats, cheeses, and bread. Dismissing the food, he lifted a tankard of warm mead and drained it in one long swallow, then went to the tent opening and looked out.

He spotted Walter across the way where he was delivering instructions to the man chosen to ride north to Chesne to warn of the possibility of retaliation from Gilbert Balmaine. Although Ranulf's impression of Lizanne's brother was less than flattering, he had decided it wouldn't hurt to exercise a bit of caution.

Lizanne awoke slowly, believing herself at Penforke. But her eyes contradicted her, opening up the window of her consciousness to remind her exactly where she was—and who she was with. She swallowed and turned her head to the soothing breeze wafting through the tent.

Instantly, she saw Ranulf. Though her recollection of her escape was hazy, she clearly remembered the riders descending upon her, that soul-wrenching moment when she had stepped into empty space, and then strong arms encircling her, promising to keep her safe from all harm. They had been Ranulf's arms. . . .

She did not attempt to delve further. It was far too disturbing to dwell on the comfort her enemy had offered. A comfort she had willingly accepted.

For now she had to consider her present situation. Knowing hate was her best defense, she drew on it. It would help her through the violation she knew he intended to visit upon her.

Lowering the tent flap, Ranulf stepped back inside and removed his belt. He tossed it aside, then bent and pulled off his boots. As he lifted the hem of his tunic, his gaze fell upon Lizanne, and his hands stilled. She was watching him. Frowning, he folded his arms across his chest, spread his legs wide, and stared back.

Silent minutes passed, then Lizanne sat up. Reflexively, her hands opened, and she looked questioningly at the severed root that had fallen from one of them. When she raised her head again, she was scowling.

Ranulf's own frown deepened. There was no remorse

whatsoever on her face. In fact, she fairly emanated hostility. In quick response to her change in demeanor, he felt his emotions surge.

"Have you nothing to say for yourself?" he demanded.

Sighing loudly, she pushed to her feet. "I did warn you."

"Warn me?"

Smoothing Geoff's tunic over her thighs, she nodded. "Aye. I told you 'twould not be easy to hold me." Her words trailed off as she looked down and noticed the absence of the belt and its dagger. When she looked up again, Ranulf's self-satisfied smile greeted her.

"Missing something?" he asked derisively.

Squaring her shoulders, she boldly stepped near him and reached to the tray of food. After some consideration, she decided on a chunk of hard white cheese and idly popped it in her mouth. Her hunger had been a pretense to avoid confronting Ranulf head-on, but the taste of food suddenly made it very real. Swallowing, she reached for another morsel, even as her belly rumbled in agreement.

"You cause one hell of a lot of trouble, woman. Did you truly think to escape so easily?" Ranulf demanded.

She looked over her shoulder at him. "Nay, I thought 'twould be far more difficult than it actually was. Mayhap the next time you should send four to fetch me. After all, I do enjoy a challenge."

Engaged in an inner battle with emotions he was unaccustomed to experiencing, Ranulf did not immediately respond. "You will not be given another opportunity to escape," he assured her some moments later. "I shan't underestimate you again."

Her laugh was hard and short as she turned away. "Aye, you will—most assuredly."

He ignored her taunt. "I would hope you have

learned something from your failure to escape. And do you not forget that you did, indeed, fail."

Pulling her bottom lip between her teeth, she attempted a nonchalant shrug. "I would have made it if not for that little ravine."

His eyebrows shot straight up. "Need I remind you that you very nearly broke your neck in that *little* ravine?"

She rounded on him. "If your men had not thought to chase me down like so much common game, I would not have lost my footing!"

"You ran from them?" He was incredulous.

"Certainly! Did you think I would simply throw up my hands and surrender? I went to a lot of trouble to escape you." Angrily, she swiped a hunk of dried meat from the tray and lifted it to her mouth.

Ranulf swiftly crossed the tent, his hand closing around her wrist and denying her the morsel.

She looked up at him. "Do you mind?" she asked sarcastically, attempting to pull her hand free.

When he did not relinquish his hold, she simply leaned forward and picked the morsel from her hand with her teeth.

Where was the frightened woman who had all but ravaged him on the ride back to camp? Ranulf wondered. He shook his head, then pushed her away from him. His back to her, he raked his fingers through his hair and rubbed at the back of his neck.

"Will you give me no peace, witch?" he grumbled.

"Nay," was her answer.

Slowly, he turned to find her sitting on his wooden chest, her hands clasped between her knees as she looked about the tent.

"You do not play fair, so why should I?" she asked without looking in his direction.

He moved closer. "Nay, Lizanne, 'tis you who do

not play fair. The rules of this game are yours. Do not forget that!"

"There was nothing unfair in what I did," she denied. This time she did look at him.

"Nothing?" He gave a short bark of laughter as he closed the distance between them. "You attacked me downwind, abducted me, chained me to a wall, stabbed me. . . . Think you that fair?"

Lizanne jumped to her feet. "I had my reasons!" she declared. Reasons, she admitted, that were not as clear to her now as they had been a week past.

"Reasons you prefer to keep to yourself," he reminded her, moving to stand before her. Though he did not touch her, the heat from his body radiated across the space to warm her.

"I give you this one last chance to explain yourself," he said.

She had already considered that, yet knew she would only be jeopardizing herself further were she to explain. Most assuredly, he would feel threatened by her knowledge of his marauding exploits. It might even mean her death.

"Would you release me?" she asked.

Unexpectedly, he reached out and grasped her chin. "You belong to me now," he said, his thumb grazing her lower lip, his eyes following the movement. "I went to great lengths to have you, and I intend to keep you."

Rooted to the spot, she stared at him, unable to fathom the strange feelings his caress evoked. She knew only that it was not entirely unpleasant as it should have been.

Of its own volition, her tongue darted out and tasted him. She closed her mouth with a resounding snap of her teeth. She was positively horrified.

Ranulf's surprise was evident as well. As if burned, he jerked his hand away and retreated a step, his gaze never leaving her face.

A long silence ensued as both opponents faced each other.

"Aye," Ranulf said, at long last breaking the silence, "when I am done with you, mayhap I will send you back to your brother, but not before."

When he was done with her . . . Lizanne closed her eyes so he would not see the fear there. When he was finished bedding her, perhaps even getting her with child, then he might allow her to return to Penforke. A fortnight, a month, a year? When?

Meeting his gaze once again, she pushed her chin into the air. "Then I have nothing to gain by enlightening you," she said. Stepping past him, she retreated to the far corner of the tent, where a washbasin was set upon a stool. She snatched up the thick cloth beside it, dipped it in the cool water, and began scrubbing at her face. She took her time, her senses alert to Ranulf's movements about the tent as she fought for a composure that had slipped so far, she did not think she would recapture it that night.

When he moved behind her, her nerve endings rose to a frenzied pitch, yet she kept her back to him.

"Have a care," he said near her ear, his breath stirring her hair and sending piercing shivers up her spine. "I would not want you to rub away your beauty as well."

She scrubbed even more vigorously.

Reaching around her, he yanked the cloth from her hands.

She swung about, treading on his toes as she faced him.

Ranulf steadied her, setting her back as he looked down into her shiny red face. "You are clean," he said. "Now remove those filthy clothes and get into bed."

Eyes suddenly large and fearful, she backed away from him, bumping the stool and very nearly upsetting the basin of water.

He correctly read her fear. " 'Tis late, Lizanne, and

we must rise early in the morning." He continued as if speaking to a child. "You cannot sleep in those garments—look at them."

Her face whitened as she protectively folded her arms across her chest.

"I give you my word," he went on, attempting to ease her fear, yet at the same time chastising himself for the consideration. Yesterday, the thought of owning her fear had appealed to him. Strangely, it no longer did. "This night you will not suffer my attentions."

Lizanne hugged her arms tighter around herself, her mouth suddenly dry. "I—I would not bed with you!"

"As I do not wish to truss you up for the night, there is no other choice."

"Nay, I will sleep on the ground."

Sighing, he lifted his face heavenward and shook his head. When he moved, it was with an amazing speed that caught her completely off guard.

Belatedly, she struggled, shrieking as the tunic was dragged over her head and she was lifted onto his shoulder. Beating her fists against his back, she kicked her legs as he yanked the boots off and proceeded to peel the leggings from her. Her resistance did not deter him one bit.

Leaving only her thin undergarments to cover her modesty, he straightened and went about the tent dousing the candles. In complete darkness, not once did he falter as he carried her to the cot and dropped her upon it.

Lizanne rebounded to a sitting position and groped for the opposite side. She had only found the edge when a hand suddenly descended between her breasts and pushed her back down. He held her writhing body there as he removed his own clothing, releasing her just long enough to remove his tunic. Again, she did not get far before he subdued her.

Lowering himself to the cot, Ranulf flipped her onto her side, her back to him, and drew her into the cradle

of his chest and thighs. Almost immediately, his body reacted to the contact, his arousal lengthening and pressing
against her backside.

It was painful, his need. Suppressing a groan, he
pulled the coverlet over them and buried his face in her
thick hair. Though she was not perfumed, he found her
fragrant. Sliding a hand beneath her, he reached up and
slid his fingers through her hair. He felt her panting
breath against his palm a second before the scrape of her
sharp teeth.

"Lizanne," he rasped as he wrenched his hand away,
"be still!" He pulled her rigid form closer and held her
there with an arm clasped just beneath her breasts.

In quick response, she landed a vicious blow to his
shin. Cursing loudly, he threw a leg over her hip. However, it was not to his benefit, for he only grew more
aroused as she continued to wiggle against him.

"If you persist in moving like that," he hissed, "I
may be forced to break my vow to you."

It was all that was needed. Although she held herself
rigid in his arms, she ceased her struggles.

With the stillness came Lizanne's first awareness of
that part of his anatomy pressed insistently against her
backside. Though she very much wanted to, she could
not believe he would keep his word. His clothes might be
fine, but he was still the villain of four years earlier—one
who raped, pillaged, and murdered without remorse.

"I cannot breathe!" she protested, arching away
from him.

"Relax and I will not hold you so tightly," he retorted.

Grudgingly, she released the tension from her limbs,
trying to block out the disturbing feel of his hard, muscled body pressed against her softer one.

Though he retained his hold on her, he loosened his
grip as promised.

She shivered then, not from the cold, but from her

wakening senses. What was wrong with her? she wondered. Was this not her enemy? Aye, though her mind recognized him, her body did not, reacting shamelessly to his touch. To her horror, another shiver of awakening coursed upward from her feet to her scalp.

"You are cold?" he asked, running his hand over the prickly skin of her forearm.

She tensed and drew her arm closer to her body. "Nay, I am quite warm, thank you. Too warm." Even as she spoke, her body quaked traitorously.

In the dark, Ranulf frowned. If she was not cold . . . Knowingly, he smiled.

Both lay wide awake for what seemed like hours, Ranulf from desire and Lizanne from something that was only part fear. Not until Ranulf felt the last bit of tension flow from her and heard her deep, soft breathing, was he finally able to sleep himself.

Chapter 7

It was only growing light when Lizanne opened one bleary eye to peer at the shadowy room. Muttering, she closed the eye again and turned her face into the warm, firm pillow beneath her cheek. Liking the feel of it, she nuzzled closer.

Something tickled her nose. Lifting a hand to push it away, she ran her fingers through the springy mat of hair beneath her and felt a steady thud against her palm. Frowning, she lifted her head and looked up at Ranulf's sleeping face.

She did not draw back as she realized his chest had served as her pillow, but she did come fully awake. Turning her head, she colored to find herself draped halfway across him, her left leg thrust between his two, her hip riding on his. She would have pulled away, but his arm was curled possessively around her waist, his fingers splayed across her ribs.

Swallowing nervously, she dragged her gaze up over his bare chest, noting the deep golden color of the skin stretched tautly over firm, sinewy muscle. She was momentarily fascinated by the dark aureole visible among the wiry chest hairs, and her fingers ached to touch it.

Clenching her hands into fists, she looked back at

his face and, at her leisure, studied it. His sharply chis-
eled features appeared softer, his hard mouth fuller, the
bottom lip retracted slightly to reveal even white teeth.
Her brows drew together as she stared at his mouth.
Something vague tugged at her memory, allowed her a
frustrating glimpse, then receded.

It struck her then that he had kept his word to her.
He had held her throughout the night to ensure against
her escape, but he had not violated her.

Why? The enemy she knew would have no remorse
in breaking his vow to her. Nay, he would not even have
given her his word in the first place. Had he truly
changed then? What force was so great as to turn a man
from such an evil path?

As she stared at the face that was not as familiar as
it had once seemed, he turned his head, presenting her
with his strong profile. At the same time, his hold on her
slackened and his hand shifted downward to rest lightly
upon her abdomen.

Seizing the chance to slip free, she reached across
him and, planting a hand on the cot, slowly leveraged
herself up. His hand fell from her.

Holding her breath, she lifted her leg from between
his and started to roll away, but she did not get far.

In one fluid motion, he rolled atop her, pinning her
beneath his greater weight.

Gasping, she looked up. Although his face was
shadowed by the curtain of hair that fell forward and
skimmed her cheek, she easily found his glittering black
eyes.

"Going somewhere?" he drawled in a voice thick
with sleep.

She raised her hands to his chest and ineffectually
pushed at him. "Get off me," she demanded.

Grasping her wrists, he raised them above her head.
"I would first claim a kiss."

"You vowed you would not violate me," she reminded him, her voice rising in panic.

"Aye, and I kept my vow yestereve, but this day the rules change."

So he did still intend to rape her. He had not changed, after all. She lowered her chin and met his eyes. "Do you intend to make me your leman? Is that to be my punishment?"

Ranulf smiled. "Nay, that will be your privilege—and mine. I will exact my revenge in other ways." He was not about to admit he'd already abandoned each of the carefully plotted punishments he'd earlier constructed. Truly, beyond installing her at his home, he was not at all certain what, exactly, he was going to do with her.

His arrogant words inflamed Lizanne, bringing forth a deep tumult of emotions that forced her body to sudden stillness and deepened her voice. "I assure you, your rape of my person will suffice. Have done with it and release me."

"Rape?" He all but spit the vile word. "Nay, Lizanne, I have no need of such methods. You will beg me to take you. And when I am ready, only then will I accommodate you."

He would not rape her? But had he not said the rules had changed? In a great quandary, she turned to the only line of defense open to her—hate. "Then you will wait an eternity," she ground out from between clenched teeth. "You repulse me."

He did not react, his face a mirror of detachment. "You will become used to my touch, and you will like it."

She strained against his hold. "I could never desire you."

"Ah, but you already do. I have seen it in your eyes, felt it in your touch. Do you really know so little of passion you cannot recognize it? Or do you simply play another of your games?"

"You arrogant beast—I despise you!" The tightly

coiled emotions were surfacing, causing her to tremble
with the effort of containing them.

"Aye, that you do," he agreed, "but more deeply,
methinks you desire me."

She sucked in a deep breath. "I would rather slip a
blade between your ribs."

"That I do not doubt, but in the end you could
not." His warm breath stirred her hair. "Tell me, how is
it I know you better than you know yourself?"

"You do not—"

"Now, I will have that kiss," he said, and lowered
his head to capture her lips.

She jerked her head aside in time to evade him, his
mouth finding her cheek instead. Without hesitation, he
trailed his lips across to her ear.

When she felt his warm, moist tongue begin a sen-
sual assault of that sensitive area, she screeched loudly
and twisted her head the other way.

He laughed, then proceeded to minister to the other
ear before seeking the vulnerable spot below it, and
lower, the hollow of her throat.

A delicious, forbidden shiver crawled up Lizanne's
spine. Squeezing her eyes closed, she became aware of a
deep, rhythmic beat growing louder in her ears, as if
she'd run a great distance. She felt warm—feverish, actually.

Something was happening to her, she realized with
growing alarm. Her rage was turning on her, abandoning
her as it transformed itself into something that both
thrilled and frightened her.

Her mind at war with her body, she whimpered as
her self-erected barriers began to slip. Nay, it could not
be. She hated this man. . . .

Sensing victory, Ranulf lifted his head and took
control of her mouth, patiently seeking a response.
When he felt her awakening, he released her wrists and
ran his hand downward to claim her breast.

She shivered at his bold touch and arched against him, sweet, rasping breaths issuing from her lips.

"Open your mouth," he ordered thickly, his body aching for release.

Bewildered by the new sensations assaulting her as her traitorous body reacted to his bold caresses, Lizanne was too overwhelmed to comply.

Forcing his tongue between her teeth, Ranulf tasted her, drinking in the sweet nectar he found in the hidden recesses.

He heard her moan of surrender, felt her hands that buried themselves in his hair, and mated with the tongue that tentatively met his. The effort it took him to pull back amazed him, but withdraw he did, leaning on an elbow to study her flushed countenance.

"Lizanne, look at me," he commanded.

The corners of her mouth lifting, she raised her lids to reveal dazed, impassioned eyes, their green a vibrant shade he had not seen before. He was momentarily mesmerized by the effect. Then the color darkened to that familiar, angry green.

It was all it took, Lizanne realized as loathing replaced the waves of shame sweeping her. She had but to open her eyes and look upon his face to conquer her body's response to him. Her mind rejoiced in the discovery.

She smiled bitterly, her lips a thin line. "Are you finished?"

His eyes narrowed, his brows nearly meeting as he stared at her. Then he gripped her shoulders. "What do you see when you look at me?"

She winced. "I fear you would not be pleased by my observation."

If he had lunged for her then and throttled her, she would not have been surprised. Perhaps not even blamed him. But he didn't, which did surprise her.

Cursing, he released her and rolled away.

Lizanne threw herself in the opposite direction, and in her haste tumbled off the cot to land on her rear end.

"I will discover that which you hide from me," he threatened, stalking around the cot.

Rubbing her backside, Lizanne scrambled to her feet and stepped back so she would not be forced to lift her head to meet his gaze. It was the cool morning air touching her skin that reminded her of the scanty undergarments that served as her only clothing. Feeling exposed, she crossed her arms over her breasts.

"What does not belong to you cannot be hidden," she retorted. "My secrets are my own, Ranulf Wardieu. I share them only with those I choose. I do not . . . choose you." This last she punctuated.

In the ensuing silence, he leaned toward her but did not step closer. When at last he spoke, his voice was dangerously soft. "I weary of your mockery," he said. "Henceforth you will address me as 'my lord'—for that I most certainly am now. Only in bed will you use my given name. Do you understand?"

Years of verbal sparring were responsible for Lizanne's impulsively foolish rejoinder. "Then will you address me as 'my lady'?" She did not have to see the dark cloud that settled over his features to regret the words the moment she said them.

Now, she thought, he would beat her. With a muffled cry, she jumped out of reach and ran across the tent to the opening. Throwing back the flap, she dashed outside, only to skid to a stumbling halt.

Geoff, bearing a tray, also drew himself up short, his mouth falling open at her dress—or, rather, lack thereof. Others were milling about in the dawn's soft light, and they, too, paused to gape at her.

Rooted to the spot, she could only stare back at Geoff. She offered no resistance when Ranulf dragged her back inside the tent.

Away from prying eyes, he swung her around and

gave her a quick, forceful shake. "Have you no sense? Think you it permissible to run around near-naked? . . ."

"I did not think . . ." she weakly interjected, tears pooling in her eyes. Too late, she looked down so he would not see them.

Sighing wearily, Ranulf pulled her to the cot and pushed her down on it, then proceeded to wrap the coverlet about her. Shaking his head, he strode to the tent opening and beckoned Geoff inside.

"Godspeed, my lord," the young squire greeted him, brightly flushed as he carried his burden across the tent. Keeping his eyes carefully averted, he removed the supper tray and replaced it with the smaller one.

Ranulf gathered the items Lizanne had taken from his squire and returned them to the shamefaced young man before sending him on his way. Turning to Lizanne, he saw she was peering over the edge of her wrap at the food.

He broke off a piece of bread and grabbed a small apple, then crossed the tent and handed them to her.

She hesitated only briefly before accepting the offering. "Thank you," she murmured, and took a loud, large bite of the apple.

He was surprised at her civility. It occurred to him that, though in his revenge he denied her the title of "lady," she did indeed offer glimpses of such breeding. Frowning, he turned to his chest and, throwing back the lid, removed fresh garments.

Curious as to the remaining contents of the chest, Lizanne leaned forward to better see inside, but only caught sight of other garments before it was closed.

Catching her show of interest, Ranulf swept his hand toward the chest. "You will find nothing in there to 'slip' between my ribs, Lizanne. Do try to restrain yourself from snooping among my belongings."

Shrugging, she looked away. "Do not flatter yourself," she muttered. "You have nothing that interests me."

Taking another bite of the apple, she leaned back on an elbow and swung her legs.

Reminding himself that he was a patient man, Ranulf strode to the cot and made quick work of disrobing.

Glimpsing his lean, muscular body stripped bare of all clothing, Lizanne felt her breath catch in her throat. Hot color rose in her face, and she quickly looked away. Only then did she realize she'd inhaled a small piece of apple. Wheezing noisily, she tried to draw enough air into her lungs with which to expel the object.

Immediately, Ranulf was there, dragging her to her feet and thumping her on the back. Slack in his arms, she wondered which was worse—the lack of air or his blows. The apple popped free a moment later.

Drawing in deep, ragged breaths, she straightened and glanced over her shoulder at him. "Bad apple," she quipped, then smiled.

It was on the tip of Ranulf's tongue to inform her he saw no humor in the situation, but her smile dispelled all thoughts of a reprimand. Like nothing he'd ever seen, it lit her entire face, turning her eyes an entirely different shade of green shot through with sparkling gold, bringing a warm glow to her cheeks, curving her mouth into a full bow that exposed two neat rows of pearly teeth, and revealing, for the first time, a single dimple in her left cheek. He was mesmerized.

"I would have you smile more often," he said, touching the indentation with one finger. Instantly, he regretted the words.

"Is that an order?" she asked, her old self once again.

He shook his head and firmly set her away from him. "An observation, 'tis all."

"Good." Grabbing the coverlet, she tossed it over her shoulders and walked to the tray of food. Her back to him, she picked at the morsels while he completed dressing.

Pulling up a stool, Ranulf joined her shortly thereafter, but not another word was spoken between them until Geoff was given permission to enter once again. Removing a bundle from beneath his arm, the squire handed it to his lord, picked up the tray, and left without a word.

"Your clothes," Ranulf explained, extending them to Lizanne.

She looked disdainfully at the folded bliaut, chemise, and shoes he held. She had thought herself well rid of them, and now here they were again.

"I would much prefer chausses and a tunic," she said, planting her hands upon her hips. "These are far too cumbersome." She flicked her fingers at the garments but did not take them from him.

"A fact I am well aware of," he said, "and one which I find particularly convenient where you are concerned."

Scowling, she crossed her arms over her chest.

He shrugged and tossed the garments on the cot. "If you are not dressed when I return, I will do it myself."

He left her standing in the middle of the tent.

She wasted the first few minutes vacillating between defiance and grudging capitulation. In the end, she frantically threw off the coverlet and rushed to pull the garments over her head. She was struggling with the laces when Ranulf reentered.

Wordlessly, he crossed to her, pushed her hands away, and effortlessly knotted the laces. Then he stood back and examined her from top to bottom.

Indignant at his perusal, she lifted her chin. "Well, do I meet with your approval?"

He shook his head. "Hardly."

Striding to his chest, he tossed back the lid, and a moment later returned with a comb and small mirror.

"You must see to your grooming," he said, dropping the implements on the cot. "You are truly a mess."

After settling the girdle about her hips, Lizanne lifted the mirror to view her reflection. "I see nothing amiss," she lied, though in fact she was quite dismayed with her appearance. As usual, that damnable hair.

"See to it," he ordered. "We depart within the hour." Then he was gone.

Ignoring the order, Lizanne could not resist the temptation to investigate her state of confinement. When she felt sufficient time had passed for Ranulf to make himself absent, she crept to the tent opening and poked her head out. Leaning against a tree directly across the way was the squire Geoff. Smiling thinly, he lifted a hand and waved, then pointed to the two men-at-arms positioned on either side of the tent.

Glowering, Lizanne retreated from the opening, and with loud mutterings grabbed up the comb and began yanking it through her hair.

An hour later, with Lizanne seated before Ranulf on his great destrier, they broke camp and headed north.

Although Lizanne was intensely curious as to their destination, she maintained a rebellious silence, ignoring Ranulf's occasional comments as they passed through the changing countryside.

Inasmuch as the ride was less rigorous than the one the day before, she quickly tired of holding herself apart from him. By noon, when they stopped alongside a clear stream to water the horses, her muscles were fairly screaming for ease. When Ranulf reached up to assist in her dismount, she fought down the impulse to reject him. Her muscles creaked betrayingly as he set her on the ground.

"You are a stubborn woman, Lizanne Balmaine," he said before turning and stalking away.

Kneading the sore muscles of her shoulders, she

looked about her. To her left and right stood the two men who had guarded the tent earlier that morning, their eyes trained on her. Geoff, too, watched as he fed a handful of oats to his horse.

She smiled prettily at him, then stuck her tongue out. The young squire blinked in surprise, then returned the gesture.

It was Lizanne's turn to be surprised, though she should not have been, considering the deception she had played upon him on the night past. Closing her mouth, she turned her back to him and came face-to-face with Sir Walter.

He was not smiling. Apparently, he had witnessed the brief exchange, and his mouth was grimly set, much as it had been when he'd been forced to carry her the day before.

"What do you want?" she asked flippantly in a sorry attempt to mask her embarrassment.

His frown deepening, he held out a skin of water to her, clearly finding it distasteful to have to deal with her again.

Lizanne felt a sharp pang at his attitude but shrugged it off. Drawing on years of experience that had taught her the best defense against men was to cut them to the quick with her venomous tongue, she clasped her hands behind her back and raised her eyes to his.

"Am I to take it you would offer me a drink?" she asked in an exaggerated, disbelieving voice.

His face darkened, but still he said nothing.

She took a step nearer and placed herself at eye level with him, for he was no taller than she. " 'Tis a kindness I would not expect."

"I assure you, my lady," he snarled, " 'tis not out of kindness I offer it to you. 'Tis by order only."

She was taken aback by the depth of his animosity but was nevertheless pleased that she'd forced him to speak. Shrugging, she took the skin from him. "You do not like me?" she asked before taking a long swallow of the cool, sweet water.

He met her eyes over the skin. "I bear no affection for vipers, my lady."

She nearly choked on the liquid. A viper? Was that how he thought of her? The remark wounded her to the quick, but again she suppressed the outward expression of her pain.

For the first time, she took a close look at him. He was older than Ranulf by at least ten years, his once-dark hair liberally interspersed with silver. Though his face was marked by the ravages of a childhood illness, he was nonetheless attractive, his piercing blue eyes like chips of ice beneath full, dark brows. Very much like Gilbert's eyes, she reflected.

After taking a last swallow, she handed the skin back to him. "I cannot say it surprises me," she said, "though methinks you mistake fear for dislike."

"Fear?"

From the look on his face, she knew he was tempted to strike her—or at least take her in hand. Stepping away from him, she nodded. "Aye. 'Tis not uncommon for men to be frightened of that which they do not understand," she explained. "I forgive you, though. 'Tis obvious your misplaced loyalty to your lord casts shadows upon your good judgment."

There, let him chew on that a while!

A stunning shade of red suffused the man's face and fanned outward to set his ears aflame. Clenching his fists, Walter turned on his heel and stalked away.

Mayhap she had pushed him too far, Lizanne considered as she watched him leave. After all, an enemy was of little use to her, but an ally. . . . She pondered that possibility a moment, then shook her head. Nay, it was not likely Ranulf's man would play him false. She would gain nothing by befriending him.

Sighing, she strolled to the bank of the stream and,

hiking up her skirts, squatted at the edge. Pushing back the troublesomely long sleeves of her bliaut, she leaned forward and dipped her hands in the cool water, letting it flow over her wrists. After the long, hot ride, it was wonderfully refreshing.

Cupping her hands, she scooped up some water and splashed it over her face. Gasping at its cold bite, she splashed more over her throat and let it trickle down the front of her dress. Soaking through to her skin, it trailed a cool path between her breasts and lower to her abdomen. Smiling contentedly, she grabbed a handful of skirt and patted her face dry.

"What did you say to Sir Walter?"

Lizanne started, very nearly sending herself headlong into the stream. She had not heard Ranulf's approach. For such a large man, he moved with incredible stealth.

Recovering, she peered over her shoulder at him. "Naught really. We simply agreed to dislike each other."

His eyes narrowed. "I will not have you causing strife among my men, Lizanne. Henceforth you will refrain from speaking to them."

"I have done nothing wrong."

"I have seen how you treat your inferiors. Do not think you can treat my men the same."

That gave her pause to stop and search backward for such an occasion. Only one came to mind. Though she rebelled against offering an explanation for her unseemly behavior, she found herself doing so anyway. "If you are speaking of the servant at Lord Langdon's castle, then I would have you know that miserable woman slapped my maid."

He held up his hand. "I will not argue with you."

Too angered to be mindful of the interest their talk was generating, Lizanne scooped up another handful of water and threw it at him.

He sidestepped, easily avoiding much of the spray.

"I begin to wonder whether you be woman or child," he said. Without waiting for a response, he caught hold of her and roughly pulled her to her feet.

With a sudden twist, she jerked free and stepped back, defiantly thrusting her chin in the air.

Albeit sorely tempted to give her the slight push that would land her in the stream, Ranulf merely shook his head. "Follow me," he ordered, turning away.

Squaring her shoulders and putting on a show of dignity, she grudgingly obeyed.

"You may relieve yourself here," he said a few minutes later, having led her to a secluded area away from the others.

Her brows arched. "How thoughtful of you."

He let her sarcasm slide. Pointing to a grove of trees, he motioned for her to go ahead. "Do not try my patience," he warned as she stepped past him.

In a foul mood, she thought perhaps she might.

Turning his back on her, Ranulf crossed his arms over his chest and focused on his squire, wondering what task he might set the young man so that he could redeem himself. It was obvious his pride had taken a grievous blow, and that Lizanne would not so easily dupe him a second time.

When several minutes had passed without her reappearance, Ranulf grew uneasy. Turning, he scanned the area for a glimpse of her green garment. Then he silently cursed. He had not thought how easy it would be for her to blend with the surrounding vegetation in that color.

"Lizanne," he called, "do not dawdle."

He received no answer. Closing his eyes, he shook his head with disbelief. Surely, she had not attempted another escape? Had he underestimated her again?

He called again, but still no reply. A harsh invective issuing from his lips, he strode briskly forward, then broke into a run. She could not have gone far.

"God's rood!" he bellowed, coming to the place he'd last seen her and finding her absent.

Though she made no sound that would have alerted him to her whereabouts, he instinctively raised his head. Shading his eyes against the sun's glare, he scanned the branches of the trees around him. A moment later, he located her where she perched precariously on a limb midway up an ancient tree.

How had she managed to climb so high—especially hampered by her voluminous gown? he wondered as he walked over to the tree. She was like a boy, a contentious, uncontrollable little boy constantly getting himself into trouble.

"You are not very quick, are you?" she said, grinning mischievously down at him. "Had I known you would take so long, mayhap I would have tried to escape after all." Her legs dangling amid her skirts, she offered an enticing glimpse of firm calves and fine-boned ankles.

"What are you doing up there?" he demanded, ignoring her barbed remark as he chastised himself for the stirrings in his loins. He did not care for the danger she had placed herself in.

" 'Tis a lovely view," she answered, sweeping a hand before her to indicate the panoramic scene. "Why, I can see—"

"Come down."

Her lips twisting, she looked back at him. "I rather like it up here. Mayhap you should come up."

To her great surprise, he unbelted his sword and began to scale the gnarly tree.

Watching him, she could not help but admire the apparent ease with which he accomplished the feat. Even without her burdensome garments, she could not possibly have made it appear so effortless. She was immensely grateful he had not witnessed her ascent.

A minute later, he heaved himself up to the branch she was balanced upon. Since he couldn't venture out

upon the limb—his weight might snap it—he reached
for her. "Give me your hand," he said. "I will help you
down."

"You are not angry?" she asked with disbelief and
disappointment.

"Nay. You hoped to make me so?"

She nodded. "Aye."

"For what reason?"

She dropped her head back and looked up at the
sky. "For that miserable ride, of course."

He nearly laughed aloud. "If you relaxed, 'twould be
more comfortable for you."

"I would have a horse of my own," she suggested,
turning her head so quickly in his direction, she teetered
on the branch.

Instantly, he sobered. "We will speak of this matter
when we are on the ground. Now, take my hand."

She edged farther away. "As I got myself up here, I
will get myself down."

"You will break your neck is what you will do!" he
retorted. Now he was angry. Damn her for her ability to
unleash that emotion! It was a weakness he could ill afford.

She looked him squarely in the eye. "Would you
care?"

Although he had no intention of admitting it, he realized he would care a great deal. And not simply because his revenge would be curtailed.

At his protracted silence, she shrugged. "I have been
climbing trees, shooting bows, and engaging in swordplay for years, Ranulf Wardieu. I do not need to be res-
cued."

Taking a deep, calming breath, Ranulf leaned back
against the tree trunk and considered her words. When
he spoke, his tone was gentle. "Tell me of your childhood, Lizanne."

She regarded him suspiciously. "Now?"

He shrugged. "Unless, of course, you are ready to climb down."

She considered his request thoroughly before answering. Deciding there was no real harm in the telling of it, she acquiesced. "Though you may not believe this, I was brought up to be a proper lady. At one time, I could even sew a fine stitch." She grimaced at the remembrance of that womanly skill gone by the wayside. For the very first time since she had set it aside, she felt an unexplainable loss.

"Still, I was always interested in those things considered the domain of men." She laughed at a particularly vivid memory. "Once I even challenged Gilbert to a duel—my stick against his sword. He was not amused." Grasping her bottom lip between her teeth, she shook her head.

Ranulf was intrigued. One question after another came to mind, but he remained silent, wanting her to continue.

"When I was fourteen, shortly after my father's death . . ." Her voice caught in her throat. Swallowing, she continued. "Gilbert finally relented and began secretly instructing me in the art of warfare."

"Why?" Ranulf could not resist asking, wondering at what kind of man would allow himself to be coerced into something so dishonorable.

Of a sudden, her demeanor changed, her playful smile fading. She stared down at her hands. "To defend myself, of course."

Confused, he shook his head. "That is the responsibility of men, Lizanne."

She turned grief-stricken eyes to him. "But sometimes they fail." Her voice was barely a whisper.

Ranulf was jolted by the look on her face. He had the sudden, overwhelming urge to comfort her. "Who failed you? Gilbert?"

Her eyes widened, then that mask of indifference

fell into place like the slamming of a door. "I am ready to get down now," she said, avoiding his probing gaze.

Ranulf was not ready, but he held his hand out to her anyway.

She scooted along the limb toward him, not hesitating in her acceptance of his aid this time. Wordlessly, she placed her hand in his and allowed herself to be drawn against him.

"Lizanne," he said, tilting her face up, "what am I to do with you?"

"Let me go home," she whispered.

He shook his head. "I cannot. 'Tis done."

She smiled bitterly but made no attempt to evade him when he lowered his head and covered her mouth with his. The kiss was sweet but brief, and when it was over, she buried her face against his neck and tried very hard not to think about it.

Chapter 8

*R*aging, *Gilbert Balmaine* swept the long table clear with one stroke of his arm. Pitchers of ale, platters of viands, and unfilled tankards flew across the room like errant missiles. All within range either ducked or fled in search of cover, further enraging their baron.

Bellowing loudly and spitting vile profanity, the likes of which he had strictly forbidden his sister, he swung around to face the captain of the guard and the steward where they stood before the assembly of knights at the edge of the hall.

His color high, his breathing ragged, he strode across the rush-covered floor, his limp more prominent than usual. Reaching the two men, he hauled them up by the fronts of their tunics.

"I will have both your necks if any ill befalls my sister as a result of this ... atrocity!" he roared. The blast of his breath stirred their hair; the expression on his face cowered them. "Best you pray to your God for her safe return."

In the face of such fury, neither man was capable of speech. Moments later they found themselves thrown aside as their lord set off on a new tangent, scattering his knights about the hall as he went. A sideboard burdened with an array of pastries was sent crashing to the floor, and a bench along the wall collapsed beneath a well-placed kick.

Few could remember a time when he had been so intensely alive with emotion, albeit such an ominous one struck uncertain fear in their hearts. This was indeed a rare, momentous display.

Although considered a just and honorable lord, Gilbert Balmaine was typically sullen, with a quiet, brooding manner none dared take offense to. Only around the Lady Lizanne was the hidden side of his nature ever glimpsed. He indulged her every whim, even to the point of instructing her in the use of arms. Behind his back, the castlefolk frowned and shook their heads at such exploits, but none dared dispute the improprieties.

Still, some remembered the humorous and enthusiastic young man Gilbert had been prior to inheriting the barony following his father's death. Even his sister had been a different sort of person then.

The events that had led to these changes in brother and sister, though vague in detail, were common enough knowledge among the castlefolk, but never spoken of—not even in private. It was strictly forbidden.

"Who is this black-hearted knight who holds her?" Gilbert shouted, returning to tower over the subjects of his wrath.

Robert Coulter regained his feet first, nervously brushing away the litterings of the rushes as he straightened before his lord. With much effort, he willed his eyes to meet Gilbert's.

"He called himself Wardieu. Ranulf Wardieu, my lord."

Wardieu? His jaw working, Gilbert considered the name and found it recently familiar. Of a sudden, he remembered the large, fair-headed knight who had sat at the king's table more than a fortnight earlier. The white knight, the ladies had whimsically named him.

Not one for women's prattle or gossip, Gilbert had turned his attention elsewhere, but it had been impossible not to be aware of the intense speculation the man raised among the people at court. Still, he had gleaned little from the snatches of conversation he had involuntarily been privy to. He knew only that this Wardieu held vast lands to the north—Chesne—and that he was recounted to be a formidable adversary.

Vaguely, Gilbert remembered a group of younger ladies twittering over the recent death of the man's wife. They had unashamedly vied for his attention, and he had not even seemed to notice.

Gilbert fisted his hands at his sides and tried to make sense of the events that had led to the taking of Lizanne. Why had this Wardieu deigned to carry her away? What could have possessed the man to such an action? Aye, his sister was beyond lovely, but her belligerent disposition was easily recognized, and most men found it far outweighed her looks.

Apologetically, Ian, the steward, broke into his lord's madly churning thoughts. "Samuel knows more, my lord. 'Twas he who tended the man when the Lady Lizanne held him prisoner."

The words pricked Gilbert's volatile temper. At once, he thrust his face near the smaller man's. Had he heard right?

"Prisoner?" he repeated. "My sister held this Wardieu prisoner? A knight?" At the steward's sullen nod, Gilbert clapped a hand to his forehead. "Bring Samuel to me!"

"I am here, my lord." The huge bald man showed himself, skirting a group of knights to stand before him.

Gilbert knew the man well. He and his wife were favorites of Lizanne's. "Samuel," he said, fighting to regain control of his emotions. "I would speak with you in private." He glared meaningfully at the other occupants of the room.

"And send that wench, Mellie, as well," he commanded as an afterthought.

Wordlessly, the horse-weary, travel-fatigued knights left the hall, taking with them the steward, the captain of the guard, and the few brave servants skulking about.

Rubbing his aching right leg, Gilbert crossed to the raised dais and dropped heavily into his high-backed chair. He lifted his good leg and laid his booted foot against the edge of the table. Pressing backward, he tilted the chair onto its two back legs.

Following, Samuel sat on the bench opposite that his lord indicated with an impatient sweep of his hand.

"Tell me everything," Gilbert commanded. "And do start at the beginning!"

Respectfully, Samuel began his narrative, commencing with the return of Lizanne from Lord Bernard's castle and her giving of the unconscious prisoner into his care. He left out nothing, pausing only when the baron spewed profanity and pounded his fists upon the arms of his chair.

Halfway through, Mellie crept into the hall and trepidatiously approached the raised dais.

Leaning precariously toward Samuel, his chair on the verge of overturning, Gilbert acknowledged her by jabbing his finger toward the bench the bald man was perched upon.

She sank down upon it and, clasping her trembling hands in her lap, bowed her head and stared at her nibbled nails.

"She did what?" Gilbert roared, his sudden outcry startling poor Mellie so that she slipped off the edge of the bench and only managed to upright herself after much ado.

Neither man appeared to notice.

"Aye," Samuel said. "She faced 'em alone and loosed her arrow on the man."

"Did she wound the bastard?"

Samuel shook his head. "Nay, though had she meant to, I do not doubt she would have. As you know, her aim ..."

Impatiently, Gilbert waved the man to silence. "So she went willingly, without breach of the castle's walls?"

Samuel nodded, his bare pate gleaming in the midday light streaming through the windows. "She had no choice, milord. We were greatly outnumbered, and the knight claimed to have taken you captive."

"The deceitful villain! I—" Gilbert halted his words as another thought that had been niggling at the back of his mind sprang forward. "Curse King Henry!" he blasphemed, remembering the monarch's seemingly indifferent inquiry into his sister's whereabouts. With a resounding crash, his chair landed back on its four legs.

Samuel and Mellie exchanged looks of uncertainty, shrugged, and turned their attention back to their baron. Gilbert was leaning forward, his hands clenched into tight, whitened fists.

Unsuspectingly, Gilbert had told the king of Lizanne's stay with her cousin at Langdon Castle. Henry had smiled—almost gleefully, then he had mumbled something about finding a worthy knight who could take her in hand. Was it this Wardieu Henry had had in mind?

Curiously, one delay after another had been thrown into Gilbert's path over the past fortnight until, finally, he and his retainers had been allowed to return to Penforke. At the time, Gilbert had seen it as nothing more than a coincidental nuisance, but now he thought it more likely he had been the victim of delay by design—the king's.

"He is behind this," Gilbert concluded with dire certainty. "But how is it Lizanne took this Wardieu prisoner—and why?"

Ranulf Wardieu was a man of immense proportions, after all. How had she managed to fell him? Most important, why would his man-hating sister go to such lengths? He dropped his head back and pondered the ceiling.

"Milord," Mellie said softly.

Gilbert looked at her. "What know you of this, Mellie?"

He had calmed considerably. For the first time since hearing his sister had been abducted, his thoughts were ticking logically again.

Mellie wrung her hands. "Well, milord, 'twas I who lured the knight into the trap."

Gilbert's brows dropped over his startling blue eyes. "You?" he asked disbelievingly, sitting straighter in his chair. "And why would you do such a thing?"

"Why, at my mistress's bidding, of course," she wailed, looking away.

"Make sense, girl!" Gilbert brought his open palm down upon the tabletop.

Her bottom lip trembling, she looked back at him. "Lady Lizanne did not tell me why, milord, but she had me lure the man down a darkened corridor at Lord Langdon's castle. He was near upon me when she sprang from the shadows and dealt him a blow."

"Single-handedly?" Gilbert asked, a frown marring his otherwise-handsome face. Well he knew his sister's abilities, but he could not reconcile the size and apparent strength of Wardieu with that of hers.

"Aye." Mellie bobbed her head earnestly. "He was well sated with drink, milord. Though he tried to fight, milady was too quick for him and knocked him unconscious with the second blow. 'Twas like a great oak he fell."

Gilbert imagined the scene and could not help the small smile curling his lips. What in God's wrath had possessed her?

"And how did she deliver him to Penforke without alerting Lord Bernard? Surely, he was suspicious?"

"Why, we hid him in one of the wagons and left before dawn the following morn. He was not missed at that time, milord."

"And he did not awaken? 'Tis a full day and a half's journey to Penforke," he reminded her.

A mischievous twinkle entered the maid's eye. "Aye, but soon as he stirred, I had but to wave one of me mistress's potions beneath his nose and"—she snapped her fingers—"he went right back to sleepin'."

Still trying to make sense of it all, Gilbert groaned and tugged at his new growth of beard. "Lady Lizanne told you naught of her reasons for abducting this knight?"

Mellie shook her head. "Alls she said was he'd greatly wronged her family, and she intended to punish him for his sins."

It sounded like her, but still ... "How many days does this Wardieu have on us?" he asked as he wrestled with the questions uppermost in his mind.

"He rode north three days ago, milord," Samuel answered.

Three days? Was he returning to Chesne? Suddenly exhausted, Gilbert ground the heels of his palms against his eyes. He would need to allow his men rest before following, but follow he must. The thought of failing Lizanne a second time burned in his gut like the sharp spark off steel.

Heaving his tired body out of the chair, he strode across the hall and mounted the stairs to his solar. Though his belly gnawed with hunger, he ignored the discomfort and began to pace the floor.

"Why, Lizanne?" he asked the walls. Getting no response, he lengthened his stride until his leg protested with a wrenching throb that flared upward to his hip. Grimacing, he threw himself into a heavily worn chair and massaged the impaired limb.

You allowed her too much rein, he reproached himself, his mind returning to his sister's motive for imprisoning a man like Wardieu. Why had none gainsaid her?

Never had he known Robert Coulter to back down from a challenge. The man had, after all, held his esteemed position as captain of the guard for nigh on twenty years. He had served Gilbert's father well during the time of King Stephen's reign when conflicts between neighboring barons had been commonplace events.

Why, then, would the man allow Lizanne to surrender without putting up at least a token resistance? Had he gone soft in the intervening years of relative peace? Mayhap Penforke could have held out long enough for him to return and do battle.

Because, a persistent voice in his head admonished him, you allowed Lizanne to supersede the authority of others, including your own, time and again.

Gilbert closed his eyes. There would be changes, he determined, when he brought his little sister home.

It was time for her—and him—to put the past aside and assume their rightful roles at Penforke. For too long, they had allowed their futures to be governed by the forces of past aggressions.

His eyes flew wide at the inevitable remembrance of that grisly night four years earlier when his blood had been spilled. Grappling with a sense of impending discovery, he reluctantly immersed himself in the memory, reliving every detail of his failure.

A full score strong, they had swept down on the camp from the woods, their blades already seasoned with the blood of the guards they had slain. Immediately, Gilbert and his men had awakened and reached for their swords, but too late. Even as they had struggled to gain their feet, weapons rose and fell against them.

All around him, Gilbert had heard the cries of his men as they fought, their shouts of agony as they fell. He had tasted the blood that sprayed the air and flecked his clothing, but had not paused in his fight to defeat those who would see him dead.

His blade sheathed in blood, the first who had dared to challenge him dead at his feet, he turned his attention to the two advancing upon him. Rage was his faithful ally, lending him the strength to match blows with them as they fell upon him simultaneously.

Refusing to surrender any ground to the miscreants, he forced them back. However, the satisfaction he felt when he buried his sword in the flesh of the smaller man's neck was short-lived. The other's blade sliced through his chausses, flaying open skin and muscle and driving him to his knees.

The pain was excruciating, but his need to protect Lizanne was stronger. The fury of battle raging through his veins, he struggled to regain his feet, swinging his sword up to deflect a blow intended to bring a quick end to him. But torn by escalating pain and weakened by the loss of blood, he was unable to stand again. Instead, he was forced to fight from the ground.

As he defended himself, he caught a glimpse of another swiftly approaching—pale hair that slashed light across the darkness of night. However, he didn't have time to fix his gaze upon this new adversary, for his assailant was bearing down on him.

Though his thrusts had grown labored and his vision dimmed, his warrior's mind rebelled against his body's weakening and bade him to continue seeking the other's steel. He did so almost blindly, his other senses guiding his arm.

Once again, his sword made contact, though he could not say with what. At nearly the same moment, he felt a white-hot pain explode within his chest. Protesting loudly, he collapsed, still holding tight to his sword. As consciousness fell away and a dark hand urged him to explore the depths of a void theretofore unknown, he heard a scream that cleaved his soul.

Lizanne!

He struggled to rise above the darkness, but it proved stronger than his mangled body. Even as he was dragged under, he clung to a single thread of life.

A greater purpose . . . Promises to keep . . .

His breathing ragged, Gilbert sat forward in the chair, his knuckles white where he gripped the padded arms.

The pieces finally fit. Although he had caught only the barest glimpse of the man who had led the attack upon their camp, Lizanne had been adamant about his appearance. Could it be? Such colorless hair was not common.

He shook his head. Why would a landed nobleman disguise himself as a common villein? It was absolutely preposterous, but he could think of no other reason for Lizanne's actions. Had she not vowed with all her heart to one day unleash her revenge upon the miscreant for all the wrongs done her family?

Was this Wardieu's reason, then, for stealing her away? If so, what did he intend to do with her? Gilbert knew the answer. She could not be allowed to live. Did she still?

Shoving to his feet, he strode from the solar and descended the stairs two at a time. There was no time to rest. This night he and his men would ride.

Chapter 9

"You've never before tended a wound?" Ranulf asked disbelievingly, ignoring Lizanne's silent appeal to be relieved of the task.

"Mayhap a scratch or two," she said.

He frowned. " 'Tis common for the lady of the donjon to be accomplished in such things."

She refused to meet his eyes. "Aye," she admitted, "but I gave up those duties long ago."

Ranulf knew otherwise. Samuel had been very clear on this. Still, he would play her game—for a short while. "Then I will have to teach you," he concluded. Amusedly, he witnessed the indignation that flitted across her face.

"Nay." She shook her head and started backward. "I take to fainting at the sight of blood. You would not want me swooning, would you?"

He reached out and caught her hand. Urging her down beside him, he drew her palm over his bared leg and placed it upon the bandages.

" 'Tis nearly healed," he assured her. " 'Twas a clean cut—do you not remember?"

She looked away. " 'Twould not have happened had you not attacked me," she muttered.

"Nay, 'twould not have happened had you not imprisoned me."

Pressing her lips together, she reluctantly set about removing the bandages a strip at a time until the evidence of her infliction lay before her.

Leaning forward, she examined it, her training as a healer taking over and replacing all other concerns. The wound was indeed nearly healed, the flesh seamed neatly together with Lucy's fine stitches. And there was no redness or swelling—a very good sign.

When Ranulf offered her a small pot, she took it unthinkingly and was immediately struck by its familiarity. Frowning, she removed the lid and peered at the creamy salve within. She sniffed its distinctly pungent odor. It was one of her preparations.

Her head snapped up. "Where did you get this?"

He grinned. "Lord Bernard's wife gave it to me. Her cousin, whom I understand to be a lady with a gift for healing, prepared it for her household.

He knew.

She sat back on her heels and considered the hateful man, her brow furrowing, her lips pinching white. "What else did my cousin tell you?"

"You concede too easily, Lizanne," he said with mock disappointment. "I had thought we could play this game a bit longer."

She ignored the taunt. "You did not answer my question."

He prolonged her torment a moment longer. When finally he spoke, he leaned conspiratorially forward and whispered in her ear, "I would not dare repeat her exact words, but I must say the lady appears to have no great love for her cousin."

Lizanne's head snapped around. She saw that his dark eyes sparkled with barely suppressed humor, his lips twitching. The cur was laughing at her!

"You are despicable—and deceitful!"

Instantly, the laughter disappeared from his face. Reaching out, he grasped her chin. "Nay, Lizanne, 'twas you who tried to deceive me. Now, I want your word you will cease with these lies and start behaving more reasonably—like a lady."

She pushed his hand away. "I will do what I must to protect myself," she declared. "And that does not include behaving like a lady!"

His eyes narrowed. "Your word."

"If you think I would keep vows made to you under order, then you are more a fool than I first thought." She angrily placed the flat of her hand against his chest and pushed him back. Then, dipping two fingers in the salve, she scooped up a generous amount and bent over his thigh again. She began working it into the wound with a vengeance.

Leaning back on his elbows, Ranulf laughed loudly. He knew he should be angry with her continued defiance, but her reasoning was simply too amusing.

She threw him a look of disdain. "I will need fresh bandages," she informed him, smoothing in the last bit of salve.

Sobering, he reached for the strips of clean cloth and handed them to her.

She took them and efficiently rebandaged the leg, perhaps a bit too tightly. "There," she said, straightening. "I will remove the stitches in two days' time."

"Then you are not planning another escape?"

She hesitated, then shook her head. "Nay, I plan for naught. I simply await another opportunity. You are bound to give me one."

"There will be no more opportunities." Standing, he reached for his leggings and pulled them on. "You will not play me for a fool twice."

"Is it only once, then?"

"Lizanne!" He took a step toward her.

She was narrowly saved from his wrath by a call from outside the tent. "My lord, may I enter?"

Ranulf shot her a warning look, then moved past her. "Aye, Walter," he answered.

The knight threw back the flap and strode inside. He spared Lizanne only a cursory glance, his mouth tightening perceptibly, before turning his full attention upon Ranulf.

"The patrol has returned," he informed his liege lord.

In two long strides, Ranulf bridged the distance between them. "And?" he prompted, purposely turning his back to Lizanne.

Walter sent a meaningful look in her direction. It was not lost on her.

"No sign, my lord."

"No sign of what?" Lizanne asked, unable to suppress her curiosity.

Walter was taken aback by her effrontery, his jaw slackening as he looked beyond Ranulf to where she stood with hands on hips.

" 'Tis none of your concern," Ranulf harshly reprimanded her.

"But 'tis my concern," she protested. "I would know if my brother rides for me."

Slowly, he turned toward her. "Do not argue with me."

She was tempted to but decided better of it. Swinging around, she stomped over to his wooden chest and dropped down upon it. Drawing her legs up, she sat cross-legged, facing the two men.

Suppressing the urge to instruct her in the proper behavior of a lady, Ranulf turned his attention to the remains of the meal brought earlier. Between bites he carried on a discussion with Walter that shifted between the topics of provisions, disputes, and preparations for the next day's ride.

"Where are we going?" Lizanne asked when she

heard mention of Henry and Eleanor. A leaden silence descended.

Bluntly ignoring her question, Ranulf accompanied Walter to the tent opening. A few hushed words were exchanged, then the knight departed.

Ranulf rounded on her then. "You will not question me again! If naught else, you will show me respect in front of my men."

"Aye, *my lord*. As soon as you earn it."

He was across the tent in seconds. He hauled her to her feet, then sat down on the chest himself and threw her over his knees.

Lizanne was too surprised to react immediately. Then, realizing the ground was bare inches from her face, she began thrashing about on his lap.

Steadying her with one hand, Ranulf raised the other and brought it firmly down upon her rounded buttocks.

She squealed at the stinging contact and fought harder.

"That is one," he counted, then brought his hand down again. "And that is two. Will you obey me?"

"Nay!"

He brought his hand down again. "Will you obey me?"

Though she stilled, she shook her head emphatically.

He spanked her once more. "Now?"

This time she hesitated. "Nay," she finally answered, tears choking her voice.

He wavered, his hand in midair. Then, sighing harshly, he turned her over and pulled her into his arms. Though she resisted, he pressed her head against his chest and held it there.

"You hit me," she said sniffling.

"Nay, I spanked you—there is a difference." He offered her the sleeve of his tunic to wipe her eyes.

"Why didn't you?" she challenged him. "After all, you are a coldhearted beast, Ranulf War—"

"Ranulf," he reminded her. "And I am neither cold

nor a beast, Lizanne. Any other man would have beaten you for your improper behavior."

"Why didn't you?"

Having never before considered his aversion to hitting a woman, he did not immediately answer her. It was something he simply did not do. "Though I have had to kill many men," he said, "I have never hurt a woman."

She stiffened in his arms. "You do not consider forcing yourself upon a woman harmful then?"

He held her away from him. "I have not forced myself on you, Lizanne, and I will not. When we make love, and we will, 'twill be with your consent."

She averted her gaze. True, as promised, he had not forced himself upon her. No more intimacies had he stolen. And, until this most recent argument, he had been quite tolerant of her barbed remarks and taunts. Disturbing as it was, it was becoming difficult more and more to believe this was the same man who had attempted to violate her so many years ago.

"I would like some fresh air," she announced, unsettled by the path her thoughts were drifting down.

Accepting her sudden change of topic, Ranulf released her and reached for his boots. "Come, I will take you," he said, crossing to the tent opening.

Overhead, the sky was a deep purple, pinpoints of lights sprinkled liberally upon its canvas. Lizanne paused to stare up at it, wondering whether Gilbert saw the same sky. It was three days since she'd been taken from Penforke. Surely, he had arrived home to find her absent and was, even now, searching for her.

"Hurry, Gilbert," she whispered, then lifted her skirts and hastened after Ranulf.

Directly ahead, a group of men were gathered around a fire. As Lizanne and Ranulf neared, the steady buzz of conversation halted.

Lifting her chin to afford herself some dignity in an extremely undignified situation, Lizanne refused to look toward the group as Ranulf led her past. She heard the talk resume at once behind them.

At the outskirts of the camp, Ranulf leaned back against a tree and watched as his men boisterously broke into song.

Though the trunk was wide enough for two, Lizanne chose to stand away, clasping her hands behind her back as she and Ranulf shared the rare moments free of quarreling. It was blessed, this peace, almost enough to make her forget how she had come to be there.

"What is it they sing?" she asked some time later. "I have not heard it before."

Ranulf looked at her, then back to his men. "I am surprised you do not know it. 'Twould appear your brother finally did something right by you." He heard her sharply indrawn breath but did not look at her again.

"Unlike you," she retorted, "my brother is an honorable man. He has done nothing wrong."

Knowing the direction the conversation was fast heading, and dreading it, Ranulf pushed off the tree and strode away, leaving her standing alone.

Regretting the harsh words that had seen their peace shattered, Lizanne followed, drawing even with him as they neared the fire. This time she did not look away from the men. Instead, she favored each with a level stare.

Spurred on by her impertinence, the men ribbed one another and exchanged knowing winks, then one of the younger knights began a bawdy song that told the story of a great baron and his mistress.

Unlike the other, Lizanne had recently heard this song during the late-night watches at Penforke, though it had been an earl, not a baron. Her anger rising to the fore, she squared her shoulders and plodded ahead. Though Ranulf did not appear to understand the relevance of their choice of song, she most certainly did.

At the edge of the group, she gave over to the impulse nagging at her and swung around, her skirts flaring outward to allow a brief glimpse of ankle. Instantly, the raucous voices faded and all but died.

When all eyes were upon her, she propped her hands on her hips. Smiling, she finished the lyrics of their song for them.

"Ere he goes agin afightin' on yon green hill, she will take him to her breast, an' he will take his fill!" She finished with a thrust of her chin and a snap of her fingers.

A deafening silence, save for the crackle of the fire, fell over the group at the conclusion of the lewd verse.

Pleased with herself, Lizanne smiled wickedly and curtsied. In the next instant, she found herself dragged away. It was worth it, she told herself all the way back to the tent. No matter Ranulf's anger, it had been wildly humorous.

Ranulf pushed her ahead of him into the tent, then yanked the flap closed and wheeled around to face her. Immediately, his annoyance flared.

Her shoulders shaking with mirth, she opened her mouth and voiced the laughter she could no longer contain. Harder and harder she laughed until she fell to the cot clutching her belly and rolling from side to side.

Ranulf could only stare at the spectacle. He had never before seen such a true expression of humor in a lady. Men, aye, but never a lady. But, he must remember, she was not a lady.

"Are you mad?" he bit off, stepping nearer.

Through tears, she looked up at him. "Do not . . ." she gasped, "tell anyone . . . but aye, methinks I am."

"Have done with this foolishness this instant!"

Grinning, she rolled her eyes, then took a deep, calming breath. "Ahh," she sighed, rubbing the heel of her hand across her eyes. "Pray do not lecture me, Ranulf. 'Tis the only enjoyment I've had all day. Such a small thing to ask."

He glared at her.

"Did you see their faces?" she blurted out just as it looked as if he was going to speak.

"Too clearly," he grumbled.

"Oh, you make too much of it." She pulled herself to a sitting position. "I suppose now you will tell me how dishonorable you think Gilbert. The one redeeming quality proven false."

"Should I ever meet this brother of yours, I fully intend to have words with him regarding your upbringing."

She cocked her head. "You will meet him. That much I can promise."

Ranulf was as certain of that as she, though he did not say so. "I want no more improper displays, do you understand?"

"You have no humor," she said, then nodded when she saw his brows draw together. "Very well, I give you my word. I will not sing with your men again. Is that all? I'm really quite tired."

"Nay, but 'twill do for the time being. Now remove your garments and get beneath the cover."

"But 'tis too cold not to wear them," she protested, dramatically clasping her arms about herself. She had done the same yestereve when he'd told her to remove her clothes.

"Argue no further," he said. "Take them off." Having given his order, he went to his chest and lifted the lid. When he turned and found her still fully dressed, he glared menacingly.

She held up her hands. "I know . . . I know. If I do not, you will. Am I right?"

He nodded.

Sighing, she loosed the laces and tugged the bliaut over her head.

He indicated the chemise. "That too."

Making no attempt to hide her irritation, she quickly removed the second garment and, clad only in her undergarments, dived onto the cot and pulled the coverlet up to her neck.

"You may wear this." He held up the tunic he had removed from the chest and tossed it to her.

She was surprised. Why the consideration? He had not allowed her a covering before. Knowing it useless to attempt to fathom his motive, she graciously accepted the offering and quickly pulled it over her head.

"I have business to attend to," he said as he crossed the tent. "Get some sleep. We have another long day before us tomorrow."

"When will you return?" she asked, attempting to sound as indifferent as possible.

"Shortly, but do you not worry. Aaron and Harold will be just outside if you've need of anything."

She took his warning exactly as it was intended. "They need not lose sleep on account of me," she retorted, slipping down beneath the cover. Turning onto her side, she presented her back to him.

Hours later, Ranulf returned. Light-headed from his attempt to drink away his sexual frustration, he stumbled into the tent. Only one candle still burned, though it flickered uncertainly in its puddle of hot, melted tallow.

Discarding his garments as he went, he reached the cot and lowered himself to its edge. Waveringly, he focused on Lizanne's still form. Huddled on her side, her long, bare legs drawn nearly to her chest and her firm backside brushing his thigh, she immediately awakened his desire.

He ran his hand over the curve of her thigh and down her calf. She was unusually warm, her skin moist to the touch. Drawing his hand back, he rubbed his thumb across his fingertips. Slowly, his inebriated mind registered that something was amiss.

Frowning, he laid his palm to her shoulder and felt her feverish body quake at his touch. Then she whimpered, a low, miserable sound that haunted him.

"Lizanne," he called as he turned her onto her back. A tightly curled ball, she rolled up against him.

Realizing she still slept, Ranulf considered whether or not he should awaken her. He touched her hair and found it damp as well, strands of it clinging to her face. When he reached out to brush them away, she reacted violently, crying out and slapping at his hands. A moment later, she slumped and began sobbing.

Grasping her shoulders, he gave her a firm shake.

"Nay!" she cried, trying to pull away.

He called to her again and shook her more forcefully, but again she struck out, the ring on her finger catching him alongside the jaw.

He clapped his hand to the small gash and felt blood trickle over his fingers. Merciful God, she had done it again! Wondering at the probability of further wounds from her, he gently lifted her onto his lap.

Still weeping, she gripped his tunic and held fast.

"Lizanne," he whispered, stroking his hand over her hair and down her back. "You are safe."

He thought she shook her head but couldn't be certain. Tilting her face up, he pressed light kisses to her temples and over her damp eyes. Gradually, the weeping subsided, and she leaned into him but still did not awaken.

Holding her to him, Ranulf lifted his legs onto the cot and lay back. Immediately, she snuggled closer and threw a leg over him, her thigh brushing his manhood, which rose in immediate response. Groaning, he urged her leg lower.

She muttered something unintelligible and drew it back up.

Silently cursing the drink he had consumed, for the wine and mead had done little to counteract her effect upon him, he accepted that he would get little sleep that night and settled himself in for the duration. He stared up into the darkness, wondering if he would ever get a full night's sleep with Lizanne in his bed. A slow smile spread across his face. Under different circumstances, he certainly hoped not.

Chapter 10

Ranulf pondered Lizanne's nightmare during the next day's ride. He did not speak of it for, although she had inquired as to the cause of the newly acquired cut on his jaw, she seemed to have no recollection of the incident.

By early afternoon, they reached the castle of Lord Bernard's vassal, Sir Hamil Forster. It was a formidable structure, recently constructed of stone and rising grayly against a backdrop of craggy, barren slopes.

Even though Ranulf wanted nothing better than to return to his own lands, he was obligated to finish the king's business first. Nevertheless, he was determined to conclude swiftly the negotiations between the two parties.

Recently, Sir Hamil had taken it upon himself to claim this, Baron Langdon's property, as his own. If not for the vassal's close familial ties with King Henry, Langdon could have resolved the dispute simply enough with a show of force, likely resulting in Sir Hamil's capture and subsequent death. But Langdon had wisely appealed to the king to assist him in removing the errant knight from his lands. Occupied elsewhere, Henry had sent Ranulf in his stead after arriving at a compromise he felt would appease both parties.

Since they were expected, Ranulf and a fair-sized retinue were allowed entrance within the castle's walls, but most remained without.

"I expect your complete obedience, Lizanne," Ranulf said after they'd dismounted. He beckoned to Geoff as he pushed her behind him.

Catching sight of a short, stocky man who, flanked by his knights, confidently strode forward, Lizanne hopped out of Geoff's reach and peered around Ranulf.

Walter pulled her back. Pushing her into the squire's arms, he took his position beside Ranulf, effectively blocking her view.

Sputtering indignantly, Lizanne tried to pull free from Geoff, but to no avail. Opening her mouth to protest, she found Geoff's hand clapped over it as a rather vicious warning was growled in her ear.

Incensed at his callous treatment, she tried to bite his palm, but only succeeded in biting the inside of her cheek. She winced at the pain and ceased with her useless struggles, resigning herself to waiting.

"Baron Wardieu," she heard their host say. "Welcome to Killian."

"It has been a long journey," Ranulf said, taking a step forward to meet the man. "My men are tired and hungry. I would see them settled quickly."

"They will be seen to forthwith," the other replied. "I have set the cooks to preparing an early meal."

Ranulf nodded approvingly.

"I must apologize for the reception," Sir Hamil continued, "but we expected you days ago and had nearly given up on your coming."

"I was delayed," Ranulf curtly explained.

"All is well with the negotiations?"

Ranulf's disapproving silence hung uncomfortably in the air a moment. "We will speak of them later," he said sharply. "Now I would like a bath."

"Certainly," Sir Hamil agreed. "Come, I will show you inside."

Together, Ranulf and Walter walked forward and climbed the steps to the donjon.

Removing his hand from her mouth, Geoff pointed a finger at Lizanne. "Not a word," he warned her, then pulled her along behind the group of men that surged forward.

The main hall of the donjon was impressive and, unexpectedly, Lizanne found herself appreciatively eyeing the tapestries that hung about the room. Sir Hamil's next comment, though, distracted her.

"My daughter, Elspeth, will see you to your chamber, Baron Wardieu."

Still held fast by Geoff, Lizanne craned her neck to better see the woman Sir Hamil had drawn forward. Though she was half-obscured by Ranulf's bulk, Lizanne did not need to see more to know the woman-child was beautiful.

Smooth, flowing brown hair that immediately sparked envy in Lizanne framed a heart-shaped face dominated by large, liquid eyes. Though well proportioned, she was petite—the top of her head barely reached the middle of Ranulf's upper arm—and so incredibly feminine, it set Lizanne's teeth on edge, though she could not say why.

"I trust your journey was without mishap, my lord?" Elspeth inquired, her voice so sickeningly sweet, Lizanne was certain there was a hive nearby.

"Would that it were," Ranulf said. He bent over her hand and pressed his lips to it.

Lizanne did not understand her reaction to the gesture but knew a sudden, tearing sensation.

"Jealous?" Geoff whispered in her ear.

She whipped her head around and fastened her gaze upon him. The squire did not back down. "Better that beast you call your lord bed her than me," she whispered back.

He grinned. "'Tis not likely he will. After all, she is a lady."

His barbed remark wounded Lizanne deeply. Fighting back sudden tears, she bowed her head and stared unseeingly at the rushes beneath her feet.

Elspeth's next words brought her head up again. "My lord, you travel with a lady?"

As if he'd forgotten her, Ranulf turned and sought out Lizanne. His disdainful gaze swept over her, then he turned back to Elspeth. "Nay."

"Then who is that?" Elspeth crooked a finger at Lizanne.

As one, all eyes turned to her. In that moment, made painfully aware of her state of disarray, Lizanne would have liked nothing better than to flee.

"A servant," Ranulf replied after some consideration.

Lizanne gasped in outrage but was prevented from disavowing Ranulf's claim when Geoff dug his fingers into her arm. Grimacing, she clamped her teeth together and unwaveringly stared at the woman.

Blinking prettily, Elspeth looked back at Ranulf. "You must be a great baron to be able to clothe your servants in such finery," she said, fluttering her lashes at him.

Sir Hamil moved forward. "Elspeth, show Baron Wardieu to his chamber—and take a girl with you to attend his bath."

"'Twill not be necessary," Ranulf smoothly interjected. "My servant Lizanne sees to all my needs."

Elspeth's brows arched as she glanced from Ranulf to Lizanne. Then, smirking knowingly, she turned and led the way to the stairs.

With a seething Lizanne in tow, Geoff followed.

"'Tis not large," Elspeth was saying when Geoff and

Lizanne came down a short corridor, "but well appointed as you can see, my lord."

"'Twill do nicely," was Ranulf's reply.

On the threshold of the chamber, Geoff pulled Lizanne back from the doorway and forced her to stand behind him.

"I will send hot water for your bath," Elspeth continued. "Should you need anything else, do let me know and I will try to accommodate you."

Lizanne felt the roots of her hair stand on end. Her fists clenched as she considered delivering a blow to the lady's small nose.

Followed by Ranulf, Elspeth quit the chamber, smiling broadly and swinging her hips as she passed Lizanne.

At least my teeth are even, Lizanne comforted herself, having noted the way Elspeth's overlapped.

"Lizanne!" Ranulf brought her abruptly out of her mind's wanderings.

"What?" she said belligerently.

"Come inside."

Geoff pulled her around him and gave her a push toward Ranulf.

Rubbing her arm where the squire had held her, she strutted past Ranulf and into the chamber, exaggeratedly swinging her hips in mockery of Elspeth.

Ranulf and Geoff exchanged looks, their faces mirroring each other's.

The bed was large, dominating the room. Though it beckoned to Lizanne, she strode to the middle of the floor and planted herself firmly on that spot. Arms crossed over her chest, she waited until Ranulf entered and pushed the door closed behind him. Like two adversaries, they faced each other.

It was Lizanne who made the first move, flying across the room and launching herself fully against Ranulf. Her sudden thrust of weight sent both of them back against the door. Ranulf barely retained his footing as he contended with the onslaught.

Reining in his anger, he ignored the havoc her teeth, nails, fists, and legs were inflicting upon him. Grasping her securely about the waist, he lifted her off the floor and carried her across the room.

Lizanne soared through the air and landed on the bed, the soft mattress enveloping her and drawing her down into its stifling embrace.

Gasping, she threw her arms out, found uncertain purchase, and pushed herself up on her elbows to face her enemy. She might have come at him again, but he lifted a booted foot and, placing it squarely upon her chest, forced her back down.

"Suspend your hostilities this moment," he commanded.

Ignoring him, she grasped his leg and attempted to push his foot off her . . . to no avail.

Not for the first time, Ranulf wondered at her incredible level of stamina. Lord, did she never fatigue?

He smiled wryly. Aye, she was angrier than he'd ever seen her, and here he'd thought he'd already seen the worst of that emotion.

Could it be jealousy was responsible? he pondered. He had seen the way she looked at Elspeth—and her mockery of the woman.

Her chest heaving, Lizanne abandoned the struggle and turned her face into the mattress. "How dare you call me a servant?" she croaked past a throat gone hoarse. "And . . . and insinuate I am your leman. Deny it you may, but I am a lady!"

"Since what time?"

She looked back at him. "I am Lady Lizanne Balmaine of Penforke."

Shaking his head, he warily removed his foot. "Nay, Lizanne. Though I would have you behave more like a lady, by your behavior you have renounced that title."

Denying herself the comfort of tears, she pushed up into a sitting position. "Though you may not think me a lady, neither am I your servant—or your leman."

"Aye, that you are," he disagreed. "Do not forget you are my prisoner. As such I make you whatever I wish—be that servant, leman, or both."

A knock at the door precluded any further argument.

"Enter," Ranulf called. He turned to watch as three servant girls scurried in, each toting a large pail of steaming water. Eyes averted, they emptied their burden into the wooden tub before the hearth and quickly retreated.

Neither Lizanne nor Ranulf spoke over the next several minutes as the servants returned twice more to complete filling the tub.

Ranulf thanked them the last time, smiled at their girlish giggles, and closed the door firmly behind them. Then, without a glance in Lizanne's direction, he crossed to the tub and, with his back to her, quickly disrobed.

Lizanne gaped at his virile nudity, blushed furiously, and looked down at her hands. It was not simply fear that trembled its way up her limbs and flushed her with warmth. It was something else. Something new and wakening that frightened her more than the thought that he might force himself upon her. Why he should disturb her so, she did not understand. Was he not her enemy?

Not until she heard the water lap against the sides of the tub did she look up again. He was submerged in the steaming water, his long hair darkened and dripping.

Over the next few minutes, he thoroughly scrubbed himself clean, and during that time, his wooden chest was delivered to the chamber.

"I require your assistance to wash my hair," he said, bringing Lizanne out of her quiet.

It was not his order that compelled her to comply. Rather, it was the sight of the dagger among his discarded clothing on the stool beside the tub—the one she had defended herself with at Penforke. With its ornately carved hilt and inset jewels, it could be no other.

Why had she not noticed his wearing of it before? she wondered. Not once since that night she had gone in search of it had she thought of it again. He'd had it then, she was certain. And in the meadow where they had battled with swords. She remembered the look in his eyes when he had advanced on her, demanding she fulfill their bargain. Finally, she understood . . . and was angry.

Rolling off the bed, she slowly advanced, her mind working furiously. Eyes averted, she lowered herself to the rushes and took the soap he handed her. As she placed her hands to his scalp and began to work the soap through his hair, she considered the speed she would need to retrieve the weapon.

But what would she do with it once she had it? she wondered. Was there freedom to be had in the possession of it? Unlikely, but she had to try.

"There," she said, sitting back on her heels. "You may rinse now."

He pointed to the pail beside the stool that contained clean water. "Use that."

Momentarily put off, she stared at the pail before forcing herself to action. Hefting it, she tipped the entire contents over his head at once, sending torrents of water and soap coursing down his face. Tossing the pail aside, she sprang to her feet and reached for her dagger. But she did not have time to withdraw it from its sheath before Ranulf's hand descended on her and wrenched her off balance. Crying out, she grasped at the air and toppled facedown into the tub atop him. The water sloshed wavelike, thoroughly drenching her.

Coughing up water, her nasal passages stinging, she emerged to find Ranulf's face inches from hers. He looked positively furious.

"I would have killed you!" she declared, though it was more of a lie than she had ever told.

Ranulf stared hard at her and wondered at his earlier conclusion that she could do no such thing. But nay, he still did not think she could. "'Tis good you warned me to watch my back, witch," he ground out. "I owe you for that piece of advice."

Cursing his arrogance, she began thrashing about in an attempt to release his hold on her, disturbing the water and sending it slopping over the sides again.

He gave her no warning. Cupping her head, he pressed it beneath the water and held it there for the count of ten. When he released her, she arched upward and sent a spray of water around the room.

"How dare you! You black-hearted cur—you—"

Seeing the lesson had not deterred her one bit, he reached to push her under a second time.

She sprang back and landed hard on her rear end between his feet.

Water streaming down her face, she locked gazes with him. He looked ready to pounce should she move another inch.

Slapping the hair out of her face, she thrust her chin high. "That"—she pointed to the dagger—"belongs to me!"

"Nay, no more." Reaching out, he unsheathed the weapon and held it before him. "'Tis mine now, Lizanne, and I will not soon forget how I came by it."

His threat hung on the air between them for long minutes before Lizanne gathered the courage to speak. "I hate you!" she declared.

"That much is obvious," he agreed, his nostrils flaring. "But you would do well to remember, Lizanne, hate is as strong an emotion as love. Be careful lest you mistake one for the other." That said, he extricated himself from her and stepped from the tub.

Silenced by words that greatly unsettled her,

Lizanne lowered her head to avoid viewing his nude body.

What had he meant by those words? Did he think her in love with him? Did he think she could ever feel such an emotion for a man she had once thought to see dead? Never could she love a man like him. Desire, perhaps, she finally admitted, but love? She squeezed her eyes closed. If only he were not the man who had wreaked such pain upon Gilbert and her. If—

"You look like a wet rat," he said bluntly, scooping up his clothing. "Wash yourself and get into bed. I do not wish to find you still sitting there when I return."

She refused to look at him as he dressed. Only when he came to stand beside the tub again did she venture a glance upward. His toweled hair gleamed pale again, his black eyes hard in a face set with displeasure, his fresh clothes crisp and flattering to his physique. She fixed her gaze on the dagger belted at his waist.

"I will wash when you have left," she said.

"See that you do," he said, then turned on his heel.

She caught a glimpse of the two guards posted outside the door before it closed again.

In the corridor, Ranulf hesitated. Ignoring the curious stares of his men, he strained to catch a sound from within the chamber. A sound that might prove Lizanne to have the same emotion of other women—the emotion of tears.

He heard her muffled sob a moment later. Though he had never had any liking for a woman's tears, especially if he was the cause of them, it heartened him that Lizanne did possess such a vulnerability. He had begun to think her made only of anger, hate, defiance, and, of course, a fear she refused to allow him more than a glimpse of.

Drawing a deep breath, he opened the door and quietly stepped back inside. Lizanne did not hear him, her head buried in arms propped on the edge of the tub.

Easing the door closed, Ranulf stood a long moment and stared at her dark head and shoulders that shook with emotion. Twice he heard a miserable, mewling sound that escaped her lips, but neither was allowed to fully vent her sorrow.

When, finally, another sob broke from her throat, he moved forward and lowered himself beside the tub. Still, she did not notice his reappearance.

Certain she would react violently to his being witness to her tears, he held his breath as he stroked a hand over her damp head. But she did not throw off his touch. Instead, her body went completely still.

Lizanne was too stunned by Ranulf's presence to react. Opening her eyes wide, she stared at the water below her as she searched frantically for her composure. Why had he returned? she wondered. To witness the humiliation of her tears? To taunt her? Was he pleased to have reduced her to such a weakness?

Nay, she did not think so. The hand resting upon her neck was comforting, not threatening, and the compassion emanating from his great body was so tangible, she could taste it upon her lips.

Damn his patience! The anger she had driven him to was far too short-lived for the kind of man he had once been. Where was that heartless being who had turned her world upside down?

Drawing a deep breath, she slowly lifted her head, raising questioning eyes to his.

He returned her gaze, then smoothed away a tear that clung to her jaw. "Is it really so bad?" he asked, a reassuring smile lifting one corner of his mouth.

She blinked. Bad? Nay, it was not bad enough. And therein lay her dilemma. "I would not have killed you," she whispered, her voice trembling.

The other corner of his mouth lifted. "I know," he said. "Though I do not yet understand exactly what you are, this I do know. You are not what you try so very hard to be."

Frowning, she pulled her bottom lip between her teeth. "Nor do I understand you, Ranulf Wardieu. I thought I did, but you are not at all as you should be."

"And how should I be?"

Lizanne knew she should say no more but could not prevent the uncertain words from spilling from her lips. "Evil," she said. "A man without conscience. A man bent on taking his pleasure no matter the pain others are made to suffer. That is the kind of man you should be. The kind I—" Sealing her lips, she looked away from his penetrating gaze and stared at knuckles that had grown white where she gripped the rim of the tub.

"The kind you imprisoned to exact revenge upon," he finished for her. Uncurling her fingers, he encased her hands in his. "Tell me, Lizanne. Tell me what it is you believe me to have done to hurt you."

She lifted her face to his and contemplated his eyes, nose, mouth, and lastly, his pale hair. So handsome . . . Halfheartedly, she chastised herself for the traitorous feelings that lanced through her. Changed or not, he was still the same man. If only she could convince her heart and body of it. Neither accepted what her eyes demanded they recognize. And since when had her heart become involved in this dangerous web her body had spun?

She shook her head. "I cannot," she said, too emotionally exhausted to keep the sorrow from her voice.

Though disappointed, having been fairly certain she would finally confide in him, Ranulf denied himself the anger his pride urged him to. "One day you will come to me, Lizanne," he said, pulling her against him. "You will trust me."

Her face pressed to his tunic, she was silent a long time. "I know," she finally said. "'Tis what I fear most."

Though she could not see him, he smiled. She did

not know it, but already she was beginning to trust him, to abandon whatever preconceived ideas she had about his character. It was a start.

"I am expected in the hall," he said as he drew away from her.

Avoiding his gaze, she pulled her hands from his and settled herself back into the water.

"I will send a servant with your meal," he added as he stood.

She nodded. "Thank you."

Though he would have preferred to stay with her—to see her clean himself—he had obligations to fulfill before he could see to his own desires. Wordlessly, he turned and left the chamber.

Chapter 11

$\mathcal{T}$*he lack of* warmth brought Lizanne fully awake the next morning.

Only to herself would she ever admit her sense of loss at not having Ranulf's body pressed to her back upon awakening. Expecting to find him beside her, she lifted her head and looked over her shoulder. She was the only occupant of the bed. There had been no other during the night. The realization unsettled her in a way she did not care to reflect upon too deeply.

Frowning, she twisted around and sat upright. The covering she had stolen from the window the night before slipped down, exposing her breasts to the chill morning air. Shivering, she tugged the cloth up and clutched it more tightly to her as she surveyed the chamber.

Bathed in the first light of morning, the shadows gradually receded as the sun rose outside the curtainless window. Colorful prisms of light, like those that arched against the sky after a long rain, fell across the floors and creeped up the walls.

Confirming that she was indeed alone, she could not help but ponder Ranulf's whereabouts. Clearly, he had not returned last night.

Unknown to her, her mouth tightened and her nostrils flared at the thought of him having spent the night with one of the maids—perhaps even Elspeth. Strangely, she felt no comfort at the likelihood that he had sought another to ease himself with.

She chastised herself for the traitorous emotion that reared its ugly head but refused to name it jealousy.

Pushing her wayward thoughts aside, she scooted to the edge of the mattress and lowered her feet to the thick rushes. She tucked the end of the cloth more securely between her breasts, then crossed to where her garments were draped over the mantel and felt each in turn to see if they were dry.

Though the bliaut still felt damp, the undergarments and chemise had dried completely. Remembering the sorry state of her garments the night before, she delighted in their renewed crispness, even impulsively pressed her face to them. They smelled and felt clean again, something she had not realized she'd missed until that moment. A smile of pleasure traced her lips and drew forth the briefest glimpse of the solitary dimple.

Sighing, she unwrapped her makeshift gown and let it fall to the floor. Her skin reacted instantly to the pervasive chill of the room, raising the fine hairs along her limbs. She rubbed her arms briskly, then, shivering, reached for her soft braies. Bracing herself against the mantel, she stepped into them and pulled them up over her hips.

More slowly, she donned her shift, then reached for the chemise. Pulling it over her head, she settled it upon her hips and made quick work of the laces, then began combing her fingers through her hair. As she worked on a tangle, she wondered if Ranulf had locked the comb in his wooden chest.

She grimaced. No amount of effort had budged the lock the night before, so she would simply have to make do with the next-best thing.

Having worked the last of the tangles free, she swept her hair over her shoulder and began braiding it. She was halfway down its formidable length when the sunlight cascading through the window shifted, falling upon the man reclining in the chair facing the hearth.

Her fingers stilled instantly. With a deep sense of foreboding, she moved her gaze along Ranulf's outwardly thrust leg, over his slowly rising chest, and looked straight into his penetrating black eyes.

He had not spent the night with another, then? Her relief was short-lived as she realized he had been witness to her nudity. Dropping her arms to her sides, she simply stared at him. He sat unmoving, his chin propped in the palm of his hand, one leg thrown over the arm of the chair.

The beginnings of a smile curled his mouth. "You are more lovely than I imagined," he said in a tone thick with longing.

She tried to voice her anger but could find no words to serve her.

Ranulf smiled broadly—sleepily—his eyes narrowing as he visually caressed every part of her. Having viewed her in her full glory only minutes earlier, he was spellbound, powerless to move from the chair. Though he had seen a good deal of her these past days, he had not guessed at the incredible beauty of her sleek yet womanly body.

Beneath her skin, toned muscles rippled like those of a predatory cat. Her long legs, so perfectly shaped, were at once firm and curvaceous. And those breasts ... High, round, and tipped with dark aureoles, they begged a man to suck them. Both hard and soft curves combined to produce an incredible combination of strength and womanliness he had never before seen.

They continued to stare at each other, and the air fairly vibrated with a cadence of desires too long unan-

swered, swelling up like great waves and breaking forcefully over them both.

Lizanne's spark of anger at having been spied upon
was gradually supplanted by another fathomless emotion
she did not want to know the name of. Instead of her
enemy, she saw the man who had come to her yestereve
and offered her comfort. She saw a man who not only
made her body react, but who had also managed to
touch her heart.

Valiantly, she fought to keep from drowning in the
treacherous waters pulling at her. Backing away, she shook
her head even as she came hard up against the hearth.

Desire, her cruel mind labeled it. Desire for your
enemy. Look at him, it urged her, he is the one. Her
hands splayed against the stones at her back, she looked
closely. She told herself this was the man responsible for
all the pain. Told herself it was he who had tried to rape
her. Had spilled Gilbert's blood . . .

Her body and heart refused to acknowledge it. They
saw another. A man capable of tenderness and patience.
A man of honor and word. A man who would never take
what was not given him freely. Dear God, how could he
look exactly like he who haunted her dreams, yet be another?

Having watched the range of emotions pass over
Lizanne's face, Ranulf did not speak again. He simply
dropped his head back and reached out his hand in silent invitation.

In the thrumming quiet of the room, Lizanne's
breathing grew shallow and labored as a spiraling sensation raced down her spine and suffused her lower limbs
with a liquid warmth. It stole her breath and made her
heart quicken until she felt sure he could hear its frenetic
beating. It assailed her senses, weakening her knees and
alerting her to a strange, insistent ache in that region below her abdomen. She did not understand it.

Though her mind weakly rejected her surrender, her

willful body had no such misgivings. Of their own accord, her legs carried her across the room and brought her to stand before Ranulf.

His eyes never leaving her face, he slid his leg off the chair arm and, grasping her hand, urged her down between his thighs.

On her knees, Lizanne stared questioningly at him, her mouth suddenly dry as she read the hunger in his deep eyes.

Hunger? she wondered. Was that what it was, this insistent ache that ran strife through her and set her pulses slamming, until all she could hear was the roar of blood coursing through her veins?

He lifted his hand, his fingers hovering a hair's breadth from her face before he pressed them to her flushed skin.

She accepted the light caress that moved with deliberate slowness over her eyes, her nose, the curve of her jaw, her neck, and back up to trace her lips. She shivered, panting softly beneath his touch.

"Beautiful," he murmured.

When he pulled her bottom lip down and slid his finger between her teeth, her breath caught in her throat. She was overwhelmed by the unsettling feeling that she was falling from a great height, plunging recklessly to a destination she could not even guess at, though desperately wanted to reach. Swaying, she gripped him above the knees and dug her fingers in to steady herself.

His face came closer, his breath warm against her mouth as his eyes locked with hers in silent understanding.

She drew a shuddering breath as his finger traced a circular pattern over her sensitive tongue, withdrawing once to moisten her lips before slipping back inside.

Moaning softly, her lids fluttering downward, she reflexively closed her teeth and drew his finger farther inside.

Ranulf groaned, eased his finger out, and lowered his mouth to hers.

He was amazed by her response. She opened to him, her tongue tentatively seeking at first, then with growing fervor, touching and exploring the inner recesses of his mouth. In that moment, he realized he had unleashed a storm and found at its heart a passionate woman.

One hand entwined in her hair, the other cupping her buttocks, he pulled her closer until she was settled at the juncture of his thighs. His growing need, a tight ridge of desire, pressed against her belly. Tightening his thighs around her, he slid his hand upward to cup a firm, swollen breast, his thumb finding the erect nub where it strained against the material of her chemise.

Beneath the ecstasy of his touch, Lizanne cried out, wrenching her mouth from his and throwing her head back.

Gathering her closer, Ranulf trailed his lips over her throat, licking a path of fire to the neckline of her garment. Whimpering, she convulsed against him, her hands clenching and unclenching in his hair.

Both chemise and shift gave way easily, their rending whisper-soft in the charged room. Drawing a ragged breath at the sight of the forbidden fruit, Ranulf stared at the faint, thin line his blade had drawn across her skin when she had forced him to swords. Aye, each bore the mark of the other. But it would be he who did the taming. . . .

A breast in each palm, he sucked one, then the other, as she writhed, her hips beginning a slow, uncertain gyration against his throbbing desire. He thought he might explode then and there.

Hiking up her chemise, he ran his hands up over her quivering thighs and slid the undergarment down. He slipped a hand between the welcoming thighs she opened to him and found her soft and moist. Breathing heavily, he closed his hand over her.

She shuddered and arched against him, and as if from a distance, her pleading voice reached him. "Ran ... Ran ..."

He lifted his head and looked into her beautiful, passionate face, her glorious eyes. "Say it," he demanded hoarsely.

Too enthralled by the new sensations he aroused in her, Lizanne did not hear him at first. Never had she thought to experience such things. Had she really sneered when she heard women speak of their sexual proclivities? Now she was soaring, reaching for something higher. If only she could find that place ...

Ranulf gave her a shake. "Say it," he repeated with gruff urgency.

She shook her head, confusion flitting across her features as she focused on him. Frowning, she touched his lips with her fingers, then leaned forward to press her mouth to his.

He pulled back just as their lips touched. "Nay. I would hear it. Tell me you want me, Lizanne."

Trying to make sense of his rejection, she blinked, her eyes pooling with unexplainable tears. "I—I do not know what I want."

She was so damned innocent! Ranulf drew in a ragged breath. "Do you want me to ease that ache you feel when I touch you here?" he asked softly, his fingers caressing that wild, sweet part of her that betrayed her mind.

She quivered and moved against his hand. "Aye, Ranulf. I burn so." In the back of her mind, she acknowledged that what she did was wrong but could not think clearly enough to discern why.

Satisfied with her earnest confession, Ranulf reluctantly withdrew his hand. He gripped her waist, turned her, and pulled her onto his lap.

Instantly, she melted against him, her arms going about his neck as she pressed her lips to his throat.

Fighting down his raging desires, Ranulf pulled her head away and eased it against his shoulder. Though he wanted nothing better than to ease her ache—and his—he instinctively realized the timing was not yet right.

He wanted more from her than a moment of passion. He wanted her to ache for him as constantly as he did for her. He wanted her thoughts so preoccupied with him, she could barely function. After all, had she not done that very thing to him?

Nay, there was far too much pleasure to be found in a woman's body, and he would not deny himself the pleasure of her for much longer. But he would take nothing less than her total surrender—providing he could keep his ardor in check.

"Is it better?" he asked some moments later.

She nodded. "Aye, some." Her voice was small with disappointment.

Sighing, he lowered his chin to the top of her head and closed his eyes.

"Ranulf?"

"Hmm?"

"Did—did you not ... I mean ..." She shook her head.

"What?" he prompted, unwilling to aid her.

She squirmed. "Did you feel it?" she asked in a rush of words.

He smiled. "Did I feel what?"

She let go a heavy sigh. "I suppose not."

He drew back and looked into her large, anguished eyes. Taking her hand, he pulled it between them and settled it over his manhood where it throbbed just beneath his tunic. "There is the evidence of my desire, Lizanne."

She gasped at its size, then raised widened eyes to

his when it swelled and hardened further beneath her fingers. It frightened her, but when she tried to snatch her hand away, he held it fast.

"Do not doubt that I want you," he whispered hoarsely, placing his lips against her temple. "When the time is right, I will satisfy your needs, but not before."

Lizanne was having difficulty concentrating on his words, the member beneath her hand rearing and radiating fiery heat that made her palm tingle. Experimentally, she closed her fingers around it.

He growled low in his throat and pulled her hand away.

"When?" she asked breathlessly.

Aching fiercely, he rasped, "When you come of age."

This last bit shook her out of her trancelike state. Pulling back, she looked at him, her brows drawn together. "I am eighteen years old."

"Aye, but you are still a child."

"Nay, I am a woman."

He merely shook his head and watched as her eyes narrowed and the corners of her mouth tightened. It was the old Lizanne he glimpsed.

"Is this your revenge?" she asked, sounding exactly like the hurt child she denied being.

He pondered that before answering. Truth be known, he had not regarded it as such, but it was, indeed, a sweeter revenge than any he'd previously entertained—even if it meant he, too, must suffer.

"Aye," he said, "but 'tis a cruel revenge I have sentenced us both to. Know that you do not suffer alone."

Moving out of his unresisting arms, Lizanne went to stand before the hearth. Her back to him, she dropped her face into her hands. "I do not understand," she said, her voice muffled. "I hate you, yet my body betrays me. How can it be?"

She heard the creak of the chair as Ranulf leveraged himself out of it.

"Do not fight it," he said, close to her yet not touching. "You will only fail, as I did." Turning, he left her standing there as he went to change his rumpled clothes.

Unable to face the reality of her body's illicit wants, Lizanne yearned for a dark hole in which to hide and wail out her grief. It was wrong—so wrong—for her to desire Ranulf. She chastised her body for the grievous weakness, once again dredging up the crimes he was responsible for. But even as she did, she wondered if his black heart had healed.

"Lizanne," he called to her. "Finish dressing, and you may accompany me to the hall for the morning meal."

There was nothing at that moment she wanted to do less. She needed time to sort everything out, to take her body in hand and exorcise its misplaced loyalties. She must find her hate.

Drawing a deep breath, she lowered her hands. Faced with her torn bodice, she found the excuse needed to decline his offer. Gathering the pieces of her chemise and shift together, she turned and faced him. "I cannot," she muttered. "I must obtain a needle and thread to repair my garments."

A brow lifted, Ranulf looked across the room at her. "Your outer dress will cover it."

She shook her head. " 'Tis damp still."

Exasperated, he crossed and pulled the bliaut from the mantel and shook it out. " 'Twill do," he pronounced. "Lift your arms."

She hesitated, but there was naught she could do. Obediently, she lifted one arm, the other still holding the pieces of her undergarments together.

Grimacing at what he considered unnecessary modesty, Ranulf lowered the bliaut over her head.

Under cover, Lizanne released the undergarments and thrust her arms through the sleeves. She stood still as he tugged the bodice over her head, smoothed it over her hips, and pulled the laces tight.

"Shoes," he reminded her.

Stepping into them, she turned to face him.

"You are ready," he stated as he turned toward the door.

"My hair," she protested, pulling it over her shoulder and beginning again to braid it.

Irritated with her delays, Ranulf stared hard at her, but she did not look up. Folding his arms across his chest, he leaned against the door and waited for her to finish. He frowned when she knotted her hair to end the braid.

"Have you no ribbon?" he asked.

She shook her head. "But 'twill not come undone. 'Tis the nature of my hair."

"Aye, were it fine like Elspeth's, 'twould unravel quickly." He knew the moment he spoke the words, he had guessed correctly about her feelings toward the younger woman. Although she looked away, she could not hide the livid color that suffused her face.

Ranulf was delighted. It was surely a fit of jealousy she was experiencing. He could use it to his advantage. . . .

Lizanne's disposition was not improved one smidgen when, upon entering the main hall, Elspeth materialized at Ranulf's side and placed a familiar hand upon his arm. Her short veil perfect upon smooth hair that could not possibly hold a knot, she looked entreatingly up at Ranulf. "You will sit next to me again, won't you, Baron?"

"I would be honored," he said, turning to the dais at the far end of the room.

Lizanne stared dumbly after the couple, uncertain as

to whether she should follow or retreat. A touch on her arm brought her around.

The smug smile on Geoff's face faded when he caught sight of her miserable expression.

He cleared his throat. "You may sit with Roland and me." He indicated the long table behind.

She nodded and followed him.

Refusing to look her way, Roland moved down along the bench to make room for her.

Seated between the squires, Lizanne bowed her head as the chaplain said a hasty grace. Immediately following, the hall erupted with the sounds of fifty or more voracious men and women.

Picking at the simple meal that was placed before her, Lizanne continually looked across to where Ranulf was seated between Sir Hamil and his lovely daughter. Each time she felt her color rise, and each time she regretted the weakness that impelled her to gaze in his direction. The woman was absolutely fawning over him, touching his sleeve as often as possible and giggling at his every word.

A child! Lizanne thought, grabbing at a piece of cold, overcooked meat and stuffing it into her mouth. Now that was a child. Lizanne did *not* giggle—had not since she was ten and four. How dare Ranulf make comparisons!

She looked again at Elspeth and disliked her the more for the beguiling smile she turned upon Ranulf and even more for the taunting smile the petite woman pulled when she turned and looked straight at her. Lizanne smiled tightly back, refusing to be the first to look away. With a tinkling laugh that carried clearly across the room, Elspeth tossed her head and leaned again toward Ranulf.

Fuming, Lizanne chewed and chewed until she'd finally pulverized the tough meat well enough to swallow.

It went down like a lump. Pushing away the remainder of the meal, she sat back and folded her hands in her lap.

Moments later, she felt a telling prickle crawl up her spine. Looking around, she found Geoff watching her intently.

Pushing an errant lock of hair from her eyes, she regarded him with raised brows and a hint of a smile. "I don't suppose if I smiled at you, you would think it genuine?" she asked.

He frowned, then shook his head. "Save your smiles for Lord Ranulf. He would appreciate them more than I."

She glanced at the subject of his words, grimaced, then looked back at the squire. "I do not think so."

"Then you are wrong."

She raised her brows higher, but Geoff gave her a dismissing look and craned past her to catch Roland's attention.

"Mayhap we can practice with the slings this morn," he suggested.

Roland leaned forward to get a clear view of his friend without having to look at Lizanne. "I would prefer swords."

Geoff smiled. "You will never master it if you do not try."

"A sling is but a toy. Now a sword . . ."

It was as if Lizanne had completely vanished. Neither squire acknowledged her, even when she purposely leaned forward and blocked their view of each other. They simply sat back and continued with their conversation.

"I am still a better shot than you," Roland boasted.

"Ha!" Geoff grunted.

Lizanne pursed her lips and looked from one to the other. "I can help," she offered, at last gaining their attention.

"Truly," she assured them. "I am quite adept with a sling. Have you one along?"

They exchanged looks, then simultaneously turned their attention back to the meal.

Refusing to be put off, Lizanne clutched Geoff's arm.

He looked disapprovingly at where she held him, then back up at her face.

Apologetically, she released her hold. " 'Twill hurt naught for me to show you," she said.

"Have a woman instruct me in the use of arms?" he asked disbelievingly, then remembered the true aim of her arrow. Her piercing of the banner from such a great distance had surely been an intentional act. Though he had wanted to believe it had been only chance, he had not quite convinced himself of it.

"You would trick me again?" he asked.

She shook her head. "Nay, I vow 'tis not my reason for offering."

He considered her for a minute, then abruptly rose from the table and stalked off.

Dejectedly, Lizanne watched him depart the hall, thinking she must have angered him, reminding him of her earlier treachery. When he disappeared altogether, she turned her attention to the occupants of the large room.

Unequally, they consisted of Sir Hamil's and Lord Ranulf's men, each group set noticeably apart from the other. Though Ranulf's men were generally better mannered than Sir Hamil's, they were coarse—the lot of them.

Distastefully, she shifted her eyes away from a particularly disgusting old man who was obscenely thrusting his hips at a young serving wench. When her gaze fell upon a handsome, flame-headed man seated at the far end of Sir Hamil's table, she was surprised to find his attention riveted upon her. Having caught her eye, he offered her a wide smile.

Pleased to see one friendly face among the many,

she obligingly returned the gesture before looking away. For the first time since their arrival in the hall, her eyes met Ranulf's. His expression told her he'd seen the exchange and was displeased.

Defiantly, she tossed her head and looked away. How dare he! Having abandoned her, there he sat with that harpy practically in his lap and thought nothing of it. But a mere smile between strangers—and it had been only that—and he looked fit to strangle both of them. It was not as if the man had propositioned her. A blight on Ranulf!

"Here," Geoff said, resuming his seat and discreetly dropping a strip of leather in her lap.

Lizanne stared down at the sling, then at him, eyes wide with surprise.

He smiled as he picked up a piece of cheese and handed it to her. "No stones," he said. "I would not trust you to refrain from launching one at Lady Elspeth."

Lizanne looked across the room. Ranulf had returned his attention to that lady. Aye, with a stone she might well have been tempted. A well-placed lump would do wonders for the chit's disposition.

"Well," she began, idly running her fingers over the smooth leather, " 'twould be easier to instruct you out of doors."

"Surely, you needn't cast a stone in order to show us how to use it?" Roland challenged.

"Aye, 'tis the best way," she murmured, moving back so he could see as well.

Rolling the cheese into a compact ball, she pressed it to the center of the leather. "Assuming this to be a stone, you must place it just so."

The squires exchanged looks of amusement, Roland snickering behind his hand.

Lizanne wagged a finger at them. " 'Tis important, the placement. You would want it to find its mark, would you not?"

Rolling their eyes, they nodded and leaned closer.

"Place your fingers through the loops . . . see?" She slid her own through them and turned them over to demonstrate. "Not too tightly, for when you arc it . . ."

Nodding his head at something obtuse Elspeth was saying, Ranulf glanced toward Lizanne, and his brow furrowed at the sight that greeted him. Roland and Geoff sat close to her, their heads bent over her lap, nodding as she spoke animatedly to them.

When she lifted her hand above the level of the table, he caught only a glimpse of something long and narrow she held before it disappeared again. He could not tell what the object of their intense discussion was, but decided he did not like it.

He grew even more annoyed when he heard Lizanne's laughter minutes later and turned to find her smiling gleefully at Geoff and Roland. The squires beamed back at her, under her spell once again.

For the remainder of the meal, Ranulf kept a close eye on the far table but never discovered what Lizanne hid. When the damnably long repast was finally concluded, he excused himself and headed straight for her, only to be brought up short by Walter.

"I must needs speak with you, my lord," the vassal said, loud enough only for Ranulf to hear.

Tearing his eyes from where Lizanne was being helped to her feet by the squires, Ranulf glared at Walter. "What is so urgent it cannot wait?"

Walter looked knowingly to the object of Ranulf's agitation. His jaw hardening, he stepped closer. "King Henry's negotiations," he reminded him.

Ranulf scowled. "Very well, but first I must see to another matter. I will meet you at the stables shortly."

Walter nodded and removed himself from his lord's path.

Geoff, followed by Lizanne, and finally Roland, met Ranulf halfway across the hall.

"Godspeed, my lo—" Geoff began.

"You have enjoyed yourselves?" Ranulf interrupted, widening his stance and folding his arms over his chest.

His smile falling, Geoff looked to the floor. "My lord, Lady Lizanne was merely showing us how to hold a sling. She knows much about—"

"A sling! Did you learn nothing from her first deception? Did it not occur to you she might turn it on you?"

Lizanne stepped around Geoff and raised herself up on the tips of her toes. "Unlike some men, your squire is not a fool twice, my lord." Reaching for his hand, she pressed the sling into it, then haughtily turned her back on him.

Ranulf opened his fingers and looked down. His lips twitched as a ball of cheese rolled from his hand and to the floor. Immediately, it was snatched up by a thin, scraggly dog that scurried off to a corner to enjoy its booty.

"You have learned well," Ranulf said to Geoff, clapping a hand to the young man's back. "But in future, leave your training at arms to men."

Grinning, Geoff nodded and took the sling his lord held out to him.

Taking Lizanne by the arm, Ranulf tossed over his shoulder, "And do not call her 'Lady.' She is no more."

By the time they reached the chamber, Lizanne had forced herself to a calm she did not feel. Crossing to the bed, she sat down on its edge and waited for the lecture.

"What are you up to this time, Lizanne?"

She crossed her ankles, clasped her hands before her, and began swinging her feet.

"Nothing to say?" he asked at her continued silence.

She shook her head, pressed her lips together, and raised her gaze to the ceiling.

" 'Tis just as well," he said unexpectedly. "I haven't

time to discuss this with you now, but I assure you we will later."

She heaved a great sigh and nodded.

Eyes narrowed, Ranulf looked pointedly at her, then turned on his heel and quit the room.

Wondering what she could possibly do with the time yawning ominously before her, Lizanne flopped back on the bed.

It was boredom that drove Lizanne to undertake an exploration of the chamber. Having mended her garments, straightened the room, watched a group of young squires tilt at a battered quintain in the yard below, and taken a nap, she had nothing left to do.

The uneventful search did not take long. Plopping back down on the bed with a disgusted sigh, she pondered a scene depicted on a ceiling to floor tapestry. A sudden thought struck her as she lay there.

With renewed interest, she bounced off the mattress and lifted the edge of the tapestry. A cloud of dust particles flew into her face. She sneezed, rubbed her nose, and lifted the tapestry higher. Just an accumulation of dirt, she concluded.

About to retreat, she became aware of a draft of cool air. Was it possible? she wondered, running her hand over the wall. It was a facade, she realized some moments later when her fingers located the obscure groove of a portal. Excited, she ducked behind the tapestry and, unmindful of her clothing, searched for the hidden catch. It was located at the base. She pressed it, and the door creaked inward to reveal a darkened pit.

Without hesitation, she stepped forward and pushed the door closed behind her.

As it was a narrow passageway, she was able to place her hands on opposite walls to assure her safe descent. Along the way, she found two other landings with doors, but, eager to find what lay at the end, she moved past them without satisfying her curiosity. She could explore them on her return, she decided.

That thought stopped her in her tracks. On her return? Nay, if she found a way out of Killian, there would be no need to return. Determinedly, she pressed on.

There were things in the passageway that did not bear thinking about. At the same time, one hand caught in the moist, diaphanous threads of a spider's web, something scuttled over the other hand. Still she continued downward.

Nearing the bottom, she glimpsed a thin line of light ahead. Taking the final steps with a reckless excitement, she came to the last landing and pressed her face to the crack in the door. Through the narrow opening, she caught a glimpse of greenery.

She released the catch and slowly pulled the door open, revealing a wall of thick rosebushes. It was a flower garden. Stepping cautiously into the bright, glorious sunshine, she eased the door closed behind her and stood silent for several minutes as she listened.

Naught.

Pressing herself against the donjon's stone wall, she moved along it until she spotted a break in the overgrown bushes. Bending low, she peered out at an enclosed, unkempt garden.

With an eye to escape, she surveyed the possibilities. The walls were high, but not so much that they could not be scaled if need be. As there appeared to be no one about, she carefully squeezed between the thorny branches and straightened on the opposite side. After brushing off the leaves and loosening the thorns from her skirts, she enthusiastically began an exploration of the grounds.

She soon discovered it was laid out like a maze, its paths winding, merging, and often ending abruptly.

Momentarily forgetting her plans for escape, Lizanne plucked a particularly lovely rose and wove it into her braid as she rounded a corner. Immediately, she came to a shocked standstill. There, sitting on a bench in the middle of a grassy, rectangular courtyard, was the redheaded man who had smiled at her during the morning's meal.

Stunned, she retreated a step, but not before he turned and caught sight of her. Instantly, he jumped to his feet.

"I—I am sorry," she stammered. "I did not mean to intrude."

"Nay, you are not," he was quick to respond, taking a step toward her. "Mayhap you would care to join me?" Smiling warmly, he gestured at the bench.

She backed away another step. "I must return to my chamber."

He followed her, his eyebrows arching inquisitively. "How came you to be in the garden?" he asked. "There is but one entrance." With a nod of his head, he indicated the door across the courtyard.

Only one entrance, and it led back into the donjon. So, she would have to scale the wall after all. . . . Staring hard at the ground, she shifted uncomfortably and changed the subject. "Who are you?"

He strode the last steps to her side and gallantly bowed. "I am Sir Robyn Forster, eldest son of Lord Hamil."

That surprised her, for, unlike Elspeth, he did not resemble his father in the least. "Lady Lizanne Balmaine of Penforke," she introduced herself with a quick, unpolished curtsy.

The smile slipped from his face. "Lady?" he echoed. "I understood you to be the . . . uh, servant of Lord Ranulf."

She had momentarily forgotten she bore that distinction as well. "Well, I suppose I am that too," she grudgingly conceded, her color rising.

Robyn cocked his head. "Forgive me if I appear

rather dull-witted, but I fear I do not understand the situation." He lightly gripped her arm and pulled her toward the bench.

"Perhaps you could explain it to me," he invited with another charming smile.

Lizanne's temper flared at his handling of her person. It seemed of late she was always being pulled along after some man—and she was fast growing weary of it. She very nearly swatted his hand away but thought better of it. Perhaps here was an ally whose aid she could enlist, she reasoned.

Albeit reluctantly, she allowed herself to be pulled down beside him upon the cool stone bench.

"I would like to know more about you," he said, enfolding her hand in his and lifting it to his lips.

That was the scene Ranulf came upon.

Chapter 12

$\mathcal{H}$*is heart slamming* in his chest, Ranulf froze in the doorway and stared disbelievingly across the courtyard. He blinked to remove the impossible vision from his sight, but it remained. As yet unnoticed, he watched as the redheaded bastard lifted Lizanne's hand to his lips.

Anger, deep and volatile, spiraled upward from his bowels and obliterated all rational thought. It was simply more than he could take. Slamming the door with such force, it hummed on its hinges he stepped forward. In the resounding silence, he gripped the hilt of his sword.

Startled to their feet, Lizanne and Robyn turned to face his rage. To their wide-eyed regard, he looked murderous, his unspoken challenge hanging in the still air.

Breath checked, Lizanne raised her eyes to meet Ranulf's. Even when he had been chained to a wall and she had taunted him, and when she had defended herself with the dagger, his anger had not been equal to the emotion she now glimpsed. Like an animal, wild and dangerous, he stood before them, his lips pulled back, his muscles bunched in readiness.

Glancing from Ranulf to Lizanne, Robyn protectively stepped in front of her, effectively blocking her view.

"Robyn of Killian," Ranulf said, his voice rolling like thunder in the dead silence of the garden. "Take up your sword, for I would have you feel the bite of mine this day."

Robyn stood motionless before an opponent such as he had never before known. Truthfully, he was daunted by the prospect of a duel with the king's man, but honor bound him to conceal his unease. Summoning a smile that fell far shy of his eyes, he raised his hands, palms up. "I go unarmed, Baron Wardieu."

"Then get you a sword, whelp."

Shifting his weight, Robyn remained where he stood and slowly lowered his arms. He did not think it wise to make any sudden movement. "What manner of transgression would you accuse me of?"

"Trespass," Ranulf barked. "I demand satisfaction for your insult to me."

"Insult? If you refer to my being with Lady Lizanne, then you are mistaken. We have but talked—naught else. No insult have you suffered from our innocent meeting, nor was one intended."

"Do you think me blind and dim-witted?" Ranulf snarled, stepping closer. "Get your sword, man."

Deciding she did not care for the role of helpless, shrinking female, Lizanne slipped from behind Robyn to face Ranulf's full wrath. She had to draw forth every last scrap of courage she possessed as she braced her hands on her hips and walked forward, coming to stand a bare foot from him.

Up close, he appeared even more savage. The muscles of his jaw worked steadily as he turned his face to hers, the veins in his forehead enlarged and pulsating. And those eyes, like slick, bottomless pools of pitch, bore into her and dared her to defy him.

Swallowing hard, she raised her chin. "There will be

no bloodletting," she said in a voice she feared sounded far from certain. "If you must blame someone, then blame me, for 'twas I who intruded upon Sir Robyn's sanctuary."

"Do not doubt for one moment I hold you responsible for this treachery, Lizanne. I will see to your punishment later—after I have dealt with this whelp." Pushing her aside, he stepped toward Robyn. "Your sword!"

The young knight looked from Ranulf to Lizanne, his face suffused with bright color. "Aye," he said, his voice strained. "I will fight you."

"Nay!" Lizanne cried, throwing herself between the two men.

"Do not make a coward of your lover!" Ranulf bit off.

She paled at the accusation. "Ranulf," she pleaded, " 'twas nothing. Sir Robyn speaks the truth." She laid her hand on the muscular arm that gripped his sword.

Stone-faced, he refused to look at her.

She curled her fingers halfway around his forearm. "I beseech you, do not."

As if she were a bothersome pet, he shook off her hand and reached to push her aside again.

Unthinking, she lunged at him and threw her arms around his neck, prepared to hang on for dear life if need be. "Ranulf," she whispered, "I want only you— you know that. I only thought to use Sir Robyn to further my means of escape. 'Twas nothing more."

She sensed his hesitation, a barely perceptible easing of his constricted muscles, but still he did not look at her.

"I am not worth dying for," she reminded him.

His words came back to haunt him. Aye, he had said them, and thought he had meant them, but now he was not so certain. In spite of her maddening nature and stubborn resolve to hate him, he wanted this woman more than he'd ever wanted anything else, and if it meant fighting for her, so be it. The admission stunned his sensibilities.

He looked down into her face, remembering how she had pleaded with him that very morning for something far different. "I do not plan on dying," he said, his anger abating, "not even to please you."

"I do not wish your death," Lizanne breathed, realizing for the first time the truth of her words. No matter the disservice done her family, the thought of his death tore at her. Certain her eyes reflected her confusion, she searched his face. "You do know me better than I know myself," she admitted.

His eyes narrowed as he studied her.

Realizing he was in the grip of indecision, she pressed the advantage. "Please," she whispered.

He looked to where Robyn stood watching them, then scowling mightily, looked again at her. "Will you stop fighting me?" he asked.

She gasped at the condition he was forcing upon her. "This I cannot promise. There is too much that has gone before."

His brows lifted, then he nodded. "Very well, I will have my duel." Unfastening her arms from about his neck, he set her from him.

"Nay, I will try," she said in desperation, pressing her hands to his chest. "I will try not to fight you."

Ranulf did not wish her to know it, but his anger had all but subsided, his patience returning to the fore. "And you will attempt no more escapes."

Her face washed of all color, but she acceded. "Aye, no more escapes. But if Gilbert—"

"You will agree to stay with me until I am through with you."

Swaying unsteadily, she nodded. "You've my word."

Hardly believing his ears, Ranulf turned to Robyn. "The challenge is withdrawn. Leave us now."

Wordlessly, the young knight stalked to the donjon, leaving the two to their privacy.

In the tense silence that followed, Lizanne returned to the bench and sank down upon it. Ranulf followed but remained standing as he considered her forlorn expression.

He finally spoke, pulling the single bloom from her braid. "Did he give you this?"

Reflexively, her hand came up to snatch it back from him but only grasped air. "Nay," she said, snapping her jaws together as she remembered her vow to him. She clasped her hands in her lap and focused on the pink ovals of her thumbnails. "I picked it myself."

"How came you to be here? I would not believe you single-handedly outwitted the guards I posted." Momentarily, he contemplated that, then sighed at the absurdity of his statement. To his detriment, he kept forgetting she was like no other lady he had ever before encountered. "Or maybe I would," he added upon reflection.

She shook her head. "I doubt they even know of my disappearance."

Ranulf raised his eyes up the vertical face of the donjon. "You cannot have climbed from yon window," he concluded, though it would not have overly surprised him had she lowered herself down from it upon knotted bed linens.

"Nay, 'twas by a secret passageway that I found myself in this place."

Of course! Ranulf berated himself for not considering the existence of such a passage. It was common for hidden stairways to be incorporated into a donjon as a means of escape should it come under siege, though it was more often used for trysts among the nobles. It unnerved him how careless he was becoming.

"And you thought to escape, eh?" he asked, tilting her face up.

She shrugged. "Initially, 'twas simple boredom that bade me venture outside."

"But later . . ." he prompted knowingly.

She nodded. "Aye, it did occur to me 'twould be the means by which I might escape you."

His lips thinned. "Our new understanding precludes any more attempts, Lizanne."

Her lashes swept down. "You are not likely to let me forget."

Frowning, Ranulf lifted her off the bench and drew her into his arms. "Prove to me your words—unless that is all they were."

Her hands splayed against his chest, she shook her head, not quite understanding what he asked of her.

He obligingly lowered his mouth to hers and ran the tip of his tongue over her bottom lip.

She gasped at the brief intimacy and wondered at her body's response. Would she ever understand it?

"Show me you want me," he ordered.

She realized with a start that he referred to her admission when she had pleaded with him to withdraw his challenge to Sir Robyn. Aye, she had spoken true. They had been more than words of desperation. They had come from that hidden place within her that she had not yet discovered the meaning of—that treacherous spot that had born something other than hate for this man.

Eyes closed, she tilted her head and kissed him as he'd shown her earlier that morning. Like a flickering flame fueled by the sudden stillness of the air, her wakening hunger grew steadily until her limbs quaked with the unfulfilled promise of his possession. She clung to him, thrilling when she felt the evidence of his mounting passion. Utterly lost, she drew her fingers over his scalp, pulling his soft pale hair through her hand.

When he suddenly set her away from him, she nearly collapsed and had to be steadied by his grip on her shoulder.

"I am satisfied you spoke the truth," he said. "Unfortunately, this is not the place for further demonstration." Dropping his hand from her, he turned and started down the path. "Now, you will show me this secret passageway."

Taking herself firmly in hand, Lizanne hurried after him. "Through here," she said, indicating the low opening in the rosebush wall before ducking and disappearing beneath it.

Though it was a tighter squeeze for Ranulf, he followed and caught up with her just as she was stepping through the hidden doorway.

"Our chamber lies three flights above," she said as he pushed the door closed behind him, throwing the landing into complete darkness.

He reached out and grasped her arm. "Did you not bring a lantern?"

"Nay, I did not think to," she whispered, sensing his face was only inches from her own. "But the dark does not frighten me so much."

"I am not thinking of your fear, Lizanne—God knows you have little enough of that—but of your neck!"

"Oh, that . . ."

Pushing ahead of her, he slid his hand down over her arm, threaded his fingers with hers, and drew her up the winding steps.

At the first landing, she tugged insistently on his hand and prevented him from continuing up the next flight.

"Just a peek," she whispered, turning to the door.

He started to refuse her, but something, perhaps it was the childish excitement that had supplanted her dismal mood, stopped him. "Very well," he agreed on a long sigh.

Slipping her hand from his, she bent and easily located the catch. The barest light filtered into the passageway as she quietly pulled the door open a crack and peered at the back of a tapestry. As she opened the door wider, the sound of voices fell upon her ears.

Ranulf's hand closed over hers. " 'Tis enough," he whispered, starting to push the door closed.

Sir Hamil's voice rose loudly from within. "You are betrothed to another, Elspeth."

"That old codger!" Elspeth retorted.

"He will make you a good husband. He is wealthy—"

"As is Ranulf Wardieu. He would make me a better husband." Her voice was shrill with anger. "I would marry him."

Lizanne's head jerked back and bumped Ranulf's chin.

"He will offer for me, Father. I know he will."

"Nay, Elspeth, I do not think so. Methinks he is well satisfied with the lady who shares his bed."

"That whore! She is no lady, but a harlot. He has said as much himself. See you how her eyes follow him everywhere?"

Lizanne felt as if she'd been slapped. Tears pricking the backs of her eyes, she moved away from the door and pressed herself against the cool stone wall.

"Elspeth," Sir Hamil said reprovingly, "you know not what you speak of."

"Do I not? She is but a bed warmer for him. Soon he will think to taking another wife and will throw her back whence she came."

Trembling, Lizanne watched Ranulf's still figure where he stood in the muted light of the doorway. Though she could not see his reaction, she felt the tension that flowed from him.

"Enough, Elspeth. The man is recently widowed, for God's sake. I doubt he is ready to assume the burden of another wife. I would not."

"Aye, but you have your heirs. He has none."

Though she wished to hear none of it, Lizanne realized that, painful as it was, she had learned more about Ranulf in these last minutes than she had in the past four days. Odd, but she had never even considered the possibility of there being a wife. . . .

"We will speak no more of this, daughter." Sir Hamil decisively ended the conversation. A moment later, a door slammed loudly, its vibrations felt through the stone beneath Lizanne's hands.

Ranulf eased the passageway door closed, then reached out and captured her arm. "Come," he said, pulling her after him up the remaining steps.

Lizanne swallowed hard against the tightness in her throat and tried to concentrate on her footing. However, only a few steps from the landing to their chamber, she stumbled and started to fall backward. His grip tightening, Ranulf pulled her into the safety of his arms.

"Shh," he breathed, hearing the beginnings of her misery surface.

She bit her lip hard and drew air in through her nose in an attempt to vanquish the tears from her brimming eyes.

"No good ever comes of listening in on conversations not meant for one's ears," he said softly as he swept his thumbs beneath her eyes and wiped away the moisture he found there.

She drew a shuddering breath and leaned away from the comfort of his large body. "I lied," she stated simply, her voice strained.

"Again?" He sounded almost amused by her untimely confession.

She nodded. Then, remembering he could not see her, answered, "I do fear the dark."

"Why?" he asked. "There is nothing in the dark that is not there in the daylight."

"You are wrong," she said, evading his attempt to press her nearer. "There are dreams and memories I cannot escape lurking there."

Dreams? Ranulf remembered the nightmare he had witnessed. "What haunts you, Lizanne?"

She hesitated before answering. "I—I fear that someday Gilbert will be taken from me," she began, her voice a bare whisper in the echoing passageway. "And then I will truly be all alone."

Ranulf was surprised at the jealousy engendered by her words. Her brother possessed that part of her he did not dare hope he ever would—intense loyalty. Aye, and love too. He was shocked by the self-admission. Was that what he wanted? Her love? Immediately, he rejected the idea, but it came back to him.

"Life is never certain, Lizanne," he said gruffly.

She was silent, only her breathing audible in that small space. It was minutes before she spoke again. "Most of all, methinks I fear you, Ranulf Wardieu."

He had guessed as much, had seen it in her eyes more than once, but till that moment had not realized the depth of her emotion. It went beyond reason. And the answer lay in that which she so adamantly held back from him.

"What of the past?" he asked, knowing it was there he would discover the key to her elusive mystery.

"You *are* the past ... the present ... the future. ... You are everywhere, and I can't seem to escape you." Her voice had risen. "Why did you have to come back? I was content!"

At the vehemence of her words, he pulled her roughly against him. "Were you, Lizanne? I do not think so."

"I was," she declared, sounding very much as if she was trying to convince herself of it.

He found her face and ran his fingers lightly over it. "At Penforke you spoke of a previous meeting between us. Tell me, what are these sins you have accused me of? I do not recollect ever having seen you before that day in

Lord Bernard's hall, and 'tis not likely I would have forgotten you if I had."

She wavered, but ultimately withdrew. He felt it in the stiffening of her spine and the tightness of her jaw. "I cannot, for then I would only have more to fear from you."

Patience, he reminded himself before that other emotion he detested burst forth. "God's mercy!" he bellowed. Angrily, he turned and pulled her up the remaining steps, then bent to search out the door's catch. Finding it, he pushed her ahead of him.

She crossed the room and went to stand before the window, clasping her hands behind her.

Ranulf threw her a quelling look before advancing to the opposite door and throwing it wide. The two guards outside turned, their tolerant grins wiped clean from their faces as they beheld their lord.

"My lord!" one gasped. "But . . . how . . . ?"

"Send for Geoff," Ranulf growled before slamming the door in their faces.

Seething, he came to stand over Lizanne. "I have much business to complete this evening, and 'twould be best if you were not underfoot. Geoff will stay with you to ensure you do not find yourself in any more mischief."

"I have given you my word I will not attempt to escape you again," she protested.

"Aye, that you have, but, regrettably, I will not feel able to trust you until you place your trust in me. Is that clear?"

She nodded.

"Good." He turned and stalked across the room.

"And do not test the boy overly much," he added, moving to the basin and splashing handfuls of water over his face. "God willing we will depart this place on the morrow," he muttered.

"Where are we going?" Lizanne spoke from directly behind him.

He swung around to face her. She stood holding a hand towel. "That need not concern you."

She nodded, then reached up to blot the moisture from his skin.

He was too shocked by the gesture to do anything but stand rooted to the spot and stare at her.

"There," she said, stepping back.

He studied her a moment longer, then said, "Do not think I require your complete submission. I want your fire, especially in my bed. I would simply have less arguing between us."

"I am not submitting to you," she said quickly. "I but perform the duty of a servant. I am, after all, no lady."

His brows lifted. What was she up to now?

"You should take a comb to your hair," she suggested, eyeing his unruly mane.

Smoothing his hand over it, he stepped past her and went to the wooden chest. He unlocked it and removed the comb, then secured the chest once again. Sitting down upon it, he beckoned to her. "Another duty a servant performs for her master," he explained.

Gritting her teeth, Lizanne stepped forward and took the comb from his outstretched hand.

"Gently," he instructed her.

Kneeling beside him, she pulled the comb through his hair and methodically worked her way upward to his scalp. Unlike her own hair, his easily fell into place and gave to the persuasive tugs. It was almost pleasurable, this task.

When Ranulf suddenly pulled her onto his lap, his face was so incredibly near hers, her heart tripped over itself. "I have been wondering about this," he said, taking her right hand in his and running a finger down her crooked thumb. "How came you by it?"

Tensing, she tried to pull her hand from his grasp, but he would not allow it. "An accident," she said, attempting to close her mind against the painful flood of memories. She did not wish to dwell on that particular incident any longer, for it was far too unsettling in light of the battle she was waging between body, heart, and mind.

"Tell me of your wife, Ranulf," she said, abruptly changing the topic.

He regarded her warily, his lids lowering so that his eyes were dark, narrow slits. "You already know more than I would have you know of her," he said.

"I but know that she is no longer living."

"And that is sufficient," Ranulf muttered, his mood blackening at the memories churned up by mention of the faithless Arabella.

"But—" A sharp knock on the door sounded, halting Lizanne's next words.

Glowering, Ranulf lifted her from his lap and set her on her feet, then moved to open the door.

"Godspeed, my lord," Geoff greeted him.

Ranulf motioned him inside but remained in the open doorway. "Geoff," he said, "I must needs have you stay with Lizanne while I conclude my dealings with Sir Hamil."

The squire looked confused, craning his neck to view the two men still posted beyond the chamber.

"It seems," Ranulf continued, "she has discovered a secret passageway that leads from this room to the gardens below. I would not want her to undertake any further explorations."

Lizanne scowled.

Geoff nodded. "I will see no harm befalls her, my lord."

Catching her eye one last time, Ranulf charged her with a look of warning, then quit the room.

"Well," Lizanne said when several minutes had

passed and neither had spoken. "Would you like me to show you how to use that dagger?"

Fingering the weapon, Geoff grinned. "Methinks a game of chess would be safer."

"Chess?" She grimaced. "Moving a bunch of funny little pieces around a checkered board? Do you ask me, 'tis a senseless game."

Geoff's interest piqued. "You do not know the game, do you?"

"I am familiar with it," she said offhandedly. "I have just never been interested enough to engage in a match."

"Then I will teach you," the squire declared. Opening the door, he spoke with one of the guards, then turned back to her. "With any luck, Aaron will be able to locate a board for us."

Lizanne shrugged. "Very well. But I warn you ... I am a fast learner."

Chapter 13

They left Killian the following day before the first light of dawn had spread its tentative fingers across the night sky.

For reasons unknown to Lizanne, Ranulf kept his distance over the next three days' ride. On the second day out, he even allowed her an old packhorse of her own that, in the end, made her rides with him seem like too much comfort.

More than once, as she urged her horse to a quicker pace, she caught herself dwelling on how Ranulf's arms had felt on either side of her, his thighs cradling hers, and the comfort of his broad chest against her back. It was, admittedly, more than just her body's comfort she missed.

Though Ranulf was generally kind and forced no more intimacies upon her, even deigning to sleep on the ground next to the cot each night, he seemed to have detached himself emotionally. He was wearying of her, she guessed, and tried to feel pleased with the knowledge.

In the late afternoon of the third day, they set up camp on the outskirts of London. Eager to sell their wares, peddlers descended upon the camp offering sweetmeats, new wine, cloth, ribbons—anything and everything. It was quite a sight to behold.

Perched upon a large boulder, Lizanne watched the good-natured haggling between a knight and a purveyor of small pastries. In the end, it was the purveyor who held out and obtained a price just below that which he had originally asked. Still, he grumbled as he exchanged three of the little pies for the coins the knight dropped into his palm.

A large, aproned woman approached Lizanne, holding up a handful of colorful ribbons, her toothless smile entreating. Lizanne's eyes lit with enthusiasm as she beheld the assortment, but she had no coin with which to purchase a single item.

Regretful, she shook her head and turned her attention to where Ranulf stood with Walter near the horses. Although they were too far off for her to hear their conversation, she surmised they spoke of matters of grave importance. She had noted Walter's return from the city earlier; he no doubt carried word from the king.

"Milady," the large woman persisted, tugging at Lizanne's sleeve, "this 'ere one would look nice wi' yer pretty black 'air."

Tearing her gaze from the men, Lizanne looked back down at her. "I have no coin." She showed her empty palms.

The woman considered her a moment, pressed her lips tightly together, then flounced away with a massive swing of her hips. Geoff and Roland laughed loudly, winking at Lizanne when she turned a distressed face to them.

She slid down the smooth face of the boulder and went to Ranulf's tent, where she collapsed gratefully upon the cot. After the long day of riding, it felt wonderful.

It was fully dark outside when Geoff arrived with the evening meal. In comparative silence, they ate a

sumptuous variety of foods bought from the purveyors.
When they were finished, he brought out a small chess
set, and they played another game on the floor of the
tent. Not surprisingly, Lizanne lost again, for the fifth
time.

"You are improving," Geoff praised her, scooping
up the pieces and settling them in the bag.

She shrugged. "It seems such an easy game. I do
not understand why I continue to struggle with the
moves. There are too many pieces, don't you think?"

Laughing, he stood and reached out a hand to assist
her to her feet. "Practice," he said. "Lots and lots of
practice."

She smiled. "One day I will beat you at this game,
you know."

"Then you plan to stay with Lord Ranulf?" was his
quick rejoinder.

She recovered, but not before Geoff saw the confused wonder that swept her face. "I have not much
choice in the matter," she said.

"Methinks you have more choice than you realize,
my lady."

Lizanne absorbed his words in silence. Finding
them far too disturbing, she promptly pushed them to
the deep recesses of her mind. She tossed her head back,
smiling again. "Then I will have to defeat you soon."

With a bark of laughter, Geoff threw back the tent
flap. "I do not doubt you will," he said, and grinned at
her before stepping out into the cool night air.

Clasping her hands behind her back, Lizanne disciplined herself to mentally retrace the moves he had used
to place her in checkmate. He had been so cunning!

She jumped when Ranulf entered minutes later.

"You've eaten," he said, noticing the cluttered tray.

"Aye, Geoff and I," she answered, "but we left
plenty for you." She turned and went to the washbasin.

Seating himself, Ranulf pulled his boots off and began picking at the leftovers, all the while watching Lizanne move about the tent as she prepared for bed. His pulses stirred when she began to remove her bliaut. As he had not slept with her these past nights, she had worn the thin chemise to bed for added warmth. It was quite creased from the abuse, he noticed.

He continued to watch as she went through the nightly ritual of trying to bring some semblance of order to her wild hair. She growled when the comb became hopelessly ensnared in the tangles, and he smiled. With a muffled invective, she tugged the comb free and continued with the task.

Pushing the food aside, Ranulf crossed to stand beside her.

She looked questioningly up at him, then yielded him the comb when he reached to take it from her. Lowering himself to the cot, he pulled her unresisting body into the V of his thighs and began drawing the comb through her thick tresses.

He gently worked the tangles out until her hair shone like a starry night and fell in thick curls down her back. Tossing the comb aside, he ran his fingers from her chin along her jawline and loosely gathered her hair together at the nape of her neck. Then, clumsily, he tied a bright green ribbon around it, lower a vivid blue one, and finally, a red one the color of ripe pomegranates.

Throughout, Lizanne had kept her eyes closed, her imagination running rampant as she centered on the heat from his muscled thighs penetrating her clothing. It seemed such a long time since last he'd touched her. She had truly missed it.

His sudden quiet pulled her back to the present. Suspicious, she turned her head and looked at him. He smiled, then leaned forward to plant a brief, warm kiss on her lips.

She did not fully understand her sense of loss when he drew back, her insides stirring alarmingly. Looking away, she reached behind herself and touched her bound hair. Immediately, her fingers found the bowed ribbons, their silkiness sliding coolly over her skin. She eagerly pulled her hair over her shoulder and eyed the trail of color. She touched each in turn.

"Oh, Ranulf," she crooned, "they are lovely." Her smile revealing her dimple, she raised her eyes back to his.

His mouth lifting into a smile, too, Ranulf lightly traced the curve of her jaw. Truly, she was special, this wild-eyed woman who fought like a man yet yielded to his touch. More than anything, he wanted this moment never to end. He wanted the smile upon her face never to fade. The twinkle in her lovely eyes to shine only for him. He wanted to hear the words women spoke to ensnare a man's heart. Aye, that was what he wanted—for Lizanne to declare herself his. If she did, he would never let her go. Would not surrender her when her brother came for her. . .

Wondering at the heat she saw in his eyes, Lizanne continued staring at him. He was so handsome, she thought, her heart straining in her chest at the confession wrung from it. The circumstances that had brought them together seemed no longer to matter. They belonged to a past she was no longer certain of.

Twisting around, she impulsively threw her arms around his neck, sending them both over backward.

His hands captured her around her waist, holding her to him as he gazed up at her.

Leveraging herself up on her forearms, she smiled at him. "Thank you, Ranulf," she said, her voice grown curiously husky. " 'Twas sweet of you." Then, moistening her lips, she angled her head and lightly touched her mouth to his.

Her voluntary initiation of intimacy baffled him. For days he had hungered incessantly for her, his loins growing heavy each time he looked at her. But, determined to give her time and space to sort out her feelings, and for him to better examine his own, he had repeatedly denied himself any further intimacy, knowing his resolve to wait on her could not withstand any more contact.

Whether or not she had discovered anything in the intervening days, he knew not. All he was certain of were his own riotous feelings and the way they constantly defied intense scrutiny.

He welcomed her deepening kiss and returned it with enthusiasm, feeling his manhood swell and press against the soft juncture of her thighs. God, but he needed her! All the restraint and patience of the last few days quickly dissolved as if they had never been, setting loose the dam of passion he had carefully hoarded.

Sliding a hand up over her spine, he took hold of that splendidly thick hair, pushed his fingers through it, and cupped her head. With growing urgency, he pressed her closer, bruising her lips as he worked his tongue past her teeth and drew hers into his mouth. Tasting of honey, she moaned and flicked her tongue over his.

When he felt her hand slide over his chest and down to his hip, he captured it and pulled it between them to cover his hard warmth. Without hesitation, her fingers curled around him, and a soft whimper rose from her throat as he surged against her palm. Tentatively at first, she moved against him, her hips beginning a maddening undulation that pushed him nearer the edge.

Not even with his first woman had he felt such uncontrollable desire. Every fiber of his being was ablaze with need, gathering momentum and focusing entirely on that part of him that strained to be free. Groaning loudly, he rolled over, pulling her beneath him and causing the cot to rock precariously before it settled back.

The last shred of his self-control before him, he lifted his head and looked searchingly at her. He needed to assuage his fleeing conscience before he took final possession.

Sensing his gaze, Lizanne lifted her lids and smiled at him. "Have I come of age?" she asked, her voice a bare whisper in the expectant stillness of the night.

He expelled a grating breath and nodded. "Aye, this night you are mine, Lizanne. Body and soul."

A flicker—of fear, perhaps—sparkled in her eyes as her reckless desire began to abate at his choice of words.

"I am ... frightened," she admitted, lowering her lashes over those brilliant green orbs of light.

Feeling her slipping away, Ranulf kissed her again, probing and coaxing her flame back to life until she responded anew. When she was writhing in his arms once more and panting softly, he lifted himself from her soft, welcoming body and quickly dispensed with his clothing.

Turning back, he was arrested by the disbelieving expression that surfaced through Lizanne's passion as her gaze moved upward from his swollen shaft. Her eyes riveted to the firm flesh of his belly, she shook her head.

"Lizanne, what is it?" he asked, lowering himself back to the cot and pulling her into his arms. Clearly, he was losing her again, her body gradually stiffening until it was near impossible to hold her.

Her gaze slid up over his chest, lingered overly long on his parted lips, then completed the journey to his eyes.

"I do not understand," she said, her voice breaking as she entreatingly fastened her eyes upon his. "I cannot have been mistaken. . . ."

His body's needs overcoming his mind's, Ranulf did not even attempt to decipher her hidden meaning. In desperation he gathered her against him and sought her lips again.

At first she evaded him, turning her head away and pushing ineffectually against his chest, but her body would not be quieted.

Taking advantage of the weakness of her flesh, Ranulf systematically laid siege to her battered defenses, trailing paths of fire over her flushed skin until her breathing grew ragged and her body began to tremble with want. His persistence to recapture those lost moments finally conquered her resistance, and she melted against him with renewed desire.

She was like the sweetest honey—one that filled his veins as it wound its way to his heart.

Deftly, he removed her garments and threw them to the dirt floor, beholding again the beautifully hard and soft curves of her body. Watching the play of emotions cross her face, he touched her, running his hands across her bare soles, her high arch, up her calves, and to her thighs. There, he lingered, trailing his fingers over her smoothness and threading them through the lustrous black hair at the apex.

She gasped and quivered at his touch, her skin suffusing with warmth when she met his gaze. With deliberate slowness, he smoothed his hands up over her belly to the taut peaks of her breasts. Settling her fullness in his palms, he brushed his thumbs lightly over the hardened nipples.

"Ran," she sighed, "ease this ache."

"You are sure?" he asked, unable to believe the words once they left his mouth. He did not think he could stop even were she to exhort him to.

"Aye," she breathed.

It was all Ranulf needed. Pushing a leg between hers, he covered her with his hard, muscular length, golden, matted skin meeting pale, smooth skin.

She arched against him and gripped a hand to his buttocks, instinctively seeking his entrance.

His fully erect member pressed expectantly to her soft woman's mound, he denied himself the immediate satisfaction his body urged him to. He could not bear to see her hurt any more than was necessary for her body to accommodate his.

"We must needs go slow to prepare you better," he rasped. " 'Twill hurt less that way."

Uncomprehendingly, she stared up at him, then groaned with delight when he took a rigid nipple in his mouth and began to tease it. A deeper heat sprang up between them, dampening their bodies where skin touched skin. His hands and lips played expertly over her, making her arch and groan with ecstasy.

When, finally, he raised himself and reached down to cup her mound, she cried out and pushed against his hand. Gently, his fingers parted the petals guarding the entrance to her core of heat. Finding her slick and quivering, he guided himself to her passage and, trembling with the effort of holding himself back, eased himself into her tightness until he came up against the thin membrane that proclaimed her a virgin. He experienced a great relief. Though he'd hoped, he'd known there might have been others before him. After all, she was eighteen years of age, and most girls were wed by fourteen.

Unable to wait any longer, Lizanne suddenly thrust upward and took him fully into her. She cried out in surprise at the resultant pain that swept over her in great waves. He was so very large, she was certain she was being torn in two. Immediately, she tried to retreat, pulling away from his penetrating fullness. But he followed and sank more deeply into her.

There Ranulf settled, straining with the agony of giving her time to become accustomed to him. Slowly, she did, her muscles easing and inviting him farther inside.

Groaning her name, he captured her mouth and began to thrust, slowly at first, but with increasing intensity as he felt her wakening response. Her hands sliding over his warm skin further incited him, wiping away all remnants of restraint and doubt as he gripped her hips and guided her to match his rhythm.

The pain having all but subsided, replaced by an incredibly sweet ache, Lizanne instinctively matched his movements, bowing her body from the cot to take him more deeply into her. Giving herself completely over to the passion, she raked her nails across his chest and down his back, murmurings of pleasure spilling from her lips.

In the darkness behind her closed lids, she saw herself climbing, her body reaching for something so gloriously elusive it would surely be worth the journey. Higher she spiraled, that ache within her now something more—fiery and enticing, deep and insistent, demanding its culmination. She could hardly breathe, her breath coming in sharp, shallow gasps. . . .

Nearing the zenith of his desire, Ranulf heard her cry of fulfillment and felt the rhythmic tightening of her muscles around him.

He quickened his movements then, driving her upward on the cot as his need carried him to that pinnacle of satiation. Shouting his release, he threw his head back and strained into her, spilling his seed in the warm, inviting flesh of her body.

Never before had he experienced such completion in the possessing of a woman's body. It went beyond the lust his mind would have him believe it to be. It was Lizanne, a woman he had thought to take revenge upon but instead had made himself terribly vulnerable to. What was this hold she had over him?

Breathing raggedly, he lowered his chest to the pillow of her breasts and turned his face into the mantle of her damp, loosened hair as his final shudders shook his body. The heavy, unmatched thud of their heartbeats vibrated between them as they lay motionless in the gentling wake of their passion.

Returning from the heavens of her release, Lizanne turned her head and looked at him.

Muted candlelight flickered off the distinct planes of his features. In repose they had softened, his long, pale lashes throwing spiky shadows upon his cheeks, his broad mouth lax as he drew deep, calming breaths. She thought perhaps he slept.

As the implications of their act sank in with the ebbing of her passion, her brow furrowed. Ranulf had just made love to her, and she had enjoyed it, in spite of the initial, unexpected pain his entrance had wrought. She rolled her lips inward and clamped them between her teeth.

She did not understand these strange emotions that gripped her heart and made chaos of the workings of her mind. Most of all, she did not understand how it was Ranulf no longer bore that hideous scar.

It was he, though, for it could not be possible that another could look so like him. After all, nothing was common about the man—his height, build, eyes, and especially that hair!

Had her childish imagination conjured up the scar? She glimpsed it again in her mind's eye, her breath catching in her throat as those memories bore viciously back to her. When she looked again at the face beside her, panic gripped her more tightly and threatened to tear her asunder. Quick tears of remorse filled her eyes, and deep, throbbing regret closed icy fingers around her aching heart.

Ranulf's sixth sense warned him of the abrupt change in the air. Raising his lids, he looked into Lizanne's watery eyes.

Swallowing back a sob, she turned her head away.

Ranulf could hardly believe it. After their mutually satisfying lovemaking, she was going to spoil it with tears. He pushed himself up from her. "Why do you cry?" he asked, grasping her chin to pull her gaze to his.

She stared at him for a long moment, then averted her eyes to stare sightlessly beyond him.

Losing patience, he shook her. "What is wrong with you? One moment fire in my arms, and the next ice."

Arabella. His mind forced to the fore the memory of the beautiful and deceitful woman-child who had been his wife. It was the same as she had done—playing with his emotions as if they were but a toy. "God," he breathed, "you remind me of my wife."

Lizanne drew her gaze back to his. "Now that you've taken what you wanted and had your revenge, will you allow me to return to Penforke?"

Anger, quick and scorching, welled up in him. "I did not take from you anything you were not willing to give," he harshly reminded her. "I did not rape you."

Memories brought Lizanne's own anger to the surface, ready to do battle with his. "But you would have!"

"If you find comfort in that, then believe it," he ground out. "But know this—tonight was only the first of many more nights of lovemaking." Rolling off her, he sat up and threw his hand out to indicate the virgin's blood she had spilled. "You are mine, Lizanne, and when I choose to take you, I will do so. And I assure you 'twill be with your full consent."

"Then I pray you got your fill, for 'tis the last you will have of me. *Never* again will I consent to your touch!"

Grabbing the edge of the coverlet, she pulled it over her, only to have it whipped away a bare second later. Determinedly, she reached for it again, but Ranulf held it out of reach while his gaze mercilessly raked over her.

"I hate you!" she shrieked, crossing her arms over her breasts. "Hate you! Hate you! Hate you!"

"So you have made blatantly clear time and again," he said, reaching forward to splay his hand over the softly padded ribs beneath her breasts. "Still, your body does not hate me, and that is enough."

She quelled at the truth of his statement. Her body did desire his, had responded to him with barely a prick of conscience. But she could not concede that to him. Instead, she shoved his hand away and rolled onto her stomach. "I trust you will find the floor comfortable, my lord," she muttered as she curled one arm around her face.

Ranulf stood and looked down at the firm curve of her buttocks. "Nay, no more," he said, turning to douse the candles. Returning moments later, he gave her a nudge to make room for himself on the cot and lay down beside her.

Instantly, she shot up, nearly making it off the cot before he dragged her back down into the curve of his body.

She fought him, her hurt and anger powerful agents as she attempted to wrestle free.

Drawing on his small reserve of patience, Ranulf held her tightly until the fight went out of her. Now, he thought, dragging the coverlet over them, she will cry.

She didn't, though, refusing to allow him any further glimpse of her distraught emotions. He was her enemy, and she would not let him see her weaknesses anymore, for it was a weapon that he could, and undoubtedly would, use against her.

"Sleep, Lizanne," he murmured. "On the morrow, we go to see the king."

She stiffened. "We?"

He nodded in the darkness. "Aye, you will accompany me."

She twisted in his arms and came nose-to-nose with him. "You would exhibit me as your captive before the king?" she asked disbelievingly. "You would be so bold?"

"Nay, 'tis not my purpose. I would not be so foolish to take you, but 'tis the king who has requested you attend him."

She gasped. "How knows he of my presence? Surely, you did not tell him?"

"Nay, but this city has many eyes and ears. Your accompaniment was duly noted upon our arrival. I should have hidden you."

A thought occurred to Lizanne, and she could not help but voice it. "Think you the king will approve of your abduction of me?"

Ranulf squeezed her closer. "Think you he will approve of your abduction and imprisonment of my person, Lizanne—or the wounds you inflicted upon one of his barons?" At her silence, he continued, "Do not think you will escape me by appealing to him. You may be his subject, but I do not think he would hesitate to mete out punishment for your inappropriate behavior. He is not always a tolerant man!"

"How will you explain my presence then?"

"With only as much detail as needs be to ensure you remain with me," he said softly. "Do you not forget your vow to me, Lizanne. Even the king cannot release you from that."

With a deep sense of foreboding, she turned her back to him again.

"I will do my best to remember it," she grumbled, "but you would also do well to remember that not even you can refuse the decree of a king . . . or God."

"Nor can you," Ranulf responded.

Lizanne was sore and temperamental, Ranulf distant and brooding, the following day when they rode through the gates of Westminster Palace. Neither had spoken a word to the other since the night before, and their stubborn, self-imposed silence yawned uncomfortably between them.

Disturbingly aware of Lizanne's and his lord's moods, Geoff rode quietly beside her. Although he did not know what had caused this most recent rift, he knew it to be a serious one and wondered at his own distress at it. Truthfully, he had grown rather fond of his lord's leman. Perhaps too fond, he chided himself.

Ignoring the curious looks cast upon her by the castlefolk bustling about, Lizanne raised her chin haughtily and sat straighter in the horrid sidesaddle Ranulf had insisted upon. Grimacing at the press of hard leather beneath her, she shifted backward to settle her weight onto her tailbone and off that contentious place between her thighs. The ease of soreness did little to take her mind off its cause and the perpetrator.

She eyed Ranulf as he dismounted and came around his horse to assist her down. Glaring at him, she ignored the arms he raised to her and, quick as a sprite, hauled her skirts up and dismounted from the opposite side before he or the horse could protest the imprudence of such an act.

Straightening her attire, she smiled tightly at him when he stepped around the horse and gripped her by the forearm.

Though he said not a word, his eyes spoke volumes. Spinning her around, he led her up the steps to the palace.

Trying not to think about the man beside her, for his simple touch was far too disturbing, Lizanne looked up at the building that rose before her. Recently restored and refurbished following Stephen's reign, which had seen it fall into a sorry state of neglect, Westminster shone like a jewel.

It was the first Lizanne had seen of it up close. During her visit with Gilbert the year before, Henry and Eleanor had still been in residence at Bermondsey Castle, located at the busy east end of the city.

Lizanne was awed by the new palace's magnificence, so much so that for a moment she was nearly—not quite—able to separate herself from Ranulf's presence.

Inside, Ranulf exchanged a few words with a soldier.

Then, following the man, he led Lizanne up a staircase and down a long corridor. At the end, the soldier threw open a door and stood aside for the two to enter.

Pushing Lizanne ahead of him into the lavishly appointed apartment, Ranulf spoke in hushed tones to the soldier, then stepped inside and closed the door behind him.

Lizanne stood on the far side of the chamber, her back to the large hearth. "What is this?" she asked, her eyes scanning the room.

" 'Tis your apartment for the duration of our stay," he said, walking over to her.

Her brows lifted. "Our stay?" she repeated. "Will we be long at Westminster?"

He shrugged, his great muscled shoulders rolling beneath the fine weave of his dark blue tunic. "For as long as the king decrees necessary."

That last word sent a jolting shiver up her spine. "Necessary?" she said, more than a little suspicious. Why had King Henry specifically requested her presence at the palace? she wondered for the hundredth time. She was, after all, simply a noble—and hardly noteworthy at that, much less held in high regard. What warranted this treatment?

Her gaze flitted past Ranulf and over the furnishings a second time. They were much too fine. Dread poured into her heart as she realized the significance of her surroundings.

"Ah nay!" she moaned, searching frantically for a way out of this new dilemma.

Frowning, Ranulf gripped her shoulders. "What is it?"

"The king intends to wed me, doesn't he?"

He shook his head. He did not understand her ramblings. "Wed you?" He laughed. "The king is already married to Eleanor—"

"Nay!" She twisted out of his grasp and moved past him to the huge four-postered bed. "To another."

Ranulf followed her. "What speak you of?" he demanded.

"Don't you see?" She threw her hands up to encompass the room.

"Lizanne, make sense!" he ordered, pushing her down upon the bed.

Shaking her head, she fell back onto the coverlet and covered her face with her hands. "Last year he tried to wed me to Sir Arthur Fendall," she said, her voice muffled. "I did not wish to wed the man, and the king was greatly angered."

"Then you refused him? You defied the king?"

She peeked up at Ranulf through her fingers. "Not exactly . . ."

"Enough of your word games. What exactly *did* happen?"

Sighing loudly, she pushed herself up on her elbows. "I made it so that Sir Arthur changed his mind about taking me to wife. 'Twas simple, really."

Impatiently, Ranulf flapped his hand for her to continue.

"I wrestled him," she said frankly, then shoved to her feet.

"You what?" He dropped his face near hers, his brows nearly touching above his nose.

"I wrestled him," she restated, then moved past him.

Ranulf caught her by the arm and swung her back around. "You will explain yourself."

"There is not much to explain." Seeing the anger suffusing his features, she shrugged. "Shortly after King Henry announced that he would give me in marriage to Sir Arthur, that awful little man began publicly boasting about bedding me. I overheard one particularly lewd description of how he was going to . . . well, you know.

Quite by accident"—her voice rose sarcastically—"I struck him in the nose."

Ranulf's look of horror fascinated her. Reaching up, she impulsively smoothed his furrowed brow. "Don't look so concerned. He could hardly retaliate there in front of the king, though he certainly did try later. And when he did, he ended up on his backside with me astride."

Ranulf's mouth dropped open. "Truly, you wrestled him to the ground?"

She could not help herself and laughed. "Aye," she said, temporarily forgetting her more immediate problems as she reveled in the memory of that little man's utter embarrassment. He had been pompous and arrogant, and she had bettered him without much effort. She was quite proud of it, actually.

"In all fairness, though," she continued, "he was not large like you, Ranulf. He was actually shorter than I am, and slight of build. 'Twas not much of a challenge really."

Ranulf shook his head. "I'm sure."

"Needless to say, he thought better of wedding me and withdrew the offer. Fortunately, Gilbert spirited me away that very evening before the king could attempt another match."

Ranulf shook himself out of his stupor, not understanding why he should be so surprised by her disclosure. It was, after all, the kind of behavior she had indulged in up until their departure from Killian. Only in the days following had he begun to see another side to her.

"And you think he intends to try again?" he concluded, not caring for the implications. He had no intention of letting his catch go to another man.

She sighed wearily. " 'Twould seem likely."

"You suspected this yestereve?"

"It did cross my mind—the possibility. Now, I am

very nearly certain of it. Why else would he place me in a nuptial chamber?"

For the first time, Ranulf looked about the lavish room. Then, muttering to himself, he strode to the door and pulled it open.

"Where are you going?"

" 'Twould not be appropriate for us to share the same room," he informed her, gripping the doorjamb as he turned to face her.

"I know that. 'Twas not my question."

"My quarters are just down the hall. Should you need me, I will be there."

"I will not need you."

He shrugged. "I've asked that hot water be brought for your bath. Freshen yourself, and shortly I will collect you for the midday meal."

Staring at her hands, she nodded. When she heard the door close behind him, she looked up, a frown marring her features. What would he do, she wondered, if the king gave her to another man? He could hardly hope to claim her for himself without also offering marriage. . . .

Chapter 14

*A*ttired *in the* borrowed garments Ranulf had sent to her chamber, Lizanne walked quietly beside him as they entered the main hall for the midday meal. At the far end, seated on a raised platform, was King Henry, and beside him, his queen. Noting their approach, the king motioned them forward.

Lizanne looked first to Queen Eleanor. In her early thirties, the woman was a dozen years older than her husband—a man who had been crowned king of all England less than two years before. In spite of her age, Eleanor was still the legendary beauty the troubadors sang of. Though she'd only recently given birth to Henry's third child, the princess Matilda, the birthing appeared to have laid no waste to her beauteous face. She was so incredibly feminine and strong at the same time that Lizanne could not help but envy her, especially the intelligence that shone from clear green eyes.

She offered Eleanor a tentative smile, then shifted her gaze to Henry's square, bearded face. He looked much the same as she remembered, though she had forgotten the intensity of the close-cropped red hair that matched his freckled complexion. Still, he was a handsome man.

Reluctantly, she met his large gray eyes and inwardly

cringed at the look of disapproval he leveled upon her, his mouth visibly tightening. Aye, it was obvious he was remembering their last encounter.

Nervously breaking the eye contact, she looked farther down the king's long table. Unseeingly at first, she fixed her gaze on a man who was staring at both her and Ranulf. Blinking with sudden recognition, she refocused on the boyishly handsome face of Philip Charwyck and felt her color rise in her cheeks—not from embarrassment or any other mild emotion, but consuming anger.

It was beyond ironic that she now found herself in the presence of both Ranulf and Philip, her two most hated enemies. Six years had passed since last she had seen her formerly betrothed—two years prior to the wedding that had never taken place. She was surprised that her memories of him had remained so intact over time. Except for the premature graying at his temples, he appeared much the same as when last she'd seen him.

A fire sprang up in the pit of her belly. Did he recognize her? she wondered. She tore her gaze from him as she and Ranulf reached the king and queen. Ranulf's gentle tug on her arm brought her kneeling beside him.

A short silence followed; then they were commanded to stand.

"Baron Wardieu and Lady Lizanne, you are most welcome at my court," King Henry said, then leaned expectantly toward Ranulf. "I trust you bring me worthy news."

"Aye, Your Majesty, that I do."

Henry grinned. "Then let us enjoy the meal and speak of it. Come." He motioned them toward the empty chairs to his right. "Seat yourselves beside me."

Lizanne and Ranulf had to walk the length of the table to get around it to the proffered seats. Passing behind Philip, Lizanne boldly met the eyes he turned to her, letting the full weight of her hostility shine through.

Philip smiled at her even as he swept a degrading

look down her figure that Ranulf could not possibly have missed.

The hand on Lizanne's arm tightened perceptibly as she was led past. "Mayhap you would like to set yourself upon his lap?" Ranulf hissed.

Glowering, she met his disapproving stare but kept her lips firmly sealed against the thoughts that were attempting to transform themselves into loud, inflammatory words. She hoped Ranulf appreciated the effort she was making not to cause a scene.

"Behave yourself," he warned as he helped her into her chair. Seating himself beside her, he became immediately engrossed in conversation with his overlord.

Feeling sorely excluded, Lizanne clamped down on the temptation to look along the table to where Philip sat. Instead, she lifted the goblet that had been filled to brimming with warm, dark wine. She savored the wine's fullness, settling it in her mouth before swallowing. It was a fine wine, and before she even considered touching a morsel of the food laid before her, she had drained the last drop. Directly, it was refilled.

Lifting the goblet again, she finally acknowledged the persistent sense of being watched. And indeed she was—by more than a few pairs of curious eyes. Doubtless, they were pondering her relationship with Ranulf.

Absently crumbling a piece of bread between her fingers, she slowly leaned forward and looked down the length of the table. Immediately, she encountered the particular gaze she had felt, most tangibly, upon her person.

She raised her chin and narrowed her eyes on Philip Charwyck. Truly, she did not believe he recognized her, for surely he had never looked at her *that* way. Nay, he had only ever been mildly tolerant of her.

Ranulf's hand closing over her clenched one brought her head around. She was beginning to feel the effects of the wine, but her senses were not so dulled she couldn't recognize his anger as he leaned past her and turned his full ire upon Philip.

"Remember, Lizanne," he whispered as he stared down the man he perceived to be a rival, "you belong to me."

Lifting the goblet to her lips, she boldly leaned into his line of vision, breaking the staring duel between the two men.

"For the moment," she recklessly taunted before returning her attention to the meal.

With a growl that rumbled low in his throat, Ranulf lifted his hand from hers and turned back to the king.

When the tedious meal was at last finished with, Lizanne felt exceedingly light-headed from the two or more goblets of wine she had consumed without benefit of adequate food. She said not a word as she was led across the hall to where Geoff awaited his lord.

After passing Lizanne into his care, Ranulf turned and strode away.

From a shadowy alcove outside the main hall, Philip watched the transfer, noting again the possessiveness the baron exercised over the lady who was certainly not his wife.

Like the others, he was deeply interested in their relationship, but for an entirely different reason. It was lust that burned in his loins.

The moment he had laid eyes upon her, he had determined he would have her, no matter her relationship to the king's favored baron. Her wild beauty set her so far apart from the other ladies of the court, they paled to insignificance. There was definite promise in those firm, rounded hips, and pleasure to be had between those breasts. She would be a most pleasurable ride, this one.

Feeling pained discomfort at his desirous musings, he shifted his thoughts to the matter of Baron Wardieu. The man's striking likeness to another more than unsettled him. He had seen that pale hair before, those eyes, and the imposing stature . . . and he knew exactly where.

Already he had considered the possibilities for a resemblance that was certainly not coincidental. There was power to be gained in the knowledge. Though he did not yet know how he would use it to his advantage, he most assuredly would.

Breaking out of his ponderings, he stepped from the alcove and hastened after the squire and the lady. Tactlessly, he placed himself squarely before Geoff just as the two reached the stairway.

"I am Sir Philip Charwyck," he announced to the squire. "And you are . . . ?"

Geoff straightened himself to his full height so he was nearly level with the other man. "I am Geoff, Baron Ranulf Wardieu's squire."

"Hmm," Philip murmured, then shifted his attention to the lady, turning his body so that Geoff was forced to look at his profile.

Lizanne stared up at the man whose brows were drawn in unspoken question and very nearly laughed aloud. It was as she had thought. He had not recognized her. Had she really changed so much?

"I would have the pleasure of your name, my lady," he purred, grasping her hand and drawing it to his lips.

When he bent his head to lay a kiss upon her fingers, he suddenly found himself clutching air. Surprised at her rejection, he lifted his gaze and met her green eyes. Though he did not understand it, a chord of familiarity knelled within him. Was it possible he knew the lady after all? Had he met her before?

His brow furrowing, he wondered at the thick air of antagonism falling off her.

"But we have met before," she informed him in a smooth, frosty voice as she made a show of wiping clean her hand.

Philip's frown deepened. "Nay, I do not think so," he said.

In silence Geoff looked from one to the other, fascinated by the scene unfolding before him. Although Lizanne seemed out of sorts, swaying slightly on her feet, he recognized the telltale signs of her devilment. Like Sir Philip, he, too, wondered at her thinly veiled hostility. How did she know this man, he wondered, and what had he done to incite such emotion?

Lizanne curtsied, her smile tight. "Lady Lizanne Balmaine of Penforke," she said, her eyes never leaving the man's face.

She was rewarded by a suffusion of purplish-red color, a gaping jaw, and eyes grown round as a full moon.

"Lady Lizanne?" Philip repeated disbelievingly, taking an involuntary step backward.

"Aye, formerly your betrothed, Sir Philip. Though it pains me you would forget your commitment so easily, I daresay I am not terribly surprised by it."

Geoff's breath caught in his throat at the revelation, his own face mirroring much of the other man's astonishment.

"I believe I owe you something," Lizanne added, raising her hand from her skirts.

Her drink-induced sluggishness gave Geoff the time needed to fathom her intent. Just barely, he caught hold of her wrist as she flung her arm out to strike the knight.

Having missed her mark by bare inches, Lizanne swung around to face Geoff. An expression of hurt flitted across her features as she looked at the young man whom she'd come to regard as a friend.

"Nay, my lady," he said, gently urging her arm back to her side. " 'Tis not prudent."

She would have argued with him, but the wine had numbed her tongue and made it feel large and awkward. Instead, after a brief hesitation, she conceded with a nod and wordlessly turned to mount the stairs.

Steadying her, Geoff walked beside her.

They were a mere half-dozen steps up when Lizanne stopped abruptly and turned to look at the man below. "I regret I cannot say it has been a pleasure to meet you again," she said, then continued up the remaining steps.

When they were out of sight, Philip leaned back against the stone wall and contemplated the encounter.

The Lady Lizanne was fortunate that the young squire had stayed her hand, he thought, for he would not have refrained from like retaliation had she struck him. It was obvious she bore him a mighty grudge for his refusal to marry her.

With some difficulty, he dredged up his remembrances of the gangly, dark-haired child who had continuously vexed him during his training as a squire at her father's castle. Never had he dreamed she would become such a beauty.

He shook his head in wonder, feeling again the restless stirrings in his loins. He had thought himself fortunate to have escaped marriage to her, but now he was not so sure he should have put forth the effort that had been required to forgo the obligation set to him by his father.

But it was not too late, he reassured himself. If she could play mistress to the enigmatic Baron Wardieu, she could certainly entertain him as well. The thought cheered him considerably.

Ranulf found Lizanne sprawled upon the bed. Lying on her stomach, her feet dangling over the edge, one shoe on, the other lying amid the rushes, she looked like a child.

Quietly, he lowered himself to the mattress and leaned over her sleeping form to examine her face. A fist was curled against one brightly flushed cheek, her features relaxed as the eyes beneath her lids traveled from side to side.

She did not look as if she had been weeping, as he'd expected her to be. Indeed, she appeared quite content, most likely a result of the wine he had watched her consume.

His shoulders slumped with relief. When Geoff had told him of her encounter with Charwyck, he had been greatly unsettled by the news that the two had once been betrothed. He had also been reassured by the hostility Geoff had reported Lizanne had displayed toward the man.

Reaching out, he fingered the ribbon that bound her freshly washed hair. He could not help but be pleased she had chosen to wear his gift in spite of their most recent altercation. Mayhap she truly was growing up.

She stirred but did not awaken.

Deciding he would let her sleep off her stupor, he lay down beside her. He stared up at the softly draped material overhead as he thought back to his meeting with the king.

Henry had been receptive to the bargain struck between Lord Bernard and his vassal—quite pleased, in fact. Oddly though, he had been less interested in the mission he had sent Ranulf on than the circumstances surrounding Lizanne's accompaniment.

Although Ranulf had been brief in the telling of the story the king had demanded, he had been honest. Suspicion creeping up his spine, he had quickly become watchful, catching the curious glances between Henry and Eleanor throughout the accounting.

When Henry had asked whether or not he had bedded Lizanne, Ranulf had been shaken by the forward inquiry. He had declined to answer, and surprisingly, the king had not pursued it.

Ranulf's greatest shock had come near the end of his interview with the young, mischievous king. Offhandedly, Henry had asked him whether or not he intended to wed the lady. Ranulf's immediate response had been to deny any such consideration.

The king had looked disappointed but had quickly recovered and set himself to ticking off the names of eligible knights he could match Lizanne to, including this Charwyck.

The accuracy of Lizanne's prediction, coupled with the realization of his imminent loss of her, had shaken Ranulf.

Prior to being dismissed, Henry had slyly suggested he reconsider his decision to offer for Lizanne and informed him a choice would be made soon if no offer was forthcoming.

Had he not been king, Ranulf would have throttled the man, but he had withdrawn with his head still firmly planted upon his shoulders, a rage building in him.

Of a sudden, Lizanne rolled onto her back and threw an arm across his chest. Groaning, she turned her head and peered at him through the narrowed slits of her lids.

"Oh, 'tis you," she muttered, rubbing a hand over her face.

"Did you expect Sir Philip?"

"What?" She blinked, then forced her eyes wide to stare at him. "Oh." She shook her head as everything came rushing back to her in a kind of hazy fog. "Geoff told you, then."

"Naturally."

"Naturally," she echoed. Raking a hand through her rumpled hair, she leveraged herself to a sitting position. She squeezed her eyes shut at the pounding sensation caused by the sudden movement. It was undoubtedly a strong wine she had partaken of. She opened first one eye, then the other.

"Tell me of your broken betrothal to Charwyck," Ranulf prodded, his jaw hardening.

She regarded him with something akin to disbelief. Through the dissipating fog, she forced herself to acknowledge that it was Ranulf who had been responsible for the broken promise he now asked about.

Desperately, she grasped at the earlier pain and anger that had so fueled her hatred for this man, but was only able to recapture the barest measure of it. The treacherous emotions he caused to envelop her had overpowered the others, she conceded with dismay. That she could have such feelings for her enemy at the cost of her very soul, was nearly the most difficult blow she'd ever had to take.

" 'Tis none of your concern," she finally answered, thrusting her chin high in the air.

"You are wrong," Ranulf said, amazed at the firm grip he maintained on his composure. He sat up. " 'Twould seem the king does intend to see you wed, and this Charwyck is among the knights considered likely candidates. As you are still under my guardianship, I would know."

At his words, Lizanne dropped her head to her chest, her hands fisting in her lap. Looking at her bent head, Ranulf was overwhelmed with the longing to embrace her and offer the solace she seemed so in need of. Squelching the impulse, he crooked a finger beneath her chin and lifted it.

She met his steady gaze. "And were you considered a likely candidate as well?" she asked.

He was surprised at her directness but dismissed it. "Aye," he admitted, "but I have declined the offer."

It was as if he'd slapped her. Drawing back, she dropped her feet to the floor and stood, averting her face so he could not read her emotions.

"Are you disappointed?" he asked, rising to follow her across the room to the small window.

"Disappointed?" She laughed, swinging back around to face him. Tears shone brightly in her eyes. "Think you I would want to marry you?" She stabbed a finger to his chest. "Think you I wish to wed any man?" She threw her hands out for emphasis.

Beginning to tremble, she turned to the window. "Mayhap you do not yet understand," she said. "I do not like men. They are the pestilence of the earth."

Before she could protest, Ranulf disengaged her fingers from the window ledge and turned her around. "What of Gilbert?" he asked. "You hate him as well?"

"Nay!" she said, vainly trying to pull free of him. "Gilbert is different—"

"Different from other men? How can that be?"

"He is my brother . . . and a good man."

"Ah," he muttered. "And Geoff?"

Her eyes flared wider. "He . . . he is . . ."

"And what of Roland? You do not hate him either."

Wrenching herself free, she jumped out of his reach. "They are boys!" she declared. "They have not yet learned the treachery of men."

Calling on his exhausted patience, Ranulf cocked his head. "And treachery . . . is this an exclusive trait of men? What of women, Lizanne?" He was remembering the woman he had been wed to for five miserable years. With a determined set to his mouth, he advanced upon Lizanne, driving her back until she came hard up against the wall.

"Methinks," he said, pressing a hand to the stone on either side of her, "women can be far more treacherous than any man."

"I do not speak of matters of the heart, but of needless pillaging and murder," she said. "And rape," she added, as she pressed a hand to her temple.

Rape? She always came back to that. Staring down at her pain-drawn features, Ranulf shuffled through the varied pieces of Lizanne's character. In the long minutes of silence that followed, he methodically analyzed each and attempted a fit that would give him the insight constantly eluding him.

Of a sudden, everything fell into place, and a dread realization swept over him. In that instant, he discovered what it was that drove her. Focusing again on her face, he saw the fear that had risen there while he'd been lost in speculation. Frowning, he laid his hand over her jaw and brushed her parted lips with his thumb. She recoiled from his touch, but he followed and pulled her face closer.

" 'Tis what this is all about, isn't it?" he murmured. "Someone tried to steal your virtue."

Her eyes dilated, nearly obliterating the bright green color ringing her pupils. Beneath his hand, he felt the muscles of her jaw contract and the sudden warmth of blood that flushed her skin.

"Who was it?" he persisted.

She drew in a sudden, sharp breath but continued to stare at him.

"Was it Charwyck?" he asked, the very idea constricting his throat.

She reacted so violently to his words, it was as if he had struck her. "Philip?" she cried, shaking her head wildly. Her breath came in short rasps as she slapped his hand away. "Nay, he is a far more honorable man than he who tried to rape me. Philip is the man I wanted more than anything to wed."

Ranulf winced. She had loved Philip then—at least thought herself in love with him. "And why didn't you wed with him?"

Keeping her gaze steady with his, she lifted her chin. "Believing me to have lost my virtue, he decided he no longer wanted me."

Ranulf ground his teeth together. Philip Charwyck was every bit the bastard he appeared to be. Though Ranulf very much wanted to put his arms around Lizanne, he held himself away from her, knowing his touch would not be welcomed. "If 'twas not Philip, then who?" he pressed. He had to know.

Lizanne exploded then. " 'Twas you—Ranulf Wardieu!"

Chapter 15

It was Ranulf's turn to react. His incredulity staggered him back a step. It explained so much—her imprisonment of him, her hate, her mortification over her body's response to him. . . .

Through a haze, he heard her speaking again and forced himself to concentrate, understanding her words were elemental to the complete puzzle.

"Do you know what you have wrought?" She pushed away from the wall, no longer the prey but the predator. "Everything that was ever dear to me you destroyed—my father, Philip, Gilbert. . . ." Her voice caught in a throat thick with unshed tears. "You might just as well have killed Gilbert when you attacked our camp, for he is forever lost to me and everyone else."

She pressed her hands to her temples. "Now," she continued, "I would know if you are going to deny it."

Ranulf shook himself out of his self-imposed quiet. " 'Tis a mistake," he said. "Believe me, Lizanne, I could not have done this thing."

When her hand flew up and made stinging contact with his face, he did not move. " 'Twas you!" she declared, feeling less than satisfied with the rush of bright color that marked his face.

His jaw hardened. "Nay, it was another," he insisted.

She laughed with great bitterness. "I do not blame you for denying it, for it cannot have sat too well with you to be bested by a woman."

"Again, I know not what you speak of."

"This," she hissed, lifting her right hand between them. "You wanted to know about this." She flexed the crooked thumb. "Foolish. I should have had my thumb on the outside rather than the inside of my fist when I struck you. But I can hardly complain, for it achieved the same end and stopped you from taking what I would not give. Now do you remember?"

He shook his head. "Not until I saw you at Lord Langdon's had I ever before laid eyes upon you."

Ignoring the shooting pain behind her eyes, Lizanne reached forward and, grasping a handful of his hair, drew it into his line of vision.

"There is no other with hair the color of new snow." Her gaze moved from the mane she held to his eyes. "Nor eyes so black they are but one color." She dropped her hand and stepped back.

"And your size," she said in a bare whisper, " 'tis unmistakable." She turned away. "Nay, I have not erred."

"Aye, you have," he retorted, pulling her back around. "I am not this man you speak of."

"You have not the scar, 'tis all," she spit. "But you are one and the same."

Ranulf latched on to that. "Scar?" he repeated. "What scar do you speak of?"

When she suddenly raised her knee between his legs, her aim apparent, he sidestepped and avoided her angry attack. In one smooth motion, he bent and swung her up into his arms. He carried her to the bed, where he dropped her upon the mattress. When she attempted to raise herself, he leaned forward and pushed her back down.

Holding her there, he placed his face near hers, his breath mingling with hers.

She stilled and looked up at him.

"The man who tried to violate you would not have been patient, Lizanne," he said in a soft voice. "He would not have waited until you were ready for his touch."

He saw the confusion that creased her brow and lightened the green of her eyes. Hope flared within him. She was uncertain.

Bringing his face closer, he stared unblinkingly into her glittering eyes. "Nor is it likely you would have desired him as you do me." To demonstrate, he lowered his mouth to hers.

Her battered defenses falling around her, Lizanne closed her eyes tightly and lay still, trying not to feel the warmth of the lips that gently coaxed a response from her. Futilely, she sought to focus her thoughts elsewhere, but his touch kept drawing her back to the present and the feel of his lips and tongue caressing her mouth.

The keen, unnerving sensations began in the small of her back and spread up and outward like a warm breeze. Though her mind cried out its weak protests, her body drowned them and swept her away on the heady tide of desire. Whimpering, she yielded and drew his tongue inside her mouth.

Immediately, he lifted his head and stared at her.

She raised her lids and met his heated gaze.

He smiled bitterly. "Though you refuse to accept the truth, your body knows," he said, his gaze shifting to her swollen mouth. "With or without your consent, that other man you accuse me of being would take you this very moment."

He straightened and strode to the door. "Think on it," he said, then was gone.

His words struck something in Lizanne—an element of truth she had been wrestling with for days.

Though her eyes told her differently, her heart was adamantly resistant to the belief that Ranulf was responsible for that horrible night.

Clasping her hands before her face, she looked entreatingly to the canopy above her and prayed to the God who had abandoned her all those years ago.

As Ranulf had expected she might, Lizanne pleaded illness and did not put in an appearance for the late meal. In her place sat Walter, his expression dour as, in a confidential tone, he related to Ranulf the information he had obtained about Charwyck.

Ranulf leaned closer at the mention of Philip's knight service to the king, or rather, lack of it.

"He pays the shield tax to avoid military service," Walter said.

"So he is a coward as well?" Ranulf murmured, his eyes flicking past Walter to the object of their discussion. Charwyck didn't notice, engrossed as he was in staring at a particularly curvaceous serving wench.

"So 'twould appear," Walter said, "but I am also told he is not inexperienced. The first three years following knighthood he did fulfill his knight's service. 'Tis just in recent years he has declined to do so."

Consideringly, Ranulf raised his goblet and drained the last of his wine. "What else?"

Walter shook his head. "Shortly after Philip broke the marriage contract with Lady Lizanne, he wed a landed widow, nearly doubling his family's holdings."

Ranulf's brows rose at this bit of information. "She is no longer living, I presume?"

Walter confirmed the assumption and leaned closer to his lord. "Two years ago, she died under rather suspicious circumstances." At Ranulf's nod, he continued, "Sir Philip says she fell down the stairs and broke her neck, but 'tis gossiped 'twas broken prior to the fall."

The knuckles of Ranulf's hand whitened as he

gripped his meat dagger. "Do you think it just lurid gossip?" he asked.

The vassal shook his head, feeling his lord's tangible anguish. "I fear 'tis likely true. The rumors of his cruelty abound unlike any others I have heard. There must surely be some substance to them. . . ."

Ranulf pondered this. Lifting a tankard of ale to his lips, he turned his head and looked again at Sir Philip. As he swallowed a mouthful of the warm liquid, he met the icy blue of the other man's stare over the rim of the metal vessel. Without breaking the contact, he drank from the tankard once more before setting it back upon the table. Outwardly dispassionate, he watched as Charwyck's lips slowly curled.

So, they understood each other, Ranulf thought. Excellent! He looked back at Walter. "I cannot allow Lizanne to wed him," he said with unwavering conviction.

As Walter had expected. Tentatively, he broached the only other alternative. "Then you will marry her yourself?"

Aye, Ranulf mused, he had delivered Lizanne unto this, and he would deliver her out of it—whether or not she liked it. It mattered not that she had made it perfectly clear that afternoon her preference still lay with her former betrothed. She would be his.

"Aye," he said, "I will offer for her."

To his surprise, Walter grinned broadly. "Though the woman surely bedevils you, my lord, methinks you will not soon tire of the novelty of her company."

Ranulf frowned. "I gathered you did not care for her."

"I did not," Walter admitted, "but I have watched her closely since we left Killian and think I may have misjudged her—though only because she wished to be misjudged."

"And what of your agreement to dislike one another?"

Walter frowned. He knew not what his lord referred to. "Did she tell you that?"

Ranulf nodded. "Aye, she made it clear you had reached some sort of understanding."

The memory of his confrontation with the Lady Lizanne beside the stream came back to Walter with sudden clarity. Shaking his head in wonder, he chuckled. "Aye, I suppose we did reach an agreement, though 'twas certainly unspoken."

"Ranulf," the king said, breaking into their conversation.

"Your Majesty?"

Henry leaned forward, a conspiratorial gleam in his eyes. "I have made my choice, and a fine one at that."

Knowing with dread certainty Henry spoke of the man who was to become Lizanne's husband, Ranulf stiffened. He felt an answering tension emanate from Walter. It was said the king was not always a good judge of character. "I would speak to you on that," Ranulf said. "I have reconsidered and would offer to wed with Lady Lizanne myself."

Henry looked surprised, then regretful. "I fear 'tis too late, Ranulf," he said, frowning. "I have already approached Charwyck, and he has agreed to take her to wife. Did you know that the Balmaine and Charwyck lands adjoin?"

As if he did not notice the stricken look that shifted across Ranulf's face, Henry continued, "Odd thing, but I have learned that Lady Lizanne was once betrothed to the man." His frown deepened, his eyes drifting upward as he tried to recall the details.

Ranulf was struck again by the desire to throttle the king. Again he suppressed it. "I would ask that you reconsider," he pressed.

The king raised his wine goblet and drained the

contents in one long, deep swallow. "There is nothing to reconsider," he said. "I have already made my decision."

Where in God's name was his patience? Ranulf wondered as quick fire coursed through his veins. He was overwhelmed by the desire to strike out. Wisely, he redirected that urge to Lizanne's newly betrothed. He would deal with the man personally.

Smiling beautifully, Eleanor leaned forward and placed her hand upon her husband's arm. "Mayhap you should let the Lady Lizanne choose for herself," she said, her eyes sparkling with something Ranulf did not understand. "After all, 'twould seem either man would be a suitable match for her." In that instant, the queen's power was unmistakable.

Henry considered the suggestion for some minutes, then leaned back in his chair, one hand dangling from the armrest. "Aye," he said, favoring Eleanor with a lazy smile, "methinks 'twould make for an interesting diversion."

He tapped his fist to his mouth, then nodded. "The Lady Lizanne will make the choice herself on the morrow." Suddenly, he laughed. "Mayhap she will be more agreeable than before."

Ranulf was not pleased, but the king was finished and was shoving to his feet, signaling an end to the long meal.

His eyes sweeping the hall, Ranulf located Philip among the throng of nobles eager to depart. He pushed his chair back and left Walter gaping after him.

With much effort, coupled with decided rudeness, Walter caught up with him and barred his way.

"It seems," Ranulf growled, "you are intent upon continually deterring me from reaching my destination." He reached to set the smaller man aside.

"Nay, my lord." Walter firmly stood his ground. " 'Tis as the king has decreed. Let Lady Lizanne decide her own fate." Boldly, he gripped his lord's arm. "She *will* choose you."

Ranulf was jolted by the conviction in the man's voice. Would she choose him? After her accusations and her affirmation of the feelings she had once had for Philip, he did not believe she would.

"Unhand me, you vermin!" Lizanne shouted, straining against the two men holding her. Neither spoke; they simply dragged her into the hall, pushed her none-too-gently forward, and retreated.

Regaining her feet, she swung around just as the doors came together with a resounding thud.

"We thought perhaps you had decided to leave us early, Lady Lizanne." The king's booming voice reached her from across the hall.

With a queer sense of doom, she slowly turned and looked across to where King Henry sat in an elaborately carved chair high upon a raised platform. Beside him sat Eleanor, arrayed in a voluminous gown that reproduced, exactly, the color of blue sapphires. To the queen's left stood a stout priest, a psalter clasped between his hands. To the right of the platform were Ranulf and Philip.

Lizanne looked suspiciously from one to the other, but her eyes ultimately came to rest upon Ranulf. Though he was some distance away, she recognized the tight-lipped expression he wore and the hard glint in his eyes. Something terrible was afoot, she acknowledged, though she was hardly surprised.

"Come, Lady Lizanne," Henry ordered. "You have kept us waiting far too long as it is."

No doubt. The soldiers had come for her while she had strolled through the gardens that morning, and without any explanation had dragged her back inside the palace to deliver her to the king.

Squaring her shoulders, a distressful frown marring her features, she walked forward and came to stand directly before Henry. Confronted with his thunderous expression, she took but a moment to remember the proprieties. Lifting her skirts, she knelt before him.

"Enough," he said.

Glancing at Ranulf, Lizanne straightened.

" 'Tis time you wed, Lady Lizanne," Henry began. His tone was similar to one her father had used with her whenever she misbehaved. "For too long, you have been a burden to your brother, but now 'tis time for that burden to be passed on." He smiled at that.

Lizanne's frown deepened. She did not find his witticism amusing in the least, but knew she dared not say so.

"Once again," he continued, "I have taken it upon myself to find you a suitable match. This time, though"—he pointed a warning finger at her—"you will not challenge me. I intend to see you wed this day, and hence, I expect to hear no more of your unladylike escapades. Is that understood?"

She swept her gaze to the priest, her jaw working as his presence in the hall became indelibly clear. It was most certainly understood that the king intended to wed her before she could foil his attempts a second time.

She glanced again to Ranulf and Philip, and her entire being filled with dread. It was Philip he intended to wed her to, and it would seem Ranulf was prepared to hand her over himself.

A wave of nausea and dizziness struck simultaneously, washing her face of all color. Why would Philip consent to a marriage he had years earlier refused? she wondered. She was less pure now than she had been all those years ago.

She simply could not help herself. "But, Your Majesty—"

"It is understood, Lady Lizanne?" Henry bellowed, his face reddening.

Eyes downcast, she nodded.

"You will look at me when I address you!" His booted foot struck the platform to add emphasis to his words.

Drawing a deep breath, Lizanne lifted her eyes and nodded again. "Aye, Your Majesty . . . 'tis understood."

Triumphantly, he smiled and leaned back in his great chair. "I am pleased we finally understand each other." Sighing loudly, he leveled his gaze first upon Ranulf, then Philip.

"In spite of your most recent behavior, I have decided to be generous with you. The queen believes 'twould be fitting to give you a choice in the matter of whom you will wed. Thus, I give you the choice between these two knights."

Uncomprehendingly, Lizanne stared at the king. Then, with a muttered oath, which she quickly clapped a hand to, she spun around to face Ranulf and Philip. Ranulf was offering for her as well? But had he not told her he had declined? She could hardly believe it. Surely, the king had forced it upon him. Her heart heavy, she met those black eyes.

Arms folded over his chest, Ranulf stared unwaveringly at her. She read tension there—anger. Aye, he did not do this willingly.

Sweeping a tongue over her lips, she shifted her gaze to Philip. He looked self-assured, a charming smile on his face. Though she had once thought him the most handsome of men, in that instant she could not help but compare him to Ranulf. He paled considerably.

"Well?" the king pressed when she remained unmoving.

Brows knit, she shook her head. "I—I cannot," she whispered. As if from a distance, she heard Philip's sharply indrawn breath.

Henry leaned forward. "I have given you a choice, Lady Lizanne. I warn you not to test me further. Either choose one of these men to wed or prepare yourself to enter a convent." He gave his words a moment to sink in, then jabbed a finger toward the men. "Now be quick about it. I am a busy man and have other, more pressing matters that must needs be attended to."

A convent? In desperation, she latched on to the horrid alternative he had thrown her way. "Then I choose the convent," she said, throwing her chin into the air.

Henry turned a deep crimson that made it difficult to discern where skin ended and hair began.

All too aware of his displeasure, Lizanne nervously sought out the queen, but the woman had turned her attention elsewhere, staring off into the distance as if uninterested in the discord that hung thickly upon the air.

Slowly, Henry regained his natural color. "Hmm," he mused, rubbing his hand over his beard. "Then I withdraw the option of the convent."

Lizanne took a faltering step forward. "But you cannot!"

"What?" He came straight up out of his chair. "You dare question my authority? I may do anything with you that I please, and that includes beheading you for your insolence."

She quelled beneath his anger. "Forgive me, Your Majesty. 'Tis just that the other option does not so much appeal to me."

Henry turned and stared hard at Ranulf and Philip. "I see before me two worthy men with whom you can bear children, Lady Lizanne. Now, either you choose or I will do it for you—and I cannot guarantee you will be pleased with my choice."

Knowing there was nothing left but to have done with it, Lizanne drew a deep, calming breath and contemplated each man. "One is as bad as the other," she muttered, although she already knew whom she would choose.

"Did you say something?" the king asked in a voice grown tight with irritation.

She shook her head. "Nay, Your Majesty. I will make my choice now." But she would make certain there was some measure of humiliation for the two knights to suffer as she did. Squaring her shoulders, she walked first to Ranulf. Planting her hands on her hips, she tilted her face close to his. "'Tis out of your hands now," she whispered, loud enough only for him to hear.

Her words were met with a perceptible narrowing of his eyes, but otherwise he remained motionless.

Consideringly, she stepped back and ran her gaze down his muscled length. Then, round and round him she walked, her jaw firmly set as she appraised him in much the same way she'd seen Gilbert measure the worthiness of a stallion.

Boldly, she reached out and touched his hair, rubbing it thoughtfully between her fingers. Then she tested an arm, her hand spanning less than half its bulging diameter. "Hmm," she murmured.

Tapping a finger to her lips, she walked around him once again and, as a final insult, leaned down to test his calf.

Throughout the entire ordeal, Ranulf forced himself to utter stillness, but his eyes, when Lizanne met them, belied his calm and warned of dire consequences for her degradation.

She smiled thinly. Then, shaking her head, she moved across to where Philip stood. He looked positively confident, smiling lazily at her.

She smiled back, though it did not reach her eyes. She subjected Philip to much the same appraisal she had given Ranulf. He, too, grew still, his bearing emanating increasing outrage as she examined him.

Hands on her hips, she rounded Philip a last time and came to stand before him. "Do you wrestle?" she asked, her voice carrying to the other occupants of the hall.

Remembering the story she had related to him of her encounter with Sir Arthur, Ranulf nearly choked on his tongue. Pressing his lips together, he glanced at Henry and Eleanor. Although the king looked thunderous, the queen appeared to have enjoyed Lizanne's thinly veiled taunt, pressing a hand to her lips to hide the evidence of her amusement.

Initially, having found Lizanne's display entertaining, the king had been tolerant, but of a sudden, he grew annoyed. "Enough of your games," he roared. "Choose!"

Sighing loudly, Lizanne placed her hand on Philip's arm and stiffly turned to face Ranulf. Her brows lifting, she offered him a self-satisfied smile and a shrug.

Ranulf could not remember seeing her look lovelier, or more untouchable. His anger grew to immense proportions. Her choice was obvious. As he had suspected, she would wed that bastard Philip.

Lizanne's next words took a moment to sink in.

Philip roared for clarification.

Chapter 16

I choose," *Lizanne* repeated, disdainfully removing her hand from Philip's arm, "Ranulf Wardieu." Her eyes found Ranulf's and held them as she walked toward him.

If the circumstances had not been so tragic, she thought she might have enjoyed the look of utter confusion and disbelief on his face. However, she only pitied him his predicament. He had wanted this no more than she, but he'd had no choice in the matter. Placing her hand on his tensed arm, she turned to face Henry and Eleanor.

"A fine choice!" the king exclaimed.

Ranulf was as dumbfounded as Philip was infuriated, every last particle of his anger draining from him as he stared at Lizanne's determined profile. Immense relief poured through him. So Walter had been correct. . . .

When Lizanne had taken such humiliatingly precise measure of him, he had berated himself for becoming a party to such antics, especially knowing she would not choose him. Was it possible she hated Philip more strongly than she hated him? Or, perhaps, she had realized the error of her accusations?

She turned and looked unwaveringly into his eyes.

"I have kept my vow to you," she said softly. "I only hope you do not rue it as much as I."

In the presence of God, King Henry, Eleanor, and a modest gathering of Ranulf's men, Lizanne and Ranulf stood before the priest an hour later and exchanged vows. It would have been sooner, but the queen had been adamant about the proper attire such an occasion warranted, and Lizanne's borrowed garments had been deemed entirely unacceptable.

Three seamstresses had quickly altered one of Eleanor's own gowns to fit Lizanne, a cream-colored samite heavily embroidered with silver and gold threads, to which a flounce had been added to accommodate Lizanne's height. Despondent, she had sat unmoving while her hair had been tamed and arranged beneath a light veil secured to her crown with a garland of flowers.

When Lizanne had been escorted across the hall, she'd had no notion of the comely picture she presented until she'd met Ranulf's gaze. She did not think she would ever forget the way his eyes had settled upon her. It was almost as if he were seeing her for the first time.

Throughout the entire ceremony, Lizanne stared at her fisted hands where they rested in the voluminous skirts, looking up only once to repeat the vows given her. She did not understand why she should be, but she was increasingly pained at having forced Ranulf to this travesty of a marriage. It had been wrong of her, she knew, but she could not have chosen Philip. What her childish eyes had been blinded to years ago, she had clearly understood when she had seen him yesterday.

When Ranulf lifted her chin to drop a kiss upon her lips, she hadn't time to respond before he drew away again. She swayed, then steadied herself, and focused on the smiling faces moving in from all sides.

Geoff was the first to make it to her side. Grinning

broadly, he gave her a quick, affectionate squeeze. "You are truly my lady, now," he said.

She tried to smile but failed miserably. Instead, her eyes pooled with hot tears that caught in her lashes. Of a sudden, a hand extending a small square of cloth emerged from the throng of people. Glancing in that direction, she looked into Walter's face and stilled. Although the corners of his mouth were only slightly curved, he was definitely smiling.

Smiling at her? But why, for God's sake? She would not have thought him to be pleased with this marriage. Did he not dislike her?

The cloth fluttered beneath her nose again, breaking her out of her reverie. Grateful, she accepted the offering and dabbed at her eyes, then lowered her hand to the folds of her skirts, her fingers crumpling the soft linen square.

Sensitive to her churning emotions, Ranulf turned from the well-wishers and caught her hand. Gently, he pulled her against his side.

Swallowing convulsively, Lizanne looked up at him and was surprised to find him smiling as well. Her heart tumbled over itself.

He pulled her closer, turning her body into his, and touched his lips to her temple. "Let us make the best of this, hmm?" he whispered, the warm sweep of his breath raising the hairs along her arms.

She nodded. "I will try . . . husband."

Although she could not see it, he smiled, liking that word on her lips.

A moment later, they were swept along to the main hall where a hastily prepared but worthy feast was laid out to honor their marriage.

Lizanne was overwhelmed by the throng of people awaiting them. It seemed as if all of London had turned out for the occasion.

The men were quick to congratulate Ranulf, slapping

him on the back, cuffing him on the shoulder, and muttering words in his ear that Lizanne could only guess at.

In contrast, most of the women seemed less than enthusiastic, especially the younger ladies who gazed at the handsome groom with eyes full of longing and regret.

Frowning, Lizanne turned and looked at Ranulf's strong profile, her eyes narrowing as she tried to see him in a different light from the one corrupted by the anger and hate of her past. Through new eyes, she saw for the first time what others already knew. Not only was Ranulf peculiarly handsome with that shock of long pale hair, but he was young and virile. And he was a baron held in high regard by the king. He was honorable . . . patient . . . kind. . . .

Aye, it was envy that held the other women from her. No doubt each thought herself more worthy a match for Ranulf than she with her wild black hair and bothersome height that topped the majority by inches.

Her musings were hauled up short as her last observations returned to her with a suddenness that seemed to turn her whole world upside down. Honorable, patient, kind?

The acknowledgment that he possessed such inconceivable qualities thoroughly shook the foundation upon which she had built her case against him. Whence had come these beliefs? The man who had tried to defile her had not possessed any of those qualities, yet the one she had wed truly seemed to.

"Lizanne?" Ranulf's voice reached her as if from a great distance.

Startled, she lifted her gaze to his. "Hmm?"

"All is well?"

She nodded and forced a stiff smile. "Aye, I am fine."

He did not believe her but had no time to pursue the matter when the king suddenly appeared.

"Come, Baron Wardieu," he said, "do not keep your bride to yourself. Share your good fortune."

Seeing Ranulf's obvious reluctance to abandon her, Henry laughed. "I will not keep you long," he said. "I would just have your opinion on a matter that vexes me. Come."

Ranulf offered Lizanne an apologetic smile before following the king to do his bidding.

Dismayed, Lizanne watched the two men disappear among the crowd. Finding herself alone, though still under intense scrutiny, she edged her way among the people in search of the friendly comfort of Geoff and Roland. Surely, they were nearby?

She did not find them, but Walter found her.

"My lady," he said, "your husband has not so soon deserted you, has he?" A sympathetic smile showed his teeth.

Lizanne was truly grateful to see a familiar face among the crowd, even if it belonged to the redoubtable Sir Walter. "I fear the king has taken him off," she said, her own smile rueful.

He grimaced. "On his wedding day?" At her nod, he sighed. "Then perhaps you could suffer my company for a few moments."

Untold relief sweeping her, Lizanne offered a genuine smile, her lone dimple turning inward.

Walter was momentarily fascinated by the indentation. He had not known that such a canted smile could be so lovely and captivating. It completely transformed her features.

"You do not trust me alone?" she bantered, as he led her out of the press and to an unoccupied corner of the hall.

His brows shot up, but still he smiled. "Truly, I had not considered that," he said, leaning back against the wall. "But, since 'tis you who has brought it up, mayhap you can tell me if you intend to continue bedeviling my lord now that you are wed?"

Her smile fell. "Though you will not believe me, Sir Walter, 'twas not evil which drove me to my transgressions against Ranulf. At the time, I felt my actions were more than justified."

He considered the return of anguish to her features. "Hmm," he murmured. "And now?"

She lowered her eyes and stared at the toes of her shoes. "Now I am not so certain. Mayhap I have erred," she admitted, "though logic dictates otherwise."

"Then which will you follow?" he asked, silently imploring her to look at him. "Your heart or your head, my lady?"

Lizanne was surprised by his unexpected question, staring wide-eyed at him as she attempted to sort through her feelings. "Perhaps both."

It was obvious he was not overly pleased with her vague answer. "At least lead with your heart," he suggested.

Warmed by his concern, she smiled again. "I will think on it. But tell me, do you lead with your heart?" Something told her it was more than casual advice he offered.

Immediately, he looked away, shifting his feet and loudly clearing his throat. "You would like something to drink?"

She laughed. "Your heart or your head, Sir Walter? You have not answered me."

"Nay, and I do not intend to."

She grimaced but backed down. "All right, but it seems hardly fair that you expect me to take advice that you yourself have not proven worthy."

"I did not say I have not. . . ." His voice trailed off as he realized she had very nearly led him down the path he was trying so hard to avoid.

Seeing she had lost the battle, Lizanne sighed and

settled her folded arms across her chest. "Why, of a sudden, are you so kind to me?"

"Am I?"

She nodded. "Aye. As I recall, you not so long ago took great pleasure in calling me a viper."

He pulled a face. "Did I? Aye, I suppose I did."

"And what has changed your opinion?"

"I have not said it has changed," he teased.

Her dark, arched brows shot upward. "You still think me a viper, then?"

He laughed at her mock indignation. "Nay, I do not."

"I am pleased to hear that." She wrinkled her nose. In the silence that followed, her stomach rumbled alarmingly. Embarrassed, she pressed a hand to it and shrugged.

"You have not eaten, have you?"

"Not since yesterday."

Rolling his eyes, Walter motioned to the tables laden with every delight imaginable. "There is food aplenty here. Wait you here and I will bring you a plate."

Aye, Walter thought as he walked off, the Lady Lizanne was not so bad after all. He only hoped she and Ranulf could resolve their differences and set about making a peaceable life together. Ranulf needed an heir for his vast properties and, unlike the beautiful Arabella, Lizanne would probably beget him many strong sons and daughters.

Alone again, Lizanne looked around her. Nowhere did she see Geoff or Roland, although she recognized several of the Wardieu knights. With growing interest, she watched as they vied for the attention of the serving wenches and unwed ladies who were far outnumbered by men in the hall.

It was quite interesting, this ritual, she thought as she studied the beautifully clothed ladies weaving in and around the groups of men.

Looking down at her wedding gown, Lizanne was suddenly grateful the queen had had the foresight to provide her with such finery on this, her wedding day. The garment was splendid, emphasizing her narrow waist and flattering—

Abruptly, she caught herself, disturbed that she should appreciate such feminine attire with the depth of feeling she had been experiencing. It had been years since she'd last taken any real interest in her appearance. Was this what marriage did to a woman?

She shook her head. Nay, it was what a man like Ranulf did to her. She groaned inwardly. What had happened? Where was the cloak of masculinity that had served her so well during the past four years? Should she not be wishing for a loose, comfortable tunic and the freedom of chausses and boots? It simply did not make sense.

"All alone?" a derisive voice said at her side, breaking her out of her churning thoughts.

She snapped her head around, her eyes coming level with Philip Charwyck's glacial stare. He stood not two feet to her right, his expression clearly born of resentment and barely contained anger.

She felt a tremor of unexplainable fear course through her. "Nay," she managed. "Sir Walter has gone to fetch me something to eat."

Although her announcement was meant to serve more as a warning than be informative, Philip deigned to ignore it. "Not your husband?" he asked, sarcasm lacing his words. "Curious, but mayhap he is as averse to used goods as I. Think you he is seeking his pleasures elsewhere?"

Indignant, Lizanne turned to fully face him. That he would throw into her face the reason for his rejection of her all those years ago deeply pained her. It was beyond cruel. Her first instinct was to launch herself at him, but, with clenched fists and a firm resolve, she quelled it.

Knowing that to remain might mean an unpleasant confrontation, she straightened herself to her full height and started to step past him.

Immediately, his hand shot out and captured her wrist. He halted her departure and pulled her nearer. "Think you I wished to wed with a woman who so freely gave herself to another?" he hissed. "Nay! I am grateful for your consideration in choosing that great white beast."

"You sound as if you are trying to convince yourself of it," Lizanne retorted, glaring into his reddened eyes. "You seemed all too willing to take me to wife earlier, and more than a little disappointed at my rejection of your offer." Any moment, she thought, he was going to begin frothing at the mouth.

"Do not mistake my desire for your body as anything but that," he said. "Just because you are now wed to another does not mean you cannot share my bed as well—and I do intend to have you in it."

She tugged to free her arm. "Release me!" she ordered, fighting down the urge to scream it for all to hear.

His fingers bit into the fine bones of her wrist. Frantically, she looked about, but for once, all eyes were elsewhere. Should she risk causing an unpleasant scene?

"Not a soul would notice if we slipped away." His moist breath fanned her ear. "Come with me now, and I will teach you the pleasures of the flesh."

Bile, thick and burning, rose in her throat. Swallowing to force it down, she turned and looked at him. "You desire me? After I have whored myself all over England?"

His eyes widened. He looked thoroughly taken aback by her declaration. "So 'tis true you were Baron Wardieu's leman," he concluded.

She swallowed again but refused the impulse to look away. Her insides were all jumbled, first anger, then revulsion, and finally fear struggling to the fore. Her pride would not let the weaker two of the three emotions prevail. Grasping hold of the anger, she shoved her face near his.

"Think you I would deny it?" She laughed bitterly. "Nay, I am proud to have lain with him. He is an expert lover. You think I would let you touch me when I have him to satisfy my needs?"

She watched his face deepen with color. "Nay," she finished, "I would not lower myself to your touch—or your canine slaverings. Though were I to, I daresay there is little you could teach me that my husband has not already done."

Slowly, Philip recovered from her verbal onslaught. "I will have you, Lizanne Wardieu," he said, his breathing harsh and shallow. "And when I have disposed of your husband, 'twill not be marriage I offer you."

Although his threat shook her, she forced her face to an impassiveness she did not feel. He was no longer looking at her, though, his attention turned to something beyond her.

"Unhand me," she said, and was surprised when he did, viciously throwing her hand away from him. Glancing over her shoulder, she realized he had only done so because of Walter's return. And beside him strode Ranulf, his expression thunderous as he looked from her to Philip.

"Your husband," Philip said, capturing her gaze one last time, "does he not remind you of someone—a common villein, perhaps?" Then, with a wickedly knowing smile, he turned and immersed himself in the throng of people.

A common villein—Darth. Staring after him, Lizanne felt the walls close in around her, their thickness suffocating as her anger fell away, replaced by the weaker emotions she had earlier discarded.

Clasping a hand to her throat, she drew in ragged breaths of air as the floor began to shift and yawn beneath her feet.

Nay, she could not faint now—not here. A cold chill breaking over her, she spun around to face Ranulf and Walter.

Through the narrowing field of her vision, she saw they were nearly upon her, their faces mirroring alarm as they caught sight of her. She blinked rapidly to bring Ranulf back into focus, but he blurred and then disappeared altogether. She was falling, she realized, instinctively throwing her hands out before her.

In the darkening haze of her consciousness, she felt strong arms come around her.

Chapter 17

'Tis a fine night for a raid, my lord," the squire, Joseph, pronounced, his voice pitched higher than usual at the prospect of the venture about to be undertaken.

It was indeed a fine night, the young man's lord thought, propping his hands on his hips and turning his dark head to assess the situation.

Though warm, the night was cloaked in the tenor of a bracing wind that stirred the leaves of the trees. He and his men stood on the edge of a glade, from which a mighty stronghold rose against an inky black-blue sky. The wind howled hauntingly across the open grassed land and buffeted the unsuspecting castle. With a vengeance, it churned the water in the wide stretch of moat surrounding the stone walls.

Though near full, the moon slid in and out of thick, intermittent cloud cover that had stolen in just before dusk. When obscured by the billowing white-gray mass, it would shed only enough light to facilitate passage over the hilly terrain. Although this favored the raiders, it would likely prove a hindrance to the men-at-arms who walked the parapet along the crenellated walls.

Still, the lord concluded, turning back to his squire, they would have to be cautious, for the castle appeared to be in a state of readiness. There could be no mistakes this night.

Shifting restlessly in their saddles, the many soldiers watched with mounting excitement as the chosen few were given final instructions and their weapons secured fast to avoid any unnecessary noise.

They set off when the moon was completely obscured behind a long bank of clouds, and when next it briefly appeared, they were halfway to their destination. As the moonlight shone down, each man threw himself facedown in the long, waving grass and waited for the protection of darkness to come again. They waited a long time, but they were at last able to make it to the bank of the moat.

At the most likely point of vulnerability—the southernmost wall—they gathered before the lapping water and knelt in the thick, sheltering undergrowth at the precise moment the moon reappeared. Again they waited, their eyes searching for signs of movement among the crenellations. They found it.

When darkness fell once again, the lord was the first to enter the bone-chilling, muddy water, steeling his mind against the discomfort that penetrated his clothing and pierced his skin.

Their progress was mercilessly slow, the mud sucking at their feet as it attempted to pull them under the murky depths. At the midpoint, the ground dropped sharply beneath them, and they were forced to swim. To avoid losing the benefit of their blackened faces, they paddled awkwardly, struggling to hold their heads above the agitated water.

At the sloping base of the great wall, they once again found treacherous purchase for their feet and dragged themselves up the side. Water swirling about their hips, the wind whipping around their wet torsos, they waited for many minutes, listening for the sound of the guard who patrolled that particular stretch of wall above them. Finally, they heard him, his boots scraping the walkway as he passed overhead. When his footfalls faded, the young squire was urged forward, two men-at-arms holding him steady in the shifting mud.

Deftly, Joseph fit his bow with the prepared arrow, to which a padded hook was attached. Trailing behind this was a coil of light, albeit wet, rope, which one of the knights laid across his arms to ensure a smooth ascent.

None could dispute Joseph's skill. It was the very reason he had been chosen for this all-important task. Although not particularly skilled with any other weapon, he was nearly unrivaled with the bow.

Drawing the string taut, the squire raised the weapon and gauged the air's erratic movement, waiting for the brief stillness that would best ensure the arrow's accuracy. In readiness for its release, he lifted up a silent prayer that his hand would be steady and his aim true. When he let go the string, the arrow sailed upward, higher and higher, struggling to maintain its course as the wind revived itself and shifted directions. Miraculously, the feathered shaft dived in a graceful arc over the wall and fell with a dull thud.

The lord was the first to go. His arms strong and able, he wasted no time scaling the wall and shortly lowered himself to the parapet on the opposite side. Crouching low, he made the rope secure, then yanked on it. He felt it grow taut as the first of his men began the journey upward.

The torches placed about the outer bailey gave him a good idea of the castle's layout, though he had already gathered much from the man he'd had slip through the walls earlier in the day with a group of peasants. The news that the baron had not yet returned had baffled him, but it had also offered a rare opportunity to capture the hold with the least amount of resistance.

One by one, the soldiers came over the wall and scattered to their preassigned positions. The squire, Joseph, was the last. He dropped down beside his lord, and the two promptly made their way from the parapet to the bailey below. It was no simple task, for there were many guards about, and thrice they had to silence a wayward guard in their progression toward the donjon.

Leaving the squire to watch outside, the lord entered the great, darkened hall, dagger in hand. The sound of sleeping men, women, and children guided him over the dimly lit, rush-covered floor. Warily, he mounted the stone steps, flinching at the echo of his sodden advance that seemed to bounce off the walls of the narrow passageway. At the first landing, he craned his neck around the corner and studied the wide, torch-lit corridor stretching before him.

All was quiet.

Too quiet? he wondered as he crept to the door of the chamber he had been informed the lady of the keep occupied. His ear to the door, he listened. All was silent, so with a barely perceptible grating, he pushed the door inward, revealing a room softly lit by the glow of a dying fire. His gaze fixed on the large bed where the still form of his prey lay. Easing the door closed behind him, he quickly assessed the situation, then moved forward.

On a pallet at the foot of the bed slept the lady's maid. He subdued her first, shoving a wad of cloth into her mouth before trussing her hand and foot. Eyes wide with terror, she stared up at him. One side of his mouth lifting derisively, he gave her a pat on the rear end, then straightened and crept around the bed.

As he drew near, the lady beneath the coverlet suddenly sat bolt upright and turned sleep-laden eyes on him. Immediately, she drew a breath to scream.

Launching himself across the bed, he pounced on her, pushing her back into the mattress. His forceful lunge knocked the breath from her and left her gasping for air even as he fit his hand over her mouth.

He listened, and within moments he heard the

alarm being raised throughout the stronghold. He prayed his men were in position and the reinforcements riding to cross the lowered drawbridge. If all went well, within minutes the castle would be under their control—with or without this woman.

Regaining her breath, the lady began to struggle beneath him, her legs flailing, her hooked hands flying.

He muttered an oath when her knee slammed into his leg. His anger flaring, he threw himself off the bed and dragged her with him. He kept his hand firmly clamped over her mouth and pressed her against his damply clothed body, encircling her with his free arm. Still, she fought him.

When she finally stilled, he pulled her into the light of the fire. Its pulsing warmth felt wonderful against his chilled body, but he could ill afford to enjoy it.

Defiantly, the lady lifted her head and stared at him, eyes glittering like black chips of coal that spoke loudly of her outrage and . . . fear.

For her age, Baron Ranulf Wardieu's mother was still a lovely woman, the lord realized, her skin relatively smooth and clear, the figure beneath his hands decidedly slender—not skeletal but softly rounded. Her long hair was nearly as light as her son's, but interspersed with darker strands of gray. There the resemblance to the bastard ended, for her features were delicate and refined, and she was nowhere near the height or breadth of him.

It was difficult to believe this petite woman could have borne such a son. But her hair was testament to that unfortunate distinction.

"If you behave yourself, you need not fear me, Lady Zara," he found himself reassuring her, and wondered why he felt he should even bother. "I come only to recover that which is mine . . . and to repay your son a very old debt."

The woman's eyes widened in silent question, but he deigned not to waste any time enlightening her. Instead, he raised the tip of his dagger to her slender throat and slowly removed his hand from her mouth.

Her eyes shifted downward to the weapon; she did not utter a sound.

Taking her arm, he pulled her to the door, and together they stepped out into the long corridor. The other members of the household were rushing frantically about, spilling from their chambers as he drew his captive past them. They could only stare in horror as the great, blackened man made for the stairs with their lady in tow.

In the main hall, which had been hastily though poorly lit by torches, the invader halted and waited for all eyes to turn to him. Beyond, through doors thrown wide open, came the thundering of hooves as his men descended upon the inner bailey. There would be resistance, he knew, but his skilled soldiers would soon put order to their invasion, and the threat to the Lady Zara would mean less bloodshed.

It was only moments before his presence was noted, a great hush falling over the people as they stared from him to their lady, and the dagger pressed to her throat.

"Send word to your garrison leader that I hold the Lady Zara," he shouted. "Only if he agrees to a complete, unconditional surrender will no harm befall her."

"My son will slay you for this injury," the lady spit.

"Not if I slay him first," he returned.

Ignoring the blade near her throat, she began to struggle. "Unhand me, you villain!" she demanded, then swung her hand and connected with the side of his face.

Rage shot through him, but he did not retaliate. "Villain?" His voice came dangerously soft as he tightened his grip. "I am Baron Gilbert Balmaine of Penforke."

Eyes ablaze, she stared up at him. "Aye, I know who you are," she snapped, "though I would not deign to bestow such an esteemed title upon one such as yourself." Disdainfully, she swept her gaze over him.

Gilbert laughed, a harsh, grating sound. "Then 'tis true you were forewarned. That surprises me. Truly, I do not think much of the defense of this holding. 'Twas far too easy to breach."

"You are vile," she said indignantly. "Had you come but a day earlier, 'twould have been a far different ending to your attack."

" 'Twas foolish to let your guard down so quickly."

"One would not expect a seasoned knight to dally so long," she retorted. "You are seasoned, are you not? Or did you obtain that limp chasing about your mother's skirts?"

She truly had no way of knowing how very close to the edge she had pushed him. Reaching deep within himself, Gilbert found the strength to pull back from the precipice.

Chapter 18

Leaning forward, Ranulf rested a palm on the stone-work framing the window and looked out at the starry night. It had been hours since Lizanne had collapsed in the hall, but still she slept.

He was angry with himself for having let the king convince him to leave her side in the first place. Dammit, he had known better! he berated himself, and not for the first time. She had been in no state to fend for herself among those people.

He had been dismayed, and aye, jealous, to come upon her conversing with Philip Charwyck, their bodies so close as to be nearly touching. The other man's swift retreat and Lizanne's subsequent faint raised questions that, as yet, remained unanswered.

His men had been unable to locate Charwyck, but word had finally come that the man had left the palace forthwith, taking his small retinue with him. Ranulf had wanted to go after him but had chosen to stay with Lizanne.

Wearily, he looked over his shoulder to where she lay upon the bed. The candlelight flickered over her face, made even paler by the tumble of black hair spread around her. Straining, he could hear her slow, even breathing.

Queen Eleanor's personal physician had shrugged off his concerns and told him that, when she was ready to awaken, she would. It was exhaustion and excitement, he had said, not to mention her disregard for nourishment.

That last had bothered Ranulf. Although he'd had a tray sent to her the night before, the chambermaid had reported that nothing had been touched. Knowing the state she had been in when he'd left her yestereve, he upbraided himself for not having made certain she ate something. Especially after the pitiful way in which she had picked at her midday meal.

Still, he could not shake the feeling there was more to it than the physician's diagnosis. He was certain her faint had to do with the exchange he'd witnessed between her and Charwyck.

Rubbing a hand over his face, he crossed to the bed, then lowered himself into the chair he had dragged beside it. Leaning forward, he brushed the hair from Lizanne's face. Her lids flickered, and he thought he heard her moan, but he couldn't be sure.

"Lizanne?" he said, touching the back of his hand to her cool cheek. Her breathing changed perceptibly as she turned her face and nuzzled his palm.

Lifting himself out of the chair, Ranulf leaned closer and ran his knuckles over her jaw, brushing his thumb across her softly parted lips. Her lashes fluttered, revealing the sparkling slits of her eyes.

"Ran . . ." she sighed, a smile working its way across her lips. Lifting her lids higher, she reached up and touched his face.

Relief, quick and warm, flooded through him. Turning his face into her palm, he kissed her cool skin. Her fingers curled around the heat he left there, and she lowered her arm back to her side.

"How are you feeling?" he asked, settling himself upon the edge of the bed, his thigh pressed against her side.

"Tired," Lizanne answered, then frowned as the remembrance of her confrontation with Philip flooded back to her. The deep, terrible shock she had felt at his parting words had been her undoing. "Your husband, does he not remind you of someone? A common villein . . ." Abruptly, she pushed the memory away. She did not want to think about it now.

"I am sorry if I embarrassed you," she muttered with distress. "I do not know why I fainted."

Lifting her hand, Ranulf cradled it in his larger one and rubbed his thumb across her pulse. "Don't you?"

"I—I suppose I should have eaten more," she lamely confessed, "and I did not sleep well yestereve."

"Hmm. And the wedding, of course."

Grasping at his offer of yet another viable excuse, she nodded. "That too," she agreed, encouraged by his understanding smile. Then her brow furrowed. "I'm also terribly sorry for that, Ranulf."

His hand stilled. "You are?" he asked, his smile slipping. But of course she was, he reminded himself. Had she not voiced her preference for entering a convent over marriage to either him or Charwyck?

Lowering her eyes, she nodded, then struggled to sit up.

Ranulf assisted her.

"Aye," she said, leaning back against the bed support, unaware of the provocative way her thin shift outlined her firm, thrusting breasts. Clasping her hands in her lap, she stared at them before continuing. "I should not have forced it upon you, but there was no other alternative. You understand, don't you?"

Nay, he did not understand, but he intended to. "No alternative? But the king gave you a choice— Charwyck or me."

Shaking her head, she laughed bitterly. "A choice? Nay, Ranulf, that was no choice. I would never have married Philip, even if the king had given me no other option. Methinks I would have died first."

"Why?"

She wavered, uncertain as to the course she was setting for herself.

Ranulf covered her hands with his and leaned toward her. "I am your husband now, Lizanne. You must share these things with me if we are to live in peace. You must trust me."

Trust him . . . It would take no great effort to do so, she realized with wonder, and she so wanted to.

Drawing a deep breath, she nodded. "If there was anyone I hated as much as you, Ranulf, it was Philip. I grew up loving him. I idolized him, followed him everywhere. To my childish eyes, he was so perfect and so handsome." She dropped her head back and stared up at the canopy, chewing her bottom lip as she fought to regain her slipping composure.

Ranulf waited, his insides twisting at the emotion in her voice and the jealousy that surged through him at her admission of love for another man.

"He was never really very kind to me, though," she continued. "I was tall for my age—awkward—and cursed with this black horse's tail for hair." She flipped her hand through the tangled mass. "Doubtless, he found me less than appealing." She sighed. "Beneath my nose, and my father's, he trysted with the women servants of our castle."

Ranulf watched with unease the myriad emotions sweeping across her lovely face.

"Though it hurt deeply to see him behave in such a manner, in the end it hardly mattered. You see, Philip belonged to me. There was never any question that I would one day become his wife and bear him children. 'Twas my destiny, and I embraced it as only a child could." She leveled her gaze to his. "For two years, I had not seen him but had thought of him every day. I was on my way to the wedding. Gilbert was with me when—when our camp was attacked. We were taken by surprise."

Her jaw clenched. "When I saw Gilbert, I was sure he was dead. There was so much blood everywhere. . . ."

"But he lived," Ranulf said.

She bobbed her head. "Aye, he is strong-willed—more than I." A faint smile flashed across her face, quickly disappearing.

"And when Philip refused to wed me," she said in a rush, "it killed my father."

"And you still think 'twas I who maimed your brother and tried to take your virtue that night?" Ranulf interjected, his voice harsher than he intended it to be.

She looked away from the pain etched in his features, her face beginning to crumple. Raising her hands, she covered it. "I don't know anymore," she said, her voice choked. "I was so certain 'twas you, but now . . ."

Hope blossomed within Ranulf.

Shaking her head, she lowered her hands and stared into his eyes. "Trust is not so easy for me, Ranulf. I have lived too long with these painful memories to so quickly discard them . . . though I want to."

It wasn't much she offered, but it was more than she'd previously allowed. Wordlessly, Ranulf stood and strode across the room to the hearth. He returned moments later and placed a tray of viands on the bed beside her.

"You are to eat everything," he said, then lowered himself into the chair again.

Solemnly, Lizanne tucked her legs beneath her and reached for a meat pie.

Not until she had consumed a goodly portion of the meal did he voice the question uppermost in his mind. "I would know what Sir Philip said to upset you so."

She blinked.

"Lizanne." His tone was admonishing. "Do not think to tell me he said naught, for I will not believe you. Now tell me."

She raked her teeth over her bottom lip and shifted her eyes to look past him. " 'Tis not important."

Grasping the tails of his patience, Ranulf folded his arms over his chest and stared grimly at her. "I will be the judge as to whether or not 'tis important. Now you will tell me what he said."

Realizing he was not going to back down, she acquiesced. "He was angry," she began, her fingers working restlessly over the coverlet. "He said it mattered not that I was wed to you. That he would still . . . have me." She looked up to gauge his reaction, but only met his unreadable black eyes.

"And?" he prompted, knowing there was more.

"He said he was going to dispose of you."

"Dispose of me?" Ranulf laughed, as if the very idea was farcical. "He intends to try to kill me?"

"Aye, I am sure of it."

"What else?"

Philip's parting words echoing in her mind, Lizanne looked away. She did not fully understand her reluctance to share them with Ranulf but knew she could not. The implications frightened her terribly. She would first have to think on it some more.

" 'Tis all," she said, slipping down beneath the covers.

Nay, it was not all, but Ranulf did not pursue it further. Leaning forward, he pressed his lips to hers before she could offer a protest, then drew back. "Get you some sleep," he said, and turned to leave.

Wide-eyed, she reached out and caught his hand. "You are not staying?" she asked disbelievingly. It was, after all, their wedding night. He had every right to claim it. And besides, she truly did not want him to leave.

He looked back at her. "Were you well, wife, I would take what your eyes offer, but 'tis better that you do not suffer my attentions this night. We will have our wedding night when we reach Chesne."

What her eyes offered? Lizanne's indignation flared for but a moment before she allowed honesty to douse the flames. Aye, whether or not Ranulf was the villain she had believed him to be, she still wanted him.

"I—I do not wish to be alone," she said softly. "Won't you stay with me?"

That she would allow her pride to be trampled by the admission that she desired his company was so unexpected, Ranulf was momentarily dumbfounded. When at last he spoke, his voice sounded strained to his ears. "And where would you have me sleep?"

Blushing, she looked to the chair he had just vacated, then smoothed her hand across the bed. "Here," she said.

Ranulf could not help but smile. "Think you it safe?"

She still could not bring herself to meet his gaze. "You could just hold me," she offered, then raked her teeth over her bottom lip as she awaited his reply.

"Ah, torture," Ranulf breathed. "Is that what you have in mind for me, wife?"

She looked back at him to find his dark eyes twinkling with suppressed laughter. " 'Twas not my intention," she said, then smiled. "Would it really be so bad?"

He nodded. "Aye, but so long as you do not plan on chaining me to a wall, I am willing."

Hiding her smile, Lizanne folded back the covers and invited her husband to share her bed.

Chapter 19

Chesne," *Ranulf announced,* his voice filled with emotion for the land spread before him. The three days' ride from London had seemed like a dozen. Not only because he longed to be home, but because he had not yet exercised his husband's rights over Lizanne. At Chesne he would have her again, though, and their life together would finally begin.

"What do you see, Lizanne?" he asked.

She frowned at the unexpectedness of his question. "Land," she answered simply, then added, "fertile land." Shrugging, she looked over her shoulder at him.

He was obviously not pleased with her answer. "And?" he prodded.

Gnawing her lip, she looked again. " 'Tis all," she concluded. "What would you have me see, my lord?"

He grasped her chin, urging her face around to his. " 'Tis not Penforke," he said. "Nevertheless, it is your home now. I would have you see that . . . and accept it."

Her gaze focused on his lips a moment, then lifted to the eyes regarding her with such intensity. "I have accepted it, husband."

"That pleases me," he murmured. He lowered his head and pressed a brief, warm kiss to her lips.

When he started to pull back, Lizanne followed, sliding an arm around his neck and bending his head back to hers.

He responded but broke the contact moments later, leaving her staring disappointedly up at him. "Your heart knows the truth," he murmured. Then, settling her back against his broad chest, he reined the destrier about and led the descent toward Chesne.

The sun was nearing its zenith when one of the men from the small party Ranulf had sent ahead broke from the trees and rode wildly toward them, undecipherable words spilling from his lips.

At once alert, Ranulf's soldiers halted their horses. The ring of swords being removed from scabbards echoed in the nervous silence that descended.

"My lord," the man gasped when he reached them.

"What is wrong, man?" Ranulf demanded, his insides churning. "You have seen my mother?"

"Nay, my lord." He drew in a deep, sustaining breath before continuing. "Chesne has been taken and all within held prisoner."

Ranulf began his analysis of the situation calmly, rationally. "And what of the rest of your party?"

"We were set upon, my lord, and taken within the walls. I was sent back to deliver you a message."

Ranulf nodded for the man to continue, only vaguely aware of Lizanne's stiffening.

"I was told to inform you 'tis Baron Gilbert Balmaine who holds Chesne, and that—"

"Gilbert?" Lizanne exclaimed.

Ranulf's eyes narrowed on her upturned face. "It changes nothing," he snarled, then turned back to the messenger and commanded him to continue.

"He said if you wish to see your mother alive again, you will return his sister to him and hand yourself over."

His words were met by a long silence that seemed

to stretch without end. "And?" Ranulf asked finally, sensing there was more to the message.

Swallowing, the man pulled a cloth pouch from beneath his tunic and handed it to him. "He said this would convince you of his intent should you think to disregard his demands."

White-lipped, Ranulf turned the object over in his hands, feeling its weight. It was light. Something quite small, he thought with growing unease. Nostrils flaring, he looked again at Lizanne. "What kind of man is your brother?"

Lizanne had heard of sending body parts of an adversary's loved ones to mark the seriousness of the captor's threat, but she could not for one instant believe Gilbert capable of doing such a thing. It was nothing short of preposterous!

"He is not an animal," she declared, reaching out to take the pouch from him. He would not relinquish it.

With eyes turned as cold as a winter's night, Ranulf stared at her. "If he is," he said, "I will have to kill him like one."

His words squeezed Lizanne's heart, and she retaliated without thought. "Gilbert will not give you a second chance to do so."

"I do not ask for a second chance—only a first," Ranulf ground out, his muscles bunching visibly through his clothing as his fury grew.

Either way she would lose, Lizanne thought, finally admitting to herself what she had refused to acknowledge for days.

She loved Ranulf.

It was pure madness, but she knew the emotion she felt for him could have no other name. Never before had she felt such depth for another. Briefly, she closed her eyes against the pain. When she lifted her lids and met Ranulf's gaze again, her eyes were wet with unshed tears.

He was unmoved.

"Open it," she whispered.

It was as if the world stood still as he peeled back the folded cloth. Not a man moved in the tense, silent moments following the unveiling.

"God's mercy," Walter exclaimed, though few heard his sputtered oath as they waited for their lord's reaction.

Only hair—a long pale lock that lay starkly against the dark cloth. Ranulf barely had time to feel relief before his anger consumed him. How dare the man lay a hand on his mother. "I will kill him for this!" he roared.

" 'Tis but hair," Lizanne protested, placing a hand upon his arm. "He is my brother!"

"And she is my mother!" He thrust her hand away. Looking past her to Geoff, he beckoned the young man forward. "Take her up before you," he commanded.

Frantically, Lizanne looked from one man to the other. "What do you intend, Ranulf?" she demanded as she was lifted from her place before him and settled on Geoff's mount.

Ranulf pinned her again with those steely black eyes. "You are my wife, Lizanne . . . and you will remain so."

"What of your mother?"

"Do you not worry. I will have her back shortly—and Chesne."

She shook her head. "Let me speak with Gilbert," she pleaded. "Blood need not be shed over this. I can make him see reason."

"Aye, but whose?"

"Nay, Ranulf!" she cried, but he was no longer listening, having turned his attention elsewhere.

Tears again flooding her eyes, Lizanne watched as the men donned their armor of chain mail in preparation for the battle that lay ahead. They were efficient, remounting minutes later and following Ranulf, who, wearing his great hauberk, set the course for the short ride to the castle. Visible, but out of range of fire, they gathered at the far end of the glade surrounding the stronghold.

Behind the ranks of men, Lizanne stared up at the impressive fortress that was Chesne. It was entirely of stone, the great rectangular donjon rising high above walls that bordered on a wide expanse of wet moat. Although the drawbridge was lowered, the large portcullis of the gatehouse was firmly in place.

She lifted her eyes upward again. From this distance, she could only just make out the men who dotted the crenellated walls. Gilbert, she knew, would be among them. Which one? she wondered.

There was a pervasive restlessness throughout the ranks of Ranulf's soldiers as each man readied himself for that which he had been trained.

Lizanne was experiencing her own restlessness, knowing that it was only a matter of time before many of these men, and Gilbert's, lay bloodied upon the ground. Frantically, she searched for a solution to the ominous problem, only to return time and again to one.

She had to speak with Gilbert, to show him she was well, and convince him she stayed with Ranulf of her own free will. Surely, it would make a difference once he discovered she was wed. . . .

"Geoff," she said, shifting her body around so she might look at him, "take me to Lord Ranulf. I must needs speak with him."

"Nay, my lady, he would not want you any closer. You are safer here."

"They are going to kill each other," she vehemently declared. "Can you not see that?"

He looked at her, his expression woeful. " 'Tis my lord's decision, this. Your brother has done him a great offense in taking his home and threatening his family. He has a right to defend both."

"And what of the offense done Gilbert?" She was desperate, her hands clenching and unclenching.

Geoff's face hardened. "Though I know not the details, my lady, 'twas you it started with. You dealt the first offense."

More than anything she wanted to refute his claim, to explain to him why she had done what she'd done, but it would be futile. Geoff would remain intensely loyal to Ranulf in spite of his fondness for her.

Pressing a hand to her mouth, she turned back to survey the changing scene before her. Through the ranks, she glimpsed Ranulf and Walter, their heads bent toward each other as they conversed. Shortly thereafter, the messenger of earlier spurred his horse toward the castle.

"What is happening?" Lizanne asked.

"I know not, my lady," Geoff answered tightly. Clearly, he was as frustrated as she not to be included.

The messenger was not allowed within the walls, though he was permitted to cross the drawbridge and deliver his message through the portcullis. Minutes later, he turned and started back to Ranulf.

As the man drew nearer, Geoff, unable to resist his curiosity, urged his horse forward until he was backed up to the ranks.

"He will meet you, my lord." The messenger's voice carried to Lizanne and Geoff. "He has agreed upon swords."

"Nay!" The cry was wrenched from Lizanne.

Grasping her tighter in anticipation of trouble, for he was fast becoming accustomed to her moods, Geoff prudently withdrew, but not before her outburst was noted by all.

First she chattered incessantly, then she took up sobbing, and finally, she attacked the poor squire with every available part of her anatomy. He knew not how to handle her, barely managing to stay astride during the tirade.

When Ranulf appeared beside him and promptly

relieved Geoff of her, the young man was too grateful for words.

It took Lizanne some moments to realize she had changed hands, but when she saw it was Ranulf who held her, she stilled. "Nay, Ranulf," she pleaded, "do not fight Gilbert. He is an excellent swordsman—"

"You are worried for me?" he asked, his face softening as he set her to her feet.

She reached up and placed her palm to his face. "I am worried for both of you," she admitted, her eyes searching his for assurance.

" 'Tis your chance to free yourself of me," he reminded her, "and have that which you had intended all along without soiling your own hands."

She gripped the chain mail of his hauberk. "Ranulf, I do not want your death anymore. I do not think I ever did."

His brows drew together, but he remained silent.

"Don't you see?" she went on. "Gilbert only does this to retaliate for your taking of me from Penforke."

Ranulf thrust a hand through his hair. "The insult has been given and the challenge issued, Lizanne. I have done naught against your family without provocation, but have borne another's punishment. Now, however, 'tis time for Gilbert to pay for his misdeeds."

"Let me talk to him first. I am your wife now. There is nothing he can do to change that. I will make him understand."

"Nay, Lizanne, 'tis done." He pulled her to him and, his back to his men, lowered his head and captured her lips. The kiss was one of fire, breathtaking in its intensity, and then it was over. As he set her from him, their eyes clashed momentarily, then he was walking away.

Lizanne watched mutely as he remounted his great destrier and nosed it through the ranks, Geoff close behind. When she could no longer see him, she turned and looked to where Roland was mounted. Offering her a grim smile, he beckoned her forward.

Forcing down the panic she knew would only hinder her, Lizanne walked slowly toward him, setting in motion the workings of her mind in an attempt to solve this very real, very ominous dilemma. She hit upon an idea even as Roland offered his hand to her. She had so few options and little time to search for alternatives. Still, she was grateful it was not Geoff she must take advantage of in order to achieve her end.

Sitting before Roland, her spine rigid, she searched out Ranulf and found him at the outermost margin of his ranks.

All timing, Lizanne told herself, measuring the distance to the castle. "Roland, can we not move closer?" she asked.

"Nay, Lord Ranulf would not wish it."

"Then just to the outer edge so I might better view the duel," she compromised. "I would see for myself that 'tis fairly fought."

Roland hesitated, but then shook his head, his regret evident. "You can see well enough from here, my lady."

"Nay." She threw her hand out to encompass the wall of soldiers before them. "They move about too much and block my line of sight."

Lips compressed, the squire looked from the soldiers to the castle, then to the middle ground where Lord Ranulf would meet the interloper.

He was wavering, Lizanne realized, and pressed the advantage. "Please, Roland." Allowing her distress to show in her eyes, she squeezed his arm.

He sighed, then nodded. "All right." Slowly, he guided his mount to the far left edge and positioned them diagonally across from the castle and just in back of the soldiers.

Craning her neck to look down the forward rank,

Lizanne saw that both Walter and Geoff had moved back and left Ranulf alone before the gathering. He faced outward, staring straight ahead, his helmet on, his chainmail hood drawn beneath his chin and buckled.

It was exactly how she remembered him from the day he had returned to Penforke for her. Aye, he was perfectly matched for Gilbert ... perhaps too much so. Although her brother had learned to adjust to his lameness, it was a certain disadvantage that could mean his downfall in the face of a man like Ranulf.

She was surprised at the sudden inner calmness she was experiencing, the unexpected emotion fueled by certainty that she would be able to put an end to this senseless duel.

Then the portcullis of the castle was raised, and a single horse and rider rode out onto the drawbridge. Behind him, the portcullis fell back into place.

It was Gilbert, Lizanne knew. Did he see her? In her green dress that blended with the scenery behind, it seemed unlikely. Turning her head, she looked to where Ranulf was guiding his own horse forward at a slow canter.

Now!

She gasped loudly enough for the squire to hear, then fell forward, draping herself over the horse's neck in as close to a dead faint as she could manage.

"Lady Lizanne!" Roland exclaimed, pulling her limp form back to him.

Purposely, she inclined her body to the side and allowed herself to start a downward descent. As expected, the squire centered his attention upon keeping her astride, shifting her back over the midline of the horse's neck.

Wondering if any of the others had yet noticed Roland's predicament, Lizanne gave a low moan and shifted her weight to the opposite side.

Roland muttered an oath as he steadied her with

one hand, then he carefully swung out of the saddle so that he might pull her safely down beside him.

Without hesitation, Lizanne shot backward in the saddle and brought her leg up. Thrusting it to the side, she connected with Roland's chest, the force of her kick sending him into the grass.

"I am sorry," she said, grabbing the reins as she met his look of astonishment. Digging her heels in, she spurred the horse past the ranks of men, hearing the wave of surprised utterances that swept over them as she shot forward.

Knowing Ranulf would try to stop her, she stayed to the far left as she guided Roland's mount through the long grass, heading toward Gilbert. As she drew nearly level with Ranulf, she worked one hand hurriedly through her hair, releasing the long braid. Like a river of black, turbulent ink, the strands flowed out behind her. It was calculated, for Gilbert would immediately know it was she.

Distracted by the commotion he perceived more than heard, Ranulf turned his head to search out the cause. Far behind, he saw that a number of his men had broken rank and were riding rapidly, veering to the left in clear pursuit of someone. He swiveled his head around.

Lizanne! Even with him, though farther out, she was making a course straight for her brother.

"Nay!" he bellowed. Cursing a thousand times, he changed directions and urged his destrier to a full gallop.

Although he was gaining on her as she arced inward, he was all too aware that her precipitous course was drawing them dangerously close to the castle's walls. Soon they would be within range of fire. Digging his heels more deeply in, he pushed the destrier to its limit.

Though she was intent upon Gilbert, who was now riding swiftly toward her, Lizanne was all too aware of Ranulf's approach. Glancing at her husband, fast bearing down upon her, she knew he would reach her first. Roland's horse was no match for Ranulf's beast, and Gilbert was still too far off.

Nonetheless, she pushed forward. If nothing else, at least she might delay them long enough to speak to Gilbert and explain before the two men locked themselves in mortal combat.

Because of Ranulf's pursuit, she was forced to alter her course to avoid meeting him head-on and gain for herself some extra time. Jerking the reins, she guided the horse back to the left, toward the moat. The move gained her only seconds, for suddenly Ranulf was alongside her, his arm snaking out and tearing her from the saddle.

Shrieking, her arms and legs flailing, she was roughly dragged across his leg and onto the fore of his saddle. Her tailbone struck the pommel, but she hadn't time to consider the resultant pain before the air around them was displaced with the shrill whistle of a dark shaft. Ranulf's body was flung backward, and they both flew through the air.

Ranulf took the brunt of the fall on the damp-softened ground that rose up to meet them, his arm still clamped tightly about her waist.

It took Lizanne a long moment to regain her bearings and suffer the terrible realization that it was an arrow Ranulf had taken.

Vaguely, she heard the approach of horses as she twisted around in Ranulf's hold. Though he did not completely release her, she was able to slide off him to kneel beside his supine body. She swept her gaze from his pain-contorted face to the feathered shaft protruding from the links of his hauberk. Just below his right shoulder, the blood was already seeping through the chain mail and spreading outward.

"Ranulf," she called to him, cupping his face between her palms.

His lids lifted, pain-shadowed eyes staring into hers. "Lizanne," he rasped. Lifting his head, he looked at the shaft, then back at her. "Why?"

Tears flooded her eyes and dropped to his face. "I did not want this," she said, swallowing convulsively to keep her voice from breaking. "I wanted only to speak with Gilbert, to explain. You would not allow me to. . . ."

His eyes flicked past her to where Gilbert was fast approaching, and beyond to where his own soldiers were hurrying to his defense. With a muffled groan, he forced himself into a sitting position, pushing her away from him and reaching up to snap the arrow to a point just above its entrance.

Lizanne reached for him, but he again shoved her away, setting her upon her backside.

"Nay, Ranulf," she pleaded, scrambling upright. "We must needs attend to your wound. You will lose much blood if it is not seen to."

Another arrow sliced through the air as he straightened and reached for his sword. It missed him by mere inches, cleaving the ground to his left.

"Nay!" Lizanne cried, launching herself in front of him as he awkwardly used his left hand to pull his sword from its sheath.

Knowing Gilbert's men would not fire upon him with her in their path, she wrapped her arms tightly around his waist and clasped her hands together at his back. Through her bliaut and chemise, she felt his life's blood soak through to her skin.

Ranulf tried to shake her free but was unable to without losing his sword. "Get back!" he ground out. "I do not need your woman's skirts to shield me."

Vehemently, she shook her head. "I would not have you die for me, Ranulf. Do not do this thing."

He searched her lovely, fearful face. Aye, she could run from him now, but she did not.

"I . . . care for you," she whispered. "Do not ask me to explain it. I just do."

"Lizanne." Gilbert's voice carried to them as he reined in his destrier and leaped to the ground, sword in hand. "Move away."

Ranulf looked to the very tall man advancing upon them, then back to the woman he was risking all to have. "I was wrong," he said huskily, his deep voice barely audible. Lifting his pained right arm, he grasped her shoulder. "You *are* worth dying for."

His lips brushed hers so fleetingly, she could not be sure he had actually kissed her. As she grasped at the memory, he pushed her away so forcefully, her hands broke free.

His unexpected words echoing through her mind, she stared uncomprehendingly at him as she struggled to sort through the hail of emotions descending upon her.

Moving away from her, Ranulf swung his heavy sword upward. He scowled, though pain was less responsible for his expression than the ungraceful movement. Aye, the familiar weapon felt more than simply awkward in his nondominant left hand. It felt foreign.

The barrage of arrows from atop the castle's walls kept Ranulf's men at bay as Gilbert, his limp subtle, advanced upon his opponent, weapon-ready.

Lizanne looked from one man to the other, then chose what seemed the most sure course. Lifting her skirts, she ran to her brother and threw herself into his arms.

He gave her a brief hug but spared her only the barest of glances before setting her away. He continued marching toward the man he intended to draw blood from.

"Gilbert," Lizanne cried, grabbing hold of his sword arm. "Stop this now. Ranulf has done nothing wrong."

Her words had the desired effect, bringing him to an abrupt halt. Only paces remaining between the two men, Gilbert looked down at her, a puzzled expression transforming the formerly determined set to his face.

"Is this not the man who tried to defile you, Lizanne?" he asked, inclining his head toward Ranulf.

Knowing both men were awaiting her response, she quickly, desperately, accommodated them. "N-nay."

Gilbert stared at her as if she had just struck him. "What?" he roared. "Look at him! Does he not have the pale hair you described to me? Is he not the same breadth and height you spoke of?"

"Aye," she agreed, looking over her shoulder to where Ranulf observed the two of them with predatory stillness. "But it cannot have been he."

Her words rocked Ranulf. Fathomless relief flooded through him as he met her beautiful eyes. Was it possible she finally believed him?

Beyond, Ranulf's men had drawn closer, but were no longer attempting further progress. Instead, as it appeared the situation had lightened, they waited to see what would happen next.

Gilbert wavered, his gaze flying between his sister and the man she defended. He saw again the way she had shielded him from the possibility of further fire only minutes earlier. Though it had been clear she had not wanted this Wardieu to capture her as she had ridden toward the castle, when he had been wounded, she had not run from him either.

He wondered what, exactly, the situation was. Had he misunderstood?

As if hearing the unspoken question, Lizanne obliged him with an answer—one that thoroughly shook him. "He is my husband, Gilbert."

Involuntarily, Gilbert took a step back, the point of his sword lowering. "You have wed this . . ."—he searched for the word, his eyes locking with the black orbs of the other man—"this miscreant?"

Lizanne decided it best to ignore her brother's jibe.

"Aye, I am Ranulf's wife," she said, and bit her lip as she watched the range of emotions sweeping her brother's embittered face.

"You were forced into this marriage?" He was remembering the king's deviousness at keeping him at court.

She hesitated, then said, "The king wished it so. But I was given a choice," she hastily added. "And I chose Ranulf." She took a deep breath and, placing herself squarely before Gilbert, lifted her chin. "And I choose to stay with him, Gilbert. I will not be returning to Penforke."

He saw the truth in her eyes and heard the conviction of her words. His brows set low over his eyes, he looked past her to the man she now called "husband."

Ranulf met his stare, his own expression hard and challenging even as he felt the drag of weakness from his loss of blood, felt the sharp, tearing pain radiating outward from just below his shoulder.

"Answer me this, Baron Wardieu," Gilbert addressed him. "Did you or did you not lead a raid against an encampment near Penforke four years past, and in doing so, slaughter nearly all?"

"I did not," Ranulf answered without hesitation, gripping the hilt of his sword tighter as he began to feel its weight. He had never before thought it heavy, but it was fast becoming so.

"Has my sister not accused you of this deed?" Gilbert pressed on. Measuring Ranulf's state, he knew it was only a matter of time before the last of the man's strength was subdued.

"Aye, that she has."

Lizanne saw Gilbert's fists clench, his color heightening as he stared at the other man. It was a discussion that was leading nowhere—except to trouble, she realized.

"Can you not see he is hurt, Gilbert?" she said.

"Have a care and let us take him within where I may tend his wound."

"Aye," he agreed. "We must needs speak further on this, and he is no good to me dead—yet. Mount up, Baron Wardieu."

Ranulf was torn between outright refusal and his need to stem the flow of blood that now stained nearly the entire front of his hauberk. He looked to Lizanne, saw her tremulous smile, and reached a decision. Lowering his sword, he signaled his men to ride forward.

"Nay," Gilbert barked, countermanding him. "Only you."

Eyes narrowed, Ranulf stared at his opponent. His surge of anger brought with it a renewal, albeit short-lived, of his strength.

" 'Tis my home," he snarled, "and I will take with me whom I wish."

"Then I cannot allow you within," Gilbert retorted, planting his legs firmly apart as he attempted to stare him down.

It was Lizanne who decided the matter. Leading Ranulf's destrier, for the great beast would not allow her to mount him alone, she came to stand between the two men.

"I will not go without Ranulf," she said. "There can be no harm in allowing him an escort, can there?"

Gilbert wanted nothing better than to refuse, but he knew Lizanne would have it no other way, and more than anything, he needed to ensure her safety.

Nay, even though she was now wed to this Wardieu, he could not leave her.

"All right," he said grudgingly as he swung up into his saddle. "He may choose two."

"A dozen," Ranulf countered.

Lips twisting, Gilbert shook his head. "Six," he bargained.

Ranulf nodded and signaled for Walter to ride forward. Then, returning his sword to its scabbard, he awkwardly mounted the destrier and reached out a hand to assist Lizanne.

"Lizanne, you will ride with me," Gilbert called.

"Nay," she said, slipping her hand into Ranulf's. "I will ride with my husband."

Gilbert snapped his jaws together but said no more.

Inside the outer bailey, the small party was greeted by a gathering of Gilbert's men, who quickly and efficiently relieved Ranulf's escort of their weapons.

From among the gathering, a small, fair-headed woman emerged whom Lizanne knew instantly to be Ranulf's mother.

"Ranulf!" Lady Zara cried, reaching up to grip her son's thigh. Her eyes widened as she took in his blood-soaked hauberk. She seemed not to even notice the woman mounted before him.

"Mother," Ranulf said, closing his hand over her much smaller one, "you are well?"

"Of course," she answered. "But you ... What has happened?"

"A flesh wound, naught else," he reassured her, though he knew it went far deeper than that.

"We must needs get him inside," Lizanne said. "He has lost much blood."

Seeing her for the first time, Zara looked at the raven-haired beauty seated before her son. Her eyes narrowed as she realized this was the one responsible for all the trouble.

"Get you down from there," she demanded. "I will see to him myself."

Lizanne flinched but shook her head. "Nay, I am a healer—and his wife. 'Tis I who will tend him."

Lady Zara stumbled back a step, her mouth gaping wide, though more from her new daughter-in-law's unexpected announcement than the chit's outright defiance. Suddenly, Walter was there beside her, leaning down from his saddle to grip her shoulder.

"Come, 'twill be explained later," he said. "First we must needs see to Ranulf's well-being."

Walter and Geoff assisted in Ranulf's dismount. Though still conscious, he was weakened and did not object to the succor offered him.

Having decided to ignore the devil-headed woman who called herself Ranulf's wife, Zara led the way through the donjon to the lord's solar. Once Ranulf was lowered to the bed, his men unmindful of the fine linens there, Lizanne took over. She pushed her way among them and tossed orders over her shoulder as she leaned over Ranulf to begin a thorough inspection of his wound.

When Lady Zara started to protest what she perceived as an invasion of her rightful domain, it was Walter who again quieted her, pulling her away before she could cause any trouble.

"I will also need a cauterizing iron once the shaft has been removed," Lizanne said, her voice exceedingly calm in the face of the critical task that lay before her. "And do set a fire."

"You are a truly dangerous woman to associate with," Ranulf muttered, lifting his lids to peer at her. "Methinks I may yet die for you."

She smiled weakly at him, her heart pounding in her chest. "Not this time," she said.

His lips curling faintly, he closed his eyes and sank into a deep, painless sleep.

Chapter 20

"Where is your son?" Philip demanded of the woman whose years of hard work in the service of the Charwycks had aged her far beyond her forty-five years of life.

Unnerved by his sudden appearance, Mary cowered against the rickety table upon which she had been kneading bread dough when Baron Edward's son had flung open the door and entered her small cottage. Though it had been many years since last she had been so near him, she still held no liking for the man. After all, she blamed him for her son's wild, sometimes vicious disposition. Too many years of Darth's impressionable youth had been spent in the company of Philip Charwyck.

And now that Philip had been given control of his family's estates, though his father yet lived, life at Medland had become very difficult for its people. The past two years had seen much hunger and sickness among the common folk. Fields that should have been producing abundant food for the winter ahead lay fallow. Only those who'd be given plots of land by the baron— the villeins—had enough to eat and to barter with. Even they despaired, though, for Philip Charwyck was not averse to taking from his people that which his neglect failed to provide for his household. Nay, the baron's son had no conscience.

"I-in the fields, milord," she stammered, clutching the skirt of her apron to her ample bosom.

Scowling, Philip stepped closer until he was towering over the rotund serf. "Then fetch him," he spit.

Nodding, she skirted him and flew out the door, scattering coarsely ground flour from her hands as she went.

Smiling, Philip turned and watched her lumbering flight toward the fields. When she disappeared from sight, he propped himself against the table and scooped up a handful of the pasty dough. He popped the whole of it into his mouth, then another a minute later. He was halfway through the mound of dough before the mismatched duo appeared in the doorway.

Entering ahead of his mother was the large man called Darth, his dirty pale hair pulled back and secured at the nape of his thick, corded neck.

"Milord, ye wished to speak with me?" he asked, moving to stand in the middle of the small room that immediately shrank around him.

Wiping his hands, Philip pushed himself off the table's edge and strode across the short space. He pushed his face near the other man's and inspected the weathered features that spoke of years of heavy toil in the sun and wind.

Philip's tight smile grew wider, showing his teeth as he confirmed what he'd already guessed. Reaching up, he gripped the man's chin and turned his head first to the right, then the left. Issuing a short bark of triumphant laughter, he stepped back and nodded.

"Well, Baron Wardieu," he said, carefully enunciating the name, "what do you in the fields working like a serf?"

It was Mary, Darth's mother, who responded to the query. She did so with a strangled gasp, then collapsed to the floor in an unsightly heap.

Immediately, her son was beside her. "Mother," he

called, giving her a shake. In response, she moaned and blinked her eyes open and shut again.

Grunting impatiently, Darth lifted her and carried her to her pallet. There he laid her down, then settled himself beside her.

With a decidedly smug expression, Philip set himself upon a stool and watched as Darth lightly slapped Mary's cheeks and called to her in a gravelly, unrefined voice that bore no resemblance to that of his look-alike. Finally, Darth turned his ebony eyes to him. There was intelligence in the man's face, Philip realized for the first time. Mayhap too much.

"Ye called me Baron War . . . dieu," Darth said, testing the strange, unfamiliar name upon his tongue. "What mean ye by it?"

Drawing a deep breath, Philip leaned forward and pointed to the woman who now stared at him, her face fearful. "Methinks 'tis your mother who could answer that."

Darth looked down at her. "Ye know what he speaks of?"

Mary shook her head.

Philip heaved a disgusted sigh. "I know not the details, but she does. Mayhap I can refresh her memory. . . ."

"Go on," Darth urged when Philip's long pause threatened to persist past Darth's short threshold of patience.

"To the north, at Chesne, there is a baron by the name of Ranulf Wardieu. You know the name, do you not, Mary?"

Swallowing loudly, the woman turned her head to the wall.

"Oddly enough," Philip continued, folding his arms across his chest, "the man has hair as fair as Darth's and eyes every bit as black. He is as tall and nearly as wide." He threw his arms out to emphasize the point. "And were it not for your son's hard years in the fields, one could say the two men were, in fact, identical. Twins. Now do you remember, Mary?"

Thoroughly agitated, Mary looked at Darth, who was staring down at her with narrowed, calculating eyes. "I know not what he speaks of!" she said vehemently.

"Hmm," Philip purred. His lips twisted side to side as he made a show of considering his next words carefully. Were it not for Darth's presence, he would surely have beaten the woman. "The way I see it, Mary," he said, "is either Darth is of noble birth, or his brother is of peasant stock. Now which is it?"

Mary pulled herself to a sitting position, her grip tightening on Darth's arm as she leaned toward him. "Darth, I must needs speak with ye alone," she entreated, her lips trembling and white-edged.

Darth looked from Philip to his mother, his mouth hardening. "Answer him," he demanded in a voice grown cold as the first frost of winter.

"I can explain, my son," she whispered, great tears beginning to roll down her full cheeks.

He shook her hand off. "Then do so."

Philip muffled the chuckle that rose to his lips. It amused him, this.

Mary shook her head. "'Twas so long ago," she muttered, hanging her head and staring unseeingly at her bent, fleshy hands. "I was barely sixteen—"

"First answer this," Darth interrupted, his thoughts whirling madly. "Am I of noble or peasant birth?"

Whimpering, Mary reached up and grasped his face between her palms. "You are my son."

Again he pushed her hands away. "Answer me!"

She clasped her hands together and stared past him to the open door of the cottage. "Noble birth . . ." The admission was torn from her tear-filled throat. "You are the second-born son of Baron Byron Wardieu."

Darth shoved to his feet. "And who is my real

mother, then—who bore me? You?" His tone was disbelieving.

"Nay," she sobbed. "The woman who gave ye birth is Zara Wardieu."

"Zara? Then who are ye—the woman who has called herself my mother all these years?" he demanded, his face flooding with color as the injustice of his falsely assumed station in life was fully realized.

Perfectly content to let the scene play itself out without his interference, Philip silently observed the two, knowing there were useful revelations yet to be spilled from the old woman.

"Though I did not give ye birth, Darth, I am yer mother. Is that not enough for ye? Have I not cared for ye and loved ye as only a mother could? Have I not—"

Growling low in his throat, Darth waved aside her words. "Nay, 'tis not enough. Who are ye?"

Mary closed her eyes against the pain of her next words. "I am the bastard sister of Lady Zara. And I was her husband's leman."

Something violent was building inside Darth. The two other occupants of the room sensed it—one fearful of it, the other delighted by it.

"And how came ye by me—aunt? Did my mother abandon me?" He stormed about the room, throwing out a leg and toppling a small table beside Mary's pallet.

Nervously, Mary shifted her cumbersome body around and lowered her feet to the floor. With a great heave, she stood and faced him, tears running down her cheeks, coming faster as she faced the anger—aye, and the hate—she saw in his face. All of the love, or rather, the bare semblance of that emotion that this man was capable of feeling, was gone—snuffed like a windblown flame. Dejectedly, she hung her head.

"I gave birth to Lord Byron's son the night before Lady Zara birthed ye and yer brother," she began. "My child died the next day. I was heartbroken at my loss. Ye understand, don't ye?" Finding no sympathy in Darth's face, she looked away.

"Then here Zara has two fine, healthy boys when she needed but one to give Byron his heir. I hated her. She had everything I ever wanted—noble birth, beauty, and Byron." She paused, gathering the courage to finish her story.

"So I switched my dead boy for one of hers—you, Darth. 'Twas simple, as my babe looked so much like ye. Then I left. Hardly since have I thought of it. I raised ye as if from me own body—"

"And reduced me to the station of a commoner!" Darth shouted, catching her shoulders in a cruel grip. "I am a nobleman! Look what your greed and jealousy have done to me, old woman."

"Ye were second-born!" she protested, wincing at his rough handling of her. "There would have been nothing for ye anyway."

"Nothing? 'Twould surely have been better than this existence. I could have become a knight and made my own fortunes."

"'Nay, Darth, ye know not what ye say. Ye love me! I am yer mother."

"A lie!" He thrust her away from him, sending her toppling to her pallet. She huddled in the corner of it, her shoulders racked with great wrenching sobs.

Darth rounded on Philip, who greeted him with a toothy smile and a nonchalant shrug. "Why would ye tell me this?" he asked, jabbing a finger at the man. "Yer up to somethin', aren't ye?"

Philip rubbed his stubbled chin. "Four years ago you served me well—somewhat," he added, remembering that both Gilbert and Lizanne Balmaine lived. "I would but repay my debt to you."

Darth knew immediately to what he referred—the raid upon the Balmaine camp.

"But I do, in fact, have a proposal for you," Philip admitted, raising himself from the stool.

"And what would that be, *milord*?"

Philip's brows lifted. "Come now, 'tis no longer necessary to address me as a superior. We are, after all, very nearly equal as nobles. You may call me Philip."

Darth moved nearer him. "Well, Philip, what is this proposition ye speak of?"

Philip walked to the door. "Come, we will speak elsewhere. And bring your possessions, for 'tis not likely you will be returning to this hovel."

"Nay," Mary cried, springing up from her pallet. "Do not leave me."

Smirking, Philip stepped outside and crossed to his horse. He climbed atop the thick-limbed stallion to wait. From within the cottage came the sounds of sobbing, pleading, objects thrown about. . . .

It was only minutes before Darth appeared in the too-small doorway and strode toward Philip, a sack flung over his shoulder.

Mary did not follow. In fact, there was only silence in the cottage where moments before there had been upheaval. Philip wondered how Darth had quieted the old woman but didn't bother to ask. "Follow me," he said, turning his horse's head away from the village.

Neither man spoke another word until, in a secluded area beside a swiftly running stream, Philip dismounted and seated himself on the moist bank.

Wordlessly, Darth slung his sack to the ground and lowered himself a goodly distance from Philip.

Leaning back, his hands clasped behind his head, Philip looked over at Darth. "Would you like to take back that which was stolen from you—and perhaps more?" he craftily suggested.

Darth heaved a great, disgusted guffaw. "'Tis a question that hardly bears answering. Think ye I would prefer to live out the rest of my years doin' the stinkin' work of a commoner?"

"Of course not." Philip laughed. "I was simply prefacing my proposal to you."

"And what is this proposal you have for me?"

Philip closed his eyes and turned his face to the heat of the sun. "'Tis simple," he murmured. "You will become the baron of Chesne."

"That does not sound so simple to me. What of this brother of mine? Is he not the baron?"

"For the moment," Philip said, idly pulling a blade of grass through the small gap in his front teeth.

"And how am I to take his title from him?"

Philip turned and looked directly at Darth. "You know the answer to that."

Aye, he did, Darth thought. It had been a foolish question. For too long he had been around Philip Charwyck to have asked the means by which he should dispose of another. "This brother of mine, we look alike, ye said."

"Aye. Were it not for the hard life you have needlessly suffered, old friend, 'twould be impossible to tell you apart."

Darth ran a probing hand down his face, feeling the deep sun and wind-cut ridges there. His resentment at the blow his life had been dealt burgeoned. "And how am I to kill him?"

"How would you like to kill him?"

"My brother?" Darth shrugged. "First I would meet him."

"Ah, so sentimental . . ." Philip sighed. "But you most certainly will meet him.

"When?"

"Soon, but do you not worry. I will be at your side."

Darth nodded. "I had figured as much. And what think ye to get out of this fer yerself?"

"You know me well, old friend. I want but one thing—the baron's wife."

Darth frowned. "That is all?"

"'Tis enough, though I am sure your deep gratitude will serve me well for years to come."

Of course. "Why is this woman so important to you?"

Philip rolled himself up and propped his arms on his raised knees. "I want her for my bed . . . and there is the matter of revenge that is my due for an insult she gave me."

"She is beautiful?"

"Aye, but mayhap I should be the one asking the questions."

Confused, Darth stared at him.

"You know her better than I do, Darth. 'Twas you who bedded her first. Tell me, how was she?"

Darth's confusion grew. "I know not what ye speak of."

"Of course you do. Do you not remember Lady Lizanne Balmaine?" At the slow widening of Darth's eyes, Philip slapped his thigh and sprang to his feet. "Aye, one and the same. Ironic is it not, that she would wed a man who looks exactly like he who violated her? I look forward to having the full story from her myself . . . soon."

Darth didn't know what to say, but he did know he couldn't possibly tell Philip the truth—that the wench had knocked him senseless before he could have his way with her. "And why do ye want her now," he asked, "when ye did not want her before?"

With a swagger, Philip came to stand over him. "Had I known she would become so beautiful, mayhap I would not have been so hasty in trying to dispose of her." He propped his hands on his hips and smiled. "Are you with me, Baron Wardieu?"

Chapter 21

The first light of dawn was etching its warm, silky fingers across the walls when Ranulf opened his eyes to the familiar surroundings of his solar. At first he thought it was a dream, these last weeks, but when he turned his head and saw Lizanne sitting beside the bed, he felt a surge of unspeakable relief.

He looked at her smooth profile, her head propped upon crossed arms resting on the mattress. Even in repose, she was the loveliest thing he had ever seen.

Still, she was very nearly white, the dark smudges beneath the sweep of her lashes standing out in stark contrast. Further, running from her right temple down to the curve of her jaw was a dark smudge of dried matter.

Blood, he realized. His blood.

Frowning, he looked at the clean bandages secured over his wound and wondered at the curious absence of pain. He would have expected much after the serious injury he had sustained. Instead, there was only a dull throb, naught else.

He looked back at Lizanne, recalling Samuel's praise for his lady's gift of healing. Aye, she was indeed gifted.

Moving slowly so as not to awaken her, he lifted a lock of the abundant black hair spread over the coverlet.

Free of the weight of the mass, the strands sprang to life, finding a new shape as they curled around his fingers. Smiling, he lifted another lock and watched as it, too, coiled.

A sound from the hearth stilled his hand. Coming to full alertness, he lifted his head and looked beyond the foot of the bed to the chair filled to overflowing with the watchful Gilbert Balmaine.

Impassively, the man met Ranulf's eyes, and the two stared at each other for countless minutes.

At last, Gilbert slid his leg off the arm of the chair and stood. Throwing his shoulders back, he stretched and rolled his head, then walked toward the bed.

His eyes never leaving the other man, Ranulf lowered his head back to the mattress and watched his approach, his hackles rising as Gilbert neared. Seeing the barely restrained anger in Gilbert's erect bearing, he could not help but wonder what weapon might be at hand that he could use to defend himself. A fist would do, he decided.

"Thanks to my sister's skill," Gilbert said in a hushed voice, "it appears you will suffer little from your mishap. A pity." His lips tightened as he stopped beside Lizanne.

A muscle jerking in his jaw, Ranulf shifted his gaze to Lizanne, then back to Gilbert. "So, you do not trust me alone with my wife," he said, his voice husky as he struggled to keep it low.

Gilbert's eyes narrowed. "Not when your *wife* is also my sister," he hissed.

A silent battle raged between the two, so tangible upon the cool morning air that Lizanne stirred, muttered something unintelligible, and turned her head on her arms before falling back into her deep, exhausted sleep.

Breaking the stare, Gilbert bent over and gently lifted his sister from the chair she had occupied throughout the long night.

"Ran . . ." she mumbled, her lids flickering but never fully opening. Reflexively, she grasped a handful of tunic and nudged her face against her brother's chest, seeking and finding his warmth. Then she quieted and returned to her slumber.

Fierce jealousy fired through Gilbert as he met the other man's eyes. She had never called for anyone but him, and now suddenly there was another in his stead.

Gilbert tightened his hold on her. During the long night, he had discovered there was something very different about Lizanne . . . yet very right. It was as if time had turned about, reversing somewhat the effects of that nightmarish night they had shared four years ago. Curiously enough, the loss of its burdensome familiarity was unsettling to him. He had lived too long with it.

What had brought about this change? he wondered, as yet having no explanation from her. The only thing he knew for certain was that she cared deeply for this man, mayhap even loved him, and it infuriated him to no end. In his eyes, Ranulf Wardieu was still the enemy, and would be until he proved otherwise. Walking around the bed, he carefully lowered Lizanne onto it.

"She has not left your side since you were brought here," Gilbert said, glancing at the other man. Flipping the coverlet over Lizanne, he tucked it around her, then walked back around the bed.

He settled himself in the chair most recently occupied by his sister, leaning back and steepling his fingers upon his chest. "If you are up to it—and you most certainly appear to be—I would hear from you the circumstances that led to the taking of Lizanne from Penforke."

"She has not told you herself?" Ranulf asked in disbelief.

"Nay, though I do have it from my people that 'twas not entirely unprovoked. She abducted you from Langdon Castle, did she not?"

It was an embarrassment that he had been abducted

by a woman, but it was certainly the truth. "Aye, that is how it started," Ranulf admitted. He was having a difficult time keeping his voice low, and more than a little annoyed at having to. "I do not think, though, that now is the time or place to discuss this."

"My patience has worn quite thin, Baron Wardieu," Gilbert said, shoving forward in the chair. "I would know it all! Think you cannot control yourself?"

Patience, Ranulf warned himself, feeling the glowing embers of his anger struggling to spring upward into flames. Grinding his jaws, he eyed Gilbert. "Methinks neither of us will be able to control ourselves once started."

Unexpectedly, Gilbert backed down. "Then we will wait until Lizanne awakens," he said, and began the habitual kneading of the aching muscles in his leg.

Shortly thereafter, Lady Zara, accompanied by Sir Walter, entered the solar. Rising from the chair, Gilbert moved across the room. Legs spread wide, hands clasped behind his back, he stationed himself before the great fireplace.

Scowling, Ranulf pinned Gilbert with his blackest glare. "I would like some time alone with my mother and Sir Walter."

Lips compressed in an unsmiling, thin line, Gilbert shrugged. "When we have settled this matter between us, you will have your privacy—not before."

It was enough to bring Ranulf up off the bed, his injury forgotten, his nudity given no consideration. Ignoring his sudden loss of equilibrium, he pushed past his mother and Walter and started toward Gilbert, weaving as he went.

"Ranulf, get you back to bed!" Lizanne ordered. Springing up from the bed, she stumbled forward, taking the covers with her as she went. When she crashed to the floor, her feet bound up in the length of material, both Gilbert and Ranulf rushed to her aid.

As Ranulf was barely able to stand on his own, and his right arm was fairly useless, it was Gilbert who assisted her, one hand absently picking the rushes from her skirts as he righted her.

Lizanne muttered her gratitude, then turned to Ranulf where he stood, one hand on the bedpost, an angry flush seeping up beneath his skin.

"You should not be up," she said, gripping his left arm and urging him back around the bed.

Stubbornly, he resisted. "I want you out of here," he snarled, jabbing a finger toward Gilbert.

Gilbert hardly noticed, his gaze dropping to Ranulf's unmarred abdomen. "The scar . . ." he murmured.

Lizanne started at his unexpected observation, then sobered. "I have told you, Gilbert, 'tis not him," she said, understanding his confusion. She had been explicit in every detail of her assailant, right down to that horrid scar Ranulf clearly bore no evidence of. "We can talk while Lady Zara visits with her son."

"What exactly is going on?" Lady Zara demanded. "What scar do you speak of?" None answered her.

Dumbfounded, Gilbert nodded his acquiescence and strode to the door.

Ranulf shook off Lizanne's hand and returned to the bed.

Lizanne followed, her eyes averted so she would not have to face either his mother or Walter. When Ranulf lowered himself back to the mattress, she fussed over him for a few minutes. Satisfying herself no further damage had been done, she retrieved the cover from the floor and dragged it over the lower half of his body. Ranulf said not a word to her.

Together, Lizanne and Gilbert withdrew from the chamber.

Gilbert gave instructions to the two guards posted without, then grasped Lizanne's elbow and guided her down the corridor.

Of a sudden, Lizanne halted, and when Gilbert

turned to look at her, she launched herself into his arms and clung to him.

"Ah, Gilbert," she cried, her great flood of tears the result of something that went far deeper than exhaustion.

Bewildered by her behavior, for he had not seen her cry in a very long time, he tentatively lifted a hand and smoothed it over her hair.

After some minutes, she quieted and tilted her head back to look at the bearded face above her own.

"I am sorry," she said, unclasping her hands from about his neck. "'Tis all my fault, this. I was foolish to act so rashly. I should have waited for your return before—"

"Shh," he hushed her, one corner of his mouth lifting as he cut through the torrent of her words. "Let us walk outside, and you can tell me everything."

Lizanne nodded and took the arm he proffered.

The castle's garden was redolent with the scent of roses. There was every shade of red imaginable there—from the deepest to the palest. It was a veritable feast for both the eyes and the nose.

"'Tis the work of Lady Zara," Gilbert explained.

"How?" Lizanne asked with wonder, burying her nose in a full bloom that was just beginning to shed its abundance of soft, velvety petals.

Gilbert shrugged. "I do not know how she does it, but surely as you have a gift for healing, she has a gift for flowers." During the past days, he had come to admire the strong-willed woman who was Ranulf's mother. She was fire, this small lady. In fact, were she younger, he thought he might very well have considered taking her to wife.

Eyes alight with discovery, Lizanne threw her hand out and spanned the garden. "Even the king does not have roses as fine as these."

Only as a child had Gilbert ever seen Lizanne take interest in such things, so he was surprised by her enthusiasm over such a simple thing that had nothing, even remotely, to do with weapons or strategizing.

"You have changed," he said, feeling a deep loss that he knew immediately to be purely selfish.

She turned puzzled eyes to him. "Have I?"

He looked away. "Come." He urged her forward with a hand against the small of her back. "We will walk, and you will tell me of this Ranulf Wardieu."

She nodded. "Aye, we must needs speak of him."

Though the garden was not large, they spent the next hour covering every inch of it as she poured out her tale to Gilbert, beginning with her encounter with Ranulf at Langdon Castle and ending with how she had wrested Roland's mount from him that she might disrupt the duel.

She raised her eyes to Gilbert's and sighed. "Oh, Gilbert, why the dramatic gesture of sending a lock of Lady Zara's hair? It so infuriated Ranulf."

"I thought it might," he answered gruffly. Still, a smile played about his lips as he remembered how he'd come by it. To procure the snippet, he'd had to sneak up on Ranulf's mother and clip a piece free before she realized what was happening. Discovering too late what he'd done, she'd turned her wrath upon him with the force of a sea-blown storm. Narrowly, he had escaped the coltish kick that had aimed to unman him.

"'Twas cruel of you," Lizanne said.

Gilbert's head jerked back as her sharp words sank in. Stopping abruptly, he turned her around so that she stood directly before him. "I was taking no chance of Wardieu running with you," he explained, his hands perhaps a bit too tight on her upper arms.

"But he—"

Gilbert gave her a small, barely controlled shake. "I wanted you back, Lizanne. The thought of losing you to him a second time tore at me." Breathing heavily, he shook his head, his lids squeezed tight over pained eyes. "To fail you again . . ." His voice trailed off as emotion gripped him. Then, with a great sigh, he released her and turned his back to her.

Lizanne looked at the dejected slump of his shoulders and felt his deep, raw pain. For too long, he had carried this burden, and she had allowed him to do so with nary a protest. She was deeply ashamed of the selfishness that had blinded her to his plight. The king had been correct in his estimation of her.

She moved to him and laid a hand upon his shoulder. "You did not fail me," she said in a soft voice. "There was naught you could have done to prevent what happened. 'Twas preordained, and I no longer regret it."

There was a moment of stunned silence, then Gilbert swung around to face her once again. "What?" he bellowed, causing the birds in the garden to take flight. "Explain yourself!"

Biting her lip, she stared hard at his chest. "Had it not happened, I would now be married to Philip," she began, searching for the right words. "As I told you, he is not a kind man. There is something quite cruel about him. In fact, he . . ." She stopped, rethinking whether she should plunge forward and tell him what the terrible man had revealed to her.

"What are you not telling me?" Gilbert asked, lifting her chin and staring into her uncertain eyes.

"Philip," she croaked past a throat tightened with feeling. "'Twas he who ordered the attack upon our camp. I am certain of it."

Gilbert stared at her, then slowly shook his head. "You are speaking nonsense, Lizanne. Who has filled your head with such outrageous lies? Ranulf Wardieu?"

"Nay," she said, then told him in a rush what she had earlier withheld. When she finished, she looked expectantly at him and was alarmed at the terrible fury that had invaded his face.

"Philip said this to you?"

She nodded. "Aye, 'tis clear he knows of the man

who . . ." She swallowed, then took a deep, sustaining breath and forced her shoulders back. "There is another, Gilbert, another who resembles my husband, but is not him. It could not have been Ranulf."

"Has he a brother?"

She blinked. "This I do not know. He has spoken little to me of his family . . . and truly, I had not even considered the possibility." She was ashamed at the admission, for it would seem the obvious solution.

"Then we will ask him," Gilbert said, turning on his heel and striding away.

Though Lizanne's legs were long, they were not as long as her brother's. However, with a bit of running, she caught up with him and accompanied him back inside the donjon.

Lady Zara and Walter were just leaving Ranulf's solar when the two of them came down the corridor.

Without a word, Gilbert took Ranulf's mother by the arm and, without a word of explanation, pulled her with him into the chamber. Throwing an apologetic smile to the stupefied Walter, Lizanne followed her brother inside and closed the door. Almost immediately, a ruckus commenced outside the room, and a moment later Walter burst through the door.

Gilbert spun around. "Out!" he commanded.

"What is this all about?" Ranulf thundered from where he was seated in an armchair before the fire, a rich robe belted about his waist.

"What are you—" Lizanne began to question the reason for his being out of bed but was brusquely interrupted by Gilbert's wrathful voice.

" 'Tis a private discussion I mean to have between us. I want no interference from that one." He jabbed his finger toward Walter, who was struggling to free himself of the hold the guards had upon him.

Ranulf's eyes flickered to Walter. "He may stay."

"Nay, he will go," Gilbert countered.

Lizanne watched with growing trepidation as Ranulf's eyes narrowed to fine slits. "I have said he will stay."

Knowing it was only a matter of time before blows were exchanged, Lizanne walked over to where Gilbert stood with Lady Zara and placed her hand on his arm.

"It can do no harm to have him present," she said. "Sir Walter can be trusted."

The determined set of his jaw told Lizanne Gilbert was not about to waver on this. However, Lady Zara's appeal changed his mind.

"Let him stay," she said softly, touching Gilbert's hand.

Both Ranulf and Lizanne looked sharply at Zara, then to Walter, whose face was a mask of rage and indignation.

Jealousy? Lizanne wondered. Ah, now she understood the advice Walter had given her. The man was obviously enamored of Lady Zara.

With a wave of his hand, Gilbert dismissed the guards, then, with Lady Zara on his arm, advanced toward Ranulf.

Side by side, a frown marring Lizanne's features and a scowl set firmly upon Walter's, they followed.

"Where Lady Zara is concerned, do you lead with your heart?" Lizanne asked, her voice loud enough for Walter's ears only.

The man started so violently, she thought he might be having a seizure. Then he recovered, turning eyes full of remorse upon her. "Too often my head," he admitted.

Feeling triumphant at having pieced together this particular puzzle, she nodded and went to stand beside Ranulf.

"You are feeling well?" she asked.

"As well as can be expected," he answered, his mouth set in that damnably thin line as he fixed his eyes on Gilbert, not once looking at her.

Gilbert seated Lady Zara in the chair directly opposite Ranulf, then stood beside her. Rather forlornly, Walter positioned himself to the side and between the two chairs, but his eyes never left Ranulf's mother.

Finally, Gilbert broke the uneasy silence. "Have you a brother, Baron Wardieu?"

Ranulf blinked, looked to his mother who had gone suddenly rigid, then shook his head. "Nay, I have no other siblings—that I know of. Why do you ask?"

Gilbert folded his arms across his chest. "There is the matter of the man who committed an atrocity against my family for which you have been blamed, Wardieu. Though my sister says it cannot have been you, 'tis true that you match her description in every way."

"In all ways except the scar, hmm?" Ranulf said, his eyebrows rising into the fall of hair brushing his forehead.

Gilbert nodded. "Aye, except for that."

"Lady Lizanne." Lady Zara spoke with surprising urgency, leaning forward in her chair to pin her new daughter-in-law with eyes every bit as black as her son's. "You are saying there is another who resembles my Ranulf?"

"Aye, there is another, so nearly identical that I mistook Ranulf for that one, which is why—"

"Tell me of this encounter," Lady Zara urged.

Nervously, Lizanne ran a tongue over her lips as she looked from Lady Zara to the others. They were all waiting for her to elaborate.

She gripped the back of Ranulf's chair. "I—I do not wish to speak of it. Be it sufficient to say there is another."

Lady Zara sat back and observed the stubborn set of Lizanne's jaw for some moments. When next she spoke, her voice had grown melancholy. "I gave birth to twins," she said, her eyes moving to her son. "Ranulf was the firstborn and Colin the second."

Swaying on her feet, Lizanne gripped the upholstery tighter, her nails bending backward with the effort.

"Mayhap 'tis Colin . . ." Lady Zara began, anguish etching her features.

"Colin is dead, Mother," Ranulf sharply reminded her. He tried to stand but dropped back in his chair when the effort sent shooting pains through his side.

Lady Zara clasped her hands before her face and nodded. "Aye, he died within hours of his birth."

"Then what is this nonsense about it being Colin?" Ranulf demanded.

His mother shook her head, then reached an imploring hand to Walter. Immediately, the vassal was at her side, kneeling before her and grasping her small-boned hand in his larger one.

"I never even held him," Lady Zara said, speaking more to Walter than anyone else, her eyes awash with unshed tears. "Byron said the child was diseased, but mayhap 'twas not Colin after all. . . ."

Seeing the distress on his mother's face, Ranulf decided he'd had enough of this foolery. He shoved himself to his feet and, a hand pressed to the throbbing wound, walked toward her.

"What ridiculous speculation," he said. "I will hear no more of it!"

"But 'tis possible, Ranulf, do you not see?" she asked, looking up at him.

He shook his head. "You are becoming distressed for naught."

"Nay, mayhap Colin was stolen from me."

Wearily, Ranulf shook his head and ran the back of his hand across his eyes. "Who would dare such a thing? Be sensible, won't you?"

"Know you of any other children born before or shortly after yours, Lady Zara?" Gilbert asked.

"Enough!" Ranulf roared, stepping forward to shove Gilbert aside.

Lizanne sprang across the rug and threw herself be-

tween the two men. Gilbert's retaliatory blow meant for
Ranulf narrowly clipped her temple.

Moaning, she clapped a hand to her head. "Nay,
Ranulf," she croaked, seeing the unleashed fury in his
eyes. "'Twas an accident. I am fine."

Grinding his teeth, Ranulf glared at Gilbert, who
looked positively mortified. "I have not finished with
you," he warned, then drew Lizanne back with him to
his chair. Although she protested, he pulled her onto his
lap and pushed her hand aside to examine the slight
lump, his fingers gentle as they probed the tender flesh.

"All right, Mother," he said, turning his attention
back to the matter at hand. "Let us end this speculation
once and for all. Were there any other children born during the same time?"

Zara nodded, her eyes glazing with pain at the
memories she had buried so long ago. "Aye, Byron fa-
thered another—on my illegitimate sister, Mary."

They all stared at Zara, wide-eyed with disbelief.

"When I discovered her betrayal, and Byron's, I demanded she leave Chesne forever." Zara sighed. "But she
had no place to go, and Byron convinced me I should let
her remain until her babe was born. Then, he promised,
he would send her south."

Although Ranulf had known of his dead twin, he
had never heard a word of his mother's sister. He sat in
stunned silence as she struggled to continue her story.

"She hated me, though I did not know it until she
had lain with my husband and got herself with child.
'Twas torment day in and out to see her about the castle.
She flaunted her pregnancy and openly speculated on
which of us had been impregnated first . . . whose child
would be Byron's true heir."

Zara dropped her face into her hands and began to
sob. Walter offered her his shoulder to lean against, and
she did so without hesitation. When she had calmed suf-

ficiently to continue, she pulled away from the vassal and offered him a weak smile of gratitude.

"Mary birthed a son the day before Ranulf and Colin were born. As promised, she was gone from Chesne when I recovered sufficiently to see my Colin given a proper burial."

Lizanne was the first to break the silence that fell over the room like a pall. "Lady Zara, forgive me, but know you what name Mary gave her son?"

"Of course," she answered with great bitterness. "She named him for Byron's father, D—"

"Darth," Gilbert supplied.

Startled, Zara looked up at him. "Aye, that was his name."

"'Tis him," Lizanne breathed. "'Tis the name of the one who led the raid against our camp—the one who looks like Ranulf."

Another stricken silence fell.

"'Twas Mary's son you buried, not Colin," Gilbert concluded. "And Mary took your second-born with her to Medland, Charwyck's home."

The mention of that man's name snapped Ranulf out of his stupor. Sitting abruptly forward, he very nearly dumped Lizanne from his lap. "Charwyck? What has he to do with this?"

Gilbert looked at Lizanne. "You have not told him?"

Ranulf grabbed her chin and pulled her head around to stare into her troubled eyes. "'Tis the reason you collapsed at the palace, is it not? What have you withheld from me?"

Lizanne struggled to free herself from his hold, thinking it best to put some distance between them, but he would not release her. When her elbow inadvertently jostled his wound and forced a groan from him, she stilled and slumped against him.

"I could not tell you," she said, unwilling to meet his eyes, knowing they would be filled with anger. "I had to first sort it out for myself." She twined her fingers together and stared down at them.

"You see, Philip was not explicit," she continued in a voice so low, the others had to strain to catch it. "He simply mentioned that you bore a resemblance to another, then he disappeared. 'Twas so confusing and frightening to think he might have been responsible for the attack—to think he would go to such extremes to avoid wedding me."

"I will stain my sword with the bastard's blood!" Ranulf exploded.

"Nay, he is mine," Gilbert countered, slapping his hand to the hilt of his sword. "And I will slay this Darth as well."

Lady Zara was instantly on her feet, pushing Walter aside to face Gilbert. "If 'tis my Colin, you will do no such thing. He is my son and cannot be held accountable for those things he has been forced by another to do. No doubt he has lived the life of a commoner when he is of the nobility."

She swung around to face her firstborn son. "Is that not so, Ranulf?"

Ranulf looked from her to the woman he held in his arms. "We will have to see," he said noncommittally. "Some things can be forgiven. Others? . . ." He shook his head, then looked to Gilbert.

"We will do this together," he said. "When I have recovered sufficiently, you and I will meet Charwyck and demand satisfaction for the pain he has inflicted upon our families."

Gilbert shook his head. "Then you had best be recovered within the hour, for I ride this afternoon." Turning on his heel, he stalked to the door.

"And how do you propose to get past my men?" Ranulf threw over his shoulder, effectively bringing Gilbert to a halt.

His boots ringing loudly in the silence, Gilbert

crossed back to Ranulf. "I will place Chesne back in your hands. Your men can have no objections to letting us leave peaceably."

A wicked grin slashed across Ranulf's face. "Aye," he said, thoughtfully rubbing his palm over the rough stubble shadowing his chin, "so long as they've a good length of rope with which to string you from the nearest tree."

Fisted hands planted on his hips, Gilbert stared long and hard at Ranulf but in the end could think of no retaliation.

"You may as well accept it, *brother*," Ranulf said, "for 'tis the only way you will leave Chesne alive."

Gilbert's face grew red, but still he said nothing.

Sliding off Ranulf's lap, Lizanne went to him and placed her hands on his arms. "Please, Gilbert," she pleaded, "do not do this alone. Wait for Ranulf."

Gilbert's teeth snapped together. "You do not trust me," he harshly bit off. "Think you I would fail you again?"

She shook her head. "Nay, Gilbert. 'Tis Ranulf's right to go with you."

Turning, Gilbert looked straight into Ranulf's eyes. "A sennight," he grudgingly conceded.

"Nay, a fortnight," Lizanne countered. "His wound is deep."

Gilbert's nostrils flared, his fists clenching at his sides. "A fortnight, then. 'Tis all you have. Then I ride— with or without you." Turning on his heel, he stalked out of the solar.

Chapter 22

Over the next several days, Ranulf remained distant with Lizanne, angry with her for having kept her knowledge of Philip from him. He allowed her to tend his wound but was otherwise unresponsive. Between Lady Zara, Geoff, and Walter, all his other needs were met without so much as a single request made of her. It pained Lizanne, his disdain, but she refused to give in to the easy comfort of self-pity, accepting Ranulf's anger as his due.

During that time, the tensions gradually eased between Ranulf and Gilbert. From a distance, Lizanne watched their animosity evolve into a tentative alliance. Though she was pleased by this turn of events, it only made her feel more of an outsider. They always set aside their conversation in her presence.

Sleeping on a bench in the Great Hall, a coarse woolen blanket her only companion, she got very little sleep, though more because of her whirling thoughts than any discomfort she experienced.

Each day, she squared her shoulders and determinedly set about familiarizing herself with the castle and its people. Though it was disheartening, she was not surprised that, as the sister of the man who had laid siege to Chesne, the suspicious castlefolk were less than friendly.

They snubbed her, going out of their way to avoid being anywhere near her. Even Gilbert's appearance could not clear a room faster than hers. It did not seem to matter that she was Ranulf's wife. Even Lady Zara, who had warmed only slightly, was short with her and ofttimes argumentative. It took very little intellect to discern that, until the woman accepted her, her people would not.

Once she had satisfied herself with exploring the castle, Lizanne spent many hours in the outer bailey, watching with great longing as Ranulf's and Gilbert's men tilted at the quintain, practiced their archery, and fiercely tested each other's sword skill. But, as usual, none were eager to offer her a turn. So she contented herself with analyzing the mistakes made by the competitors and visualizing what she would do differently in each man's place. It sustained her . . . for a while.

In the evening of her fourth day at Chesne, feeling the forced distance between Ranulf and her had gone on far too long, she climbed the stairs to the solar.

Closing the door softly behind her, she leaned back against the wooden planks and stared across at Ranulf's still form, which the darkening night threw shadows upon.

Unnerved but determined, she gathered the shreds of her courage and crossed to the bed, where she began to remove her clothes. When only her thin shift remained, she pushed the covers aside and slid in beside Ranulf.

She felt him stiffen when her naked thigh brushed his. It was nearly enough to send her bounding off the bed, but she fought the impulse and moved closer to him.

"What think you you are doing, Lizanne?" he asked with more than a little irritation.

Dragging the covers up over her shoulders, she lifted her head and, in the bare light of the room, met his sparkling gaze.

"I am your wife now," she said bravely. "It should not be necessary for me to seek accommodations elsewhere."

"So you have grown weary of sleeping in the hall with the others. Is it too cold, too crowded, or merely beneath you?"

She clamped her teeth down on the prideful reply that thrust itself against her lips. Swallowing it, she shook her head. "Nay, 'tis too lonely."

After some moments of consideration, Ranulf slid his fingers into her hair to cup the back of her head. "I did not know you wished to stay with me," he said, his voice rippling over her like fine Oriental silk.

She shivered, closing her eyes briefly on the splendid sensation before lifting her lids to stare into those ebony eyes. Nervously, she ran the tip of her tongue over her lips.

"Aye, I wish to sleep with you, Ranulf," she said, though the admission cost her a good deal in pride.

"Why?" His voice was harsh in the quiet of the room as his fingers slipped lower and he kneaded the stiff muscles of her neck.

"A—a wife should sleep where her husband sleeps," she said as the tension began to drain from her. "Otherwise, 'tis not likely there will ever be peace between them."

"And you want peace?"

"Aye, I would have peace between us."

Damn, he wanted a wedding night! At that moment, it would not have taken much for Ranulf to cross the invisible line he had drawn between them that he might satisfy his baser needs, but he managed to hold his desires in check. "What convinced you 'twas not me who committed those crimes against you and your brother?"

She sighed. "Sir Walter told me I must lead with my heart. And my heart told me it was not you."

Walter had said that? Stern, serious Walter who never led with anything but his head? What magic had this witch worked on him to bring forth such flowery, poetic advice? Ranulf was completely baffled, then he recalled the attention the man was paying to his mother and frowned. Deep down, he had always felt the bond between Walter and his mother but had never before acknowledged it.

Lizanne's next words pulled him out of his reverie.

"Even before we wed, my heart was telling me this, but I would not listen. I was too frightened." Her voice had grown tight with dammed up tears. "And when I saw you did not bear the scar, still I denied your innocence, but my heart knew . . . Ah, Ranulf, I am so sorry."

He urged her head down to his shoulder. "As am I for the suffering my family has caused yours. But why did you not tell me all this sooner? 'Twould have saved us so much pain."

She settled against his side. "In the beginning, I was so certain 'twas you." She drew a shaky breath before continuing. "The villain I thought you to be could not possibly allow one to live who knew his secrets. He was a murderer and . . ."

Silent tears spilled over and dropped to Ranulf's bare chest, beginning the torrent she had held inside for too many years.

Ranulf stroked her hair and whispered soothing words as incoherence tumbled from her mouth amid sobs. The end was a long time in coming, but when it did, she was fully curled atop him, softly hiccuping the last of her anguish.

"No more," he said, feathering his fingers down her spine. "Henceforth, you will cry no more over this. Do you understand?"

She lifted her head. "You are forbidding me the comfort of tears?"

"I do not like it when you cry," he admitted. "I would have no more tears over this. You have cried enough to last you two lifetimes."

It was true, but still she did not like being told what she could and could not mourn. "I am finished with crying . . . for now," she said, "but I cannot promise I will refrain from doing so again."

Ranulf was appreciative of the fire he detected beneath her indignity. She was going to be fine.

"You would defy me—your lord and husband?" he asked with mock disbelief.

"'Tis not defiance!" she protested, rolling off him and onto her knees at his side. "You cannot tell someone when to turn on and off their emotions. 'Tis more complicated than that. I am not a puppet, husband, and if you expect me to behave as one, there will never be peace between us."

He could no longer suppress his laughter. Loud and rumbling, it rose to fill the room.

"Why do you laugh?" she demanded.

Sobering, he shook his head. "I am pleased with you, wife. 'Tis all."

"Pleased with me? As the king forced you to this marriage, I would not think you would be pleased at all."

Clasping a hand behind his head, he looked up at her shadowy figure. The room had grown much too dark to be able to make out much more than her outline. "The king did not force me, Lizanne. I chose to offer for you."

He had chosen . . . His declaration left her speechless. "Why?" she breathed a moment later. "You said you had declined."

He shrugged. "'Tis something I am still sorting out for myself."

She clasped her hands together. "Good," she said. "There is one less thing for me to feel guilty about."

Ranulf was silent a long time, then reached out and pulled her back down beside him.

Tentatively, she settled her head on his shoulder and placed her hand to his chest. Beneath her palm, she felt the erratic beat of his heart.

After a minute, his voice came softly to her. "Each time you look at me, will you remember what that other man—my brother—did?"

"It seems farther and farther away with each passing day. When first I laid eyes upon you at Lord Langdon's, 'twas as if only yesterday it had all happened. Now it seems a very long time ago."

It was not exactly the answer he was seeking, but he tried to be satisfied with it. "'Tis unfortunate such a tragedy brought us together, Lizanne, but I am grateful for it."

She snuggled closer.

Smiling, Ranulf pressed his face into her hair and breathed its light scent, detecting the smell of the outdoors—sap, roses, herbs. . . .

"Ranulf."

"Shh. Go to sleep. We will have our wedding night later."

She started to protest his conclusion but realized with dismay that he had accurately guessed her state. She was acutely embarrassed that he had read her so easily. How had he known she desired his touch—that she ached to experience again the fire he had caused to rage within her?

Unable to sleep, she lay perfectly still for what seemed like hours. Although her mind was fatigued, her body was not. At every point she made contact with Ranulf, she was disturbingly alive with a deep, pulling ache. It did not help that Ranulf also lay wide awake, his breathing shallow, his heart beating briskly beneath her palm.

Sighing, she pushed his arm away and moved to the edge of the bed to escape his disturbing presence. It was surely the only way she would get any sleep that night.

He followed and pulled her back, curling his body possessively around hers and raising his knees to press against the backs of her thighs.

He felt wonderful—his every hard, muscled ridge sinking into her softer curves, perfectly molding them into one. Groaning her desire, she moved against him, rubbing her buttocks into the cradle of his hips.

Still, he did not respond. He merely drew himself backward a space.

Twisting around, she slapped a hand to his chest and pushed him onto his back. "You no longer desire me?" Her words were a mixture of accusation and hurt, his rejection tightening her voice to a husky strain.

"Lizanne," he said sternly, "'tis hardly feasible for me to make love to you with this injury."

"Then do not touch me!"

"What?" he bellowed.

"I said, 'Do not touch me,'" She settled herself away from him again. "I cannot sleep for being so near you."

Ranulf blinked. He had not expected such an admission from her. Damn, but it excited him. He dragged her back to the middle of the bed, threw a hard leg over her, and leveraged himself up on one elbow to look down at her shadowy form.

"'Tis your wife," she said, her misery evident. "You still love her though she is dead."

"Arabella?" Ranulf's body tensed at the mere mention of that woman. "You know not what you speak of, Lizanne."

"Do I not? You have hardly touched me since our one night together."

"I assure you it has nothing to do with her. God forgive me, but I cannot even mourn her death."

"Why?"

It was not something Ranulf cared to talk about, but he knew it needed an explanation. He sighed. "She was a cold and conniving woman, and more than once unfaithful to our marriage vows. She did not come to me a maiden, though she claimed to be one."

Lizanne was beyond relieved, but then another thought struck her. "Were you faithful to her, Ranulf?" She waited with bated breath to know what would be the fate of her own marriage. After all, his father had not been faithful to Zara.

"Aye," he said, "in the beginning."

Her heart squeezed, his words paining her more than she would ever have believed.

Sensing her anguish, Ranulf moved closer. "I cannot lie to you, Lizanne, but I can explain." He trailed a feathery light finger over her throat. "We lived separate lives, not even sharing sleeping quarters. Arabella had her lovers, and eventually I had mine."

Lizanne captured his hand and halted its downward path. "And will I be expected to share you with another?"

"Only if I have to share you." He spoke near her ear, his warm breath raising the hairs along the back of her neck. "And I have no intention of doing so, Lizanne. I would gladly kill any man who so much as touches you. You are mine."

"But, Arabella—" she began.

He removed his hand from her grasp and laid a finger across her lips. "I did not want Arabella, nor did she want me. I want you, Lizanne—more than I've ever wanted any woman. Do you understand?"

She nodded, then berated herself for daring to hope he might declare his love for her. Aye, he desired her, but that was all. She was grateful for the dark when quick tears filled her eyes. "Then if 'tis not Arabella that holds you from me, what is it?"

Lowering his head, he brushed a kiss over her lips. "I have been waiting on you."

"Me?"

"Aye," he breathed, pushing back the covers and lifting the hem of her shift. "For your consent, madam," he reminded her as his hand moved up to cup her breast.

Remembering the argument they had had following their first intimacy, and the words she had thrown at him, Lizanne smiled. "But what of your injury?" she protested weakly as a shiver of pleasure shot through her.

"There are other ways," he said. "I will teach you." Then he lowered his mouth and captured hers.

It was a different kind of kiss he stole from her—hungry, demanding, intense. For a moment, Lizanne could only lie there, her mind reeling as his tongue thrust between her lips and swept the sensitive tissues lining her mouth. Then her body took over.

Gripping his head with both hands, she boldly explored his mouth, drinking in his moan of pleasure. When his fingers caught the erect nub of one breast and rolled it between them, she gasped and arched upward, pressing herself to his firm chest.

With maddening slowness, his hand trailed lower, pausing at her firm belly before continuing on. Lower, he threaded his fingers through the softly curling hair between her quivering thighs.

"Aye, Ran," she gasped, and fastened her teeth upon his lower lip.

A rumble of satisfaction vibrated through his chest as he parted her and eased two fingers inside her moist warmth.

Moaning at the sensation, she threw her head back even as her lower body thrust against his hand. She heard the ragged cry torn from her throat but did not realize it was her own voice as she answered the primal urgings of her body and gave herself completely over to them.

Settling his mouth over the peak of one ripe breast, Ranulf let her set the rhythm, ignoring the protesting throb of his injury that was growing more and more persistent.

With a suddenness he was not expecting, her hand moved down and found his swollen member without so much as a break in the cadence of her body's movements. She held tight to him, making him groan with desire as her breathing grew shallow and sharp.

Then, with a final thrust, she drew in a shuddering breath that echoed through the room, and convulsed around him.

With barely restrained passion, he lifted his head and felt her short, panting breaths stir the hair at his temples. Slowly, the rigidity of her body eased, and her hips fell back to the mattress.

"Ah, Ranulf," she sighed. "'Tis wonderful."

Smiling, he lifted his hand and touched her face, smoothing back the damp strands of hair clinging to her cheeks. "And what is it like?"

"'Tis such a mixture—heat ... light ... breathlessness. And then a sweet death."

He chuckled.

"And you?" she asked, her hand tightening around him.

Immediately, he surged fully against her palm. "The same," he groaned. Gripping her about the waist, he rolled onto his back and lifted her atop him.

Straddling his waist, her unashamed nudity pressed to his muscled abdomen, Lizanne laughed and drew her shift off. Tossing it aside, she leaned toward him, the cloak of her hair falling forward and tickling his chest.

"Kiss me," he rasped.

Enthusiastically, she lowered her head. In the darkness, she missed his mouth, finding instead his forehead.

A giggle escaped her, but she hardly noticed as she worked her way downward. When she reached his lips, she teasingly circled them with the tip of her tongue, which told her he was smiling. Then she pressed her lips to his and easily coaxed his teeth apart to undertake an exploration of his mouth.

Throughout her plundering, Ranulf simply lay still, listening to the music singing through his body as his lovely wife attempted to seduce him. Against her firm backside, his fully erect member pressed forward as the last of his control began to slip.

Her exploration moved from his mouth to his neck, and finally, his ear. Catching it between her teeth, she bit a little too hard, then drew her lips down his neck to his collarbone.

"Here," he murmured, pressing her head to his chest.

She nuzzled his firm nipple, drawing it between her teeth as he had done hers and swirling her tongue around it. At his loud groan of pleasure, she moved to the other and gave it equal attention. Finding that she liked this new power, she continued to tease him, contorting over him as she found new places to kiss and run her tongue over, to drag her fingertips across.

Feeling as if he might explode, Ranulf slapped a hand to her buttocks and lifted her up and back.

It took Lizanne only a moment to realize his intention, then she was gliding down his thickness, gasping at the sensations aroused by her descent. When she was fully seated upon him, her hands gripping his sides, she stilled and searched him out, her unspoken question hanging in the air.

"Listen to your body." His voice grated in the silence of the room.

"Not like this," she squeaked, thinking it would be far easier if she could only get her legs out from beneath her so that she might roll onto her back without losing him.

"Aye, the same as I've done you."

Suddenly, she was very embarrassed. "I . . . can't." Placing her weight on her hands, she made to move off him.

He gripped her ribs, then thrust up into her once . . . twice.

Lizanne was too stunned to do anything but hold on as those wonderful feelings surged again, growing from a spark to a flame as they struck the very core of her.

With no more thought of embarrassment, she gave over to instinct and let it be her guide. Soon she was matching his movements.

His cry of release came before hers, but she was too intent upon freeing herself to pause. When at last she collapsed upon him, her head reeling drunkenly with the taste of a satisfied passion, she hardly noticed when he shifted her weight off his injury.

Pressed against his side, she snuggled closer, raising her leg up over his and nudging his manhood. With a gurgle of delight, she trailed her hand down his chest and brushed her fingertips over him.

"Witch," he grumbled, his spent body coming to life again beneath her touch.

Neither slept that night, but there were no regrets. However, they could not have anticipated the explosion when Gilbert walked in unannounced the following morning and found the two of them sprawled naked across each other. It was nearly an hour before he calmed sufficiently to resheathe his sword, and only when Lady Zara appeared and suggested a stroll through the rose garden did he retreat from the solar.

Somehow, Lizanne and Ranulf managed to find humor in the situation and ended up spending the entire morning abed.

Chapter 23

After *seven long* days—a full sennight—Lizanne still felt like an outsider. Though she cared for Ranulf's injury, and had spent these last nights in mutual bliss with him, there were still so many hours of the day to fill that she thought she might go mad with the restlessness eating at her. She had tried, repeatedly, to take part in the running of the household, but Lady Zara had remained unaccepting of her presence.

In the end, there was nothing left for Lizanne to do but spend her free time with Joseph, Gilbert's squire. At the back of the donjon, away from prying eyes, they set up targets and practiced their archery.

To Lizanne's chagrin, far too often the squire's skill won out over hers. It would not have been so bad, but she had taught the young man to shoot, and she could not help but be bothered by her failure even to match him.

She complained that she had not practiced in weeks and that her chemise and bliaut were far too cumbersome. Good-naturedly, Joseph loaned her chausses and a tunic, but it was hours of practice that sharpened her aim.

It was not long before Geoff and Roland discovered

their secret and convinced Lizanne and Joseph to give
them instruction in the proper use of the bow. Lizanne,
knowing that Ranulf would likely rage if he discovered
that she was practicing, secured a promise from both
squires that they would say nothing of it.

So it was that Geoff forgave Lizanne for the imprudence of her act in attempting to end the duel between
Ranulf and Gilbert and offered her his friendship once
again. Grateful to have someone else to talk to, Lizanne
set about making an invincible archer of him. He did not
disappoint her.

Roland, however, was a different matter entirely. He
had been sorely shamed by Lizanne's trickery. Though he
graciously accepted her instruction, he stubbornly withheld his camaraderie until the day the four of them
slipped outside the castle walls and went traipsing about
the woods in search of prey.

Each with hares tied from their belts, they were
emerging from the trees when a large wild boar rushed
at Lizanne as she walked confidently ahead of the others.

"My God!" Joseph shouted from behind her.

Swinging around, Lizanne faced the animal. Wide-
eyed, she quickly gathered her wits and threw her hand
over her shoulder to draw an arrow from her quiver . . .
and found it empty.

Her wits scattered. Run! her mind screamed as the
beast bore down on her. She stumbled before finding the
presence of mind to set her limbs to flight. Still grasping
her bow, she turned and fled through the long grass.

Louder and louder, the animal's angry wheezing
grew, the pounding of its hooves vibrating as it closed
the distance between prey and predator. Certain she felt
its hot breath on the backs of her legs, she pumped her
arms harder.

Then it screamed, a tortured, high-pitched sound
that cleaved the air before a blessed quiet fell.

Panting, Lizanne whirled around to stare at the

shuddering beast. It lay only feet from her, an arrow protruding from its side.

Her bow fell from her hand as she dropped to her haunches in the wake of a world nearly torn asunder. Wondering at the terrible fit of trembling that seized her, she lifted her head and focused on the one running toward her—Roland.

It was his arrow that had felled the beast.

Beyond him, Geoff and Joseph emerged from the trees.

"You are well?" Roland asked as he dropped down beside her.

She nodded but could find no words to reassure him.

"Can you stand?"

Drawing a deep breath to calm her wildly racing heart, she held up a hand in silent appeal for him to wait, then looked past him to where Geoff and Joseph stood over the dead animal.

"By God's wounds!" Geoff exclaimed, shaking his head in dazed amazement. "You could have been—"

"Splendid shot." Joseph brusquely cut across the other squire's ill-considered words. Glowering at Geoff, he placed his foot on the animal to pull the arrow from its meaty carcass.

Shakily, Lizanne raised herself, grateful for Roland's firm grip beneath her elbow.

"You are all right, my lady?" he asked, frowning with concern.

Lizanne could not help herself. Turning, she wrapped her arms around the young squire and clung to him, so incredibly grateful she could not speak past a tongue grown thick and awkward.

Feeling somewhat redeemed after the shame her trickery had visited upon him, Roland awkwardly patted her back. When the two other squires grimaced at him, he shrugged and lifted his eyes heavenward.

For several minutes, Lizanne clung tight, unwilling to relinquish her hold on him even when her fear eased sufficiently to do so.

From the walls of the castle, a sentry had watched the scene play itself out and raised the alarm. So it was that Gilbert arrived shortly thereafter.

Too angry to speak, he extricated Lizanne from Roland and carried her to his horse. After lifting her into the saddle, he mounted and headed back to the castle.

They were crossing the drawbridge when Lizanne turned and offered him a tremulous smile. "Methinks he will forgive me now," she said. As soon as the words were out, she regretted them.

A great frown settling itself upon his forehead, Gilbert reined in his horse and none-too-gently turned her around to face him. "What is going on, Lizanne? Do you play some silly game?"

"Nay, I did not ask that boar to chase me," she said, shuddering at the remembrance. "I was truly frightened. At first I could not even run."

"Then why so satisfied?"

She was reluctant to explain but knew he would not allow his question to go unanswered. "Roland's been angry with me for deceiving him when I thought to prevent the duel between you and Ranulf. Mayhap I took my fright a bit further than necessary. . . ." She silently begged him to show a little understanding.

He appeared unmoved by her appeal.

She looked at her hands. "Please do not tell him, Gilbert. He would only hate me the more."

"What I ought to do is let him paddle your behind. Or better yet, I should let your husband see to your punishment."

She gasped. "You would not!"

He pursed his lips thoughtfully, prolonging her torment, then shook his head. "Nay, your secret is safe with me, little sister. However, if he does not yet know, Ranulf

is bound to find out about your hunting. I think that
will be sufficient punishment."

She huffed loudly. "And what is wrong with that?
You have never before objected to it!"

"Aye, and I was more than foolish to allow you such
free rein. You have no business behaving as if you are a
man. You are married now, Lizanne, and God willing,
you will bear children before long. You are a woman.
Why don't you start behaving like one?"

She could not speak past the lump forming in her
throat. Never before had she seen Gilbert so angry with
her. It could not possibly get worse . . . but it did.

Suddenly, Ranulf was there, his hands braced on his
hips, his jaw sternly set as he looked up at her. Distastefully, his gaze swept over the men's clothes she wore,
then alighted upon the empty quiver protruding above
her shoulder.

Clothing aside, Lizanne knew too well the image
she presented. Her hair had all but come undone from
the hastily plaited braid she had earlier set to it, flying
out in all directions around her face and falling into her
eyes. Too, she was aware of the smudges of mud that
marked her face from when she had raced through a
large pool of stagnant water to intercept that last hare. It
was certainly not the image a baron—any man—wished
to have of his wife.

"You do try my patience," he finally said. "Now
come you down from there."

Accepting her fate, she held her arms out to him,
but he stepped back, refusing to help her dismount. His
message was clear. If she was going to behave like a man,
she would be treated as one.

Indignant, she twisted sideways and slid partway
down the horse, then dropped the last feet to the
wooden planks. Swinging about, she faced her husband.

Ignoring the warning sparkle in her eyes, Ranulf
leaned forward and cut the ropes from which her game

was suspended at her belt. Tossing the hares up to Gilbert, he resheathed his dagger, then closed a hand around her upper arm and marched her past the disapproving castlefolk.

He did not slow, not even when they entered the great hall of the donjon. Lady Zara, Walter at her side, stood when they walked past, her delicate brows rising straight up at the sight Lizanne presented.

Lizanne scowled. She had certainly dropped a notch or two in the older woman's estimation—if that was even possible.

Pulling her behind him, Ranulf mounted the stairs two at a time and practically dragged her down the corridor to the solar. Inside, he closed the door loudly and stood, waiting for her to turn around.

Feeling as if she was playing out an all too familiar scene, Lizanne accommodated him, defiantly crossing her arms over her chest.

"Now I suppose you will lecture me on hunting," she said.

"After you've removed those filthy clothes."

She looked down at them, then tossed her chin high. "I will not."

Ranulf was not about to argue with her; however, the first step he took toward her sent her racing around the bed. He stopped and stared at her, considering what her next course of action would be.

When he took another step, she did not move, but her eyes followed his progress, her body set to spring away.

He came around the bed and stopped again, less than two easy strides separating them. Still, she did not move.

Then, at the precise moment he commanded himself to lunge for her, a broad grin split her face. Bounding onto the bed, she rolled across it and sprang to the floor on the opposite side.

Still somewhat encumbered by his injury, Ranulf quickly followed. She was just passing through the portal when he caught her arm and pulled her back inside. Slamming the door so loudly its vibration seemed to go on forever, he pushed her against it and pinned her there with the length of his body.

"You truly thought to escape me?" he demanded.

She shook her head. "Nay, 'twas verily my intention that you should catch me." She laughed at his look of disbelief.

"Admit it," she said, giving him a poke in the ribs. "You enjoy the hunt as much as I. Would you deny me the same pleasure, my lord?"

"You do not take this seriously," he growled, pushing her hands to her sides.

She shook her head again, more laughter bubbling up in her throat. "I am not going to let you ruin a perfectly good day, Ranulf Wardieu. I enjoy using the bow, and as I would not ask that you give up your weaponry, I think it unfair if you ask it of me."

There were so many things he wished to say to her, but the only one that came out sounded weak to his ears. "You could have been killed!"

She blinked, then solemnly nodded.

He recognized the fleeting light of fear that entered her eyes as she harkened back to that too-recent incident. Then it was gone—replaced by another of her captivating smiles as she attempted, without much tact, to entice him out of his anger.

"Do tell. What would you have missed most?" she teased, raising herself up to blow lightly in his ear. "The excitement I bring to your life . . . or my warm thighs?"

His head jerked back, but the moment he looked into her impassioned eyes, he was completely lost. Groaning, he claimed her lips.

In the end, Lizanne obeyed Ranulf, shedding the

wretched chausses and tunic where she stood before the door.

A hand placed on either side of her, Ranulf leaned his body toward hers. "I see before me the woman beneath the man's garb," he murmured.

Eyes alight, she lifted his tunic and began loosening his laces.

Grinning, he stilled her hands and stepped away from her. As she stared at him, clearly baffled by his unexpected withdrawal, he tapped a considering finger to his lips and swept his gaze up and down her unclothed figure.

"Hmm." He moved to the side of her and craned his neck to catch a glimpse of her backside. When he reached down and drew his hand up her calf and over the back of her thigh, ending with a pinch to the buttocks, she jumped.

He was inspecting her! she realized, her mouth gaping wide in horror.

"Exquisite," he pronounced as he straightened. A smile tugging at the corners of his mouth, he shifted his gaze to her unruly hair. He shook his head and pulled the tangled mane over her shoulder. "We will have to do something about this, though."

She slapped his hand away. "How dare you!"

Pressing her back against the door, he laughed low in his throat, his teeth visible in the smile that slashed across his face. "'Tis something I owed you. Do you not remember?"

She blinked. Then, as she recalled the occasion when she had done much the same to him before King Henry, her anger dissipated as fast as it had risen. Sheepishly, she smiled at him. "I suppose you've been waiting for just the right moment."

He nodded. "Consider yourself fortunate I chose to do it in private."

"You are so considerate, my lord," she murmured, lowering her head to lick a path up the side of his neck.

"In future, if you wish to go hunting, you will wait until I can accompany you," he said, getting in the last word even as his body sprang to life.

She nodded.

They did not bother to remove his clothes, finding it sufficient to lower his chausses and braies.

Near the end of the stipulated fortnight, Ranulf declared himself fit enough to ride south with Gilbert. Together, the two men determined to leave in two days' time.

With growing apprehension, Lizanne watched as preparations were made and training for both Gilbert's and Ranulf's men escalated. All this for her, she thought, wishing there was some way to bring an end to it. Although the worry over Ranulf and Gilbert killing each other had abated, she now had the new worry of Philip Charwyck. It was a threat she took quite seriously.

As all three squires found themselves fully occupied with their lords, she spent much time brooding over the matter. When she had broached the possibility of accompanying Gilbert and Ranulf, she had been met with such angry opposition on all sides that she had fled the Great Hall.

Now, seated atop the outer fence of the corral, her hand idly stroking the muzzle of the great stallion that blew softly into her hand, Lizanne was too intent upon the training yard across the way to notice Lady Zara's approach. It wasn't until the woman touched her knee that she looked down from her perch and saw her.

"Lady Zara." She gulped, pulling her hand from the horse and clasping it with the other. Immediately, the stallion nudged her shoulder, pushing her sideways. Gripping the fence railing, she righted herself before she could be toppled to the ground and shooed the animal away.

"You have a way with horses," Lady Zara noted. "That one is far from being broke, yet he comes to you without fear."

Blinking at the cryptic compliment, Lizanne looked over her shoulder at the animal who stood watching her with great, doleful eyes. "He is not broken?" she queried. "He seems gentle enough."

Zara smiled, not a full smile, but it was a start. "Try mounting him once, then——" She caught herself and shook her head. "Nay, I should not even propose that in jest, for most certainly you would try."

Lizanne grinned. "You are right there," she said, then eased herself off the fence. "You wished to speak with me?"

With a sigh, Zara placed a hand on Lizanne's arm and guided her away from the corral. "I have just received word there is a young child in a village not far from here who has broken his leg, and that it may need to be removed. I thought, perhaps, you might like to accompany me."

Lizanne pulled herself up short. "You trust me?"

Zara gave her a look that said her question was absurd. "You have proven yourself skilled—certainly far more than I. My son behaves as if he never even sustained his injury."

Lizanne smiled. "Of course I will accompany you." Abruptly, her enthusiasm shadowed. "Think you Ranulf will mind if we go? He has forbidden me to leave the castle's walls."

Zara was indignant. "I do not need permission to see to my people. Ranulf has grown accustomed to me visiting the villages. Besides, we will have a proper escort."

"All right," Lizanne agreed. "I must needs gather my medicines, and we can set off."

"Then do so, but be quick about it," Zara said, and a smile twitched her lips as she watched Lizanne take off at a full run.

Their escort was more formidable than it would have been had Ranulf not caught word of their intent. To their ranks he added a full score of armored knights and chose Walter to lead them.

Staring up at Lizanne when she was mounted and ready to go, he pushed the hair back from his sweat-streaked face. He had been training hard to get himself back into condition.

"Lizanne," he said, gripping her knee, "pray do not challenge Sir Walter. Regardless of the child's condition, I want you back before sunset. Now, give me your word you will follow his orders without question."

"Aye, you've my word," she said, smiling down at him from the wonderfully spirited mare she had been given to ride.

Ranulf considered her a moment, then removed his belt and slid the sheathed dagger off it. Holding it by its point, he handed the bejeweled weapon to her.

Recognizing it as her own, she eagerly accepted it and held it to her breast. "Thank you, Ranulf—my lord." Lifting the hem of her skirts, she quickly slid the weapon in the top of her hose before Ranulf could protest her lack of modesty. Then, throwing caution to the wind, she gripped the pommel of her saddle and leaned toward him. Sliding her hand to the back of his neck, she lowered her mouth to his in a brief but sweet kiss, then lifted her head to stare into those black eyes.

"Though you do not know it," she whispered, "I have lost my heart to you."

At his dawning look of disbelief, she smiled and laid a finger against his lips. "I love you, Ranulf Wardieu." Then, straightening, she prodded the mare forward into the midst of the others.

It had cost her much to say those words knowing

he did not return her feelings, but it was as if in saying them, a burden had been lifted from her shoulders. As she nosed the mare beneath the portcullis, she ventured a backward glance. Ranulf stood where she'd left him, his hands planted on his hips as he stared after her.

Due to the nature of their excursion, they rode at a pace that was far from leisurely, but Lizanne thrilled to it. It seemed ages since she'd been astride a worthy mount. The wind in her face, the steady, rhythmic movement of the mare beneath her, and the smell of the land, all combined to set her senses soaring.

At the village, Sir Lancelyn, Gilbert's vassal, assisted her dismount. Until that moment, she hadn't realized Gilbert's men were among those chosen by Ranulf to accompany them. It seemed a good sign of the two men's newly formed allegiance.

She smiled at the familiar face, then pulled her bag of medicinals from the saddle and hurried after Lady Zara, who was being led to a small hut at the edge of the village. Inside the one-roomed dwelling, it was dim, and a small boy of no more than four summers lay moaning on a pallet of straw, his mother on her knees beside him.

"Lady Zara," the pretty young woman exclaimed. Scrambling to her feet, she rushed forward and touched her lady's arm.

Zara placed a comforting hand over the other woman's. "I did not know it was Lawrence who had been hurt."

The woman nodded, looking over her shoulder to where her son lay. "You have brought the healer with you?" she asked, her eyes lighting upon Lizanne, then looking past her to where Walter stood in the doorway.

"Aye, she is here, Becky." Zara reached behind herself to pull Lizanne forward. "This is Lady Lizanne. 'Tis she who healed Ranulf."

Eyes widening, Becky stepped back and stared at the

woman. "And no doubt caused his injury," she said. "So you are the one our Lord Ranulf has wed.

Though she knew dislike when she saw it, Lizanne was unwilling to give any time over to it. The boy was her first priority. Shouldering past the stiffly erect woman, she went to the pallet and dropped to her knees.

"I will need more light," she said over her shoulder, even as she turned her attention to the child.

Whimpering, the child raised feverish eyes to her, his hands clutching at his leg beneath the coarse woolen cover tucked around him.

Lizanne smiled reassuringly and laid a hand to his moist forehead. "You will be all right," she said softly before turning to her bag to remove a stout vial.

The boy was too weak to protest when she placed the acrid powder on his tongue. Within minutes he drifted off into a blessed, drug-induced sleep.

Prying the child's fingers from the covering he still clutched, Lizanne pushed it back to examine the injury. In spite of the protrusion of bone, the leg was not nearly as bad as she'd feared. With prayer and careful attention, she was confident it would heal completely and the child would suffer no lasting ill effects.

While he slept, she cleaned and reset the leg, spread a sweet-smelling unguent over it, and finally applied a heavy bandage around the splint. Throughout, Lady Zara assisted while both Walter and Becky stood off to the side watching.

Afterward, while the child still slept peacefully and the sun moved toward its final descent, Lizanne pressed a packet of medicine into Becky's hand and took some minutes to impress upon her the importance of keeping the leg clean and covered if it was to be saved.

Becky followed Lizanne outside to the waiting horses. "Methinks you will make Lord Ranulf a good wife," she said, a genuine smile wreathing her pretty face as she stared up at Lizanne atop her restless mare.

Lizanne smiled back. "I will return in two days' time to check on your boy. Do not forget that he should lie abed throughout—even if you must tie him down."

Becky nodded, then stepped back as Walter called for them to ride.

Waving to the people who had gathered at the edge of the village, Lizanne urged her horse forward, sidling up to Lady Zara as they picked up speed.

"You did well," the older woman said, throwing her a satisfied smile. "They will respect you now."

Feeling she had also earned Zara's respect, though the woman was certainly not willing to admit it, Lizanne smiled back at her.

They were within a few miles of the castle, the sun just touching the horizon, when a large group of riders appeared. At its head was Ranulf, his pale hair flying out behind him.

"He worries too much,' Lizanne heard Lady Zara laughingly tell Walter.

Spurring her horse forward, Lizanne overtook the knights at the front of the party. Though they stayed close behind, none tried to stop her. Out of breath, she reined in her horse just short of the oncoming party and beamed up at her husband as he came alongside her.

He did not smile back.

Frowning, she opened her mouth to speak, but no words came out. A moment later, her scream pierced the air.

Chapter 24

Those terribly black eyes Lizanne remembered so well bore into hers as his lips parted to reveal yellowed teeth.

Reflex was responsible for Lizanne jerking on the mare's reins as Darth reached for her. The high-strung animal reacted instantly, sidling away and rearing, its sharp hooves cleaving the air.

Throwing herself over the horse's neck, her hands clutching at the tangle of mane, Lizanne managed to hang on. When the animal finally settled back to earth, its eyes rolling with fear, ears flattened to its head, Lizanne sharply dug her heels in and jerked hard on the reins.

Too late, Walter raised the alarm. Immediately, his men drew their swords, closed formation around Lady Zara, and turned their horses about to flee the greater number of soldiers facing them. There was nothing they could do for Lizanne, who had set her own course far to the right of them.

The assailants surged forward, spreading outward in an attempt to enclose the smaller group. Escape would have been possible if not for the sudden appearance of more riders emerging from the cover of the woods. Cursing loudly as a circle was drawn around them, Walter signaled for his men to gather at its center.

Crouched low over her horse, Lizanne sped ahead, her eyes trained on the opening between two riders. Knowing that if she could make it she had a chance to reach Chesne and give warning, she fought down the fear boiling in her belly and held on.

As she passed between the two horses, her mount brushing heavily against the one on the left, the soldier astride lunged for her . . . and missed. But what he could not do, a well-placed arrow did, embedding itself in the mare's side. Screaming, the frightened animal reared, its hooves flailing as it twisted sideways.

Lizanne groped wildly for purchase as the reins were torn from her hands, then she plummeted to the ground, her head hitting something sharp. Though it did not render her unconscious, it left her dazed and hurting.

She was given no time to recover. Immediately, the soldier who had tried to wrest her from her horse was upon her, dragging her to her feet.

Swaying against him, she lifted her head and stared at the numerous mounted riders on all sides. So many . . .

Still grappling with her wayward bearings, she raised a shaky hand and probed the gash beneath her hair. Wincing, she brought her hand back down and stared at the blood staining her fingertips.

"Surrender or the lady dies," a familiar voice rang out above the clamor of restless horses and men.

Philip Charwyck! Swinging her gaze around, Lizanne searched the ranks for a glimpse of him but could not pick him out from among the other armored men. With their mail coifs, they all looked much the same.

Abandoning the futile search, she turned her attention to where Walter and his men were protectively clustered around Lady Zara. Lady Zara herself sat unmoving atop her horse, her gaze fixed upon her second-born son.

Lizanne felt her pain. Here was the son stolen from her all those years past, and now he was returned to her a villain, the veriest of knaves. And he had not even acknowledged her presence, though her hair, so like his, revealed her as his mother.

"Lay down your arms, I say," Philip ordered when Walter remained irresolute, "or I will spill her blood where she stands!" Separating himself from the others, he spurred his horse toward Lizanne.

Throwing her head back, Lizanne glared up at him when he came alongside her.

He grinned wickedly and motioned for the soldier holding her to step back. With a shove that had her stumbling forward, the man released her.

"What? No warm welcome for your lover?" Philip taunted, reaching down to run the back of a gloved hand over her cheek.

Revolted, Lizanne jerked back from his touch.

"Tsk-tsk," Philip clicked his tongue. His face was deceptively impassive, then he lunged for her and caught hold of the hair at her crown.

Deciding she could afford to lose a few hairs, she threw her head back and lashed out at him. She struck him with her bloodied hand, soiling the front of the sleeveless tunic he wore over his hauberk but achieving little else.

Without hesitation, Philip retaliated, jerking on her hair and striking her hard across the face.

Lizanne heard the distressed murmurings of Walter's men but knew she stood alone. Ignoring the pain from his blow, she swung her arm up again, fingers hooked and aiming for his eyes.

Philip knocked her arm aside and pulled hard on her hair, nearly lifting her from her feet. "I will tame you, shrew," he threatened.

"Never!" she vowed, her eyes flooding with tears of

pain as she brought her knee hard up into his horse's belly.

The destrier protested loudly, jumping away from the offender, but still Philip did not release her. Her head aflame, Lizanne gave an ear-piercing shriek and fell against the animal.

With a satisfied snort, Philip leaned forward and, throwing an arm around her, pulled her off the ground. However, Lizanne was no small thing to be easily hauled up the side of a horse, especially by a man not much larger than herself. In the end, it took the help of a soldier to seat her before Philip.

As she struggled against him, Philip pulled her head around and took possession of her mouth, grinding her lips against her teeth and drawing blood as he triumphantly proclaimed to all that she belonged to him.

If it was her wrath he expected when he lifted his head, he was sorely disappointed. Smiling thinly at him, Lizanne made a great show of drawing the back of her hand over her mouth, then turned her head and spit on his boot.

"You taste of sewage, Philip." Her daring words earned her another slap.

Lord, she thought, holding her hand to the new ache, she was not going to be a pretty sight when they got out of this. She only prayed they would. . . .

"If needs be, I will kill her," Philip warned, drawing forth his dagger with great ceremony and trailing its tip down her chest to her abdomen. "Now, throw down your weapons that Baron Wardieu's wife might live."

In the silence that followed, Lady Zara's voice carried across the cool air. "Do as he says."

As it darkened and into the night, the interlopers and their prisoners covered much ground before immersing themselves in a thick wood. And still they rode.

Only hours before dawn, they came to a clearing that was pronounced suitable to set up camp. The horses needed to rest for a few hours before continuing on.

Bringing his destrier to a standstill in the middle of the field, Philip promptly shoved Lizanne off his horse, sending her sprawling facedown in the grass.

"That," he said, amid his men's raucous laughter, "is for the spit."

Fuming, Lizanne sank her fingers into the soil, but at the last moment squelched the impulse to throw the clumps at Philip. It would only find her trampled beneath his horse's hooves.

Taking a deep breath, she got to her feet, expending her angry energy on the task of brushing her soiled skirts. Only then, when her hand brushed its hilt, did she remember the dagger hidden in the top of her hose.

"Do not exert yourself, Lady Lizanne," Philip said. "I will want you alert when you come to me."

Again there was laughter, and though Lizanne glared heatedly at him, inside she had grown as cold as ice.

"Bernard," Philip called to one of his men, "put her with the others."

Lizanne wanted to resist the large man who gripped her with such force she winced, but common sense bade her cooperate. To infuriate Philip further would only bring her closer to the time when he would attempt to claim—nay, violate—her. And the best place for her now was with the others. Mayhap they would discover a way to free themselves of their captives.

While a makeshift camp was erected, the hands of all the captives, with the exception of the two women, were firmly bound behind them. Then they were corralled together into a sort of pen constructed of ropes wound around a group of trees. About the perimeter, Philip set numerous guards. He was taking no chances.

Her legs drawn up beneath her chin, Lizanne sat

next to Zara, on whose right sat Walter. All around them were Ranulf's and Gilbert's men.

Several times during the past half hour, Lizanne had tried to talk with Zara, but the woman was too preoccupied with following her second son's progress about the camp. Lizanne turned her mind instead to searching out a viable means of escape.

"So alike," Zara finally said, her voice filled with deep sorrow, "yet so different."

Lizanne turned her head and looked at the woman. Zara suddenly seemed much older in the flickering light of the torches. "One good ... one evil," Lizanne said.

On a heartfelt sigh, Zara closed her eyes and nodded.

Lizanne touched her arm. "He has not yet spoken with you?"

"Nay, he spurns me, though he must surely know I am his mother." She was quiet for a long time before speaking again. "Tell me more of this Philip. What does he want with you?"

Though it certainly did not take Lizanne's mind off the threat of Philip's possession of her, she acquiesced, starting at the beginning and ending with her final confrontation with the man.

Sighing again, Zara reached out and touched the largest of the two swellings on Lizanne's face.

Though she did not withdraw, Lizanne flinched at the pained tenderness.

"You must not give in to him," Zara said, her voice a bare whisper upon the night air as she edged closer to Lizanne. "Have you still the dagger Ranulf gave you?"

Lizanne nodded.

"Good, and I've mine."

Lizanne started. "Have you?"

Smiling faintly, Zara bobbed her head and raised a finger to her lips. "We must needs be wise in this. Do you think you can use yours on that Philip when he comes for you?"

Lizanne nodded. "Aye."

"That is good. And could you make your way back to Chesne?"

Having forced herself to pay strict attention to the course Philip had set, Lizanne was familiar with her surroundings. "Aye."

"Then listen well." Zara leaned nearer Lizanne. "You must get to Ranulf and lead him—"

"I will need a horse."

Zara shook her head. " 'Tis not likely you will be able to obtain one without getting yourself caught again. Nay, run. I know you can do that."

Swallowing, Lizanne nodded.

"Ranulf cannot be far," Zara continued. "No doubt he has divided his men, and they are this moment scouring the area. When all is quiet, I will see the ropes are cut from the men. If we've surprise on our side, mayhap 'twill be possible for us to escape as well. Otherwise, 'tis entirely up to you."

"I will bring Ranulf back—and Gilbert," Lizanne assured her.

Zara lifted her hand and placed it over Lizanne's. "You are my daughter now. With a mother's protectiveness, methinks I judged you too harshly. For this I apologize."

Tremulously, Lizanne smiled, her tongue suddenly too clumsy to reply.

"And for the pain my family has inflicted upon yours, I beg your pardon," Zara continued, her eyes glimmering with unshed tears. "Had we but known . . ."

Lizanne squeezed her hand. "You could not have. 'Twas a cruel deception fate played on both our families."

There was silence, then Zara smiled, a small smile

that returned a measure of youthfulness to her face. "He loves you."

Lizanne gasped, her lids blinking rapidly at the woman's unexpected declaration. "Ranulf? He told you this?"

"Not in words . . . but I have seen it in his eyes."

Lizanne turned her head and stared out across the camp. "Methinks you are wrong, Lady Zara. He but desires me."

Zara chuckled, surprising Lizanne. "Nay, 'tis you who are wrong, daughter. Never did Ranulf feel toward his first wife as he does you—or any other woman. Do you love him?"

Lizanne could not bring herself to look at her. "Aye," she admitted reluctantly. "I told him as much before we left for the village."

"And how did he respond?"

"Naught." She pulled a face. "Forsooth, I did not give him the chance to."

Zara opened her mouth to say something, but closed it when a restless murmur fell over the captives. Looking up, she saw her second-born son advancing on them.

With a suddenness that startled Lizanne, Zara gave her a fierce hug. When she drew away, Lizanne felt the sharp, cold steel of the small dagger Zara had slipped beneath her hand. She gave Lizanne a look filled with meaning, then turned to confront her son.

When he came to stand over them, he simply stared at Zara, his hands planted on his hips, his jaw hardened into a square, thrusting line.

It was Ranulf, yet not him. . . .

Panic burst through Lizanne as she stared up at that face, her mind beckoning to her to relive those terrible memories. Swallowing convulsively, she lowered her gaze to his booted feet and concentrated on getting her irregular breathing under control, even as she concealed the second dagger in her shoe.

"So ye are the woman who bore me?" Darth finally said, his gaze fixed on Zara's telltale hair.

Zara pushed to her feet and stood. "Aye, and you are Colin."

He laughed. "So that be my given name. Colin. Much nicer than Darth, methinks. Noble . . ."

"You were stolen from me," Zara said in a small, apologetic voice.

"Aye, but now I am returned to ye, Mother. Rejoice in the miracle that has brought us together again."

His lips twisting, he nudged Lizanne with his booted foot. "I never finished with ye, wench," he taunted her, his gaze raking the thrust of her breasts. "Mayhap when Lord Philip is done, I might have another taste o' yer sweetness."

Bile rose in Lizanne's throat as a vivid image split her mind. Shaking it off, she put all of her hate into her eyes and defiantly met his stare. "For all your fine clothes, *Darth,* your blood still runs with that of the lowly commoner you are."

Surprisingly, he only laughed. Then, taking hold of Zara's arm, he turned her around. "Come," he said, "we have much to talk about."

Immediately, Walter was on his feet. "Nay," he bellowed, running forward, though his hands were tightly bound behind his back.

Colin swung around, his hand still firmly gripping Zara. A venomous smile split his features before his fist came up and slammed into Walter's face, sending the smaller man backward.

Walter's men reacted instantly, lunging to their feet and surging forward as one.

The guards raised their weapons, but the captives did not stop. It took one arrow through the heart of the man nearest Colin to squelch the uprising.

Crying out, Zara struggled to free herself from her son's hold, but without success.

Lizanne scrambled to her feet, and ran to kneel beside the fallen soldier.

Glassy-eyed, he stared up at her for a moment, then his lids fell as he shuddered his last breath. Hands pressed to her mouth, she shed stinging tears over one of the two men who had guarded her during those first days with Ranulf. Mayhap only a dozen words had passed between them, but she felt his death straight through.

Only a minute passed before deep anger replaced her grief and sent her into action. Standing, she walked over to where Walter sat, a number of his men gathered around him. Bound as they were, they were useless to offer any help. Stepping over them, Lizanne made a space for herself and knelt beside Ranulf's favored vassal.

"Evil," Walter croaked, his broken nose gushing great amounts of blood.

"Lie back," Lizanne commanded, pressing her hands to his shoulders. When he resisted her efforts, she bore down with her full weight, forcing him to the ground. "There is naught you can do."

Lifting the skirt of her bliaut, she wadded it and pressed it to his face to stem the blood.

"I imagine we're quite a pair," she remarked a short while later, noting that both his eyes were blackening.

Struggling to a sitting position, Walter craned his neck to search out the area beyond. "I will kill that bastard if he harms one hair on her head," he declared.

"How could you?" Zara demanded in a voice that trembled with anger and fear. Hands clenched in her lap, she shifted upon the fallen log so that not even her skirts touched the man beside her.

Darth was truly puzzled, then he understood. His mother was sickened by his violence, and most especially that he had allowed a man to be killed. Soon, though, she would learn his ways.

"I am not my brother," he said gruffly, then crooked a smile. "Though I shall soon enjoy all manner of the life that he has had these many years while I toiled in the fields. 'Tis only fitting that I now become the baron of Chesne, is it not?"

Fear's arms gripped Zara more tightly. "And what of Ranulf?" she asked, willing herself to meet his dark eyes. Truly, now that she looked closely, they were really not all that similar to Ranulf's. Aye, the color was the same, but the emotion expressed there was as unlike Ranulf's as day was unlike night. Summer unlike winter.

His lower jaw thrusting forward, Darth looked toward the campfire. "Ranulf," he breathed, then gave a nonchalant shrug. "Philip has plans fer him."

"Then he will try to kill the man who is your brother," Zara stated, knowing better than to phrase it as a question.

Darth looked back at her. "If 'tis not him, 'twill be me."

Zara's face began to crumple as the world's sorrows descended upon her shoulders. At long last, she had her second son, knew him now to be a grown man, and he was cruel and coldhearted. If it would gain him the barony, he would willingly take Ranulf's life himself. He would take from her that which she held dearest. Fighting for control of her emotions, she dropped her face into her hands.

A hand that, surprisingly, had some of the warmth of Ranulf's, descended to her shoulder. "No harm will come to ye," Darth said, his voice gentling as much as was possible for a man like him.

Tears glistening upon her lashes, she looked up at him. " 'Tis not for me I grieve," she croaked. " 'Tis for Ranulf . . . and you. That you could not have grown up side by side. That you could not have loved each other as 'twas meant to be. That your heart is so cold and your ways so cruel."

Darth's eyes hardened. "Had ye grown up a peasant and toiled as I have, worked till yer body screamed in agony, methinks ye would not look so fairly upon this world either."

"What was it like, Darth?" she asked softly.

He sneered. "Never enough food to eat, so ye had to steal from another to fill yer belly. Ever too much work to be done, so ye never could get enough sleep. Always too cold . . . or too hot. Always saying 'aye' to the lord no matter what 'twas he asked of ye—"

"Is that why you attacked the Balmaine camp—for Philip?" Zara broke in.

"Aye, he promised me a share of the dowry wagons and my own plot of land did I do it fer him."

"And you did."

"I am no fool," Darth snapped.

"Did he give you what he promised?"

A muscle leaped in Darth's jaw. "I failed him. Nay, he gave me naught but blood upon my back."

"And you think he will give you Chesne?"

Darth's eyes narrowed to suspicious slits. "I will not fail him this time," he said with conviction.

A cold chill passed over Zara. Though it was not really his fault he was the way he was, her second son was evil. Aye, it was Philip's fault . . . and Mary's. "Mary—" she began.

"Is dead," Darth viciously interrupted.

Zara stared hard at him for a long moment, something telling her she did not want to know the answer to the question formulating in her mind. Still, she had to ask. "How did she die?"

Darth shifted uncomfortably upon the log, his downcast eyes moving side to side before he finally tossed his head and met her gaze. "She fell," he said. "Fell and broke her neck, methinks."

Zara hardened her resolve to discover the truth of it. "Did you do it, Darth?"

He wet his lips, clearly discomfited by her pursuit of the circumstances surrounding Mary's death. "I would think ye'd rejoice in knowing the hag was dead," he said evasively. "She did steal me from ye."

"Aye, that she did, for which I can never forgive her. But I would still know if 'tis you responsible for her death."

Of a sudden, Darth's face twisted into an ugly mask of hate. "Aye, I pushed her," he said, his upper lip curling back to reveal his yellowed teeth. "She tried to stop me from leaving with Philip—cried about how I was her son and owed her for the years she had cared fer me." He spit upon the ground. "I was angry. After all, 'twas because of her deception I was made to suffer all these years." His large shoulders rolled beneath his tunic as he fought to contain the rage struggling to surface.

Zara wanted to cry—to scream—at the injustice of it all. Not only was her son a thief and rapist, he was also a murderer. He was so different from Ranulf that the only thing the two men had in common was looks, and even that had been corrupted by the different lives each had led. She had only ever known such great sorrow before when she'd been told of Colin's death nearly thirty years past.

"Ye are disgusted," Darth said.

She shook her head. "I am saddened for the life you were forced to live . . . that you seek your brother's death that you might obtain all that is his. Have you no feeling for Ranulf?"

Darth gave a shout of bitter laughter. "Think ye he would welcome me at Chesne? Nay, he seeks my death as surely as I do his."

"'Tis not true," Zara protested. "Ranulf has not said any such thing."

"He need not say it fer it to be true."

"He is not like that."

"And what of his wife?" Darth asked. "Ye are telling me he would not seek to avenge her honor?"

"There was naught that occurred between Lady Lizanne and you. She stopped you—do you not remember?"

Without conscious thought, Darth rubbed a hand to his head. "Aye, well I remember. As I remember laying low her brother." As if it were yesterday, he saw again the knight's anguished face. He had felt such a heady sensation when he had run his sword through the man to end his life. But Gilbert Balmaine had lived, and Darth had paid for his failure with two dozen stripes across his back. Philip had seen to the punishment personally.

"Balmaine," he said, wishing not for the first time that he had severed the man's head from his neck to ensure his death. "He seeks revenge."

Zara nodded. "Greatly you wronged him."

Darth's jaw clenched tightly. "Had I to do it again, I would not make the same mistake of leaving him alive—nor his sister."

"Nay, do not say that!" Zara exclaimed, still harboring hopes deep down of setting her second son on the right path. Impossible, she knew, but could not so readily dismiss the idea. "It is not too late," she said, gripping his arm. "Help us escape Philip, and all will be dealt with fairly. This I vow to you."

Darth pushed her hand away. "Fair would be to take my life for the crimes I have committed, and I do not wish to die. Nay, Philip will secure for me all of Chesne, and then I will have what is rightfully mine."

Rightfully his? Zara squelched the rejoinder hovering upon her lips. "Nay, Darth, Philip will see you dead. It is not only Lizanne he desires, but Chesne as well. He is not the kind of man to settle for a woman when there are riches to be had."

"Ye lie," Darth snapped. "Chesne will be mine!"

Zara shook her head, the reserve of love in her heart for this unknown son beginning to shrivel. Of her body, aye, but not of her soul. Darth was as much a stranger to her as any. She did not know him—would never know him.

"If Ranulf dies," she said, "so will you, Darth, for Philip cannot allow you to live. You have only one chance to save yourself. Give us aid."

For a moment, Darth looked to be considering her words, but then he laughed. "Ye are as deceptive as yer bastard sister. I have chosen my path, *Mother*, and soon I will be rewarded."

Zara's shoulders slumped. It would be futile to argue further. It was up to Lizanne.

"Now," Darth said, "ye will tell me everything about Chesne."

Fighting back tears, she turned her head and looked across to where the other captives remained.

Chapter 25

$\mathcal{A}$ *commotion caught* the attention of the prisoners. Lizanne turned to see, and her eyes rounded with fear as she saw Philip in the midst of his men. They were laughing loudly, raised voices making lewd, suggestive comments as he headed toward the captives.

He was coming for her. . . .

She made a hasty decision. As Lady Zara's return to the pen was uncertain, she slipped behind Walter as unobtrusively as possible and retrieved the other woman's dagger. Praying she would not cut him in her haste, she caught his hands and sliced the weapon up between his bound wrists. The ropes fell free.

"Keep your hands behind your back," she whispered when he started in surprise. Sliding the dagger up his sleeve, she closed his fingers over the hilt. " 'Tis Lady Zara's. I only regret I cannot leave you mine as well, but methinks I will need it myself."

She clamped her mouth tightly closed as Philip caught her eye. "Come," he said, waving her forward.

"I will bring Ranulf," she whispered as she pushed to her feet. Shaking her head at the men as they moved to shield her, she weaved her way toward Philip.

When he took hold of her and turned to guide her across the camp, she did not protest.

"Do you pleasure me, Lizanne," he said, not missing a step as he drew her past the campfire, "mayhap I will keep you to myself."

She stopped, forcing him to turn and face her. "I am resigned to my fate," she said. "You may do with me what you will. I will fight you no more."

He regarded her with suspicion before a smile made its way across his features. "That is good." He lightly touched the bruises he had placed on her face. "It does not please me to have to discipline you."

Only just, Lizanne contained the inner cringe that threatened to manifest itself outwardly. "Then you will not hurt me anymore?" she asked in as submissive a tone as her constricted throat would allow. When he raised his brows, she quickly lowered her lashes to hide the lie in her eyes.

He brushed the hair back from her face. " 'Tis entirely up to you."

She tried to smile but only succeeded in showing him a bit of teeth. "Then I need not worry further on it," she said.

Pleased with her acquiescence, Philip led her into the trees, announcing himself to the guard posted there before pulling her deeper into the woods.

"This will do," he said, releasing her to remove his long mantle. As he spread it on the fallen leaves, his eyes never once strayed from her. "Come," he said, unbuckling his sword. "I would see what you've hidden beneath all those clothes."

"Would—would you like me to remove them?" she asked, ignoring the hand he held out to her. "I would do that for you."

She was certain he was smiling, though with only the waning moon for light, she couldn't quite make out his features. "Aye," he said, "but do come closer."

She waited until he sank down upon the mantle, then stepped nearer. Loosing the laces of her bliaut, she bent and drew it over her head.

"You know I have always loved you, Philip," she lied, hoping to distract him that he might lower his defenses. "When you rejected me, I was deeply hurt. 'Tis verily the reason I chose Ranulf instead of you." Dropping the bliaut, she lowered herself to her knees and reached to his booted feet.

He stiffened but relaxed as she slowly drew his boots off. Thankful for the darkness that hid her intense loathing, she slid her hands up over his legs.

"Won't you help me remove these?" she said, tugging at his leggings. Eagerly, he complied. "And this," she added. She pushed the tunic up around his waist, her hand brushing the dagger he still retained.

Suddenly, he caught hold of her wrists. "Do not think to trick me," he warned, then shoved her away from him. "Now remove the rest of your clothing."

Sitting back on her heels, Lizanne began to fumble with the laces of her chemise. As the first light of dawn crept through the wood, she saw Philip slide his dagger beneath a bare buttock, then in one swift movement drag his tunic off.

"You are too slow," he complained, reaching for her.

"Nay, I will do it." She moved just out of his reach. On her knees, she smoothed her hand down over her chemise and lifted its hem. Lingeringly, she drew the garment up her legs.

"Now," she said huskily, "I will show you what my husband has taught me." The chemise raised to midthigh, she paused and sought his eyes. "You do want to know, don't you?"

"Show me," he said, his voice thickened with lust.

She smiled. Drawing the chemise higher, she slid her fingers up her thighs and closed her hand over the hilt of the dagger. With the swiftness of a wildcat, she slid it from its sheath and lunged forward, throwing herself onto Philip and swinging her arm down in a wide arc.

She felt the displacement of air and heard the dagger sing shrilly as her hand traveled to his heart. "For four years of hell!" she cried.

She was completely unprepared when an iron grip on her wrist arrested her progress only inches from her mark.

Snarling, Philip threw her onto her back and rolled atop her. Forcing her arm high above her head, he slammed her hand against a rock in an attempt to force her to release the weapon.

In spite of the pain, Lizanne refused to let go of her lifeline, knowing it was likely her last chance. It was surely by God's hand that her knee found his manhood as she writhed beneath him. With a tortured groan, he sprawled heavily upon her but did not release her.

In his moment of weakness, she fought harder, desperately trying to heave him off her, but to no avail.

When he recovered minutes later, he was furious, raging loudly as he lifted his chest from her and began to grope for something hidden among the folds of the mantle.

His dagger! she realized. Throwing her free hand out, she began to search for it herself.

Philip located it first and lay its sharp edge to her throat. "Do you wish to die now or later, bitch?" he spit, his teeth bared as he slammed her hand on the rock again.

The pain was fierce. Her bruised and bloodied fingers spasming, Lizanne lost her hold on the dagger. It hit the rock with a clatter and slid to the ground.

Philip laughed, a crude, rasping sound that echoed around the woods. " 'Twill not be easy to keep you," he said, tracing the point of his dagger down her throat. "But I will . . . for just a while longer."

Straddling her, he sat back and turned his dagger in his hand. "Now," he said, "let us see if we cannot think of an appropriate punishment for you." He laid his hand on her belly and dragged it up over her breasts.

"As I do not think I could stand to look at you were your face any more spoiled than 'tis," he went on, "I will have to be creative."

So swiftly that Lizanne barely saw him move, he lifted the neck of her chemise and cut through the thin material, baring her breasts.

"Are you not frightened?" he demanded when she remained still beneath him.

"Would it please you?"

He did not answer, for in the next instant an alarm was sounded in the camp, audible even at this distance.

Jumping to his feet, Philip grabbed his leggings and began dragging them on.

Ranulf! Relief washed over Lizanne. It had to be. That or Walter and his men were attempting an escape.

"Do not move!" Philip yelled, waving his dagger at her when she started to sit up.

Trying to remain calm, she watched as he belted his sword on over his tunic. Then, drawing the weapon from its scabbard, he reached down and hauled her to her feet.

Forgetting his mantle, he pushed her ahead of him through the trees. When he obtained a safe vantage point from which to observe the camp unseen, he halted her, keeping the point of his sword at her back to ensure her silence.

In the soft morning light, Lizanne saw the utter mayhem caused by the arrival of Ranulf's and Gilbert's soldiers, but she did not have time to seek out either man before Philip dragged her back through the trees.

Cursing loudly, he forced her to a run.

She was not completely without recourse. Doing her best to thwart his efforts, she tripped and fell at every opportunity.

They had not gone far when, from among the trees, Darth emerged, Zara seated before him on one of two destriers.

"Lizanne," Zara cried, her eyes taking in her daughter-in-law's dishevelment.

"Your horse," Darth yelled. He tossed the reins to Philip before sending his own mount flying ahead.

Wasting no time, Philip ordered Lizanne up ahead of him, then mounted behind her. He jabbed his heels into the horse's sides and set off after Darth.

"God's mercy, nay!" Gilbert bellowed, thrusting his arm heavenward, a soiled garment clenched in his fist.

Too consumed by his own raging fires, Ranulf hardly noticed the other man's outcry. Sweeping the forsaken mantle from the ground, he stood tensely silent as he visually searched the area for any clue that might lead him to Lizanne.

Naught.

South—but nay, Charwyck was too clever to continue that course ... wasn't he? East, then. The easy terrain would aid his flight, though it would offer him little cover.

As he turned abruptly on his heel, a blaze of sparkling color among the grass caught Ranulf's eye. He reached down and lifted the bejeweled object from the base of a rock.

Lizanne's dagger ... but no blood to dull its shimmering blade. Clenching the hilt, he closed his eyes. It had been his most fervent hope she still retained it. That she didn't could only mean Charwyck had discovered it beneath her skirts, confirming Gilbert's belief that his sister had been violated.

If he hadn't been before, Charwyck was no better than a dead man now. Even if it took him the rest of his days to track him down, Ranulf determined he would see the life drained from the miscreant's miserable body, drop by stinking drop. No greater offense had ever been done him.

In that moment, he finally accepted what he'd been wrestling with for days.

He loved her. It was not simply an infatuation of the body, as he had tried to convince himself, but a new emotion that went far beyond the bounds he had previously set it. If only he had told her ...

Gilbert was still hurling his curses to the sky when Ranulf noticed the dark spots on a rock's gray surface. Wiping his fingers over it, he stared down at the blood that was only now beginning to dry.

He gave no thought as to how it had come to be there, or whose it might be. Pivoting, he grasped Gilbert by the arm and urged him toward their horses and the soldiers awaiting their orders.

"They cannot have gone far," he said, showing the evidence to Gilbert.

Gilbert's eyes widened as he stared at Ranulf's stained hand. "God's rood!" he exclaimed. He ran to his destrier and mounted quickly, then waited impatiently while Ranulf divided his men, sending the smaller of the two groups south before leading the larger one east.

They rode hard, at last converging upon a level meadow that stretched for miles before rising to gently rolling hills.

Ranulf was the first to spot the riders across the distance—two indistinct forms upon the crest of a hill, one topped by a telling flash of pale hair.

"There!" he shouted.

Abreast, Ranulf and Gilbert swept forward, their men close behind. Though their quarry had the advantage of distance, it would be short-lived, for their mounts carried two each. It was a hindrance that would soon see them intercepted.

It was more a feeling than anything else that had

Lizanne peering around Philip. Immediately, her gaze fell upon the rank of riders descending upon them.

Ranulf! her mind cried, her heart soaring joyously. Determinedly, she renewed her efforts to free herself of her captor, in spite of the speed they were traveling at.

"What?" Philip bellowed. Clamping his arm tighter about her, he spared a glance over his shoulder. "Ride hard, Darth!" he shouted as he drew his sword. Veering right, he guided his mount back over the hills toward the bordering woods. There they might be able to immerse themselves and evade capture.

It was not to be. As they descended to level ground, their pursuers swept around them.

Wild-eyed, Philip and Darth drew alongside each other, forced to an uncertain halt in the midst of so many who would see them dead.

Lizanne looked at Ranulf, her heart beginning a wild beat when his dark eyes captured hers—imploring yet wrathful as he studied her disheveled state.

Ashamed, she glanced away, grasping the pieces of her bodice together as she slid her eyes to Gilbert. He wore much the same expression as Ranulf. It was clear neither man would be content until he had ripened his blade with this enemy's blood.

It was stark pale hair and glittering black eyes probing his that stole Ranulf's regard from his wife. So like— nay, identical to him. His heart thundered as he stared at the man pressing a blade to the small woman before him. A yawning chasm opened within him as he attempted to reconcile that the bastard was also his brother.

His gaze fell to his mother. She did not look well, her face pressed to Darth's chest, her arms drawn up around her head. He did not think she was aware of what had transpired. Perhaps that was good, for it would save her from that which would follow.

"Let us pass, else they die!" Philip shouted, pressing

his blade to Lizanne's midriff as his horse pranced nervously.

Ranulf and Gilbert exchanged glances. Then, swords drawn, they broke from the formation and urged their horses forward.

"I have warned you, Wardieu!" Philip yelled.

Still they came, two avengers who had set themselves the license of God.

"Release them," Ranulf demanded, "and prepare to die."

" 'Tis your wife and mother that will die do you not allow us to pass," Philip said.

When they were within fifty feet, Ranulf and Gilbert slowed their advance.

"Would that it could be any other way . . . brother," Ranulf said to that other who had yet to turn from him. Dismounting, he swept his gaze over the two men, who did not wear armor. " 'Twill be a fair duel," he said, and began to remove his hauberk. Gilbert followed suit a moment later.

Then, swords in hand, the two men strode forward.

Lizanne's brow furrowed when she saw that her brother's limp was more prominent than usual. He was in pain, she realized, her anxiety soaring. It would undoubtedly hinder him.

"Come down, Charwyck." Gilbert's deep voice echoed around the hills. "Or are you faint of heart?" When his taunt was answered by silence, he forced harsh laughter that grated upon the air. "Know you how to wield a sword, man?"

Surprisingly, it was Darth who complied first. Settling Lady Zara's limp form over his horse's neck, he swung out of the saddle and turned to face the two advancing upon him.

"Coward!" Lizanne spit over her shoulder at Philip.

"Quiet, wench," Philip muttered, squeezing her so tight, she had to struggle to draw her next breath.

"Do you think you can hide behind a woman's skirts the rest of your days, Charwyck?" Ranulf sneered. "Be warned, there is no shield tax that can save you from the service required of you this day."

Silence prevailed, and then, having turned a shade of red not unlike vermilion, Philip hurriedly dismounted, leaving Lizanne astride.

"Now you will earn that title you seek," he said to Darth.

Lizanne looked at Ranulf.

With a throw of his arm, he signaled for her to move clear. Grabbing up the reins, she guided the horse to Lady Zara. She did not ask any questions of the haunted woman, simply took the other reins firmly in her hand and told her to hold tight.

Geoff and Joseph rode forward to meet the two women. Though Geoff's sword was drawn, Joseph, as usual, carried his bow, an arrow nocked in place. Without a word, Ranulf's squire took charge of Lady Zara and guided her horse behind the ranks of men.

"How do you fare?" Joseph asked Lizanne, carefully avoiding looking at her gaping chemise, his gaze roaming her ravaged face instead.

Grasping her chemise together, Lizanne nodded and turned her horse so that she might view the combat about to take place.

"Come," Joseph urged her, placing a hand upon her arm.

She shook her head, and pulled away.

Knowing he could not win an argument with her, Joseph contented himself with remaining at her side. He draped his short mantle about her shoulders, but she did not even seem to notice. Settling his bow across his lap, he looked to the center of the field.

"Which will you take?" Ranulf asked, offering Gilbert first choice.

"Darth," Gilbert answered, pointing his sword at

that man. In truth, he wanted Philip more than he wanted Darth, but he was uncertain as to how Ranulf would deal with his newfound brother and was taking no chances. Justice would be done.

Ranulf nodded. "Very well, but first I would speak with him."

Grimacing, Gilbert waved him ahead and turned his gaze upon Philip. He did not trust the man.

"Come, brother," Ranulf said, moving toward Darth. "Let us speak ere we do battle."

Darth looked uncertain for a moment before he acquiesced, following Ranulf a short distance away from the other two men.

Each with their swords before them, neither trusting the other, the two brothers stood facing each other. During that long interval before either spoke, they studied the other's face. At first, it seemed as if they stood before a large mirror, but then the differences became clearer.

Ranulf felt a sharp pang of regret for the hard life reflected in his brother, and Darth a deepening anger and jealousy.

"Would that I could have known you, Darth—Colin," Ranulf said. "That it could have been different."

" 'Twill be different," Darth said. "Chesne will be mine, and ye will be dead."

Ranulf's brow furrowed. There was no love or compassion in this man. He was hard ... and very angry. What had his life been like growing up beneath Philip's warped tutelage? What had Darth gained by doing the man's evil bidding?

Ranulf drew a deep breath. "Nay, Chesne is mine," he said, "though had things been different, I would have shared all with you."

Darth's mouth twisted. "Ye lie as much as our dear, sweet mother."

Immediately, Ranulf's gaze swept across the distance to where Zara sat unmoving upon her mount, then to Lizanne. Back stiff, she watched their exchange, her dark hair lifting in the cool breeze. Justice must be done—for her, for Gilbert, for all those nameless others who had fallen at the hands of his brother in the name of Philip Charwyck.

"I speak the truth," Ranulf said, turning back to Darth, "but 'tis too late now." It was a risk he took in turning his back on Darth, but Ranulf turned away. With long strides, he crossed to where Philip awaited him, pausing to clasp arms with Gilbert as they passed each other.

"No mercy," Gilbert said, briefly meeting Ranulf's eyes before continuing on.

Aye, Ranulf thought, two would die that day, but which two would live? Determined it would not be he who spent his life's blood upon this field, he readied his sword and advanced upon Philip.

What followed was more bloody than any could have imagined, for Philip was more than simply proficient with a sword. He was expert.

Darth was a different matter entirely, but nonetheless not a man to be toyed with or taken lightly. Although he lacked finesse in his sword skill, he was strong and terribly unpredictable, which proved dangerous for Gilbert with his leg troubling him as it was.

Labored grunts and groans filled the air, curses hurled like flotsam upon the gentling breeze, and blows exchanged that left each man raw and bleeding.

Lizanne's wide-eyed gaze swung between Ranulf and Gilbert, each blow reflected in the tensing of her body. Hugging her arms tightly to her, she watched as Gilbert parried a thrust that would have severed his head from his neck had he not anticipated it. Roaring his wrath, he countered with a swing that caught the other man unawares and sliced through his sword arm.

Stumbling back, Darth grasped at the gaping wound, torrents of blood seeping through his fingers.

Though it was of little use to him as the injury stole his strength, he held his sword aloft as Gilbert cautiously circled him.

The death cry, loud and passionate, caused Ranulf to pause to discover the victor. He had only to see the spill of pale hair upon the grassy meadow to know Gilbert had prevailed. His sword hoisted overhead, the blood flowing down it to coat his hand, Gilbert stood over the body of Colin Wardieu.

It was as it should be, Ranulf assured himself, but could not help but feel a deep loss for one he had never known but who had been bound to him all these lost years. A glancing pain that mirrored his troubled mind shot through his side as Philip took the opportunity to make up the ground he had earlier surrendered.

The wound was not mortal—Ranulf knew without looking—but it enraged him. Snarling, he deflected the next blow and forced his adversary back a pace, then another. Steel rang against steel with increased vigor as he sought and found the other's flesh, repaying him tenfold for each injury done him. Blood flew into his eye, but he did not pause to clear it as he took another piece of flesh from the bastard.

Crying out, Philip staggered backward, losing his sword as he fell to his knees.

A white-knuckled fist pressed to her mouth, Lizanne allowed herself a measure of relief before tensing again.

"Say your prayers," Ranulf ground out between clenched teeth, lowering his sword to the man's chest.

Clutching his gut, Philip threw his head back. "I yield," he shouted for all to hear, then smiled.

Ranulf's eyes narrowed. "Either way you will die," he said shortly, "be it by my hand or the king's order. My question is, will you die honorably, or as the poltroon you are?"

"I'll take my chances with Henry," Philip retorted.

Ranulf pressed the point of his sword more heavily to Philip's chest.

Philip's gaze fell to it, but the smile on his face only widened. "You would kill a fallen knight who has offered himself up to you, Baron Wardieu?"

Jaws clenched, Ranulf closed his eyes, battling with the conflicting inner voices that seemed intent upon tearing him in two. Finally, assuring himself the bastard would meet the same end either way, he allowed chivalry to triumph.

"Get up," he ordered.

"I had her, you know," Philip taunted as he slowly rose, still holding a hand to the wound that had been his undoing. "No doubt you will benefit from everything I taught her."

Chivalry be damned!

Ranulf very nearly leaned into his sword then, but something stopped him. Every muscle in his body straining, he stepped back, lowering his sword.

Laughing exultantly, Philip straightened.

Thrusting the man ahead of him, Ranulf directed him toward where Gilbert stood. His anger was so all-consuming, he was unprepared when Philip rounded on him, his arm thrown back, the newly risen sun glinting off the blade he held.

Before Ranulf could raise his sword, Philip convulsed, momentarily frozen as he stood, poised to release his dagger. Then he toppled forward, an arrow shaft protruding from his back, blood spreading over his tunic.

Ranulf knew.

Raising his gaze, he sought and instantly found the master archer whose accuracy and unhindered reflexes had spared his life. The bow still extended before her, Lizanne faced him from atop her mount, her expression unreadable across the distance.

Stepping over Philip's inert form, Ranulf walked directly to her. As he neared, she lowered the bow, giving him his first close look at her.

'Tis not the time for rage, Ranulf sharply reminded himself, stamping down that emotion. Although he had known she had been beaten, he was grateful he had not realized the extent. It surely would have clouded his judgment, and it might be he who lay dead on the field. His eyes never leaving her face, he stopped beside her.

Her mouth worked for a moment before a strangled cry was torn from her throat. She tossed the bow to the ground and slid off the horse, into his waiting arms, clinging to him and sobbing loudly against his chest.

Ranulf simply held her, stroking her hair. Even when Gilbert appeared and spoke soothingly to her, she refused to relinquish her hold on him.

Gilbert turned and crossed to where Lady Zara still sat atop her mount.

" 'Tis over," Lizanne's voice came to Ranulf.

He looked down into her tear-streaked face and nodded.

"Can we go home?" she asked.

He cupped her face and nodded. "Straightaway." Bending, he swung her into his arms.

A smile on his face, Geoff was waiting with his lord's destrier. Ranulf lifted Lizanne onto the saddle, then mounted behind her and drew her back against him.

"I love you, Lizanne Wardieu," he said. Those words, which he had never thought to utter to anyone, surprised both of them.

Lizanne's head came around, her eyes huge. "Truly?"

Cupping her chin, he lowered his head and kissed her gently. "Aye, with everything I am, and everything I will be with you by my side." He drew back to look into the shimmering green pools of her eyes.

She smiled. "Have you loved me long, Ranulf?"

He had to laugh at that. "It seems as if forever," he said.

"But when did you discover it?" she pressed, her fingers playing in the pale hair that skimmed his shoulders.

He gave serious consideration to her question, then grinned. "Methinks 'twas when you crawled up in that damned tree and refused to come down, though I did not realize that was what I was feeling at the time. I have had very little experience with loving."

"You love your mother."

"Very different."

Pillowing her head against his shoulder, she pressed herself nearer him. "Good."

Smiling, Ranulf urged his destrier forward and preceded his men back toward Philip's camp. By now, he was confident Walter would have everything under control.

"I've something for you," he said some minutes later. Reaching to his waist, he removed her dagger. "For such a valuable weapon as this," he said as he gave it to her, "you do seem to have the most difficult time keeping possession of it."

She stared at it, running a finger idly over the jewel-encrusted hilt. "I fought him," she murmured.

Ranulf's jaw hardened. "I do not require any explanations," he said, gripping her more tightly to him. " 'Tis behind us now."

It took Lizanne but a moment to decipher the unspoken meaning behind his words. Twisting around, she raised the dagger between them. "Though I did not get the chance to carve him with this," she said softly, "it did enable me to unman him."

Ranulf stared at her hand and understood. From wrist to fingertips, it was scratched, gouged, and bruised from Charwyck beating it against the rock. "Then he did not—"

She shook her head, her eyes glittering as brightly as the jewels of the weapon she held.

Sighing his relief, Ranulf kissed her soundly. "Why do I continually underestimate you, wife?" he asked, shaking his head in wonder. " 'Tis you who saved my life ... for which I am eternally grateful not to have cut short now that I have you."

A mischievous glint entered her eyes, and her dimple emerged full force. "Then you will not object to my practicing weaponry ... occasionally?"

"Wife, if it pleases you, you may instruct every last one of my men—most especially in archery."

Chapter 26

"A girl," *Ranulf* breathed with great pride as the rather large, perfectly formed infant was placed into his arms. Cradling her with utmost care, he lifted a hand and touched the silken hair sprouting in abundance from the small head.

"Flaxen," Zara murmured, standing on tiptoe to view her granddaughter better. Cooing softly so as not to awaken her daughter-in-law, she placed a finger in one miniature flailing palm and smiled at the child's strong grip.

"Think you she will be as beautiful as her mother?" Ranulf whispered.

"Of course," Zara responded. "Save for the hair, she has the look of Lizanne."

"Do share," said a voice from the bed.

Stepping around his mother, Ranulf hurried to Lizanne and lowered the bundle into her waiting arms, then gave his wife a resounding kiss.

With a passion surprising for a woman who had so recently given birth, she returned the kiss, then turned her head to view their child.

"Oh, she is beautiful," she said. As she had barely had time to focus on her child before exhaustion had overtaken her following the birthing, it was her first real look at her daughter. Due to the baby's size she had labored through a difficult day and night.

"Gillian," she pronounced with finality. "We will call you Gillian."

Ranulf looked taken aback. "Gillian?" he repeated. "And what kind of name is that?"

Lizanne kissed the crown of her daughter's head, then lay back and smiled at her husband. "Since I can hardly name a girl Gilbert," she said, her smile widening, " 'tis the closest I can come to honoring my brother."

Ranulf looked at his mother but, seeing he would get no support from her, resignedly plowed a hand through his hair. "You are certain?"

Knowing she had already won, Lizanne nodded. "Aye. As she has your surname, 'tis only fair she has one of my family's names. But you may choose a name of endearment, if 'twould please you."

His face expressing what he thought of her generosity, Ranulf lowered himself beside her and grasped her hand in his. "I must needs think on this a while," he said with all seriousness. " 'Twill have to be something wonderful, lest she not care for her given name."

Lizanne chuckled. "Oh, she will like it all right."

"I must needs tell Walter," Zara exclaimed, doing a quick turnabout and hurrying to the door. "He was as nervous, I think, as Ranulf." Twittering excitedly, she went in search of her husband.

Lizanne sighed and beckoned Ranulf closer. "Now I would have a real kiss," she said, and giggled when he eagerly complied.

Gurgling, Gillian protested the shadow that fell across her.

Ranulf drew back, his features softening as he looked into the large, unblinking eyes of the gift Lizanne had given him.

"You are not disappointed that she is not a he?"

Lizanne asked, though she already knew what his answer would be.

He touched the new pink skin of his daughter's hands. "Never."

Gillian began to whimper then, her little round face slowly turning crimson, her legs thrusting beneath the swaddling cloth.

Lizanne and Ranulf looked at each other in silent question. Then, with a wide-eyed grin and an abashed shrug, Lizanne turned the babe in her arms and settled the little one's mouth to her breast. It took some coaxing and several failed attempts, but at last Gillian set about satisfying her hunger.

"You have sent word to Gilbert?" Lizanne asked now that they were alone—nearly.

Ranulf did not answer at first, too amazed at his daughter's voracious appetite. When Lizanne nudged him and raised her brows questioningly, he nodded.

"Aye, yestereve."

"Think you he will come?" she asked, worriedly biting her lip.

Reflecting on what he knew of Gilbert's latest troubles with the Charwyck woman, Philip Charwyck's sister, Ranulf shrugged. "Mayhap not straightaway, but he will come."

" 'Tis that Charwyck woman again, isn't it?" Lizanne grumbled, her eyes darkening.

"Aye, it seems she is not making this easy on Gilbert."

Lizanne fingered Gillian's softly curling locks. " 'Tis a pity she did not get word of her brother's death until after she had taken her vows."

"Gilbert will no doubt survive," Ranulf assured her.

"Of course he will. He is a Balmaine, after all."

And then the entire subject was forgotten as they immersed themselves in the wonder of their child.

"Are you truly happy, Ranulf?" Lizanne asked some

time later when their daughter lay asleep in her arms, Ranulf stretched out beside her.

He propped himself up on an elbow and feathered a finger down her throat. "Very." He met her eyes and smiled. "Now I have two worth dying for."

ABOUT THE AUTHOR

TAMARA LEIGH has a Master's Degree in Speech and Language Pathology. She lives in the small town of Gardnerville located at the base of the Sierra Mountains with her husband David, who is a former "Cosmopolitan Bachelor of the Month." Tamara says her husband is incredibly romantic, and is the inspiration for her writing. They have one child.

If you loved WARRIOR BRIDE,

look for Gilbert's story in

V I R G I N   B R I D E,

coming in the fall of 1994.

Over the next *three days Graeye searched for an opportunity* *to be alone with Sir Michael again. But none presented itself,* *for the man seemed determined to keep his distance.*

Time and again Graeye considered any number of the knights at Medland, but she simply could not bring herself to approach them. What was she to do, after all? She had no experience with seduction. How exactly did one go about capturing a man's desire? If she was to succeed, it seemed it would have to be with Sir Michael.

In the late afternoon of the fourth day following the arrival of the king's men, Graeye was faced with the prospect of seeing her plans forever spoiled when Sir Royce ordered her father's release from the watchtower.

Immediately Edward sought out his daughter and informed her that the arrangements had been made to see her returned to the convent the following morning. Surprisingly, he was calm—emotionless—until Graeye attempted to convince him to allow her to remain with him. Then he had begun to rage so terribly that she was sure he would have struck her had Sir Abelaard not interceded.

Search as she might, Michael was nowhere to be found, and late that evening a thoroughly defeated Graeye slipped out the postern gate and made her way to the one place she knew might offer solace—the waterfall.

It was there she had spent numerous sunny days with her mother before an untimely death had interceded to take the one person from Graeye who had loved her unconditionally.

She was not running away, for life in the church had become less daunting than the prospect of being on her own in a world she did not know ... or understand. She simply had to see the falls one last time and relive the wonderful memories left there ten years past. And on the morrow she would carry those revived memories with her on the long journey back to the convent.

Her mantle flying out behind her, Graeye left the castle walls far behind and entered the woods. She carefully picked her way down the sloping ground, and it was not long before the sweet melody of falling water led her to the glorious white veil that swept from on high and fell to a large pool below.

For the first time in days Graeye smiled, as the childhood memories came upon her and urged her to venture nearer. Without hesitation she made her way to the edge of the uppermost pool and knelt beside it to dip her fingers in its cool, soothing depths.

Tossing off her clothes, Graeye entered the pool just moments later and, with the stars and moon the only witnesses to her pleasure, clumsily attempted the strokes her mother had taught her so long ago. They were neither graceful nor efficient, but they allowed her to cross the deepest stretch of the pool without mishap and to venture into the biting spray of the falls.

So caught up in the enjoyment was she, Graeye might not have noticed the one who came to intrude upon her solitude had the horse carrying the man not whinnied loudly as it approached the bottom portion of the pool.

Panic-stricken, the past falling abruptly away from her, Graeye treaded water as horse and rider drew even with the grassy bank.

Though she was as yet undiscovered, Graeye's first instinct was to flee, but fear of discovery stayed her, for even with the width of the pool separating them, there would be little to deter the man from pursuit if he chose to give chase.

Shivering as the water lapped her bare shoulders, Graeye silently berated her foolishness in lingering so long. Glancing up at the sliver of moon, she saw that it had traveled a good distance above the trees since first she had come upon the falls.

Slowly, praying the dim light of the moon would not reveal her, she pushed through the water to the protection offered by the long shadows of the bank. Once there, she knelt in the shallows and trained her gaze upon the intruder.

Who was he? she wondered. Could he have been one of her father's former retainers, one who had heretofore gone unnoticed? She did not think so, for she would certainly have remembered such a man—even if she had only glimpsed him from a distance. And neither did she think he was one of the king's men. All she could be certain of was that this man was no wayfarer. Nay, with his fine vest of chain mail and the well-fitting raiments beneath, he was certainly of the nobility. And his mount, a highly prized white destrier, could further attest to that.

Curiously fascinated, and secure in the reckless belief she would not be found out, Graeye used the cloak of darkness to further scrutinize the man.

Dark of hair and beard and sitting tall in his saddle, he appeared every bit the gentleman warrior as he looked about him. But gentleman or no, with the breadth and certain height of him, he looked to be a formidable opponent. In fact, his strength, borne on a wave of something ominous, was a most tangible thing that caused a shiver of disquiet to course down Graeye's spine.

Beneath the water she rubbed her hands briskly over her arms as she pondered what is was he exuded—anger?

When the intruder dismounted, smoothly swinging himself to the ground, Graeye nearly gave in to the impulse to scramble from the water and flee. Eyes wide, her breathing grown ragged, she quelled the urge and pressed herself more deeply into the shadows. Soon he would leave, she reassured herself.

As the man carried himself to the pool's edge, Graeye thought perhaps he limped but could not be certain, considering it had taken little more than a single stride to carry him to where he now knelt to quench his thirst. Mayhap he was simply in his cups, she surmised with a wry twist of her lips as she conjured a vision of her father.

Straightening, the man placed his fists upon his hips and surveyed the pool before him.

Did he sense her presence? Graeye wondered as she fought down her rising panic. Surely he did not see her, for the shadows were too deep.

At last he turned back to his horse. But he did not remount. Instead he removed his belted sword and draped it over the back of the great white destrier. Then he began to remove his chain mail.

Dear God, the man intended to bare himself! Above the sound of the waterfall and in the light of a half-moon came the metallic rasp and glitter of thousands of joined rings as the chain mail was carefully laid aside. Next came the tunic and padded undertunic, leaving nothing save the gloss of night upon a broad, tapering back.

Graeye's maidenly senses protested but a brief moment before she sharply reminded herself that he who had intruded upon her sanctuary had done so unwittingly. He was oblivious to her presence, unaware he shared the dark-mantled sky that danced stars upon the veil of tumbling water with another.

When, moments later, she was faced with the sight of bare buttocks followed closely by thick legs, Graeye's pulses leapt unexpectedly, a gasp escaping her lips.

She was given no time to contemplate her wayward reaction, for in the next instant the intruder came around, his sword in hand, his stance offensive. With a snort heard around the wood and a toss of its massive head, the great animal echoed its master's disquiet.

Warrior-alert, the man's eyes sought the cloak of darkness where Graeye hid.

Were she to flee now, would he give chase in nothing save his swarthy skin? Graeye wondered, her eyes traveling up his body to his sword arm to trace the silvered length of blade thrust before him. Likely. After all, she would be fleeing cloaked in naught save her own natural state. . . .

After an interminable time that had Graeye's chest burning with pent air, the man finally turned back to his destrier. Muttering something unintelligible, he returned the sword to his sheath. However, about his waist he belted a dagger—naught else.

Her breath threading its way from her heavy lungs, Graeye sagged with relief. Only then did her eyes confide to her what they had discovered in their journey over the darkly matted chest to the undulating muscles of the man's abdomen.

She would have liked to look away—knew she should—but found herself unable to. Her cheeks warming, she settled her untried eyes lower upon that dark place between his thighs. Only just, she sealed her lips against the sound that would have been her undoing.

Clenching her teeth, she raised her gaze. Seemingly unaffected by the chill that had stolen Graeye's breath earlier, the man entered the water.

Though his great height had been obvious at the outset, Graeye was better able to gauge his measure when he stood at the center of the pool, his head and shoulders visible above the surface where she had treaded water.

He would stand more than a foot above the crown of her head—mayhap a half more, she realized, wondering at the sensations beginning to curl her insides. As she watched, he dove beneath the surface.

Now. If he stayed under long enough, mayhap she could . . . She shook her head. Nay, she could not risk it.

At his reappearance she was swept with relief. It did not even bear thinking what might have happened had he swum upstream while submerged.

Leave, she silently entreated him. But he did not accommodate her, seemingly in no hurry to finish with his bathing.

After a time, when it seemed he had no intention of exploring the uppermost portion of the pool, Graeye began to relax. Submerged up to her neck, she leaned back against the sloping bank and followed the man's movements, a soft smile curving her lips unbeknownst to her. When he turned onto his back, his darkly furred chest glistening in the moonlight, his lower extremities indecently exposed to eyes fascinated by this new wonderment, Graeye's smile grew wider.

How little she understood the heat upon her skin, she mused, upon realizing she was no longer cold. Not so long past she had been eager to don her clothes again. Now every one of the prickly bumps that had sprouted upon her limbs had softened.

Desire? she ventured a guess, then promptly rejected such absurdity. It was simple curiosity to know that which had long been forbidden her. After all, had she not been pledged to the church, she would have wed years ago.

The smile fell from her mouth. And now, too, she would not wed. Never would she lie in a man's arms, nor hear the laughter of the children she had borne him.

Tears gathered in her eyes. Hopeless. Now that she was no longer a pawn upon which to get heirs, she was to be thrown aside the same as before. On the morrow she would be returned to the abbey to profess herself a nun. Aye, truly hopeless. There was naught she could—

The coming of the thought was like a blow to Graeye, shaking her with its force.

Aye, she realized, here was the man she could offer herself to, an unknown who would not worry about her father's wrath at the deed she would ask of him.

But would he be willing? she wondered. Uncertain, she raked her teeth across her bottom lip. If he had been too long without a woman, perhaps.

A shuddered breath left her as she finally gave over to the idea. It was evil, that which she planned, but this man had to have been sent to her for a reason. Surely God would understand.

By the time Graeye had committed herself, the man had gone to stand in the shallows, his back to her. With a calming breath she forced herself forward, the silt surging between her toes as if to prevent the wicked act she was about to commit. When the ground fell from beneath her feet, she fanned her arms out and swam closer.

She was still several yards away, her heart pounding furiously, when the man spun about, his dagger violently rousing the air.

Searching the darkness for the being he sensed there, directly his eyes settled upon Graeye where her chin bobbed upon the surface.

"Who goes?" he demanded, even as his expression turned to one of disbelief. He blinked as if to dispel the unexpected vision, but when she remained, leaned forward to better see.

He stood thus with the moonlight upon him, his short hair not simply black but pitch—so much that the night bestowed a blue cast upon its unruliness. Though more attractive than Graeye had gleaned from her hiding place, he looked hard and . . . dangerous? Aye, his strength lay in the anger she had sensed.

Battling her fear, Graeye raised her gaze to his straight nose and found herself staring into the depths of glittering eyes that held no kindness. Nervously she wondered what color they might be, and if they ever shone with the light of a smile.

Shifting her scrutiny down the formidable length of his body, she easily found that which made him so incredibly different from her. Heat spilling upon her face and neck, she dragged her gaze away—lower to the thick ridge of a scar that started midthigh and curved downward to disappear beneath the water. So it was indeed a limp she had witnessed and not a state of drunkenness. Still it did not ease her mind nor lift the great burden of shame from shoulders suddenly unwilling to support the weight.

'Tis the only way, Graeye told herself as her mind urged her to abandon her plan. She must finish what she had begun. Only then would she be free to remain at her father's side. Assuring herself her hair still hid the mark, she lowered her feet, crouching so that only her shoulders were visible above the water.

"Who are you?" the man rasped.

Not knowing how she should answer and wary of other questions he might put to her, Graeye chose silence. Shaking her head, she refused him the enlightenment he sought.

His glittering eyes narrowed on her, his jaw clenching as the silence stretched.

Aye, dangerous . . . too dangerous.

A hard knot in the center of her being, Graeye's resolve began to fray, causing her heart to pound furiously and her breathing to turn shallow. Then something taut and trembling snapped within her.

Nay, she could not do this thing! Shaking her head, she took a step back, but only one more before the man lunged for her, closing a hand around her arm and dragging her up the sloping ground to her feet.

A distressed sound tumbled past Graeye's lips as she threw out a hand to balance herself, the flat of it finding the taut muscles of the man's abdomen and securing for her only the space of her arm.

"What are you?" the man hissed, the warmth of his breath reaching her from that great height.

What? The question confounded Graeye enough for her to momentarily overlook her state of undress. Drawing a shaky breath, she dropped her head back and looked into the glittering orbs that were not of any color she could recognize in the shadow of night.

Frowning, she shook her head, then blinked wide. He must think me mute, she realized.

Indeed that thought had crossed his mind. However, now he entertained the rather ridiculous imagining that perhaps this was a fairy turned woman come to tempt him with her wiles. Albeit wary, he found himself suddenly fascinated. Certainly his body was charmed.

He looked from the quick response between his thighs to the exquisite contours before him. Though she was petite, the wraith was perfectly proportioned, her small breasts high and firm, her waist narrow, her hips flared, and those soft, rounded thighs . . .

Graeye saw the softening in his face, beheld the slight curve of the tight corners of his mouth, and felt his bunched muscles ease beneath her palm. The danger was past.

An inexplicable emotion rushed through her then, taking with it the fear and shame that had urged her to flight and replacing it with something that had naught to do with the reason she had sought out this intimacy.

Her wakening senses were patient with her inexperience, gradually yielding to her their discoveries. Her palm tingled where it lay against his chest as the water that clung to him slipped through her fingers and trickled down the back of her hand. He felt splendid. And there was a scent about him. Not perfumed but of muscle and sinew. She inhaled it, her gaze sliding over him to his burgeoning manhood. She wondered at that—not understanding, yet somehow knowing. Reflexively she stepped nearer.

When a hand's breadth was all that separated them, she impulsively slid her touch to his shoulder and trailed it down his arm, her fingers alighting upon the hand that still held tight to the dagger. But he did not resist when she uncurled his fingers, allowing the dagger to fall unheeded to the water.

In size, Graeye felt like a child before this giant, but in all other ways—from the odd, insistent heat coiling up from her depth to the curious longing to be held in those strong arms—she felt like a woman come of age.

How to explain it? she wondered. Kept apart by something she did not understand, she breached the last space separating them, feeling the force of that strong male member rise between them.

Was that her breathing? she wondered at the shallow, raspy sound. What was this incredible song singing through her that made her pulses speed? She reached up and touched his face, threading her fingers through his crisp beard as she focused on the mouth hidden there.

Suddenly she wanted very much to feel those lips upon hers, and daring to hope they would be unlike William's fumblings or Michael's brotherly peck, she leveraged herself up onto her toes. But still the man was too tall for her reach. Curling a hand around his neck, she urged his head lower.

Letting go his held breath, the man encircled her waist with one strong arm and pressed her into the hard contours of his male body.

A shiver of pleasure tripped up Graeye's spine, causing every part of her roused femininity to tremble. Never surrendering his stare, she met the lips he covered hers with and felt a jolt of light rock her core as he proceeded to coax the breath from her. She gave it to him.

They were as two who had been without sustenance for a very long time—touching, caressing, each searching with wild abandonment the other.

Not until the man's hand slid up from Graeye's breast and slipped through her hair did the magic fall away, cruelly pulling Graeye back to the present. Gasping, she jerked her head back and lifted a hand to smooth her hair, relieved to find the mark had not come uncovered.

The man pulled back, a frown creasing his brow as he reached again to brush her hair aside.

Again Graeye resisted, evading him with a toss of her head. Raising her hands before her to ward off further exploration, she locked her gaze with his and shook her head.

Though his frown deepened, he accepted her entreaty with a shrug. Contenting himself with running his fingers through the length of hair that swept her hips, he molded the warm, fluid lines of her to him again and lowered his mouth back to hers.

Graeye accepted the caress that slid over her lips and then inside, responding as he had shown her only moments earlier. Though she was inexperienced in such things, she took this new and wondrous discovery to her breast and soon forgot the awkwardness driving her responses.

A sound, animallike, erupted from Graeye as those hands slid over the curve of her buttocks and inward to her woman's secret, leaving trails of flame in their wake. Now she knew . . . and wanted more.

Heat rose from the forbidden regions of her body and Graeye instinctively began to move against him. Seeking an end to the splendid torment, her fingers began to trace the contours and crevices beneath her hands. Quickly she learned the hard feel of the muscles bunched beneath his skin, unconsciously committing all to memory.

Aye, here were the desires too long suppressed demanding a release from their bonds. Though she sinned, she could not stop herself.

Through a haze of warring sensations, Graeye realized she was being lifted, her thighs settled about the man's waist. She clung to him, shivering when his lips trailed her face and lingered at the sensitive place between neck and shoulder, her breath turning to a tormented moan.

When the sudden, sharp pain driven through Graeye turned her pleasure to agony, she thought she would die. Gone was the promise of heaven and the spreading of wings that longed to fly. Here was the pain of woman the nuns had warned of.

"By my troth!" the man exclaimed.

His words did not register in Graeye's protesting mind. Seeking a desperate escape, she arched back and thrust her hands to his chest. Still the tearing pain did not ease, it only burned the more. Spilling tears, she closed her eyes against the dark and increased her struggles.

Why would he want to hurt her? she wondered as she attempted to twist out of his hold.

With little effort the man clasped her wrists in one hand and pulled her back to him, holding her firmly against his chest and affording her no chance of escape. A frown in his voice, he began to drop soothing words to her ear.

Knowing nothing of the incredible restraint he exercised as he held her, Graeye continued to writhe.

Though he wanted nothing better than to give himself the release she had offered only moments before, the man was patient and gentle. Knowing he would not rest this night, nor any other, if he could not first slake his thirst for this wraith who had set herself the task of seducing him, he determined he would wait on her.

When the burning flame up Graeye's center began to ease, she found herself relaxing, her spine softening until she turned slack in the man's arms. It crossed her mind that if this was what mating was like, it was a wonder women subjected themselves to it at all.

Had he been in as much pain as she? she pondered, then thought better of it. Nay, he would certainly have withdrawn. He had not, and it seemed he had no intention of doing so.

When Graeye felt his renewed movements and the pain, though of less intensity, returned, she resumed her struggles. But he was intent upon visiting that pain upon her.

"Shh," he breathed, pressing kisses to her moist face. " 'Twill not hurt long. There is pleasure at the end of this pain."

She wanted to believe him, but he offered no evidence that he spoke the truth. As his thrusts deepened, she continued to squirm, thinking she might find a way down from the discomfort this brutal giant was causing her.

Intent on escape, she did not notice when the pain subsided altogether, only becoming aware of the change when the pleasure he had promised arrived—a sweet, drawing ache that grew to a breath-stealing sensation. Full of wonder, she tried to match his movements, her attempts awkward yet satisfying.

How was it something so painful had turned enjoyable in so short a time?

Finally finding the hitherto elusive rhythm the man set, Graeye joined him, not quite knowing what to expect but certain there was something beyond this . . . that it was not far off. It was building, lifting her ever higher to soar on those gilded wings she aspired to. It bid her find completion.

He gripped her tighter, his large hands molding them into one as his rhythm increased. Then, as if from afar, Graeye heard his shout and felt his body shudder violently as he gave his liquid heat to her.

And she was plummeting, her own moment of satiation stolen from her.

The man's chest rose and fell heavily, his breath like a wind through her hair as the clam that followed was broken intermittently by tremors marking his subsiding passion.

Knowing she had missed something very important, Graeye leaned away, frowning her question, but he pulled her back to him, pressing her face into the curve of his neck.

"Forgive me," he said. "It has been . . . a long time."

Confused, she settled her cheek to his damp skin, warming to the feel of the strong, erratic beat of blood coursing through his veins.

He had certainly exerted himself, she acknowledged. Impulsively she touched her lips and then the tip of her tongue to the salt of his skin. She liked the taste of him and unashamedly ventured another.

Graeye did not realize he had moved until he lowered her to the bank, himself atop. Her back pressed to the moist ground, she watched as he raised himself above her to search her shadowed face.

Immediately Graeye's hand went to her hair and, to her relief, found it still covered the mark.

The man's raised brows asked the question before his words. "You are not going to tell me who you are?" he said in those deep, resonant tones Graeye found pleasing.

Denying him her voice, she shook her head. Then, her eyes lighting, she touched a finger to his chest and cocked her head questioningly.

An unexpected, lopsided grin transformed his face into one of humor. Then, with a bob of his brows, he shook his head.

'Tis for the better, Graeye assured herself following a bout of disappointment. For the first time since she had set herself this course, she reminded herself of her objective. It would be best if she did not know his identity, for she would never see him again. Still such cool logic did not stop her from wishing it could be otherwise.

She did not flinch when he cupped her chin in his palm, his thumb drawing lazy circles over her jaw and twice dipping inward to brush her parted lips.

It was pleasurable, this. Impulsively Graeye turned her head and laid her lips to his palm.

"You are real?" he asked of a sudden. "Or be you a spirit come to distract me from my labors?"

Graeye smiled but offered naught else save a lazy shrug.

Mild irritation at her continued obstinance had the man's brows snapping together, but he refrained from further coaxing.

"You are beautiful, little one," he said, his voice deepening as he lowered himself again to her and tucked her head beneath his chin. Cradling her, he missed the flash of surprise that crossed Graeye's face.

Beautiful? Truly? She reflected upon the image she had caught in the pool earlier. Aye, she was not uncomely, for certain, but to be told she was beautiful . . .

It warmed her that he desired her, and she felt a sudden sadness that this could not last—that after this night she would never see him again. Deciding to spend her last minutes cherishing him, she searched out his body again, feathering her fingers over him and thrilling when she felt his muscles tremble to her touch.

Were it possible, she thought she could stay with him forever. Though she was unfamiliar with the notion of love outside that which she had felt for her mother, there was something here she desperately wanted to hold to.

A sudden noise from the wooded area surrounding the waterfall broke through Graeye's dreamy consciousness.

Immediately the man's head came up, and a moment later his body followed. Moving so swiftly Graeye momentarily lost sight of him, he retrieved his sword.

Wrenching herself from her stupor, Graeye stumbled to her feet. But there was no cover for her, and the person moving through the woods was making good speed. He would be upon them any moment. Frantic, she stepped back into the water.

"Wait," the man called from where he stood naked upon the bank. Graeye spared him only a glance, then waded farther out. She simply could not be discovered, especially if the person approaching was one of her father's men—or the king's—come to battle the trespasser. There would be time aplenty to feel the old man's wrath, but for now she had to escape.

Looking one last time over her shoulder at the man who had become her lover, Graeye was surprised to find him following. Lunging forward, he caught hold of her and pulled her back to him.

Graeye tried to push him away, but he held fast. Desperate, she met his gaze and shook her head, entreating him to release her.

"My lord," a voice called from the trees, very nearly upon them.

Graeye felt the man's tension dissolve.

" 'Tis but my squire," he explained in that wonderfully thrumming voice. "You need not fear."

Finding no comfort in his words, again she tried to pull free but to no avail, for he had no intention of releasing her.

"Joseph," he called, "come no nearer."

The crackling of leaves underfoot ceased immediately, and a short-lived quiet fell over the wood. "But, my lord—"

"Remain where you are!" the man commanded, then looked back at Graeye. "Stay with me," he murmured. "I have yet to give you what you gave me."

It was all Graeye could do not to shout at him and demand her release, but she kept her lips sealed and obstinately shook her head.

He searched her face a long moment, then unexpectedly recaptured her lips with an urgency that vied with his earlier possession of her.

In spite of her body's yearnings Graeye was too fearful to respond, remaining still beneath his expert ministrations.

When finally the man lifted his head, he wore a puzzled expression that gradually reversed. "I will release you that you might seek cover," he said, "provided you vow to stay near until I have finished with my man."

Surprised at his stipulation, Graeye paused before setting herself to a course she prayed God would forgive her for. Placing her palm to the rapid beat of her heart, she nodded, knowing all the while it was a vow she could not keep.

She saw doubt in his eyes, but then his hands fell from her.

Fearful that he might change his mind, Graeye wasted no time in crossing the pool to the opposite side. Without a backward glance she boosted herself from the water and set her knees to the damp grass. On her feet once again, she hurried to where she had earlier left her clothes, snatched them up, and sprinted for the shelter of trees. There, immersed in the tall shadows, she peered back at the pool and saw that the man stood unmoving where he had only moments ago released her, staring straight at where she had slipped behind a great oak tree.

Graeye would have donned her clothes then, but she had the most peculiar feeling he was every bit as aware of her location as she was of his. Unmindful of the chill that raised the fine hairs along her limbs, she turned and hurried deeper into the woods, her vow to the man shredded upon the breeze stirring the leaves.

Don't miss these fabulous Bantam women's fiction titles

on sale in April

DECEPTION

Now available in paperback by *New York Times* bestselling author Amanda Quick
"One of the hottest and most prolific writers in romance today."—*USA Today*

❏ *56506-0 $5.99/7.50 in Canada*

RELENTLESS

by Patricia Potter
Bestselling author of *Notorious*
"The healing power of love and the beauty of trust...shine like a beacon in all of Ms. Potter's work."—*Romantic Times*

❏ *56226-6 $5.50/6.99 in Canada*

SEIZED BY LOVE

by the incomparable Susan Johnson
"SEIZED BY LOVE withstands the test of time... a wonderful tale."—*Affaire de Coeur*

❏ *56836-1 $5.50/6.99 in Canada*

WILD CHILD

A classic romance
by the highly acclaimed Suzanne Forster
"(Suzanne Forster) is guaranteed to steam up your reading glasses."—*L.A. Daily News*

❏ *56837-X $4.50/5.99 in Canada*

Ask for these books at your local bookstore or use this page to order.

❏ Please send me the books I have checked above. I am enclosing $ _____ (add $2.50 to cover postage and handling). Send check or money order, no cash or C. O. D.'s please.

Name _____

Address _____

City/ State/ Zip _____

Send order to: Bantam Books, Dept. FN137, 2451 S. Wolf Rd., Des Plaines, IL 60018

Allow four to six weeks for delivery.

Prices and availability subject to change without notice.

FN137 4/94